KILLER KING

Killers Inc. Book 3

by Stuart R. West

GORDIAN KNOT BOOKS

Dedication

I'd like to dedicate this book to the abused people of the world. You don't have to take it and you certainly don't deserve it. Sure, Leon's methods of dealing with abusers probably isn't the best way to handle them, but there are options for you.

And, as always, huge thanks to my suffering and supportive wife, Cydney and daughter, Sarah.

Chapter One

The elevator doors rolled open and Leon stepped inside. Stuffed into a yellow sweater, the man at the back studied his loafers as if they were a modern miracle of manufacturing. Fine by Leon. He preferred his social interaction on the down-low.

A precautionary habit, Leon stood close to the control panel, placing as much room as he could between him and his fellow rider. Not that the man radiated dangerous vibes.

But why wear a sweater in the summer?

A yellow blur of movement rippled across the steel walls. Leon glanced back over his shoulder. Quickly, the man looked away. As if guilty.

Paranoia, plain and simple. Evil didn't wear summer sweaters. Still, it paid to be careful, always on guard. An essential fact of life since Leon's strange journey with Like-Minded Individuals began.

Leon exhaled, shook his head and swept away the menacing shadows.

Still. The Montana meteorologists called for the temperature to hit the nineties today.

Why a sweater?

Leon tapped the twentieth floor button, flashed an innocuous smile at his neighbor. The man didn't return the smile. Just shifted a shopping bag into his other hand.

And just where exactly were Cody and Gaines? They'd dropped Leon off at the front door of the First Interstate Center, told him they'd be back as soon as they parked.

How long does it take to park?

The doors rolled shut with an asthmatic *whump.*

Behind Leon, the plastic sack rattled in the man's hand.

Over the speaker, the Carpenters sang, presumably to sooth. But the song set Leon's nerve ends on fire.

"Why do birds suddenly appear, every time you are near?"

Leon's watch read 12:45. Plenty of time before the meeting. Although he'd feel more comfortable if he had his support team with him.

Scratch that. Leon trusted Cody, not so much Gaines.

Six months ago, when Jasper Rasmussen's widow, Sheera, offered Leon the position of Like-Minded Individuals, Inc. CEO, he'd been blindsided by the sheer lunacy of the proposal. He really hadn't taken the time to think it through before he accepted. Not that he'd had much choice; when dealing with LMI, refusing an offer is tantamount to a death sentence. Strange how some things work out.

A year and some change back, Leon'd fallen out of favor with LMI. A covert corporation dedicated to providing protection to serial killers, LMI offered aliases, cover stories, jobs and found abusers for Leon to ply his trade. Leon had been extremely satisfied with their services. At least during the early years. All at a cost, of course. And what a cost. Leon had come into possession of several photographs of Jasper Rasmussen, the head of LMI, who favored his anonymity over Leon's life. Not to mention the unpleasant revelation that LMI had been lying about the nature of Leon's targets. Not all of them had been abusers. Some were just in the way of LMI's goal to achieve political domination and a controlling hand over the economy.

Constantly, Leon wondered why he'd accepted the CEO job. After all, LMI had been trying to kill him. But unknown to LMI, Leon still planned on taking them down. An inside job, the best way to assure his success.

And his future success depended on various factors, most of them out of Leon's control. Along with the Montana ranch and the prestige of being CEO, Leon inherited several other things.

Like Gaines.

"Just like me, they long to be close to youuu…"

Gaines. A small man with big, scary talents. He'd been

Rasmussen's go-to guy, an exterminator of human vermin. Hell, Leon didn't even know his first name. Leon harbored no doubts as to where Gaines' loyalty lay, either. One hundred percent to Sheera Rasmussen, the financial wizard behind LMI's curtain. Not a problem as long as Leon and Sheera stayed on the same team. Highly unlikely in the long run.

No doubt about it, Gaines gave Leon the creeps. The very few times Leon'd seen the man smile upon receiving orders to kill sent a chill down his back. Like giving candy to a child.

Still, they say keep your enemies close.

And, oddly enough, Leon truly wished Gaines was a bit closer now.

The man in the elevator shook his bag again. Leon jolted, caught the man's distorted reflection on the elevator doors.

Did he just move closer?

Leon unfolded his hands out of the universal polite stance while riding an elevator. Looked back at the man. The man rubbed his thick neck, dug a hand into his sack. And stared into the bag.

From Victoria's Secret. *Odd.*

"On the day that you were born, the angels got together..."

The man stood at about five feet eight inches, stout and red like a fire hydrant. Balding. Nondescript. Hardly the type to be buying his wife sexy lingerie. Stereotyping, sure, but Leon'd learned that when dealing with LMI, never discount stereotypes.

Crinkle, tump, crackle...

What the hell's in his sack that's so fascinating?

Leon watched the lights hop-scotch up the control panel. A sudden realization struck him. The man hadn't pressed a floor button.

Leon reached into his suit jacket pocket. Patted down his animal tranquilizer filled hypodermic. Never leave home without it. He clenched his other hand into a fist.

"So they sprinkled moon dust in your hair..."

The bag dropped, a nerve-wracking firecracker.

Splack.

A rush of air brushed Leon's neck. He yanked out the hypodermic. Something ensnared his neck. A strip of nylon, tightening.

The needle fell from Leon's grip.

Clink-tink.

The nylon grew taut, cutting into Leon's neck. The man grunted. The scent of onions rolled off his breath.

Leon dug his fingertips beneath the nylon. And pulled. The man tightened his grip, shaking out beads of sweat onto Leon's neck. The nylon burned Leon's flesh. His breath stuttered. A splotch of blood rode down his neck. He needed leverage.

"Just like me, they long to be, close to youuu..."

Leon screamed. At least tried to. He wheezed like a drowning cat. But it kick started a burst of energy. His back thrust against the man. He jerked his feet out and ran them up the elevator doors. Muscles ached, challenged beyond their limits. Leon bent his knees and pushed. Head forward, then cracked it back into his opponents'. *Contact!* The man groaned. The nylon fell.

Leon whirled, dropped into a squat. The large man tottered, arms waving. He slammed against the mirror. Then he planted log-like legs, arms out. Ready to fight.

"And decided to create a dream come trueee..."

Leon feinted in, tested the waters with an impotent swing. Then pulled back. Clearly, the man had the physical advantage. But sweat oozed from Yellow Sweater's forehead, his hands clammy. An advantage Leon might be able to use. Guy should've never worn a sweater.

Other than the hypodermic, Leon had no weapon. Didn't like carrying them. A rule he may have to change in the future. Especially if this battle represented his new world order.

The hypodermic lay shattered into glass crystals on the floor, the nylon next to it. He might be able to snatch the nylon, but the burly man would jump him. Every second counted.

"That is why all the girls in town follow you..."

Sweater dodged in, drew back. Another jab and duck, then the man inched away from the mirrored wall. Leon countered, fists up for protection. The man lunged. His hands wrapped around Leon's neck. Leon mirrored the move, a slow-dance to the death. The man carried more strength, muscle upon neck muscle, much stronger than his out-of-shape countenance belied. Using the assassin's neck as an anchor, Leon swung in a circle. He picked up dizzying speed, the man's weight providing heavy momentum. Leon released the man with a grunt. The man stumbled back into the wall. Shook his head and bounced back for another round. Time to take the offensive.

Leon roared. Ducked. Came up and threw his shoulder into the man. They crashed into the mirror, arms entwined. A fist came up, slammed Leon's ear. Dazed, he twisted, and wobbled back into the corner. Fully recovered, the assassin charged him. Battered his head into Leon's stomach, driving them into the doors. The air exploded from Leon's chest. He grabbed the man's sweater, yanked it up over his face. His elbow chopped down onto the man's turtled head. The killer dropped to one knee. But like a bullet, he shot up. Clearly stunned and out of breath, though. His forehead burned beet red as he peeked over his sweater's neck. Leon hoped for a sudden heart attack.

But Sweater didn't want to die quite yet.

He rushed Leon, elbow aimed for maximum impact. In a leap, he brought double fists down. Leon ducked and twisted. The man's head clanged into the elevator door, painful sounding. Leon grabbed the man's arm, yanked him up and swung him again. Sweater's sweat-covered hand loosened. He flew into the mirror.

"...they long to be, close to youuu..."

The man's hands flattened on the mirror. His breath blasted out condensation onto the glass. Leon brought back his aching elbow and cracked it onto the man's neck. He grabbed the nape of the sweater and wrenched back. Drove his head into the mirror.

Scack!

One more time.

Chack!

"Why? Close to youuu..."

Sweater's legs wobbled, then slackened. He held onto the mirror. His hands slid down the length, leaving a slug-trail of sweat with a piercing shriek.

Screeeeeeeeeee...

He folded, a less than graceful ballerina. Out cold. *Finally.*

Leon took no chances. Gave him a kick to the temple. His downed opponent's snoring suggested Leon's final kick hadn't been necessary. But it felt fitting, maybe even satisfying.

Leon needed him alive, though. He planned on having a little chat with Yellow Sweater later.

But now what do I do?

"Close to youuu..."

Ding!

Leon jumped, the bell announcing the final round of the elevator brawl. The elevator doors opened with a crisp snap.

Gaines and Cody stood in the twentieth floor hallway. Gaines looked at the man on the floor, no discernible expression. Business as usual.

Cody, on the other hand, dropped his jaw. Out of amusement.

"Yo, what the hell, Leon? Guy get up in your personal space or somethin'?"

"Didn't like his sweater." Leon took off his tie, wrapped it around his bruised and bleeding hand. He turned to Gaines. "Where *were* you? The building has a huge parking garage. Plenty of open spaces!"

"It took time, sir, to walk from the garage to the building."

The man unnerved Leon. Impossible to read. He studied Gaines' cold grey eyes, slightly magnified by his round glasses. Searched for a tell. Anything that might indicate prior knowledge to the attempt on Leon's life. Only ice flowed in his eyes.

"That true, Cody?"

"The hell? It's what he said, Leon. Took forever and a day."

"We'll talk about it later. Right now, I need you to get this guy outta' here."

"How the hell we 'sposed to do that?" Cody scratched a thumb-nail over his soul-patch. "Not like we can carry him outta' here. Not in front of the security guard downstairs. And the thousand yuppies."

"Improvise, Cody. You're good at it." Improvisation, the one thing Cody Spangler had proven a talent for. Still, the kid was a live-wire, ready to fry at any given moment. Sheera Rasmussen had given Leon grief about keeping Cody on as his second-in-command, his body-guard. Sometimes Leon wondered if she might be right. Honestly, though, he did it mainly to keep an eye on Cody. Keep him out of trouble. The one-time "Denver Decapitator" had carved his way through numerous housewives and mothers several years back due to what his horrific abusive mother had done to him. As far as Leon knew, Cody hadn't taken any more innocent lives over the last six months. Something he meant to keep status quo. And the only way to do that? Keep Cody on a tight leash. Give him something to do. And God help him, Leon actually liked the kid.

"I still don't know how—"

"There." At the end of the hallway, a door read *Janitor Services.* "Probably a janitor cart in there. Stick the guy in that."

Cody raced down the hallway. A hint of a smile broke Gaines' Mount Rushmore façade. A challenging smile. "And then what, sir?"

"You take him to the car. Keep him subdued. Sit on him if you have to." Leon tapped Gaines' chest. "But, listen to me, Gaines. I want him alive." Nothing. Not even a blink. Leon raised his voice. "You hear me, Gaines? *Alive.* I want to question him later."

The minimal smile twisted into a sneer. "Yes, sir." The way he said it sounded full of disdain, hardly respectful. One of the reasons Leon wanted Cody also watching Yellow Sweater. If Gaines had a say in the manner, he'd probably kill the man. For entertainment. Or possibly because he'd hired him.

Cody raced behind a janitor cart and rejoined them. "Yo, got it! Had to empty a buncha' shit outta it, though!"

"Cody, keep your voice down."

"What the hell, Leon? Thought you rented out the top couple floors anyway."

He had. Glad he did, too. No precautions were too extreme when dealing with LMI. And his pending meeting concerned him. Even though Cody'd embarrassed Leon before at meetings, he'd rather have him at his side. But the identity of the assassin's employer overrode every other concern.

"Don't get out on the first floor. Take the cart down the last flight of steps to the basement. Pull the car around. And dump him in the trunk."

"It's gonna royally suck carrying him down the stairs."

Leon sighed. "Just do it, Cody."

Cody grabbed the man beneath his arms. Then gave up. "Yo, Gaines, you gonna just stand there doing jack, or you gonna give me a hand?"

The thin man moved quickly and quietly, easily hefted the man's lower body up. Strong, human rebar wrapped in a three piece suit.

Leon checked his watch. 1:00. Right on time. He straightened his jacket, took off down the hallway. As an after-thought, he called out, "Cody?"

"What?"

"Make sure he stays alive."

"Yeah, whatevs…no problem."

Understatement of the year.

In front of the meeting room doors, Leon closed his eyes. Took a deep breath and listened. Murmurs drifted out, hushed voices from secretive men and women. The first international LMI board of directors meeting. He'd had contact with several board members before, usually via secure electronic methods, but hadn't met any of them. And he knew full well, one or more of them could've masterminded his assassination attempt. He'd heard a lot of griping that his unorthodox methodology had kept LMI in the red and far from the black.

As he swung open the doors, the room fell silent. Carefully, he studied the board members' faces, looked for signs of surprise that he still drew breath.

"Ladies and gentlemen, good afternoon. Many of you know me already, but for those who don't, I'm Leon Garber, the new CEO of Like-Minded Individuals, Incorporated." Several nods, a few grunts. Not a lot of smiles. Definitely no registered shock.

Leon took his seat at the end of the table. Slowly, he poured a glass of water, tried to quell his nerves. There were only eight official board members. But a menagerie of goons and bodyguards hovered not far from their employers. Leon had requested a weapon free meeting. Doubtful anyone had adhered to his demand.

"I know I've come by this position under very curious circumstances, but one thing I hope to do today is allay any fears you may have regarding my true intentions. I intend on bringing LMI into a new era of prosperity and success." *Well, no, not really.* Leon intended on taking them down. He'd had a good start six months ago. Or so he thought when he'd devastated the U.S. chapters. But as he'd found out, LMI had grown, globally so. Time to hang a face on the unseen enemy. "Before we begin, are there any questions?"

"Mr. Garber, I have concerns about the way you're directing our financial portfolio." Kaito Takihiro, the Japanese LMI affiliate. A twig of a man with a forest of cash. Takihiro Electronics had already cut a formidable swath of electronics dominance through the Eastern regions of the world. But, apparently, it wasn't quite enough. It never is with LMI. "In the past, Mr. Rasmussen had operated LMI as a customer-driven, client-focused concern. It is my understanding LMI is becoming *your* concern."

Not really a question, but a tricky complaint. One that'd take some fast dancing to get it off the floor. "Hajimemashite, Mr. Takihiro." Leon stood, bowed, then sat back down. "I certainly understand your concern. LMI is still a work in progress. I think many of you'd agree that under Mr. Rasmussen's guidance, LMI's infrastructure had weakened to the point of nearly commoditizing. He'd let his own personal political priorities override LMI's original game-plan, that of a market-based, financially lucrative operation. Something I know you'd all like to see a return to."

Takihiro solemnly nodded, as hard to read as Gaines. Leon knew LMI thrived on their buzz-words. So he'd taken a crash course, immersing himself in corporate double-speak. Even though most of it ultimately signified nothing.

"It takes time to realign, to reposition a failing concern such as LMI. That's what I'm doing, ladies and gentlemen."

A woman leaned forward and cleared her throat. For an

awfully long time. "Mr. Garber...you didn't fully address
Mr. Takihiro's concerns..." Irina Kerensky, head of a Russian
security (a scary word in the business world) corporation.
Apparently one of the most successful on the planet. Leon
wondered if LMI's all-knowing, all-seeing abilities began with
her. "We understand you're realigning LMI. But how is this
different from Mr. Rasmussen's personal interests? You appear
to have your own agenda."

Crap. Leon knew this would come up. "Ms. Kerensky, how
very nice to meet you in person. I'm empathetic toward your
concerns." His spread hands offered empathy. "I'm taking LMI
into a new direction. A paradigm shift. What has been the
overriding interest for the board members since LMI's birth?"
He raised eyebrows, waiting for greed to come to the table.
"Financial gain for all present."

Appreciative nods and agreeable grunts wove around
the room. Even Ms. Kerensky's formidable potato of a nose
couldn't hide her grin. Kill 'em with cash, lesson number one.
"Mr. Takihiro voiced concern over LMI's no longer being a
customer-driven or client-based organization. Nothing could
be farther from the truth. Mr. Rasmussen ultimately lost sight
of LMI's clients, using them as his own army of assassins. Lying
to the customers. But, as they say in the States, the customer's
always right. I intend to fast track LMI back into a client-based
firm. Without pleased customers, LMI won't turn a profit. And
without said profit, our pockets go unlined."

Takihiro's nod appeared more enthusiastic. The large men
behind him added their approval, their heads bobbing up and
down.

"There's a synergy common amongst all thriving
corporations, one running from the board of directors to
management to the end customer. Believe me, ladies and
gentlemen, like-minded individuals are a unique bunch. Some
of them extremely wealthy, our most sought after clientele.
There's no need for marketing. Too risky a proposition, too—"

"That's all very fine and well, Mr. Garber." There's always
one in every bunch. Cesaire Charlemagne, CEO of an extremely
lucrative pharmaceutical corporation. Leon'd caught a share

of his haughtiness online. So condescending, so damn French. "But the issue you keep avoiding is sales are down, the lowest in LMI history. Because you've been supplying only abusive ladies and gentlemen to our client base."

True and guilty as charged. But as long as Leon sat at the head seat of LMI, he meant for the loss of innocent lives to stop. A nearly impossible task but one he'd committed to. Constantly seeking and researching regional abusers for most of the States had drained him. And, eventually, the drain would run dry, pleasing no one. But he wouldn't tell the board the bleak forecast.

"Well, Cesaire...this is all true." Leon stood, held up a politician's power fist with the thumb up. Lately he'd also been studying politicians. They shared a lot in common with LMI board members. "There's a two-fold reason for this. One, Mr. Rasmussen had let things get out of hand. Under his management, LMI was gaining market visibility, something I think we all agree is absolutely unacceptable."

"And there was your part in all of that, Mr. Garber," interjected Cesaire.

"True. But Mr. Rasmussen had given me no choice, Cesaire." Purposefully, he called Charlemagne by his first name. Leon knew it grated on the man's nerves; he believed he should be treated as royalty. "Mr. Rasmussen instigated LMI's current red positioning. I merely inherited it. And, now, with your support..." Again with the open arms, inviting the rubes in. "...I vow to cement LMI firmly again into the black. Making everyone happy. But back to the reasons why we only target abusers? It's a way to shift eyes away from LMI, make our market invisibility solid again. Mr. Rasmussen had targeted too many high-profile individuals. With my new strategy in place, we are slowly achieving that goal once again. For without total market invisibility, LMI can't become a growing, thriving entity again. Plus, I've found that some law enforcement representatives aren't as motivated to seek out those who dispose of abusers."

Cesaire shut up, nothing to add.

"Now, allow me to lay out our year long mission statement, starting with—"

"Mr. Garber, we're dangerously in the red." Senta Rosen

stood and swept back her thick mane of hair. Enjoying the spotlight. She knew she carried a striking presence. Married to an Israeli prime minister, many thought she truly held the office in her hand. Leon believed it. "You want to start over. Begin anew. I hardly see how you can lift LMI back to its once glorious heights. Not with your little grass-roots movement."

Tough crowd. "Ms. Rosen, I agree it will be an uphill battle." Flummoxed, he reclaimed his seat, but felt he no longer controlled the meeting. "As I'm sure you all know, Ms. Sheera Rasmussen is now the true controlling head of LMI. She'd informed me that the board members were no longer interested in pursuing Mr. Rasmussen's political goals. Her only directive to me was I turn a profit, keep things—"

"And you haven't done that yet, Mr. Garber," said Charles Kruger, owner of a hugely successful South African gold mining company. Based on what Leon'd heard about his mining practices, Kruger belonged on his abuser list. Some day he might just complete that little task.

"And I've only been on board for six months, Mr. Kruger. Hardly enough time to—"

"We were doing just fine before your interference, Mr. Garber." Kruger glared at him, his blue eyes so pale, he appeared blind. The only thing missing was a James Bond villain's cat in his lap. "I believe I speak for everyone here when I say we'd like to see results."

"You'll get results, Mr. Kruger." *Just not the kind you'd like to see.* "I need a little more time. After all, Rome wasn't built in a day."

"True indeed, Mr. Garber. But once it started falling, it took no time at all for it to topple." Affirmations rose from around the table.

"What exactly do you intend on doing about the so-called Man with the Shoe-box?" Senta Rosen stood up again and swung her hair like a lion-trainer's whip. Always seeking the center ring.

"Um, what about Bartholomew, Ms. Rosen?"

The Man with the Shoebox. Aka Bartholomew, last name unknown. During last year's siege on Rasmussen's ranch,

Bartholomew had helped. Then he slipped away like a shadow in the dusk. Actually, Leon's thoughts never strayed far from the man. Primarily because he'd rather have him as an ally than enemy. His mode of operandi unsettled Leon. A killer who snuck into his victims' homes and cut off their feet. He left the bodies with a calling card of a shoebox and a mysterious smile on the victims' faces. Equally disturbing was Bartholomew's vast fortune. Something that could make him a very formidable enemy.

"It's a stipulation of my alliance with Mrs. Rasmussen that none of my team members from last year are to be harmed. I have it in writing, a contract between—"

"Be that as it may, Mr. Garber," continued Senta, "Bartholomew was our wealthiest client, paying extremely generous premiums and supplying other means of support. Now, he's vanished. Gone underground."

"That's his decision, Ms. Rosen. We can't very well force clientele to—"

"Besides his much-needed financial backing, Bartholomew knows too much about LMI. And since he's out-of-touch, this means he's no longer with us. If he's not with us, he's against us. Something needs to be done regarding him."

"No disrespect intended, Ms. Rosen, but perhaps you don't understand my arrangement with Mrs. Rasmussen. In the contract, it firmly states—"

Her hand shot up, silencing Leon. "I heard you clearly. My English is not that bad." Laughs all around. "He poses a major problem, one that needs to be dealt with. I suggest you deal with it. Otherwise..." She swayed back and forth, weighing fickle scale hands.

"Is that a threat, Ms. Rosen? I don't particularly see how threats are conducive to business practices, particularly—"

"I didn't issue a threat. Did I offer anything resembling a threat?" Senta glared at her peers with ferocious eyes. Eyes that sought "no" for an answer. The board members fell in line, shook their heads. "Again, Mr. Garber, as new CEO of LMI, it falls within your house to deal with this problem."

"I...I don't..."

Leon'd fully lost control of the meeting. He couldn't condone killing Bartholomew. Even though, in the long run, the Man with the Shoebox probably deserved it. Still, as a man of honor, Leon meant to uphold the contract and protect his allies. Hypocritical, perhaps, but that's the way big corporate business operates.

The rest of the meeting zipped by in a blur of worries. Leon's plan to expand like-minded individual targets to different types of law-breakers met with indifference, sometimes dissention. Particularly when he suggested targeting white collar criminals who had duped financially struggling people of their money. Honestly, he should've known better. Preaching to some of the biggest white collar criminals fell on deaf ears. Patiently, he tried to explain how the board's desire to go international wouldn't be the soundest decision; marketing had shown that most serial killers resided in the States. They pooh-poohed the idea (putting it nicely), thoughts of international power always at the forefront of their concerns. As Leon explained his yearlong mission plan to take LMI back into the black (a plan he had no intention of seeing to fruition), he studied the gathering of billionaire thugs and killers, wondering just which one had tried to have him killed. And why.

Chapter Two

Cody turned the radio dial and dumped Gaines' easy listening choice. About as boring as the man himself. Gaines turned the radio off.

"Yo, I was listenin' to that, brah!"

Gaines pinched his lips tight, so tight the color drained, and stared out the window. Unblinking like a store mannequin. Guy never brought anything to the party. While a better companion than the two dicks LMI saddled Cody with six months ago, the guy had the personality of white bread with the crust cut off.

Boring.

Pretty much the way Cody'd describe his current life. At first, living in Rasmussen's mansion kicked; he'd never lived in style like that before. But soon, restlessness threatened to pull him under. His sea legs needed to stretch or at least get their toes wet. Now a schedule ruled his life, demanded where to be and don't be late, dammit. He felt as lifeless as Gaines acted, just going through the motions.

Sure, Leon'd been cool enough to give him a job. Leon's bodyguard. *Respect!* But there'd been no action, no rush, and no fist-pumping excitement. Just one boring-ass meeting after another.

Tump, thump, clump…

Except today started off with a bang and just in time. They had a guy in the trunk. Some guy who'd tried to deep-six Leon.

Timp…

"Let me outta here!"

"Dude's like the Energizer bunny, yo. Never gonna give up."

Gaines sniffed.

"Look, Gaines, what's your damage anyway? You never say anything. Or do anything. Straight up, you're one wack dude."

He offered Cody a small, cutesy smile like he was doing him a favor or something.

Creepy ass dude.

Thump, bam...

"Let me the hell outta here! I got money, I got—"

Cody turned the radio on again. Cranked up the metal. Far better than listening to the guy's screams.

The back door opened and Leon slid in.

"Yo, chief, how'd the pow-wow go? Fire anybody?"

"Not today. How long was the car unattended?"

"What, like twenty minutes, tops."

"Did you check the car thoroughly? See if anyone'd tampered with it?"

"Sir, had anyone touched the car, it would've self-detonated," said Gaines. "It's equipped with a very elaborate security system."

Cody sat forward, eyes wide. "*What*? Shit, how come I didn't know that? Small comfort, yo! Like, are we sitting on a bomb or something?"

Leon sighed and said, "Take us home, Gaines."

No one said a word for most of the drive. Hell, some days Cody missed the chatty Mr. Sensitivity. *Almost.* Even weirder, Leon let Cody's music blare. Totally unlike him.

Whatever.

"Gaines, pull over here," said Leon.

The order yanked Cody out of a lull. He looked around, saw they were next to a park, one that appeared isolated.

"Drive until I tell you to stop."

They wound around a gravel road, gaining altitude into the Montana woods. At a tree-cleared turn-around, Leon instructed Gaines to park.

Leon hopped out in a hurry. One step back and he opened the driver's door. "Give me the keys, Gaines."

"Might I ask why, sir?" Gaines blinked, did it again like he didn't understand English.

"No, you may not. The keys."

Reluctantly, Gaines handed them over.

"Let's go, Cody."

Not done yet, Gaines called out, "Sir if you're going to interrogate the prisoner, I suggest you allow me to—"

Flumph. Leon slammed the door on his boy, Gaines.

"What the hell, Leon? Let Gaines do the dirty work. He gets off on it."

"Not today. Help me get this guy out of the trunk."

Like lightning struck his ass, Leon rushed back to the trunk. He stuck the key in, then hesitated. "Be ready, Cody. Guy's a pro. He'll come out swinging."

"Yeah, but you got one of your lil' needles, right? Why not just jab him?"

"I got my spare out of the glove box. But I need this guy awake."

"Let's do this, yo." Quickly, Cody ran in place, took several deep breaths. Shaking out unused muscles and warming up. He hoped the guy'd live up to Leon's warning.

The trunk opened. The man didn't disappoint. His arms thrust out and clawed at them. Cody wheeled back a fist, clocked him on the cheek. Did it again for good measure. The man flopped back into the trunk.

"I think he's ready, now," said Leon.

They hoisted out the dead weight, worse than a sloppy drunk. Each of them grabbed an arm and dragged him away from the car.

"Whaddaya wanna do with him, Leon?"

"Right now let's get him as far away as possible from the car."

The guy weighed a ton, nearly impossible to move. Finally, Leon stopped and dropped onto a boulder.

"Why didn't we just talk to him in the trunk, yo? Been hella easier."

"Because I don't want Gaines to hear."

Weird. Cody thought nothing but unicorns pranced around in Leon's new LMI-pretty world.

"And Cody...don't say a word about this to Gaines. Or anyone, for that matter."

"Yeah, no loose lips here."

"Did you search him earlier?"

"*What*? Hellz, no, you didn't tell me to."

"Do I have to tell you to do everything?"

"I don't wanna touch his, like, junk or anything."

Leon rolled his eyes, the way a holier-than-thou nun might do. But Cody stood his ground. He didn't swing that way. No way he'd touch another guy's junk, one hundred percent hetero.

No way.

"Fine, I'll do it." Leon moved fast, patted down the guy's chest, felt beneath his armpits, searched his pockets. Pulled out a wafer-thin wallet. Even took the guy's shoes off and tossed them into the woods.

Leon stood and thumbed through the wallet. He plucked out a driver's license and read the name. "Walt Baker from Billings, Montana. What's the chance that's his real name?"

After pinching up his trouser legs, Leon dropped into a squat. He slapped the man several times until he stirred. The man's fists came alive, whipping at the air.

"Get off me, dammit! I'm going to—"

Cody didn't wait for the order, punched the guy. Showing Leon he didn't need to take orders. Dirt whiffed up as the man collapsed. Cody's hand tingled. He shook it out and imagined the dude's face felt worse.

Leon slapped the man again and steadied his head with fingers pinching his chin.

"Alright. In case you feel like screaming, there's no one around. Just us."

"I don't scream." Instead he spat, barely missing Leon's shoe.

"Yo, let me bash him again!"

"No, hold on. But be ready." To the prisoner, he asked, "So, 'Walt,' who sent you? To kill me?"

"Dunno what you're talkin' 'bout."

"Mm-hmm. You accidentally wrapped nylon around my throat in the elevator, I suppose."

"Just wanted your wallet."

"Muggers don't carry Victoria's Secret bags around. Or use nylon rope to strangle their victims. Who sent you?"

The man laughed. A strand of blood stretched between his

lips. "And I'm tellin' you, you're crazy. Take me to the cops. I'll confess to tryin' to mug you."

Leon's knees cracked when he stood. Not getting any younger. He looked around like he was lost, scratched at his five o'clock shadow. Killing time while Cody felt the killing urge coming on strong.

"Leon, let me crack this yellow egg! I'll make him sing like an omelet!"

"Cody, that *doesn't* even make sense." Leon knelt again, grabbed the guy's sweater and shook him. Tightly wound today. "Walt—if that's your real name—*tell* me who hired you. And I swear I'll let you go. As long as I *never* see you—"

"Or his ugly-ass sweater!"

"—again. You leave. Disappear. And maybe you'll have a chance. You *know* what your employers are like. They'll never let you survive this. I'm much nicer than them. If you don't talk, I'm taking you back to LMI headquarters where there're a ton of sweet guys who'd just love to make you talk. *Tell* me who hired you!"

A corner of the man's mouth curled up, yellow teeth on display. "And I'm tellin' you, I dunno what you're talking about. Just a down on his luck guy, trying to survive—"

Crump.

The pain from the blow burned Cody's knuckles. A good kind of pain, one that reminded him what it felt like to be alive.

But he'd hit him too hard. Unconscious again after one punch, a personal best for Cody.

"*Dammit*, Cody, I wasn't done."

"Hey, he was dissin' you, showing no respect!"

"Just *remember* who you work for."

"Yes, Dad."

Leon stormed off, his fingers combing through his hair. Better be careful or he'll end up bald.

The world of corporate business baffled Cody. Sometimes he didn't know how to act, what people expected of him. He considered apologizing to Leon. Then again, for what? Doing his job? And he hated when the old man lorded over him, reminding him who was boss. Pissing on the little guy. They were supposed to be peers, straight up, something Leon needed to be reminded of. Cody followed Leon into the woods.

"Hey, Leon, wait up, yo! Maybe I hit him too hard. Shit happens. Get over it. I'll just bitch-slap him awake. He'll—"

"Never mind. He's not going to talk. Let's get him back in the trunk. Take him home."

"Whatever, dude. Kinda a waste of time, if you axe me. What the hell's goin' on, anyway?"

"What do you mean?" Leon groaned as he tugged the man's arm.

"Dude tried to off you, I get that. But why didn't you want Gaines to hear anything? You think Gainsey sent the guy?"

Leon dropped his load and straightened. "I don't know *what's* going on. But I don't trust Gaines. And I have to find out the truth."

"Hey, I thought everything was peaches and cream with you and LMI now. That Rasmussen babe thinks Gaines walks on water. You don't think…" Frankly, Cody didn't know what to think. He tried to fit the pieces together, but his mind couldn't get past the last death metal song that'd been playing in the car. *Damn ear-worm.*

Leon plucked out a hypodermic, stabbed it into the guy's neck. When he stood up, he winced. He massaged his back, grandpa-style. "I think LMI aren't finished playing games yet. I believe someone from LMI tried to have me killed."

"No shit?"

Leon just stared at him.

So much for job security.

Located just East of the continental divide, the late Jasper Rasmussen's ranch (more like a compound) appeared as an unnatural, fabricated eyesore set amongst the sprawling Montana mountains and bountiful woods. However, Leon liked it because of its nearly impenetrable nature, a well-protected fortress. Maybe "liking it" was a little too strong. More like Leon felt slightly less vulnerable within the ranch's gates.

For better or worse, it'd been his home for the past six

months. Sheera Rasmussen, Jasper's widow and "Brutus", had offered Leon residence in the main mansion (it had enough room to house an army), but Leon valued his privacy. He set up in one of the smaller cottages next to the main house. Not that he had many belongings. The constant man-on-the-go has very few worldly belongings. Of course he spent most of his waking hours in the mansion anyway, tending to business. A business that frankly surprised him how much he enjoyed. The marketing, the planning, the business models, the accounting… he'd missed those days when he worked and played hard as a corporate raider in the high finance valleys of Los Angeles.

What he didn't miss, however, was the target hanging on his back.

"So, Leon…you're sure this gentleman tried to kill you?" asked Sheera. Seated at the head of the meeting room table, she crossed her legs, kicking one idly beneath her form-fitting skirt. The way she always did it.

"Sheera, I have a wounded hand to prove it. Wanna see my other bruises? Take off my shirt?" Leon sat down next to her, his usual position in the LMI kingdom.

She smiled. Barely. Plastic surgery had cast her face in cement. "Promises, promises."

Leon ignored the blatant flirtation. She always did it, he always blew it off, the way they rolled. Most of the time he thought it harmless, a way for her to work out her loneliness. Besides, she scared the hell out of Leon. He couldn't forget how callously she dispatched of her late, not-so-great husband. "Of course the man tried to kill me!"

"You misunderstand me, Leon. I believe you. But…as you said, he claimed it was a botched mugging. He could've robbed any poor sap."

Time to disembark the slow boat to nowhere. Frankly, Leon found it strange Sheera had such a hard time grasping the situation. For LMI, such murderous behavior was commonplace. "Muggings don't happen in prosperous business building elevators. And the guy was a pro. A nylon cord. No noise. He knew what he was doing."

"You're sure?"

"Absolutely. It'd been set up. He knew when I was getting on the elevator. He was waiting for me."

Long fingernails rapped the mahogany table-top. "So. You *think* you were set up?" Again with a half-smile, hardly befitting Leon's situation.

"I don't just 'think' so, I know it."

"Then tell me, who's behind it?"

Leon waited. Searching for clues in Sheera's facial tics. Good luck. Her only "tic" was her accountant ticking off the cost of her constant plastic surgeries. "I thought you might have an idea there, Sheera."

She sat back and rocked in her oversized leather chair. A finger tapped her plump lips. "Honestly, I have no clue. Six months ago, of course, things were different. But, now that you're the CEO, it doesn't make sense for anyone within our organization to issue such a task. If you're asking me if I condoned this action, absolutely not. And I take offense at that assumption." Her lips pulled down in what Leon presumed to be a pout. Behind that playful girlish flirtation swam a killer shark.

"I'm not saying that, Sheera." Leon waved flag of peace hands. "I just wanted to know if you have any idea who set me up."

"Not a clue."

"What about the board members? Are you certain they've all agreed to abandon, ah, your late husband's political ambitions? Some of those people...money's not enough to satisfy them."

"You just leave the big bad board members to me, Leon." She cooed the "big, bad" part as if placating a frightened child. Then she leaned forward, her hand dropping on Leon's knee. Leon flinched. Just a tad. Unless invited, he abhorred human contact. But sometimes you have to "golf" with the boss. "I know how to handle them."

Leon believed it. But would she know if there was a coup in the works? LMI bred back-stabbing bastards. "What if they're conspiring against you, Sheera? Maybe they're not so ready to let go of their political concerns regarding LMI. After all, it was the perfect covert army for them."

Sheera brayed, tilted her head up. For some reason, the scalpels had ignored her neck, full of age-defining wrinkles. "Believe me, Leon…none of them would dare go against me. I hold the kingdom in my hands. And you're my king."

Not the first time she'd called him her king. And sometimes Leon even felt like royalty, particularly when he issued orders, making large-ranging decisions. It occupied his mind, gave him purpose. More importantly, it kept his driving need to dispose of abusers at bay. At times he thought he even contributed something worthwhile to humanity. A means to rid the world of as many abusers as possible. While never actually dirtying his hands, of course.

Sometimes it's good to be the king.

On the other hand, Leon knew—absolutely so—how power corrupts. And he had to remember his ultimate goal: the destruction of LMI. A tricky thing.

"Sheera, you hired me for a particular reason. To financially stabilize LMI and turn a profit. While steering away from the political arena. I'm trying to do that. I *am* doing that."

"I know, Leon, I know." Pat, pat, pat to his knee.

"I hope you do. I'm doing the best job I can. So if you're unhappy with my performance or—"

"I've never really seen *how* you perform, now have I?" False eyelashes fluttered like hummingbird wings.

"If I'm not up to LMI standards, fine, give the job to someone else. Just let me and my allies walk away free and alive."

"Don't be silly."

Leon wondered exactly which part of his statement she considered "silly." Paranoia often derailed his thoughts, but he had to keep on track. "Fine. In return, I expect full cooperation from you. And full disclosure. One last time…are any of the board members conspiring against me? Against us?"

All playful banter left the room. Sheera's eyes narrowed. An exasperated snort puffed out from her thin, much abused nose. "And I've told you what I know, Leon. Don't try my patience. You work for me, remember." Words that echoed what Leon'd told Cody earlier. Sludge always runs downhill. "The board members are all in alignment. With me. They respect me.

Perhaps you should take a cue from them."

He'd overreached his boundaries. History often noted kings don't last long on the throne. Time to back pedal. "My apologies, Sheera. But do you blame me for suspecting the organization that tried to kill me for a year?"

"I suppose not. But all of that's changed now."

"Okay." *Not okay.* "That still leaves the question of who's out to get me."

"I'll have my best men get on that. We can't have our CEO's life in danger now, can we?" Again, more baby talk as she patted Leon's cheek. He expected her to break out the "cootchy-cootchy-coo's" next.

"Speaking of your best men, I'd like to request a change on my detail."

"It's about time you gave up your beloved Cody. Honestly, he—"

"No, I'm talking about Gaines."

Her eyes opened wide, at least as wide as possible. "Gaines? Why, what on earth's wrong with Gaines? He's absolutely my best employee, one I can count on. It was a show of faith that I assigned him to you. Only the best, after all."

Leon retreated. A battle he wouldn't win. "If you say so."

"What possible complaint could you have against Gaines?"

And what exactly did he have to complain about? Nothing. Just his gut, a feeling. Always trust the gut. Maybe just not out loud. Leon brushed a hand between them, cleared the air. "It's just…today I thought it odd Gaines took so long to park the car. You know, while the assassin was trying to kill me. But—"

"Preposterous!"

"Well…as I said, I just thought it took longer than it should've. But Cody corroborated Gaines' story."

"Perhaps, dear Leon, you shouldn't concern yourself with those trying to keep you alive and worry more about that ruffian, Cody."

Leon couldn't get a take on the dragon-lady. She watched Leon carefully. Unmoving, a mummy. Surely she wasn't insinuating Cody might've had something to do with the failed hit attempt.

Surely not.

"Cody's exactly where he should be."

"Have it your way then," she sniffed. "Now!" She clapped her hands, signifying she'd finished with the subject. "Where's this so-called hit-man?"

"Gaines and Cody took him to the 'inhospitality suite.'"

"Honestly, Leon, must you use that vulgar name?"

One of the cottages contained several stone-walled cells in the basement, void of all sound, all light, all life. Leon'd overheard several of Sheera's guards refer to it as the "inhospitality suite," an apt description. But he'd rather not argue semantics. "Fine. He's in bunkhouse number six."

"Well, by all means, let's go have a chat with your new little play-mate."

Poolside, Nanette stretched out on the chaise. Sweat filled her belly button. From the cloud-free sky, the sun boiled the pool water and baked the pavement. In the distance, mountains loomed large and imposing, practically begging to be explored. Some day she'd like to hike up into the mountains, pitch a tent. Get away from Casa de Rasmussen for several days. When she broached the subject with Leon, he agreed under the stipulation she take a guard with her.

No thanks.

Camping with an armed guard outside the tent sort of sucked the beauty out of nature.

An hour ago, Leon returned from his board meeting. As he hurried by the pool, he nodded at her, not a word spoken. He walked quickly, determination in his step. Something had happened, Cody and Gaines manhandling a hooded man out of the trunk the dead giveaway.

It'd been six months since she'd taken up residence at the Rasmussen ranch. Six very strange months. The digs were nice enough, befitting the comfort she was accustomed to. Next door to Leon, she occupied her own comfy cottage.

But Leon hadn't been very neighborly. Since he'd accepted the position of LMI CEO, he'd grown more distant. Married to his work. Not exactly the way she'd imagined things going between them. Things hadn't always been that way. During the early days, she'd visited him frequently. They'd shared dinners, some wine (well, he watched her drink wine, ever the teetotaler). But as the days trudged on, their time together grew shorter. "I have work to do," he'd say as he ushered her out the door. The relationship she'd envisioned had fizzled out like a wet firecracker.

Six months ago, not a very long time in the larger spectrum of things. Only six months ago, passion had burned intensely between them. Perhaps it'd been the danger, the adrenaline of life on the run from LMI. But their relationship never reached those heights again. Maybe what truly bugged her was his rejection, something new and very unpleasant. She knew how to wrap men around her finger, get them to do her bidding.

Before she'd kill them, of course. Her thing. In the past, she'd only chosen men who were vile women-haters. But Leon'd been different.

Now, though? Now, she'd been relegated to nothing more than Leon's business associate.

Unacceptable.

Just last month, she'd stormed the mansion.

"Leon?" She knocked on his office door. "Can we talk?" Already she hated how she sounded, timid as a shy school-girl. Not quite the take-no-prisoners attack she'd envisioned.

"Sure. Come in, Nanette." Quickly Leon swept off his bifocals (the ones he tried to keep hidden) and stashed them in his pocket. He excused the ever-creepy, ever-present Gaines from the room and gestured for her to enter his chambers. "What can I do for you?"

Nanette strolled through the office, admiring the art on display. Planning strategy. She expected it to be a painful conversation. Although she sat across the desk from him, there may as well've been an ocean separating them.

He pursed his lips, settling into his business facade. A look that had started with his LMI tenure. It made what Nanette had to say easier. "Leon, I need to leave."

Nothing. She wanted, waited for him to ask her to stay, give her a reason. Instead, he asked, "Why?"

"Because…because I'm growing stagnant here."

"'Stagnant'. Is there something you need? I can get you—"

"No, Leon, nothing. I'm tired. I feel like I'm not doing anything. Just…chilling my heels and working on my tan."

"And your tan looks very nice." A hint of flirtation? Did the old Leon reside in there somewhere after all?

"Yeah, well, not much else to do. But it's time for me to fly. Can't keep this bird caged forever."

"I wish you wouldn't." Not much of an argument, but a start.

"Why?"

"Excuse me?"

"Why should I stay?"

Leon leaned back, looked out the window over the estate. *His* estate. Not hers. Several times he opened his mouth, then shuttered it. At long last, "I need you, Nanette."

I need you. Three powerful words. But without action to back them, they meant nothing. "You're doing fine on your own, Leon. You don't need me."

"You're wrong. I do." He stood, sat on the edge of the desk next to her. "This job is hard. It's something—"

"That's just it, Leon! It's *your* job! *Not* mine. You seem content running LMI. While I do nothing. And…I think you like it."

He nodded, slowly at first before succumbing to his LMI demon. "It's not that I like it. But I'm good at it. I—"

"You've forgotten what you're supposed to be doing."

With a sigh, his shoulders rounded. The businessman demeanor vanished. "No, I haven't forgotten." He lowered his voice. "End game? The destruction of LMI. I'm working on it."

"When?"

"What?"

"When? All you've been doing is running daily operations. I haven't seen you do *anything* to take them down. Have you forgotten what they did to you? What they did to me? They—"

"I know what they did. Look, Nanette…maybe a little of what you're saying is true. But, you also need to realize, I can't put any plans into effect until I've established myself. There's distrust on both sides. LMI doesn't trust me enough yet to let me in on all of their operations. Until I gain their trust, I don't really know what I'm—we're—up against."

Nanette noticed a slight hesitation before he included her in the game-plan. Hard not to. What she suspected: his game, his folly. Everyone close to him shut out in the cold. "I wish I believed you."

"Believe it. I'll strike once LMI shows their cards. All of them. And I hope you'll be by my side when it happens."

"I dunno…"

"Nanette…that's one of the reasons why I need you. I need you to keep me honest. Keep me in line. Let me know if I've lost sight of the big picture."

"Sounding kinda needy there, Leon. You know I don't do needy." She couldn't help herself. He was playing his role, she fell into hers. Their seductive dance. She smiled, twirled a lock of hair around a finger. Batted her eyes. Shameless, sure, but also the most fun she'd had in months.

He laughed, a nice sound. First time she'd heard it in months. "Oh, I know you well enough by now that you don't tolerate needy people. Just stay by my side. Please."

"Still not very convincing, Leon."

A stern look fell over him. Back to corporate raider killer. "Nanette, are you feeling the need to…do what you used to do?"

The implication stunned her a bit, pissed her off a lot. She expected better from Leon. Not pigeonholing her into simple psychological packages for men to understand. And control. "If you're asking me if I want to resume my black widow mantle and go out and kill rich men for money, no, Leon, I'm not considering it. Haven't even thought about it. Until now. How dare you? Just because you don't understand what I'm telling you, you want to 'father figure' me into something you can wrap your Cro-Magnon head around! Save it for the stupid little girls who need saving! Not every woman wants to be saved by the 'stronger' sex! Why don't—"

"Whoa, whoa! Easy! I didn't mean anything by it, I swear. I just…sometimes I think about…taking on another project. An abuser. In a way, I guess I miss it. I was just coming at you as a fellow like-minded individual, that's all. Nothing to do with the sexes."

A good argument, actually. She hadn't considered Leon might be fighting the urge. Old habits die hard, something she knew only too well. But she couldn't let him off the hook just yet. "Well, that's too bad, so sad you're jonzing. But that's you, not me. Don't you project your *crap* onto me. You're still seeing me as the old Nanette. I'm the all new, reborn Nanette. Maybe you don't remember what I told you before our raid on the ranch."

Solemnly, he nodded. "I remember. More or less, you said you'd made peace with your past life. Ready to move on. If we survived."

At least he'd listened. Something she wasn't accustomed to men doing in her past. "Damn straight. And we survived. But here I sit, twiddling my thumbs, doing nothing. Not exactly the new life I'd envisioned." She wouldn't give him the satisfaction of telling him he'd been a part of her dreamed-about new life.

"I understand, Nanette. I understand the desire to live your life." He stood. Grabbed her shoulders and gently guided her up from the chair. "Unlike the men from your past, I wouldn't think to strong-arm, coerce you into staying. You're free to go whenever you'd like. I respect you as a person. But know this…I do need you. For all the reasons I said…and for this…"

He leaned in, kissed her. She kissed back. How could she not? He'd pressed all the right buttons and then some. A passionate kiss, the first they'd shared in months. Her fingers crawled through his hair, grabbed a lock, and gave it a tug. She couldn't let him lead, not in her genetic make-up. His hands roved over her back, massaging, searching. Rediscovering. She wanted to continue, take it further. Wipe his desk clean like in the movies, throw him down onto it. But the voice of reason— just a tiny yip—asked if she was being seduced, used. Not on her watch.

She broke the kiss, pushed him back.

"Okay, Leon, that was nice, but—"

"Only nice?" When he grinned, she remembered how handsome he could be. Suited him more than grim and surly.

"Just nice. Don't get a big head."

"Which head are we talking about?"

"Now you're getting gross." He broke the mood. But she also saw a ray of his humanity shining through the clouds, just enough to bask in. "If I stay, there needs to be some changes."

Leon sat back on his desk. "Anything you want, Nanette. I need—"

"Don't start that crap again. This isn't about your needs. It's about mine."

"Fine. Name them." He crossed his arms. Defensively?

"If you truly want me to keep you honest, you have to be honest with me."

"I can do that."

"Can you?" He nodded. Smart man, knowing when to keep his mouth shut. "So far, you haven't exactly been forthcoming about your business dealings with me."

"Nanette, I haven't lied to—"

She pressed a finger over his lips. "Quiet. No, you haven't lied to me. But you've definitely kept me in the dark. You haven't said much of anything to me about your business at all lately."

"I just thought...you were happy as things were. I didn't want you to worry about—"

She groaned, stomped a foot. Thought about landing it on Leon's foot. "Oh, shut up! You don't get to decide what I worry about. I'm a big girl!"

"Agreed. I'm sorry."

"Yes, you are! *Very* sorry! From now on, you'll treat me as an equal, nothing less."

"Okay," he said quietly. Nanette liked the chastened school boy, much more attractive than the testosterone driven alpha male.

"And, again, you tell me everything."

"You got it. I've been unfair to—"

"Just shut up for once and accept things as they are." She couldn't help her smile, an automatic reflex. To cover it, she grabbed his ears, pulled him to her. Gave him one more kiss, fast and furious. One to remember her by. Until the next one.

But there hadn't been a next kiss.

And, honestly? There hadn't been much of a change

regarding Leon over the last month either.

Yet she held on. For many reasons. In hopes he'd eventually honor his word. But so far, there'd only been a few catch-up meetings with her. It didn't escape her attention he kept her away from his big corporate meetings.

She held on because of their last rough and tumble, kiss and tell session. At the time, she'd felt fully in charge. Empowered. A great feeling. She despised losing that feeling.

But mainly she held on for Leon. Holding on for a very different man than who he was now. He'd been special. She just hoped to see the return of that Leon. *Her* Leon.

In a way, she felt incarcerated. She may as well be a kept woman in bunkhouse number six.

Stagnant. As stagnant as the water welling in her belly button.

A shadow crossed her. She shielded a hand over her eyes and looked up. The sun silhouetted a dark figure, a chlorine-induced halo blurring around his head. But it didn't take long to figure out the identity of her visitor. Only one idiot wore a hoodie to the pool.

"What's up, what's up, what's up, hotness?"

Grnnnnd, screeeee…

He dragged another chaise next to her and collapsed into it. His feet went up and landed with double slaps on the pavement.

"How're you doing, Cody?"

"Livin' the dream, baby, livin' the dream."

And Nanette knew this to be true. Cody seemed to be the only one content living in their insular serial killer village. Sitting by the pool all day (when he wasn't on an errand with Leon), drinking margaritas and watching the twin blond young women frolic in the pool. Nanette still hadn't figured out who the blonds were or why they were there. Didn't really care either, little tolerance for bimbos and all.

A force of nature, Cody never gave up hitting on Nanette. Frankly, she tolerated it. Oh, hell, she enjoyed it. He provided a nice diversion. Most of the time. Other times he grated on her last nerve. Still, he looked as good as he sounded stupid. Dirty blond hair, blue eyes, muscles like rock and shoulders as broad as a refrigerator. At times, she considered having a little fun with him. Simply a sexual diversion, someone she knew she could tame. Nothing more. But then again, she wondered if she wouldn't be using him to make Leon jealous. Something she never wanted to do to another human being. An undeserving one, at least.

"Yo, you're lookin' hot as tarmac in your two piece today."

She looked over at him, noticed he'd shed his hoodie. Flexing his muscles with his arms over his head for her benefit. Too precious. And kinda hot.

Maybe she didn't owe Leon anything. Not the way he'd been blowing her off. And Cody practically begged her to use him.

Perhaps she'd reconsider. Soon. *Ish.*

"Not looking too bad yourself there, muscles."

He yipped. Shot up a juvenile fist and pumped it. He loved when she called him "muscles." Now that she had him lapping at the well of water in her navel, she may as well pump him for information.

"Who's the guy in the hood?"

"What? I'm the only one wearing a hoodie 'round here." Distracted by the splashing twin blonds, Cody couldn't attend to the conversation. Not unusual.

"No. The guy you and Gaines dragged in from the trunk. Wearing the hood."

"Oh, yeah, right. Dude tried to off our boy, Leon."

She sat up, whipped her sunglasses off. "Say that again."

"No shit, some guy in an elevator tried to strangle Leon."

"Is Leon okay?"

"Yeah, bitchy as usual."

"Do they know who sent him? Who the guy is?"

"They're workin' on him now. Me and Leon tried to get a lil' somethin', somethin' outta' him, but he wouldn't talk. Name, rank, serial number, that shit."

"Huh."

Rage percolated, set at a low simmer. Leon had blown by her without saying a word of the assassination attempt. Sort of an important piece of info to withhold from your partner, business or otherwise. Then fear dampened her anger. Like an endless loop, danger loomed over them. Again. They'd never be clear of LMI's imposing shadow.

Yet, along with the fear, excitement fired Nanette's synapses. A small electric tingle ran from her toes, up her legs, tickled her spine, and caressed her belly with lovely butterflies.

Maybe this would provide the diversion she truly needed.

Jackass better not cut me out of it.

"Who do you think sent the killer, Cody?" She knew better than to expect an intelligent, let alone semi-coherent, answer from him, but for whatever reason, Leon trusted him. Honestly, no one knew Leon better than Cody.

"No clue, yo. But my boy don't be trustin' on ol' Gaines."

That didn't surprise her. She didn't trust Sheera's number one goon either. Particularly since he pretty much tried to kill them in the past. And looked like he was sexually climaxing while doing so.

"Tell me more."

"Leon didn't want Gainsey around when we questioned the guy."

Smart. So Leon hadn't fallen completely into the alluring arms of LMI yet.

"Cody...do you think Leon's changed? I mean, since he became the CEO of LMI?"

One muscular leg crossed at the knee and Cody picked at his toenail. Apparently in deep thought. Or what passed for it. "Tell ya one thing, the old man's...I mean *Leon's* even more uptight than he used to be."

"Shocker."

"Yeah, check it, yo, dude never sleeps. Never cuts loose. Not that he used to do that anyway, but at least I've seen him bust a chuckle a coupla' times. He's always been more uptight than a constipated priest. But now, he's just like one of them, ya know? Stuffed LMI shirt."

Huh. She didn't think Cody had a single observational skill in his gorgeous body. "Yeah. I agree."

Clearly proud of the compliment, he hooted. "Damn straight, baby! Cody's got all the answers!"

And just when she'd gained a little insight, a smidgeon of respect for Cody, he sent toenail shrapnel flying into her face.

Gaines led the march down the hallway, the only area in the entire compound not renovated, remodeled, licked, shined and polished. LMI's architects were obviously instructed not to exert any effort or expense on behalf of the compound's prisoners. Based on the scuffed cement floor and blood stains on the stone walls, Leon guessed quite a few prisoners had passed through (and passed from) these dungeon halls.

Sheera fell in step next, a royal queen with her entourage. Flanked by two of the ever-present armed guards—his usual escort—Leon trailed behind. Sheera explained their constant presence as a way of ensuring protection for LMI's most valued asset. Paranoia passed it off as something different.

On tiptoes, Gaines peeked into the small window inset into the prisoner's door, the only window in the cell. He gasped. More sound than Leon usually heard from him. The key-chain jangled as Gaines failed to insert the right key.

Leon ran to the window, looked in. On the floor, Yellow Sweater lay curled up into a ball.

"Open the damn door, Gaines!"

"Calm down, Leon, our prisoner's not going anywhere," said Sheera.

Leon doubted he'd go anywhere again. He shoved aside Gaines, found the right key.

"Turn the light on," he ordered.

Kneeling beside the body, Leon felt for a pulse. Dead. Gaines hovered above him, arms casually crossed, death an every-day occurrence in his world.

Foam fizzled at the corner of Sweater's mouth. His eyes, milky and lifeless, stared blindly at the wall. One hand had frozen into a claw. Blood from his fingertips had filled in the scant scratches he'd made on the floor.

Leon stood, turned to Gaines. "How'd this *happen*?"

"I have no idea, sir."

"Gaines, what happened after you took the dead gentleman into custody?" asked Sheera.

"Proper protocol, ma'am. I escorted him, along with Mr. Spangler, into this cell. Locked him inside. Turned out the lights. While we left, he was shouting. The usual. But very much alive."

"Then how do you *explain* this, Gaines?"

"We won't know until a full investigation is conducted, sir, but I'd hazard a guess he's dead from poison. Suicide."

"*Suicide*? I searched him thoroughly! He had nothing on him!"

Gaines shrugged, his tiny grey suited shoulders peaking up. "No offense, sir, but are you properly trained to search bodies? I'd guess it was a cyanide tooth capsule."

"Oh, for God's... That only happens in bad spy movies! Not...this..." Leon waved a hand over the corpse at his feet.

"Leon, dear, maybe next time you'll have my man, Gaines, search the body. Let him do his job."

Reverentially, Gaines folded his hands, turned to face Leon. But he didn't present reverence. He smiled, ever so slightly, barely visible beneath the jaundiced lighting. Provoking Leon. "I'm at your service, sir."

Leon ignored him. "Sheera, I don't buy this for a minute. This man was under Gaines' protection. *His* watch. He failed."

"Now, Leon, Gaines can't be held responsible for an act of suicide. And the only other option is someone got past my guards and murdered him." She tittered, fingertips covering her blood red painted lips. "Impossible!"

"Something's not right, Sheera. If the killer meant to kill himself, he had plenty of time to do it earlier."

"Perhaps he just realized the hopelessness of his situation."

"Right. *Something* like that," said Leon.

"Okay, be that as it may..." Sheera dusted imaginary dirt from her hands. Not that she'd ever witnessed dirt before. "What's done is done. Leon, you said you procured a driver's license from the poor unfortunate man. Hand it over and I'll have my experts look into—"

"No thanks. I'll do it myself."

"Honestly, must you micro-manage every little detail? You have a corporation to lead."

"Can't lead it if I'm dead." Leon stormed out, leaving the others behind. But when he glanced through the window, Gaines had his hand cupped around Sheera's ear. Whispering into it.

Chapter Three

"Come in." Leon closed his lap-top with a sigh. As suspected, researching the board members proved to be a dead end. He needed an expert, someone he could trust. And trust didn't come easy for him.

Nanette opened the door. "Leon, you got a minute?"

"Always for you." He waved her in.

She sat down across from his desk and twirled her hair around a finger. When it unraveled, she did it again. Her gaze flit about, her head jerking like a bird's. Very uneasy and fidgety and highly uncustomary. A tough conversation lay ahead. "Doesn't seem like it," she finally said.

"Doesn't seem like what?"

"That you always have time for me."

"You know that's not true. I—"

"You weren't even going to tell me someone tried to kill you today? Just let me find out through gossip?"

"Nanette...I'm sorry. It scared me. I've been busy trying to find out the killer's identity. And who sent him."

"No excuse. If you remember, we're supposed to be a team."

"I know." Seconds of silence pounded like a throbbing headache.

"Find anything yet?"

"Nope." Leon plucked the killer's drivers license out of his pocket, tossed it on the desk. "No public records, social security information, anything. Guy's a ghost. Now in more ways than one."

"I heard." Nanette picked up the license, looked at it, and then flicked it back down. "Word is he poisoned himself."

"That's what they're saying."

"You don't believe it."

Leon rapped his fingers over the desktop, stared out the window. "I don't. I think Gaines killed him."

"Gaines? Why? I mean, he's damn creepy and all, but—"

"Because nothing else makes sense. Something's not right. And this guy had all the marks of one of LMI's killers. A 'business process outsourcer.'" Leon hung finger quotes.

"But you're the head of LMI now. They're supposed to be working for you, with you."

"So they tell me."

"You think Sheera's behind it?"

"Dunno. Maybe. But that doesn't pan out. She was hell-bent in setting me up as the CEO. I think there may be a power struggle going on with the board members. A coup in motion. They were less than friendly with me today. Maybe they're unsatisfied with what I've been doing. Maybe they—"

"And what exactly have you been doing, Leon?"

"What's that supposed to mean?"

"What've you been doing about LMI?"

"Nanette, I'm trying to run the organization! Trying to turn a—"

"Exactly. And tell me again why you even took the job in the first place."

Leon sat back, sighed. Planned his words carefully before he spoke, the way successful CEO's do. "Okay, fine. You're thinking I've lost sight of my...original goal." He lowered his voice. "To take down LMI."

"And how's that going for you?"

"It takes time, dammit! To truly do the job right, I have to find out who the major players are first. Infiltrate. Immerse. Pull the rug out from under them."

"Sometimes...sometimes I think you *like* playing the CEO. You've changed. Even Cody sees it and he can't usually see the forest through his hoodie. There's a saying, maybe you know it...absolute power corrupts."

"So I've heard. Don't mother me, Nanette. It doesn't suit you. I know what I'm doing."

Nanette laughed. "I'm not so sure about that."

"Doing the best I can."

"And maybe that's not good enough. Hey, you talked me into staying to help you. Keep you on the right path. Be your second. But you're shutting me out. *Again.* That's not what I signed on for. Maybe if you leaned on me a bit more, then—"

"Fine. You want to help? Find out who hired this guy." He tapped the license. Gave her a chilly look. "Just don't tell me how to do my job."

"Oh, your job. Sending a ton of crazy-ass killers out to nail abusers."

"I've started putting my plan into motion. I'm bringing Skeeter in."

"Skeeter? LMI's computer geek?"

"The one and same. I need his talents. Ever since our siege on Rasmussen, he's been laying low. But he resurfaced last week. Called me. Looking for safe haven."

"And you call this place 'safe'?" Nanette spread her hands. "Especially since someone just tried to kill you?"

"I don't believe in 'safe'. A myth right up there with Santa Claus. But right now, the ranch is all we have." He didn't need Nanette's badgering, especially now. Surely she realized a murder attempt trumped her needs. Of course he didn't want to alienate her any more than he already had. Far from it. But he had to keep his head clear. If he felt the need to protect her, keep her out of the line of fire, he'd become vulnerable to his enemies. "I'll try and do a better job of keeping you in the loop, Nanette." He put on his glasses, stared down at the paperwork on his desk. "Is that all?"

"Go to hell, Leon." She stood, swiftly hurried toward the door. "Hope you enjoy your job."

When she wrenched the door open, a shrill voice rose. Leon's first instinct: grab the letter opener. He relaxed his grip once he recognized the voice, a friendly one. Something lacking in Leon's life lately.

Small arms lassoed Nanette's waist. A smile disarmed her scowl.

"Nanette, my darling, you appear wonderful!"

Leon rose, whipped his glasses off. "Gustav?"

The little man strolled into the room, arms outstretched and zeroed in for a hug. "Leon, my friend! Or shall I call you Mr. Garber, now that you're the head of Like-Minded Individuals?"

"It's just Leon, Gus. It's good to see you."

Leon meant to stay behind his desk to avoid the inevitable hug. But like a heat-seeking missile, Gustav couldn't be defused. He raced around the desk, arms open like a needy toddler. The hug lasted an uncomfortably long time.

"Hey, Leon. How you doin'?" Dark in leather, Delilah strolled in. She jutted a hand out. Leon finally dislodged himself from Gus and accepted Delilah's power pump.

"I'm doing well, Delilah. And you look a lot better than the last time I saw you."

"Yeah, well, hell, Leon. Can't keep me down for long." She fell down into a chair, thrust her boots up onto the desk. "They kicked me out of Hell. Scared 'em too much."

Probably not far from the truth. Gustav and Delilah, an independently wealthy couple, comprised the "Good Samaritan Killer," a particularly macabre serial killing duo who authorities still believe to be one person. With Gustav dressed as a baby, Delilah carried him down desolate streets until a doomed "good Samaritan" picked them up. Then the knives came out. Even though their murderous deeds made Leon uneasy, he took comfort in their unexpected appearance. Allies were as rare at LMI as honest politicians. At least he *thought* he could trust Gus and Delilah. Leon's paranoia crept up on him, slapped him on the back like a sadist attacking a bad sunburn. Gus and Delilah's timing seemed...*odd*. He hated "odd."

Nanette sat down next to Delilah, her anger at Leon buried for the moment. "Delilah, I've been worried. We haven't heard from you since you nearly died."

"I almost did." Delilah tipped her head, clicked a side of her mouth. "But Gus called Bartholomew's doctor once we hit town. He patched me up. Good as new." She shifted in her chair, then winced. Her hand thumped her chest. "Almost good as new. I'm still recovering from the gun wound. We've been laying low, taking time to recover."

Gus ran to his lover's side and dropped his head on her shoulder. "It was touch and go for a while. But my angel pulled through. As I knew she would." They sealed the statement with a kiss. Delilah ruffled Gus's hair. Leon wondered if he could sustain a similar relationship. If these two unstable serial killers could find love, surely he and Nanette could. But Nanette's sudden scowl predicted a less than happy ending. Still caught up in their love-fest, Gus continued, "My dark angel is stronger than the Superman, yes? Able to withstand bullets."

"Stop it, Gus. You're gonna embarrass me."

Delilah's mention of Bartholomew dredged up something Leon needed to attend to. Even if he'd rather not. "Speaking of Bartholomew, have either of you seen him lately? Talked to him?"

Gus and Delilah glanced sideways at one another; not out of love, something far from it. Fear? Duplicity?

"I'm afraid we have not, friend Leon. Our mutual acquaintance, Bartholomew, appears to have vanished into the ozone." Delilah grinned, pressed black tipped fingernails to her similarly colored lips. "A marvelous phantom, our Bartholomew, he drifts like the wind, only to be seen when he cares to be. The perks of being extraordinarily wealthy." To illustrate his point, Gus slicked back his well-coifed hair, ran a thumb behind his tailored lapels. "Why do you ask?"

"Just curious. Everyone else seems to be turning up."

"Indeed we are!"

Leon reclaimed his throne. "It's great to see you both…but why're you here?"

Gustav straightened, smoothed out his suit jacket. Clapped his hands and spread them, dropping goodwill everywhere. A very half-glass full man. "Leon, my friend! Always so directly to the point! We were absolutely *thrilled* to hear about your appointment to CEO of Like-Minded Individuals! We could come out of hiding! A much unexpected, joyous event! We've come to offer our services."

"Well, thank you." Leon rocked in his chair, taking them both in. Weighing the plus and minus columns as his accounting background had prepped him to do. Planning on how he could use them to his advantage. "Your timing's fortuitous. I need people I can trust. Especially now." Nanette shot him a look.

"We are here to serve, my friend." Gus bowed. "Let us know what we can do for you."

"I will. Have you made living arrangements?"

Delilah and Gus shared a look, a blank one. "No, I'm afraid we have not. We were of the mind-set we could—what is the quaint Americanism—crash ourselves here."

"Wouldn't have it any other way, Gus. I'll have my men set up one of the empty cottages for you."

My men. Leon didn't catch it until after he'd said it. Flowed out naturally. It hadn't escaped Nanette's attention, though. She huffed, shook her head, disgusted. Maybe she was right. Maybe the job had become more important than the end-goal. Not for long, though. He'd prove her wrong.

"Splendid, my friend!" Gus patted his hands, an excited child at a birthday party. "Can you also have your men gather our luggage from the car? Delilah has quite an extensive wardrobe, you see."

Which surprised Leon. He'd only ever seen her wear leather and Goth chic. "Of course. I'll get right on it. But I have to warn you…" Leon leaned forward, dropped his voice.

Gus crawled up onto Delilah's lap, eyes wide and excited. Danger acted like caffeine on these two. "Yes?"

"This morning there was an attempt on my life. Things could get dangerous around here."

Gustav gasped, at odds with his cherubic smile. "How can this possibly be? You're now the CEO of our enemies!"

"Sometimes things aren't quite how they appear," said Leon.

"Don't I know it." Nanette stood, offered another smile to Gus and Delilah and walked out the door without acknowledging Leon.

It'd been a long time since Cody'd killed a mother. Way too long. Especially when he knew the evil mothers were out there, roaming in country club packs, totally deserving death by his hand. Taunting him because they knew he couldn't get to them. And that was the damn problem. His digs were kick-ass, the eye-candy at the pool even better, but Cody felt like a neutered dog. A much-pampered dog, sure, but Leon and his goons hardly ever let him out of their sight. Only when he slept. Nearly tucking him in, patting his head, telling him to dream sweet thoughts of candy-canes and crap like that, just shut up and be a good boy.

Cody didn't roll that way, just couldn't do it. He wanted to party, not toe the party-line. And of course, by "party," he meant killing a mother.

Not like he was an addict. Nothing like that. He could quit at any time. Hell, he'd been kill-free for six months now, practically gone through the twelve-step program or whatever. But keeping a talented guy like him—*a damn artist, yo!*—caged up was like asking Picasso to only paint portraits. Just ain't gonna happen, no way in hell.

But how to shake his constant shadows?

Leon kept him busy and all, but at night he had nothing better to do than kick back at his cottage. Watch TV. Surf the net.

Where his surfing splashed him onto *Hot Mothers Want to Meet You*.

Absolute agony knifed through him as he scrolled through the pages, too. Sure, some of the women looked hot. Some not so much. All of them mothers. Mean-ass mothers who abandoned their kids while they whored themselves out to strangers.

Like his own mother.

As if they could sense his presence, the women leered at him from the computer screen. Some wore sexy underwear. One disgusting mother bent herself impossibly backward over a sofa. Begging him to visit. He'd teach her a lesson she wouldn't forget. Well, hell, of course she'd forget it. She'd be dead after his not-so-jolly late night visit. *Ho, ho, ho!*

Purely out of proximity, he settled on one mother.

Shelby Shoemaker. Billings, Montana.

Cody typed in the digits from his LMI supplied credit card.

Yo, thanks, LMI!

Although the card was meant for the expenses of his job, Cody had no qualms, suffered no guilt. Considered it a necessary expense for doing hella' good work, keep him well-lubed. A perk. He'd earned it after the last six months of being a dutiful good, corporate big-shot.

Hi.

What's up, Momma? He typed.

Not much. How 'bout you?

I axed first, yo.

Just sitting here thinking about you, Cody. Mmmmm. I'll bet you're all big and strong...and just BIG.

You gots that right!

Mmmm. How 'bout you prove it to me?

Plan on doin' just that, Momma! How many kids you got anyway?

He figured more than one, judging by the stretch-marks visible in her online photo. The thought sickened him. Then thrilled him. He'd found a keeper, another notch in his collection.

How many kids do you want me to have, Cody?

He came damn close to tossing the lap-top through the window. Couldn't believe she used her kids to come on to him. But he kept cool. Cool and easy on the breezy, the way he always played it. His fingers trembled over the keyboard as he wrote back.

That's somethin' we'll talk 'bout when we meet, yo.

Mmmm. Sounds kinky. Can't wait. You close by?

Closer than you think!

Why don't we meet...say, Wednesday night? Seven p.m?

I'll be there with bells and balls on!

Billings was about thirty-five minutes away. He'd need to take one of LMI's cars, steal one if necessary. Piece-of-cake.

Sounds good, big man.

Cool! Just tell me where to be!

As she typed out her address, Cody considered asking her what she planned on doing with her children. He sure as hell didn't want them there. Although he'd make things right for her kids once and for all, he didn't want a little audience.

My fees are 300 dollars an hour and I accept all major credit cards. No checks. Payment up-front.

Total rip-off. But to Cody, well worth it. Hey, it's not his money!

Damn, baby, hope you live up to your price-tag!

Oh, you can count on it, Cody. Mmmm...can't wait! See u Wednesday!

She signed off with a boat-load of annoying hearts, kisses and emojis that Cody had no idea what they represented.

Bang, bang, bang...

Apparently a never-say-die woodpecker landed on Cody's door.

Still shaking with adrenaline, Cody closed the laptop. Quickly, he dropped, did ten push-ups to the beat of the insistent visitor at his door. Working it out of his system. On the way to the door, he admired his reflection in the hallway mirror.

Looking good, yo.

Out of breath, Cody opened the door.

"Leon! What's up, old man?"

And old he looked, much older than when Cody'd first met him. Grey tipped his temples. New lines road-mapped his forehead. And the bags beneath his eyes could hold groceries.

Leon entered, sighed. "I'm not old, Cody. Just turned forty-one."

"Hey, just calling it like I see it. Once you hit twenty-seven, it's all downhill from there, yo."

"I see you've raised your age limit since last year. What're you now? Twenty-six?"

Cody blinked, considered his age. *Shit.* Completely spaced his last birthday. He erased the thought with a flurry of hands. "Hey, I still got some good time on me, old man." He flexed a muscle, the t-shirt feeling nice and snug around his bicep. "Check out that cannon."

Leon laughed, a tired and mirth-free laugh. "We gonna arm wrestle next?"

"Hey, Cody's always up for a challenge. Bring it! Not that I 'spect you'd be much of a challenge."

"Maybe next time. We have business to attend to."

Without an invite, Leon swept by Cody. Made himself at home on Cody's sofa. The friggin' king of LMI. "Mi casa es su casa, I guess."

"Yes it is."

Cody blew off the implication, in too good of a mood. Let Leon play big man on campus. "Hey, you wanna beer, somethin' harder?" He jacked a thumb toward the well-stocked bar.

"I've told you time and again, I don't drink."

Cody sat down across from Leon. "Yo, that's the problem with you, boss. All work and no play. You look like crap. Maybe you oughta' get out more. Have some fun for a change. Hey, get stupid with Nanette. She's—"

"*That's* none of your concern."

There was a time when Cody could joke with Leon. Not now, not tonight. He folded his arms. "Fine. Whatever. Just tryin' to get you to chill."

"Chill's all I know."

Hardly! "Right. So…what's up? Got someone you need me to whack?"

Leon dragged a hand down his face, maybe considering the offer. "I want you to watch Gaines for me."

"Watch him do what? It's not like he does a lot."

"No. I mean, keep an eye on him. Let me know what he's up to."

Cody considered his new task. Not like he wanted to spend any more time in Gaines' company than he had to, but it might be an interesting job. Especially if it meant he'd get to deep-six him. Guy always did act holier than thou, like his shit didn't stink. "Cool. I'm on him like a leech."

"No, Cody, it's not cool. Anything but. I don't trust him."

"Jesus, Leon, you don't trust anyone."

"Probably why I'm still alive. Maybe you should be a little more careful who you trust."

"The hell's that supposed to mean? Hey, I'm careful. Remember, I got away with a crap-load of kills in Denver. I'm the Denver Decapitator. I'm damn nation—"

"Nation-wide. You've bragged about your resume many times. Now, can I trust you to be quiet about watching Gaines? You can't tell Sheera, Nanette, not even Gustav and Delilah. Don't—"

"Wait…what? That little dude and the hot punk chick? They're here?"

Another annoying sigh. Cody really wished Leon'd quit that habit. "Yes, they're here. Just don't tell them."

"So you don't trust them either?"

"I don't know who to trust any more. Someone tried to kill me today. I think it's an inside job."

"Whoa."

"Well said. Any ideas?" asked Leon.

"I dunno. Maybe...hell, I dunno." Cody spread his mental web wide, caught nothing. But Leon implied he trusted Cody. The only one. Didn't even vouch for his woman, Nanette. Harsh. Cody stuck his chest out, thumped it. "Count on me. I'll watch Gaines, let you know when he takes a dump."

"Um, that's not nec—"

"I mean it, you came to the right guy, yo. I got your back, brah."

"I know you do. We've been through a lot together since this whole mess started. We—"

Cody feigned falling asleep, snoring loud enough for Nanette to hear him next door. "Wha...sorry must've dozed off while you were writing me a love song. Forget all that candy-ass stuff, Leon. I already tole you I got your back."

"Fine. Tomorrow we're picking up Skeeter at the Billings Airport. I'm sure Sheera will make Gaines tag along. So don't—"

"Skeeter's comin' here? No shit?"

"Yes, Cody, 'no shit.'"

"Damn. Some kinda family reunion."

"Something like that. But I need Skeeter. To help take down LMI."

"You still plannin' on doin' that? I mean...I kinda thought you liked the status quo of everything here, all big meetings, fancy suits, cushy offices—"

"I'm still going to destroy them."

"Kick ass!"

With his final sigh of the night, Leon stood. Took him a while, too, as if his bones hurt, ever the old man. "Cody?"

"Yo."

"Everything all right with you? You seem kinda...nervous, agitated."

"No, no, brah, I'm good! You know me, just excited, ready for action! Ready to get—"

"*Don't* do anything without consulting me first." Back to being bad-ass boss, no more good times to cry over. Sometimes Cody wanted to bitch-slap him, bring him back down to earth a little bit. "You understand me, Cody?"

"Yeah, I get it. You bark, I obey. Ain't my first rodeo."

"Let's hope it's not our last."

And like the world's worst party guest, Leon finally left, leaving Cody wondering just what in the hell he'd meant.

he three of them stood in the airport lobby, shoulder-to-shoulder. Since Leon's talk with Cody last night, Cody'd taken his new task to heart. Glaringly so. He stayed glued to Gaines, sneaking blatant glimpses at the man when he wasn't outright staring at him. Covert spying apparently didn't top Cody's self-proclaimed vast repertoire of talents.

Leon wondered if he'd made a mistake. Then again, he always questioned his judgment where Cody was concerned.

Cody's itchy, agitated behavior really set Leon on alert: a lion prowling his cage, waiting for the moment to strike. Leon'd seen the behavior before. Call it "killer anticipation."

One by one, passengers departed the small plane out of Los Angeles. Leon had no idea what Skeeter looked like, although he had framed a portrait in his mind. Yet no one amongst the passengers fit into his preconception; all businessmen fueled by caffeine and impending appointments, a few bohemian types, couples hugging at the gates.

Along with Leon's expectations, the crowd thinned out. Skeeter hadn't made the plane. For some unknown—possibly deadly—reason, one Leon didn't want to think about too much.

At Leon's shoulder, a meek voice peeped. "Um, Leon. Dude? Hey Leon…"

Someone grabbed Leon's elbow. Immediately, Leon scrambled for his pocketed hypodermic. A natural reflex. He whirled. A scrawny, short teenager stood behind him. Sideways ball-cap. Faded t-shirt with an indecipherable logo. Jeans torn at the knees, either a modern stylish choice or homeless necessity.

Small dirt spots of hair speckled the kid's chin, a beard in stunted progress.

"Jesus!" blurted Leon.

The kid laughed. "Well, thanks. But you can call me Skeeter."

Leon regained his composure, left his needle in his pocket. "You're not quite what I expected." Leon almost added *and you're a kid!* Thought better of it.

Skeeter frowned. "Dude, what'd you expect? I'm a lot older than I look."

Of course Cody didn't think twice about voicing his opinion. "You ain't nothin' but a teenager!"

"And what're you, Spangler? In your late twenties? We're peers, dude."

"Ain't no peer of mine."

Clash of the titans. Leon intervened, stepping between them before an airport brawl broke out. "Easy does it. We're in a public place. Low visibility, LMI's edict."

Dammit.

It dawned on Leon how naturally he'd spouted LMI's ludicrous semi-business rhetoric. Something a true-blooded company man for a killer corporation might commit to heart.

Back to business. "Gaines, give Skeeter his welcoming gift."

Gaines didn't look too happy about it. His lip teetered on the edge of a sneer. Regardless, he offered the cooler to Skeeter.

Not the reaction Leon expected, Skeeter recoiled and wrapped himself into a tight bundle of nerves. As if cold, he rubbed his shoulders, hopped back. "Leon, you said it'd just be you and Spangler. Who's this?"

Gaines said nothing, never big on introductions. Leon played ambassador. "Skeeter, meet Gaines. Gaines, meet Skeeter." Neither man offered a hand. "Skeeter, Gaines is Sheera Rasmussen's secretary. You don't need to worry about him." *A lie.*

Paranoid as Howard Hughes, Skeeter remained curled up. "Dude, you never said anything about another guy coming. I dunno…I dunno…" He shook his head, shaking loose a ponytail from the back of his cap.

Leon wondered if Skeeter had been weaned on the

computer, never seeing the light of humanity. Could prove to be a problem, particularly with a squadron of armed men roaming the Rasmussen compound.

Hesitantly, Leon clapped a hand onto Skeeter's shoulder. He drew the kid in close, whispered, "Skeeter, I'm the CEO of LMI now. As long as I vouch for you...as long as you're with me, you have nothing to worry about. You'll be safe. *Trust* me." Easy words to say. Even harder to live up to. And immediately, Leon wanted to rephrase the implicit, nearly subliminal threat he'd delivered.

Warily, Skeeter eyed the three men from beneath his cap's bill. He dislodged himself from Leon, took another step back. A smile broke through, a shaky one. "Dude, you vouch for this guy, then I'm cool." Although Skeeter looked anything but cool.

Before Skeeter could mentally retreat again, Leon snagged the cooler from Gaines. "Here you go, Skeeter. What we talked about some time ago." A promise Leon had managed to fulfill.

Skeeter's eyes widened as he flipped over the cooler's top. "Dude! No way! You did it. Finally. Gave up on you there for a while." He stuck a hand in, pulled out a plastic wrapped package. "Omaha steaks." The parcel dropped back into the cooler. Skeeter waved his hand, blew on his fingertips. "Cold."

"Yo, Leon, how come I never got no damn Omaha—"

"Quiet, Cody."

"I'm just sayin', that's all. I never got no Omaha steaks. All I ever got was—"

"Oh, for God's sake, Cody, fine. I'll get you some Omaha steaks. Now, *please*...be quiet."

Content—for the time being, which Leon knew never lasted long—, Cody folded his arms, proud of his win. Gaines stared at Skeeter, ever unblinking.

"Gaines, go get the car. Pull it around front."

"Yes, *sir.*" Gaines hit the last word hard, a verbal scowl. He walked away, shoulders forward, arms motionless at his sides. The man walked like cement comprised his body. And Leon had no doubt cement flowed in his veins, crusted over his soul.

"Look, dude, I know I told you I'd help you and everything, but...I don't know that guy. Hell, I don't even really know you two. I just—"

"But, you know me as a man of my word." Leon pointed to the cooler, an unfair but necessary strategy. "And if I say you're safe, you're safe. But never say anything—*anything* at all—about what you're doing here in front of Gaines."

"Whoa, whoa, whoa..." Again, Skeeter backed up, bumped into a businessman. "You just said I'm safe, dude! Now you're saying don't—"

"Skeeter, try to relax. And lower your voice." Leon's hands went up, hostage negotiator style. "Remember where we are."

"Want me to grab him, Leon? Drag him to the car or somethin'?"

Of course that made matters worse. "What? *Dude*, I'm not about the violence! Now Spangler's *threatening* me?"

"No one's threatening you." Leon joined Skeeter and patted his back like a grief counselor. Cody shook his head, obviously disgusted. "Never mind Cody. He's harmless."

Cody snorted. "Harmless like a killer shark, maybe."

"Dammit, Cody, go join Gaines. You have a job to do, remember?"

As if pulled out of a dream, Cody's eyelids lifted. He mouthed, "oh," and took off at a trot.

Leon looked around, made sure no one stood within listening range. "Skeeter, I understand you're a little nervous about—"

"Nervous, shit! Dude, I'm terrified! This is way outta my wheel-house! I—"

Corporate rule Number One: Kill 'em with compliments. "And you roll the biggest wheel-house of anyone I've ever met, Skeeter." Corporate rule Number Two: Always use people's names. "That's why you're the only man for the job. Taking down LMI by—"

Skeeter flagged his hands. "No details, dude! I'll do it only because LMI sucks! I found out more about them than I ever wanted to! I learned things I wish I could un-learn! But no more details! Yeah, I'll do your work...but I don't wanna know about anything violent."

A start, Leon supposed. But how Skeeter'd convinced himself of his own innocence in all of his years at LMI confounded Leon.

With Skeeter's brilliant computer acumen, surely he knew what LMI was up to. Baby steps, though. As in dealing with children and artists, Leon found himself in charge of some of the most temperamental creatures on the planet. He strapped kid gloves on and tip-toed with caution.

"That's fine, Skeeter. You set your boundaries and I won't cross them."

Slowly, Skeeter calmed down utilizing a series of deep-breathing, closed eyes exercises. It'd been a miracle airport security hadn't flagged his peculiar behavior yet.

As Leon steered Skeeter toward the exit, he said, "I know you're older than you look. You've been with LMI since before I joined them. But…how'd you ever get involved?"

Skeeter tried to vanish into his own shadow. "Dude, weird story," he said quietly. "You know that spooky-ass Summers guy?"

Leon nodded. Mr. Summers: LMI's mysterious head-hunter, the man who'd indoctrinated Leon many long years ago.

"I was in high school. Checking out my options. Which weren't many, dude. Cause, like, no way was I ever gonna sit in a cubicle or anything, answering to the man. Get me?"

"Yes." *Sort of.*

"Well, on career day, Summers shows up in my counselors' chair. Said he had an excellent proposition for me. First thing I thought, 'dude! I'm not gay!' But Summers said his company would train me completely. See, I already had mad computer skills. I never had to study once in high school. Literally wrote my own grades. Well, this Summers, he'd heard of me. Recruited me. Handed me a huge-ass contract, told me if I signed today, I could leave high school behind, not bother with graduating. Make more money than I'd ever dreamed of. So, I thought, 'what, and leave all the glorious bullying behind?' I signed. Didn't even bother to read the small print. Flipped off everyone, teachers and students, out the door."

Leon pushed through the airport's revolving door. Skeeter stayed behind, hands folded beneath his chin. Leon came back inside, nudged Skeeter toward the side door reserved for wheelchair access.

"What happened after that, Skeeter?"

"Dude, LMI pretty much locked me in a room for a couple years straight. Didn't see anybody but a couple of stuffed shirt, old guy teachers. Finally, LMI put me to work. But they warned me to keep my mouth shut. Don't talk to anyone. They'd take care of all my needs. They didn't want me to leave my apartment. Life as a hermit."

"That…sounds awful."

He shrugged. "It is what it is. Sure as hell was better than getting beat up in high school. Only two options I ever really knew, I guess."

Leon crawled into the back seat and waited for Skeeter to join him. Skeeter stood on the sidewalk, looking elsewhere, looking for options. Leon imagined Skeeter's mind a chaotic, scary place, a place he never wanted to visit. Leon held out a helping hand. After deliberating, Skeeter grabbed it and jumped in. Before the car started moving, he gripped the "oh, hell" handle and hung on for dear life.

No matter what candy coating Skeeter glazed over his LMI indoctrination tale, Leon saw it for the truth. *Abuse*. No doubt about it.

He added Summers' name to those who'd pay when retribution day came.

Chapter Four

Nanette knocked on the door, wine bottle and two glasses in hand. A flurry of footsteps sounded from within. Hip to hip, hands held, Gus and Delilah opened the door.

"The lovely Nanette! What brings you to our cottage? Oh, dear, where are my manners? Come in, please."

"Hi, Gus, Delilah. I hope I'm not intruding."

"Nonsense! You're welcome anytime. Mi cottage es su cottage."

Delilah grinned, stayed quiet.

"Now, what can we do for you? I see you've brought liquid refreshments," said Gustav.

"Actually...I came to talk to Delilah, Gus. If you don't mind."

Gus' frown spoke volumes, disappointed he'd miss a party. He never stayed down long, though. With a firecracker clap of his hands, he said, "I see. Splendid! Girl's night out?"

"Something like that. Can I bend your ear for a little bit, Delilah?"

Leather squeaked as Delilah squirmed. As outgoing as Gus could be, Delilah remained his polar opposite. Opposites attract, so Nanette had heard.

"Ah...sure. Everything good?" asked Delilah.

"Yes. No. I'm not sure."

The lovers exchanged a glance before Delilah said, "Gus, why don't you go catch up on your TV show?"

"Capitol idea, my love! I so enjoy the binge. My story is a marvelous insight into the heart of America." Gus raced up the stairs faster than an excitable child.

"What show's he watching?" asked Nanette.

"The Dukes of Hazzard."

"Really?"

"I know, right?" A shared giggle broke ice. Nanette relaxed, just a bit. Recently, while inventorying her life (not that there was much else to do at the ranch), Nanette realized she'd never had a close girlfriend before. Few friends for that matter. Par for the lonely course of like-minded individuals.

Nanette clinked the two wine glasses together. "Wine?"

"Think I'm gonna need it."

Delilah grabbed the bottle, uncorked it in no time. They settled on a sofa, the same tan model as in her cottage. In fact, the two domiciles were identical, down to a curious lengthy scratch on the wall.

Delilah propped her feet up on the coffee table. "So. What's up?"

Nanette sighed. Took a long sip of wine, fortified herself. "Okay, this is weird, I know..."

Accompanied by a crunch of leather, Delilah adjusted herself, turned toward Nanette. "Ya' think?"

"Delilah, how do you and Gus do it? I mean you guys are crazy in love with one another. Yet...we're all..."

Delilah shrugged. "Serial killers?"

The term unsettled Nanette, an ugly label. She had always avoided it, preferring to view herself as a necessary force, one that brought balance to an unjust man's world. Someone had to stand up for wronged women. But sometimes a horse is a horse, no matter the gussied up saddle you placed on it.

Delilah must've sensed Nanette's discomfort. She whacked Nanette's shoulder, let out a brisk, uncustomary laugh. "Oh, come on! Don't be so uptight. Drink up."

Good advice. "Okay, yeah, I kill people. And because of the life I lead...I don't have any friends. Not really. But you and Gus are so close...practically one and the same. How're you able to do it?"

Delilah's shoulders went up. "I dunno, really. I think we're lucky in a way. I mean, I'm not one to believe in fate or God or any of that stuff...but the stars aligned for us when we met. Now I can't even remember life before Gus."

"Is, um…your killing what keeps you close?"

"No. Well, hell, it's how we met. But…it's not what our love's about."

"What *is* it about?"

Delilah closed her eyes, a pained look on her face. "I dunno. Tough question. Sometimes things just…*are*, you know?"

No, not at all. "I suppose. But with the lives we lead, you two—"

"Don't get all gooey on me. Look, I don't have all the answers. I just know Gus and I were meant for one another. We lucked out. I doubt anyone else would have us. Is this about Leon?"

"No. Why—"

"Oh, *whatever.* Sell it to someone who's buying."

"Okay, fine."

"So…trouble in la-la land?"

"More like nothing going on." Nanette wanted to say more. Tell Delilah how lonely life felt, how she wanted to settle down. Change. Live a normal life. But she didn't want to gooey up Delilah's path. "I guess…I thought we were headed somewhere. Somewhere different. Somewhere good. But since Leon took on the CEO position…he's pushed me away."

"Huh. Yeah…he does seem a bit different. Not that he's ever been an easy-going guy, but he seems…I dunno, darker."

"Exactly. He won't admit it, but I think he's forgetting why he took the job in the first place. Now, it's almost as if he's enjoying it."

"Nanette, why aren't you telling him this? Instead of me?"

"I've tried! He won't listen."

"Oh, for God's sake." Delilah let out an exasperated sigh, clearly out of her comfort zone. "What do you want me to say?"

"What's your secret? How do you two keep it together?"

"There's no secret! Fine. I'm the last one to be giving relationship advice. But…our relationship isn't as easy as it looks, you know. It's not built on big revelatory moments and proclamations of love. It's hard. But you work at it. Every day. Not big adjustments or huge-ass promises. Just a little maintenance, bit by bit. Day by day." Delilah topped her glass off, chugged half of it down. "That's what I got. Probably not much, but…

my advice is just go talk to Leon. Make him listen. Figure it out together. Quit wasting time with me."

Sound advice, of course. But the problem remained that Leon may've already lost interest. For whatever reason. And, frankly, Nanette wondered just how much longer she could maintain interest.

"Thanks, Delilah."

"I didn't do anything."

"No, you helped. And I know you're a little uncomfortable with—"

"I'd say I'm here for you anytime. But I wouldn't really mean it. I just don't do the whole 'girl talk' thing. Not in my make-up."

"I know. It's not really my deal either."

"Are we gonna do each other's hair and talk about cute boys next?"

Nanette laughed. "I'll go get my sleeping bag. Anyway... thanks again. I'll leave you to it."

"Cool. As long as you leave the bottle, too."

"Drink up. Tell Gus I hope he learns a lot from The Dukes of Hazzard."

Wine shot from Delilah's mouth, a classic spit-take. "Yeah. An education in daisy dukes."

As Nanette opened the door, Delilah called out, "Hey!"

"Yeah?"

"Watch Leon. Don't let him turn into one of them."

"I'm trying."

Outside, Nanette stopped, gazed at the big, uninviting house. Where Leon barricaded himself most of the day, all LMI business twenty-four seven. She considered taking Delilah's advice. March into the house and force Leon's attention.

But, really, what good would it do?

She deep-sixed the idea and headed for her cottage. And despised her weakness, pining for a relationship that wasn't happening. A guy never hung her up like this before. If there was hanging to do, she always tightened the rope, pulled the trap-door lever. She expected her head to spin, her belly to swirl, all the romantic clichés that's supposed to dominate someone in love. Instead she felt pathetic.

One way or another, something had to give. *Soon.*

The afternoon dragged on and on. Even watching the ever-present pool babes failed to alleviate Cody's tension. Just made him more uptight. He busied himself by imagining what it might be like to kill both of the water nymphs in one marathon session. Could be fun. Still, he saw no evidence of their motherhood. Too young, probably. And their deaths would be a total waste of hotness.

He still had three hours or so until his "date." But he couldn't continue to chill his heels by the pool. Time to get the show on the road. Maybe he'd hit up a bar first. Could make things more fun with a few drinks warming his gut.

Dressed in his favorite hoodie (favorite for several reasons, actually; first, it looked smokin' cool; second, the hood provided a good mask should he need it), he strolled over to the car-filled garage. Casual as could be. Had to keep it cool to get the hell off the ranch without a babysitter. He sure didn't want Gaines riding shotgun.

Last in line, the Bentley practically screamed to be taken out. Sunlight's fading rays sliced through the open garage door, rippling like a reflected pond upon the car's polished hood. A quick look around showed the garage empty. Which made Cody wonder just what in hell all of Mrs. Rasmussen's goons did all day. No matter, it'd work in his favor.

He opened the key cabinet, drew his fingers across the various keys until he scored the right ones. The key shook in his hand as he inserted it in the Bentley's door. Not from fear, never an issue with Cody. Rather, he welcomed the old familiar, kick-ass adrenaline surging through him.

"Hey!"

Dammit. Not fast enough.

The pistol-packing guard had snuck up on him, stealthy as a ninja. He slammed the car door shut, kept his hand on the window. "What're you doin', Spangler?"

"What's it to you, chief? I gots bidness to take care of."

The suit scratched at his five o'clock shadow. "Haven't heard anything about this."

"What? Like you're supposed to know everything, magic eight-ball? Just shut up and get outta my way."

"Can't do that. Not without clearance." The guard plucked out his telephone.

"Hey, you're gonna piss off the ol' man. My boy, Leon wants me to go get him somethin'."

"If that's true, I'd know about it." Cody snatched the phone away. He held it high, making the guard jump for it. "Look, Spangler, there's two ways we can do this...the easy—"

"Or not so easy way? Chill out. Last minute decision. Leon needs me to run him an errand. Now let me do it."

"The phone. Hand it over. Only take a few seconds if you're on the level."

Damn. Try putting one over on this guy. "And I'm tellin' you this came down from the LMI big dog. And he ain't in a good mood today either. You wanna keep your job? Then let me do my damn job. I outrank you, yo. So shut up and move your ass."

The guard looked toward the ranch, back at Cody, settled his gaze on his shoes. Turtles moved faster.

"Fine. But if you're lying to me, I'll make sure Mr. Gaines hears about it."

"Yeah, whatever...go cry to mommy while you're at it. Times wastin'."

"Okay, big man." The guard sneered, exposing crooked teeth. "Have it your way. Maybe one of these days we'll see just how high you rank."

"My shorts rank higher than you, dick."

The guard snorted. Cody wanted to wipe the smirk off his face. But that'd possibly screw up the Big Picture. Keep it cool, wait for the pot at the end of the rainbow.

Once Cody bypassed the equally hard-ass guardians of the gate, he thought about the garage guard's words: *Maybe one of these days we'll see just how high you rank.*

The hell's that supposed to mean?

Whatever. No big deal. Little man just wants to play in the big leagues.

Cody couldn't worry about it. Not now. He had a hot date, so hot sweat broke across his forehead.

Gaines hovered over Leon like a satellite. Quietly gathering Intel, no doubt. Waiting and watching.

"Gaines, give me some time to read these documents. Then I'll get them back to you."

Gaines shrugged. "They're just invoices, sir. And an application for a new Like-Minded Individual. If you could just sign them and give—"

"And I said I want to read them." A lesson hard learned, but these days Leon always read LMI's paperwork before signing. Something his predecessor, Jasper Rasmussen, apparently hadn't understood. Didn't work out so well for him. "I'll give them to you later."

Gaines didn't budge. Battle of the wills.

Voices rose in the hall.

"Dude, get offa' me! I gotta talk to Leon." Skeeter entered the office, a guard behind him.

"Sorry, Mr. Garber," said the guard. "You want me to escort him outta here?"

"Leon, I gotta talk—"

Leon gestured for Skeeter to come in. "No, it's fine. You're dismissed, Daniels."

"What's with the Nazi protocol around here, Leon?" asked Skeeter. "I can't go to the john without one of these bulldogs tailing me." Skeeter watched the guard retreat, ready to jump at the slightest provocation. "Gives me the creeps."

"Don't take it personally, Skeeter. It's just standard business operations."

"Yeah, standard for a prison, maybe."

Skeeter sat across from Leon. Silently, Leon glared at Gaines, hoped he'd take the hint. Gaines stood firm, arms crossed. Defying Leon. "You're not needed for this, Gaines."

"No disrespect, sir, but Mrs. Rasmussen told me I should be present for all LMI business and—"

"This isn't business, Gaines. It's a social call. Right, Skeeter?"

Skeeter ran a finger inside his T-shirt's collar, the same one he'd been wearing yesterday. "Uh, yeah, cool, cool. Sure. Whatever."

Gaines stared at Leon, then gave Skeeter the same treatment. Skeeter turned his head away, unable to weather Gaines' icy intensity. Not many people could. Finally, Gaines glided out of the office, quiet as death.

"Leon, I found out some things—"

Leon jutted a finger to his lips and stood. He walked toward the door, stuck his head out. Close by, Gaines squatted, tying his shoe. Or pretending to.

"I'll call you when I need you, Gaines."

Gaines straightened and floated off in his stiff gait.

Leon closed the door and sat. "Okay, Skeeter, let's talk quietly."

"Dude! What's with all the subterfuge? Thought you were the head honcho."

Leon knew better than to tell Skeeter the entire truth. Or at least the suspected truth. No sense in fanning Skeeter's paranoia to off-the-chart levels. "I am. But in our line of business, it pays to be cautious."

Which did absolutely nothing to alleviate Skeeter's anxiety. He moaned, rolled his eyes. "What have you got me mixed up in, dude? I mean, I came here to be safe! Not—"

"You're probably in the safest place you can be now. With me."

"Right. I just heard someone tried to *whack* you! I didn't—"

"Calm down, Skeeter. You're protected here. You have my word."

"I dunno, Leon, I—"

"You said you found out something?"

"Yeah. Okay, I've been looking into the board members' financial standings. Dudes have more off-shore accounts than Meyer friggin' Lansky!"

"What I suspected. Will you be able to hack them?"

A smile brushed Skeeter's paranoia aside. Speaking his language. "Oh, hell, yes! Gotta give me some time though. They're careful."

"I'd expect nothing else."

"Oh…and about that other thing?"

Leon nodded.

"You wanted me to track Spangler's computer trail?"

Leon sat forward, nerves jangling.

"Seems he's hooking up with a prostitute tonight."

"What? Dammit. Why didn't you lead with this, Skeeter?"

He shrugged. "Hey, I didn't think it was a big deal. Whatever gets his rocks—"

"Next time, let me know immediately!" Leon stood, worked his way into his suit jacket. "What time? Where?"

Skeeter leaned sideways, dug into his pocket. Foil gum wrappers bloomed out before he found a wadded piece of paper. "Got all the deets here. Sorry I didn't tell you earlier. But, dude, I just found out about—"

"It's fine." Leon struggled to read Skeeter's handwriting. Placed his glasses on and adjusted the paper back and forth before it came into focus. "House in Billings. 7:00."

"Yeah."

"Gives me about an hour."

Leon raced out of the office, tugging an arm through his jacket. He blew by Gaines, still within eavesdropping range.

"Sir? Is everything all right?"

"It's fine. I have to run an errand."

"I'll come with you."

"No, stay here!" Leon stopped, turned, thrust out a commanding finger.

"Mrs. Rasmussen has given me specific instructions to accompany—"

"I don't give a damn what she's said! I'm going alone." He checked his watch. "I don't have time to argue with you."

He ran down the hall and took the stairs at an avalanche of footfalls.

Good God. I hope I'm not too late.

As he raced to the garage, he dialed Cody's number. Pointless. He should've known better. Nothing would stand in Cody's way. After three rings, the phone kicked Leon to voice mail.

"Yo, you know the drill." Beeeeep.

"Cody, call me back. Now! Don't do anything stupid. Don't risk everything. Stop what you're doing! For God's sake, don't…"

Leon rambled, pleading, until the call ended.

He sped the Cadillac to the gate, horn blaring. Frantically, he waved his hand out the window. The guards didn't comply and the gate stayed sealed.

"Open the damn gate! Now!"

A guard sauntered up, lazy as a hot summer day, and leaned down. Around a toothpick, he said, "Mr. Garber, we don't have you scheduled to leave today."

"This is an emergency! Open the gate!"

"But sir, I—"

"Listen, McAleister, you like your job here?"

"Um, yes sir."

"Then if you want to keep it, open the gate!"

"Yes sir." The guard still wouldn't hustle, took his sweet time. Finally, he rolled a hand in the air. The lock buzzed. The electronic gate slowly opened.

"Hey, McAleister?" asked Leon.

"Yes sir?"

"When did Cody leave?"

"Couple hours ago. In the Bentley."

Goddammit.

"He said he was running an errand for—"

"Fine, fine."

Leon roared down the gravel road, dust and fear chasing him.

Skeeter'd said he thought Cody just wanted to get his rocks off.

But Leon knew Cody wanted to "get off" something besides his rocks.

Most of the barstools at *Jimmy's Joint* remained unoccupied and that suited Cody just fine. More time to flirt with the bartender. Rough around the edges, she'd flashed her aqua covered eyelids at him the minute he'd walked in. Old, though, too old for Cody's tastes. Possibly a mother. He considered tackling two in one night. But that might be overkill, so to speak.

Still, if he couldn't kill her, he might as well kill time with her.

He held the tenner between his fingers, baiting her like a guy in a strip club.

"How 'bout another one, darling. One for the road."

"Anything else you'd like for the road, cutie?" She leaned across the bar, wiggling her butt like a happy dog.

"Depends on what you got in mind."

"Got lots of things on my mind."

Cody's ring-tone blared out again, one of his favorite death metal slams.

"Dammit." Just when things were getting good, the caller threw his game off. Leon. *Again.* King of the buzz-kill. He'd already left about four messages, each more urgent than the last. Guy seriously needed to relax a little. Apparently, he'd found out about Cody's appointment, one Cody had every intention on keeping.

Time to bounce.

Cody withdrew his cash. The bartender met him with a sour look, one that aged her even beyond Cody's initial appraisal. Definitely a mother's disapproving, bitchy look. He'd remember her next time when visiting Billings.

"Gotta go, baby."

"What a shame."

"I know, right? But I'm worth the wait."

"Sure you are. Don't forget about me." She spider-walked fingers across his arm.

"How could I forget?" Cody slammed the last of his beer.

At the door, he turned, asked, "Hey, you got kids?"

She hesitated, then spread crimson lips over a green grin. "Yeah, I gotta couple. That a problem with you, sweetie?"

"No. It's perfect."

Confusion crinkled her forehead.

One of Cody's mottos (and he had tons of them) was always leave 'em wanting more. Like a stand-up comedian.

He hopped into the Bentley, hunkered down and checked out his hair in the mirror.

Fifteen minutes 'til seven. Plenty of time to make it.

While the beer supplied his buzz, he patted down the power saw next to him, the partner that would bring the true buzz.

Leon sped down the long gravel road. A hailstorm from hell pelted the undercarriage. Clouds of dust followed him, but as far as he could see, no one from LMI did. The fewer people involved in this fiasco, the better.

His front tires hit the highway pavement with a jerk. The back end of the car kicked. And Leon accelerated.

Just enough time.

If a highway patrolman didn't stop him.

Not fast enough.

He stepped down on the pedal, bringing the Caddy to a wobbly eighty miles per hour.

He throttled the steering wheel, a series of angry push-ups. A less than satisfactory stand-in for Cody.

Dammit! Stupid, so stupid!

For once, Cody's bragging carried truth behind it. He topped the FBI's most wanted list; or at least his nom de plume, the Denver Decapitator did. Of course the feds had no clue the Decapitator now resided in Montana. But after tonight, they would.

Up ahead, a car sat on the shoulder. Leon squinted, couldn't make out any tell-tale cherries on top, no flashy stars on the side. Not a cop. Just a motorist in trouble.

With Skeeter now on-board, Leon felt close—*so* close—to taking down LMI. But not if a major manhunt swept down upon Billings, Montana. Wouldn't be long before interest fell upon the isolated Rasmussen ranch. And like Cody, Leon knew he'd graduated to a "person of interest." The Florida detective, Keats, who he'd tangled with six months ago (and, ultimately, saved her life, but he doubted that registered in her thoughts these days) knew his real name. In his field, popularity wasn't good.

Twenty minutes to seven.

He just might make it. Unless Cody jumped the gun. And seeing as how Cody'd left hours ago, Leon didn't put it past him. He floored the gas. Ninety, ninety-five…

The steering wheel shook. His arms rattled, jarred up to his teeth. A flying rock, a scurrying raccoon, a tire blow-out could send him hurtling into the woods. Didn't matter. Couldn't think about it.

Cody'd always been sloppy in his work. Decapitating mothers. Leaving blood everywhere. Easily identifiable work.

And what would the LMI board members do if they found out Cody opened up shop again? No doubt pull the plug on Leon. Or plug him full of lead.

At all costs, Leon had to stop Cody. Stop him from destroying the careful work he'd put into effect, the seeds of uprooting LMI once and for all.

Oh, and to save the life of an innocent woman. Not in the most legal of all trades, of course, but certainly she didn't deserve a premature and agonizing death.

Never one to break his rule about driving and phoning, sometimes rules had to be bent. He called Cody again.

"Cody, dammit, *listen* to me! Stop what you're doing! You're gonna ruin *everything*! If you go through with this...who *knows* what LMI will do to you! For your own safety, stop! Now! Come home!"

His message cut off. Leon's previous tirades probably filled Cody's inbox. Not that they'd do any good. Never on Cody.

Stupid kid.

The skyline of downtown Billings appeared in the distance. Falling sunlight broke through the clouds, beamed off a skyscraper.

Fifteen minutes to go.

Come on, Cody, for once in your life, think!

With five minutes to go until killing time, the GPS directed Leon into a disheveled neighborhood, one built on foundations of decay and misery. Low income apartment buildings and one-floor, cracker box ranches lined the streets. Thatches of spare grass struggled to survive in the sun-baked mounds of dirt that passed for yards.

An old Chevrolet, up on blocks, sat in Shelby Shoemaker's driveway. Weather-ravaged toys decorated her lawn, pop art ornaments. And in the midst of the toys sat a boy. Six, possibly seven years old. Dirt smudged his face, a dirty t-shirt and torn jeans adorned his body.

Shit.

Two houses down, Leon slowed the car to the curb. Killed the engine. And wondered what in the hell he'd do with the boy out front.

No sign of the Bentley, not yet. But maybe Cody'd already come and gone, leaving behind his ghastly calling card. But, surely, not even Cody would kill the boy's mother with him in the front yard. With Cody, though, never discount the unexpected.

He had to move fast. Without a plan. He hated winging it, liked to be prepared. Not the smartest option, but his only one.

The screen door opened. A mid-thirties, haggardly blond woman stepped onto the porch. Wearing a see-through negligee. Mother of the year.

"Ricky!" she called. "Ricky, get your ass in here now!" She fell into a coughing fit, resumed her screaming. "Goddammit, Ricky, get in here!"

At first the boy ignored her, his interest in a toy truck undivided. His shoulders hunched as he drove the truck into the dirt.

"Goddammit!" The woman strode outside, her apparel apparently routine for outside wear. With arms akimbo she stood above her son. "I told you to get your ass inside!"

"No, Momma! I don't wanna go in the closet!" Ricky closed his eyes, curled up into a ball of defiance.

The woman's arm rose. A waddle of fat wiggled on the underside.

Crack.

Her open palm slapped the side of the child's head.

Leon gripped the steering wheel, his knuckles chalk white. Hyperventilation raised his heart rate. His thoughts muddied, anger boiled.

The boy shrieked. Thrust an arm over his head. Little protection from the woman's next slap. Or the next. Her abuse ended with a full-on punch to Ricky's back, square between the shoulder blades. Ricky flopped forward. His arms raised dust as he landed.

"Momma! Please don't make me go in the closet! I hate the closet! I don't wanna—"

"Shut up! Shut up! I've got company comin' over in a couple minutes. Do as you're told!" With both hands, she gripped the boy's thin arm and wrenched him to his feet. He shook like a dead rabbit in a dog's maw. "You want food on the table, you little crybaby? Then do as you're told!"

"No, Momma, please, no, no, no…" The boy's sobs stirred his words into soup. But Leon received the message loud and clear. The woman abused her son. Constantly. And locking him in a closet while she entertained her clients?

Unacceptable.

Leon's rage subsided. A methodical calmness claimed him. In control of himself. And it felt good.

He watched as the heinous mother dragged her kicking and screaming boy inside the house. The screen door slammed with a jarring snap, a guillotine's blade.

Now he faced an entire new set of problems. Absolutely he felt no empathy for the woman. She deserved Cody's planned fate for her. Just not in Cody's usual signature fashion.

But what about the boy inside?

Part of Leon—the part he hadn't been in touch with lately—demanded to do the deed himself. But he'd sworn off his old ways. *Haven't I?* And everyone falls off the wagon occasionally. *Right?*

No.

Not today. Not ever again. At least not by Leon's hand. Rather by proxy.

Leon loosened his tie. Lifted his collar. Put on sunglasses even though dusk had fallen. Slipped into his old leather gloves, fine and fitting. Not much of a disguise. But in this neighborhood where a prostitute in a negligee routinely beats her son, he doubted many of the neighbors were involved in a watch program.

As he left the car, he still had no idea what he'd do. He liked everything nice and tidy, old accounting ways hard to abandon.

One quick visual sweep up and down the street. The neighbors had barricaded themselves into their own dens of despair. Time to go to work.

A warm feeling, a sense of nostalgia buzzed his brain, zipped messages through his body. A much missed old friend.

Before he knocked, Shelby Shoemaker appeared behind the screen door with come-hither eyes. She swirled a shot glass in her hand. And opened the door.

"Hey there, Cody. You're not at all what I expected."

Buried behind a closet door, Ricky's sobs sounded muffled, but insistent. His sobs wouldn't be the only thing prepared for burial.

"Hi. Shelby?"

"That's what my daddy calls me." She twirled, the negligee flying freely. "Drink?"

"Momma, I'll be good and stay in my room...please, Momma..."

"I don't drink." No sense in dragging this on. Leon plucked the hypodermic from his pocket. Directly behind her, he wrapped an arm around her waist.

"Mmm. You don't waste any time."

"Wasting time's for the idle."

"Momma, Momma, please..."

Leon stabbed the needle into her neck. Her purring ended with a yip. Her body stiffened. Weakly, she gripped his arm, attempted to wrest it free. Leon slipped the used needle back into his pocket and clamped his hand around her mouth. Held her close to him, swaying in a slow dance. Until she relaxed. Before she went completely black, Leon whispered into her ear, "Shelby, you should never, ever abuse your child. You won't again."

Then he lowered her limp body to the floor.

Felt like old times, good times.

Dizziness overtook Leon. He couldn't catch his breath. His vision darkened. Through a flurry of stars, he stared at the unconscious beast at his feet. Grinned. *Beautiful.*

As his world brightened back into clarity, trouble came with it.

Oh, my God. The boy in the closet! The body! Cody! What the hell am I gonna do?

Clearly, he hadn't thought this through. But no way could he leave this woman's crimes unpunished. Absolutely intolerable.

The smart move would be to wait for Cody. Make sure things went properly. The woman would be out for a while.

But it wasn't the humane thing to do, not with the boy in the closet.

Leon looked around, found a pad of paper and pen on a coffee table. Quickly (but not too quickly) he composed a note using generic, blocky capital letters and dropped it on the woman's body.

In front of the closet door, Leon whipped off his tie and spoke in a calm voice. "Ricky?"

"Yeah? Who's there?" A huge *snurfff,* the boy wiping his nose.

"A friend. I want to help you."

"Help me?... Where's Momma? *Momma!*"

"Ricky, shhh... I promise I won't hurt you. Your mother's taking a nap now. She wanted me to...take you away."

"Away?" A pause. Hopeful? More than likely scared. "Away where?"

"Somewhere safe. Somewhere where your mother won't hurt you."

"But...I wanna be with Momma! Momma!"

Leon closed his eyes, leaned his forehead against the closet door. Abused children never saw abuse for what it was, particularly when delivered from the violent hand of a parent. They'd been trained to see it as parental love. Leon knew all too well.

"Calm down, Ricky. I promise you...things will get better." Mere placating words. But Leon meant to see they'd come true. *Somehow.*

"You promise?" Again, hesitation, a hint, a thought of how things might become better. Leon thought the boy hadn't been too damaged. Yet.

"I promise."

"But...will Momma come with me?"

"Maybe later." *Absolutely not.* "But I need you to do me a favor, Ricky. Okay? A big boy favor."

Silence. Another sniff. Finally, "What?"

"I need you to close your eyes. And keep them closed."

"But...why?"

"It's a game. You like games, Ricky?"

"Yeah...but Momma never plays with me."

"I will. When I open the door, I'm going to put a blindfold on you."

"I dunno..."

"It's because I don't want you to see the secret awesome place I'm taking you to."

And because Leon had no idea where in hell that secret awesome place might be.

Ahead of Cody, taillights vanished down the road. Not a problem, not tonight. Excitement drove him as surely as the Bentley had in getting him there. Probably why he got lost. Or maybe it'd been the four beers he'd knocked back.

Either way, he felt amped. And things were about to get better.

One last look through his gym bag. Power saw? Check. Gloves? Check. Cover-alls? Checkity-check! With bag in hand, he strolled up the driveway, whistling. Some stupid jazz tune Leon always listened to, old fashioned and upbeat. Just couldn't shake it from his head.

He knocked on the screen door, looked around the yard. Lots of toys. Yep, a mother alright. Made the right damn choice. He swung his arms and the gym bag bounced off his biceps.

This time he pounded on the screen door louder. "Hello?" The front door was open a crack. Louder, "*Hello!*"

Piss-poor customer service.

He opened the screen door. Gave the front door a nudge. Quietly, it floated open. Unveiling a woman lying on the floor.

"The hell?"

First thing Cody thought was someone had beaten him to the punch. Total rip-off. Then he noticed a note on her chest.

Better than Omaha steaks.

Do it right, clean & discreetly.

Do not use your regular handiwork.

Clean up.

No mistakes.

Old Man

Cody stared at the body, the letter. Dumbfounded.

What the hell?

No doubt Leon had left him the note, already come and gone. Had he killed her? Cody placed fingertips beneath the woman's nose, felt a hot plume of breath.

No. Just unconscious. But why the hell would Leon do that? And he stole the fun part. Cody always got a kick out of watching them plead, the looks in their eyes at the last minute of life.

What's the fun in offing a passed out chick if he hadn't been the one who knocked her out?

Of course, he could wait for her to wake. Could take hours, though, time he didn't have. The LMI jackasses were probably all up in a shit-storm about his trip by now.

He dropped to his knees and slapped her. Did it again. Nothing. Just a deep sigh, an intake of breath. And a really gross snore. Hardly sexy.

The hell with it.

Cody took out his power saw, his work clothes. As he thrust one leg into the coveralls, he hopped on the other foot. And thought about Leon's note again.

Do not use your regular handiwork.

The hell's that supposed to mean anyway? Sometimes Leon had a problem speaking straight up English. Dude needed some more schooling or something.

Fully dressed and ready for action, Cody yanked the cord on the power saw. The saw growled, sending jolts through his arm and warming his chest like a stiff drink.

The sound stirred the woman.

Bonus!

She looked up at him through glassy eyes. Glassy eyes that widened. Unmistakable and very delicious fear paled her face. Still groggy, she screamed, sort of like gargling. Brought up heavy hands in front of her face.

Enlightenment smacked Cody, brought on by a rush of exhilaration.

Of course that's what Leon meant! Don't use my usual tranquilizer!

No problem. Cody wouldn't knock her out. Leon'd already done that. Probably a bad interaction of drugs or something might happen. And, hey, he'd never sawed the head off a conscious mother before.

Better than Omaha steaks!

"Yo, Shelby, what's up?" Cody straddled her. The saw sizzled over his head. "They call me Cody. Nice to meet cha'. But you gotta go. 'Cause you're a terrible mother."

Her scream performed an awesome duet with the saw's hungry buzz.

What am I doing?

The longer Leon drove (going nowhere, waiting for logic to hook), panic built.

Kidnapping. A crime not far from abuse. The thought soured his stomach. Sweat dampened his armpits, his forehead.

"Mister! Are we there yet?"

"No...not yet, Ricky."

"Why do I gotta lay down?"

"Part of the game."

Some game. A deadly game with a child's welfare at stake. Not to mention his own freedom. It'd all been a huge risk. But one he had to take. No other way around it.

But what would he do with Ricky?

He couldn't very well take him into LMI's compound. Surrounded by serial killers and guns for hire. Out of the question.

Take him to a hospital, a fire department? Too dangerous. He'd already been skating on ice so thin, he could hear it cracking around him. Soon, he'd fall and freeze to death from his knee-jerk reaction to the situation.

One last option, a long shot. Leon took aim, fired.

"Ricky?"

"Are we there yet?"

"No. Do you have any other family? In town?"

"My aunt and uncle and cousins."

"Are they nice? Are they good parents to your cousins?"

"Guess so. But we don't talk to them much anymore."

Uh-oh. Warning sign. "Oh? Why's that?"

"Dunno. Something about Momma's new job."

Better. Leon smiled, felt his tension lift. "Ricky…how would you feel if you lived with them?"

Silence. A sniffle. "But…I live with Momma."

"I know."

"I love Momma. Momma…"

The boy released another crying jag. Understandable. Unavoidable. There'd be many more in his future. The young are resilient, though. "Shh, everything will be okay, Ricky."

"Promise?"

"Promise. Do you know where your aunt and uncle live?"

"Mm-hmm. In a big house."

"Ricky, do you know their address."

"No… I don't understand what's goin' on!"

"What're their names, Ricky?"

"Bart…and Sheila…*Shoe-ma-ma-ma-kerrrrr….*"

Leon pulled over on a residential street. Whipped his phone out. With LMI's advanced technology and a quick lesson from Skeeter, Leon located Ricky's relatives. Ten minutes away.

As Leon drove, he let the boy cry. Anything Leon might say would only make matters worse. Adults didn't understand how to talk to children. During Leon's childhood ordeal, the army of psychiatrists certainly didn't, the only adults Leon saw after his father had killed his mother.

The Shoemaker's neighborhood was in much better shape than Ricky's. Well-kept yards and up-scale automobiles bragged of prosperity. Slowly, Leon drove past the Shoemaker's house. Lights brightened the two-story interior, a beacon of warmth. The dining room curtains were drawn back, the Shoemaker family settled around their dining room table. A boy waved his hands about, animatedly speaking. The parents laughed. Dad ruffled his hair. At home with the Cleavers. Ricky would be in good hands. Assuming the Shoemakers would take him in. Leon meant to ensure that happened. With LMI's vast resources and deeper than black hole pockets, a cinch.

One house down the street, Leon stopped.

"Okay, Ricky, we're at your aunt and uncle's house."

"Why?" He rubbed his hand across his face.

"You're going to a sleep-over. Told you that'd be fun, right?" Leon tried to lighten his tone. But he knew he sounded less than convincing.

"I guess so. Arnie has lotsa cool video games."

"There you go."

"Can I take the thing off my eyes yet?"

"Not just yet. As soon as you get out of the car, you can. But don't look back."

"But...why?"

"Still part of the game. Then I want you to walk to their front yard and stand by the tree. Face the tree, count to one hundred. Can you do that, Ricky?"

"Yeah. I'm not a..." *Snurf.* "...baby. Like hide and seek."

"Exactly like hide and seek. Then when you're done counting, ring the doorbell and ask them if you can sleep over."

"Really?"

"Really, really."

"What if they don't want me? Only Momma wants me."

Leon nearly said she didn't. But the boy wouldn't understand. "Trust me...they'll want you. They love you."

"I guess."

"Ricky, here's the most important part. The end of the game. Ready?"

"Ready." He spruced up, the promise of excitement too much for a six-year-old.

"Tell them you don't know where your mother is. And tell them money will be coming. Got it?"

"Got it."

"Okay." Leon clapped his hands, trying to end on an up-beat note. "Time to finish the game. You can get out now, Ricky."

Without a sound, Ricky slid out. As he stood outside the car, his shoulders trembled. But he remained silent, attempted to act mature. Something Leon suspected he had good practice doing. Leon rolled down the window. "Goodbye, Ricky. You're a brave, young man. Things will get better."

"O...okay..."

Slowly, Leon cruised down the street, headlights off. In the rearview mirror, he watched Ricky take off the tie and shamble across the street. Beside the tree, Ricky crumpled to his knees, crying.

Leon wanted to go back, escort him to the door. A chance he couldn't take as much as he wanted to. He swallowed hard, bit the inside of his cheek. Welcomed the sudden sting of his world.

Larger issues were at stake, more lives to save. But he had done the right thing.

On the long drive back to the ranch, he kept repeating that to himself.

Goose-bumps rippled up Cody's arms. Warm tingles swaddled his flesh. Killing the woman had been better than sex. Even if he got a spanking when he got back to the ranch, it'd been well worth it.

Cody expected a barn-storming welcome for him at the gate, tough guys in full-on bad-ass mode. Nothing but a shake of the head, a smirk.

Jack-asses. Whatever.

He couldn't understand why he'd gotten off so lightly. Not that he was complaining, of course.

Things took a turn for the worse once he entered his cottage. Leon sat in the living room, perched on the edge of the recliner.

Mr. Intensity in the hizzy!

"Hey, Dad, waiting up for me?" Cody sprawled onto the sofa, his kicks up on the armrest.

First Leon glared at his shoes on the upholstery. Then he said, "Did you have fun, Cody?"

"Hellz yeah. I mean, check it, yo, you pretty much gift-wrapped her for me. What's up with that anyway? Thought you wouldn't want me, you know, goin' all old-school and shit."

Leon slumped back into the recliner, closed his eyes. For a minute, Cody thought he'd nodded off. "How was it?"

"Whaddaya mean 'how was it?'"

"How'd it make you feel?"

"Ohhh, I get it. You missin' it, old man?"

"I'm not sure. Cody, I helped you...the least you can do is describe how you felt."

"Ah, shit, Leon, you know I ain't a touchy-feely kinda guy. Ain't in my wheelhouse, yo."

"Try." The footrest on the recliner clunked out, hiding Leon's face in darkness. Settling in for a night-night story.

"I dunno. I mean, it's always a rush when I get to do somethin' artistic. Kinda a drag that you'd already drugged her up, but, whatevs, I roll with the changes. Forward lookin', that's me. But she came too right when I fired up the ol' work-tool and—"

The footrest banged down. *Clumph.* Leon leaned forward. Shadows peeled away. His eyes looked wild. Sweat dotted his forehead. "Tell me you didn't use your power saw. *Tell* me!"

"What the hell, Leon? I did what your damn letter tole me to do, yo! I didn't plug her full of—"

"Good God, you used it..." Leon hung his face in his hands, shook his head. Friggin' drama queen.

"Dunno why you're gettin' all up in my face, old man. Ain't no fun without a lil' buzz, if you know what I mean." Cody winked. But Leon wasn't having it. "Only way I know to operate. Anyway, quit worryin'. I did everything you axed me to do in your lil' love note." Cody ticked off three extended fingers. "I didn't use any tranq. I was clean and—"

"How clean?"

"What?"

"How did you clean up the mess?"

"What, should I have called room service? I wore gloves, coveralls. My kill suit, yo. Blood got kinda outta hand, but..." Shrug. "...shit happens."

Leon groaned. Sat back with a loud sigh. Acting all "Dad" again.

"What's the big damn deal, anyway? Didn't do nothin' that I don't usually do. And hellz yeah, it felt good. First one in a long time, yo!"

"Understand something, Cody. We do *not* want any authorities—state or feds—to realize the Denver Decapitator is now active in Montana. It's crucial we maintain *complete* market invisibility—"

"Whoa, whoa, *whoa!*" Cody sat up, clunked his kicks onto the floor. "Leon, you're beginnin' to sound like one of them! Those LMI dicks with all their bullshit corporate speak!"

"Maybe that's what it takes to keep us alive."

"Really? 'Cause where I'm sittin' sounds more like you wanna keep the big, bad LMI up and alive."

Leon brought a fist down upon his knee, did it again and again, each time the blow harder. "Don't *tell* me you know what I'm *thinking!*"

Whoa. Cody'd definitely pulled Leon's trigger. Leon's ensuing silence said it all, the way he tried to bottle up his piss and venom. Finally, he released a tea-kettle of a sigh. "Cody, whatever you think, my first goal is to keep us alive. And then take down LMI. But…if you're running around, acting like the Denver Decapitator…that's going to bring all sorts of hell onto Montana. It won't be long before the feds find our ranch. Or maybe LMI doesn't like what you've done, decides to take you out."

"Yo, you threatening me, ol' man?"

"No. Not me. But you know how LMI operates. You—"

"Oh, whatever, Leon. Jesus! Lighten up! You're the prez, the top dog. You ain't gonna let them do anything to me. Dayum… when's the last time you got laid?"

Leon ignored the question. Cody knew he would. But he thought Leon really should get nasty before he stroked out or something. Actually sounded like a good idea to Cody, too. Getting laid, not the whole stroke thing.

"I can't control everything LMI does, Cody."

"If you can't, who can?"

"Exactly."

It hit Cody hard, worse than a gut punch. Things were starting to add up. Leon wanted him to watch Gaines, Sheera's fave slave. Someone was gunning for Leon. Just by being Leon's trusted number one guy, Cody had acquired a target on his back, too.

Oh, hell no! The next round starts, yo.

Cody couldn't be happier. If he couldn't kill, do it up Denver Decapitator style (*Montana Mutilator?*), he'd settle for fighting to stay alive. Hardly hella' boring. Cody's heart kicked up a notch. His pulse pounded out a going to war drumbeat. Sometimes he lived a blessed life.

"Gotcha. So...someone's out to get us. Who? Who I gotta take out?"

Leon tapped the air, the way Cody hated. Always trying to sneak in a lesson, school him. "Take it down a notch. You're not going after anyone yet. I need to find out who's on what team first. Then...and only then...maybe I'll let you have more fun." The old man grinned, first time in months. Not a good-time, elbow into the ribs grin either. Kinda scary, really. He looked like he couldn't wait for Cody to kill again. And join him in doing it. "Back to your...ah, incident tonight. I hope you didn't leave one of your Denver Decapitator notes behind."

"What? Hell no! I ain't stupid, yo!"

"And before...in Denver...you left the heads behind, took the bodies. Um, Cody...you left the body, right?"

Cody smiled, leaned back. Stuck his cannons up in the air, fingers locked behind his neck. "You worry too much! I didn't take the body! As I said, I ain't—"

"Stupid. Yes..." Again, Leon sighed. "Finally...I hope you had the foresight to bring back my note with you."

"Yeah. Shit. Course I did!" Cody patted down his shirt pockets, came up empty. "Got it here somewhere. Hang on..." Tilted left, dug into his jeans pocket, tipped the other way, repeat. *Crap.* "Must be in my coveralls. They're in the trunk. Want me to go—"

"No, tomorrow's fine. It's late. I trust you."

Yet Cody didn't trust himself. He hoped to high hell the note was in the coveralls. He remembered putting it into his pocket. Yeah, hell, sure he did.

Didn't I? What if it slipped out? Maybe I'd better go back, check it out, make sure I—

"It doesn't matter." Leon stood, yawned. "And it's too late for a clean-up crew. I'm sure the boy's aunt and uncle have already reported—"

"Wait. What? There was a kid there? He wasn't there when I did his mom, was he?"

"No. I made sure he wasn't."

Now things made sense. Why Leon let Cody take out the bitch. Old man could never stand abusers. Not that Cody really blamed him. Pride filled Cody, a job well done on a woman well-deserved.

"There wasn't no dogs there, right?"

"Not that I saw or heard. It's after midnight, Cody. I have to get some sleep." At first Leon hesitated, then clapped a hand on Cody's shoulder. Something Cody knew he didn't like doing. Something Cody wasn't overly fond of either. "Cody, if you get...the urge again—"

"'The urge?' Just call it like it is, old man! More uptight than a nun."

"Fine. If you ever feel bloodlust coming on again...let me know. I'll see to it that things are done safely. Discreetly. And that it's a woman who merits the fate. I mean it, Cody. Let me know. Before you go running off again half-cocked."

"Old man, I ain't never 'half-cocked.'"

"And I'm not old." Leon smiled, as tired a smile as Cody'd ever seen. "Say it, Cody. Tell me you'll talk to me about it first."

"Sure, whatever. Don't get all bent outta' shape. Liable to throw out a hip in your old age or somethin'."

With a wave, Leon left. "Night, Cody."

"Later, old man."

As soon as Cody saw Leon enter the big house, he raced back to the Bentley. The keys jangled in his pocket as his feet collided with the earth. He popped the trunk. Quite a mess, his wadded up blood-soaked cover-alls wedged into the corner. Just for the helluva it, he'd ask Gaines to wash them tomorrow. Try to get a rise out of the walking dead.

After patting down the coverall's pockets, his heartbeat rat-tat-tatted.

Empty. Shit. And uh-oh.

Chapter Five

Even though awake, Leon loathed leaving the relative safety of his bed. The insistently soft, yet speedy tapping at his door identified his early morning visitor, someone he'd rather not deal with first thing in the morning. But Gaines could knock forever, knuckles of leather.

Frankly, Leon didn't care that he answered the door clad only in boxers.

Gaines stood on the stoop wearing his usual nondescript grey suit and a *you're in trouble now* smile.

"Mrs. Rasmussen would like to see you, sir. Now."

"Gaines...what time is it? I just woke up." Outside, the last remnants of night were lifting. The sun peeked over the horizon, usually a sign of new promise. Not so much today.

"Seven o'clock, sir. An emergency meeting." Gaines' gaze traveled over Leon's body, lingered too long for comfort. "I would advise wearing pants."

The rebel in Leon thought he might just attend in his boxers. But crisp morning clarity hit him like a double espresso. He'd never been much of a rebel; it drew too much attention. "I'll be there as soon as I can."

"I'm sorry, sir, but your attendance is required now. Mrs. Rasmussen said—"

"And I'm not going to some damn unscheduled meeting until I'm ready! I'll be there as soon as I get dressed." Leon slammed the door.

First things, first: coffee.

The bitter taste of the coffee soured his stomach, but jolted his brain.

What the hell's this all about?

Cody, had to be about Cody.

Leon jumped into his jeans, tossed on a shirt. No time for proper business attire. He attempted to plot out a defense for Cody's actions, kept coming up short. Hard to find rationality in last night's events in the cold light of day. Plus, there was the niggling matter of Leon's involvement.

Two guards met him at the door, their lips professionally sealed.

When Leon entered the boardroom, he froze. Based on the people gathered, they weren't here to discuss Cody's indiscretions.

Sheera. Mr. Summers, the predator who swooped down on unsuspecting LMI candidates. And a man he'd not met before, an odd duck. Dressed in a simple black suit, his jacket sleeves rode high over hairy thin arms. A plain blue work shirt buttoned up to his neck, unadorned by a tie. Suspenders hoisted up his pants. A black straw hat hid his eyes. A fringe of beard surrounded his jaw, sans mustache, ending in a long billy-goat of a tail.

He stood. In a monotone, he said, "Vee bisht doo, Mr. Garber?"

Sheera rolled her eyes. "English, Jacob. *English.*"

"It is very good to meet you, Mr. Garber, yey-us." A Dutch accent, spoken in that lilting up and down way they roll. Quickly, he sat, ignoring Leon's extended hand.

"Have a seat," said Sheera, gesturing toward the far end of the table. Far away from the three of them saddled at the opposite end. Like being at the losing end of a firing squad.

Leon obliged. "What's this about, Sheera? I had nothing on the docket about—"

"In our line of business, things come up, Leon."

"Ah, how nice to see you again, Mr. Garber." Summers' constant companion, his briefcase that held the secrets of dozens of Like-Minded Individuals, stayed locked in his lap, his hands massaging the sides. "It's been some time since our previous encounter."

"Not long enough." As the CEO, Leon had quickly learned

that false niceties and social lies weren't necessary. To be truthful, it felt liberating after living a life of lies. "Must be something big going on for you to crawl out from under your rock."

Summers smiled. "Yes, ah…a man after my own inclination. Let's get right down to business, shall we?"

"I'd prefer to." Leon stared at the new man. "And who might you be?"

Again, the Dutch man stood. "Yey-us, where are my manners?" His chin dipped to his chest, the barest of acknowledgement. "My Christian name is Jacob. But in my LMI work relationship, I am called 'The Amish.' That's what they call me, yey-us."

Of course. LMI loves their silly code-names. Especially for their hired killers.

"Hello, Amish." Leon nodded back, not wanting to offend the man. "What brings you here?"

Mr. Summers answered for him. "Mr. Garber, the, ah, Amish is currently our finest business process outsourcer…" *Assassin.* "…that is, after you, shall we say, dispatched of our previous most successful quartet." Leon flashed a smile. Anything to get Summers' goat. But it had no effect. Summers shared his small shark-like teeth in a tight grin. "He's been called in on a most urgent troubling matter, one that requires a man of his special business acumen, a problem that needs the most discreet handling—"

"Oh, for God's sake, Summers!" The Amish gasped at Leon's outburst. "Quit dancing around the issue. Who's he here to kill?"

Sheera's top lip curled up. Not much, but noticeable. "We have a problem, Leon. A huge Florida-based problem."

Click, clunk.

Summers unlatched his briefcase, dug his hand inside. His distrustful gaze flit between the others, protective over his baby. Slowly, he slid out a large photograph. His fingers flicked the photo but it didn't travel far.

With aggravated ceremony, Leon stood and walked toward the opposite end of the table. And sat. At the mention of Florida, he knew who the subject of the photo would be. A glance confirmed his suspicion.

August "Augie" Schroeder. Old school, tough as nails, retired police detective. Although not so old school as to dispose of murderers and other scum who'd escaped the more conventional American judicial system. A man after Leon's own heart, aka "The New York Vigilante." Months ago, he'd been instrumental in aiding Leon in the take-down of Jasper Rasmussen.

"Augie," said Leon. "No need for dramatics, Summers. I remember him well."

"Ah, yes, Mr. Garber, I'm sure you do." An eyebrow rose over Summers' gaunt visage. "Therein lies the problem, I'm afraid. It appears that Mr. Schroeder remembers you as well. And LMI."

"Good. Glad to hear it. Maybe he's regaining some of his memory." Leon tossed it out casually, hoping it'd wash away. Augie'd suffered from Alzheimer's or possibly some form of dementia. His short-term memory had been seriously challenged; not so much his long term. Which could pose big problems for Augie's long term life expectancy.

"I'm afraid not so good, Mr. Garber. As you well know, Mr. Schroeder resides in Miami Beach. Where he's retired, living a quiet life. However, lately Mr. Schroeder has ventured out from his previously quiet life-style. He's been conversing with others...fellow tavern visitors, neighbors, whoever's ear he can catch. We have been informed he's...rather quite verbal about Like-Minded Individuals. And what transpired here..." Summers looked up at the ceiling, closed his eyes briefly, a show of reverence. "...not so long ago."

The next thing Leon said would be crucial. His best tactic? Play Augie's loose lips down. Bury the issue before LMI buried Augie. "You're kidding, right? I'm sure everyone who talks to Augie knows the symptoms he suffers. No one takes him seriously. Put your Amish back in your pocket, Summers." Leon glanced at The Amish. Beneath half-raised eyelids, the assassin remained impassive, content to be watching. Soaking it all in. "No need to be hasty. Believe me, Augie's *not* a threat."

Sheera uncrossed her legs, brought the other one up on top. Summers watched her, ready for her final say in the matter. "Leon, I'm not so sure that's the case."

"Indeed, Mr. Garber." Summers pit-patted his fingers over his briefcase. "Of course you're fully aware of Like-Minded Individuals' policy of absolute market invisibility. Our number one management objective. To have this goal corrupted could jeopardize the entire future operations of—"

"Stop already, Summers. Again...Augie's harmless. I'll vouch for him. He'll bring no attention to us. He..." Leon's argument drifted away like ash in the wind. Everyone around the table knew it. Including Leon. Sheera tipped her head, gave Summers an impatient look. But Leon couldn't give up. "Besides...Sheera, you remember the contract we signed. It clearly states that my allies are to be left unharmed from LMI and/or any affiliates."

The tip of Sheera's shoe kicked, never a good sign. If she had a tell, her toes told it all. "Show him, Mr. Summers."

"Indeed." Summers dipped into his Pandora's Box of a briefcase again. He withdrew a thick parcel of papers: Leon's contract. "Please turn to page eighty-seven, Mr. Garber...note the fine print in article seventy-nine, subsection three, e."

A sudden headache spiked between Leon's eyes. He grabbed the contract, steadied it onto the table with trembling hands. As he flipped through the massive tome, he tried to remember anything that might've slipped by him when he signed. He'd been careful, took his sweet time. Apparently not time enough.

...under the condition that said allied parties revoke their silence agreement, the violation of contract agreement shall result in the contracts agreed upon protection being null and void. All offending issues shall be resolved by Like-Minded Individuals, Incorporated in a manner they see fit...

It went on and on and on as Leon sank lower in his seat. He hadn't missed it. But he never thought anyone would break their silence, not after the long chats he'd had with everyone. But Augie...Augie probably forgot all about it.

His voice low, uneven, Leon said, "But I'm the CEO. Surely I can...override this stipulation, come up with a better solution." No louder than a chastised child amongst adults.

Summers looked like a cat that'd just swallowed a bird. One step away from licking his lips, he leaned forward. "I'm afraid it's a binding contract, Mr. Garber. If you'll turn to the last page, you'll see that you've agreed, signed it and—"

"I don't give a damn what I agreed to!" Leon shoved the offending document away. "You're not gonna kill Augie!"

Something stirred in The Amish. On the edge of his chair, he tilted his hat back. His eyes lit up. "Ach, I can assure you, Mr. Garber, I will make a right clean sweep of things, yey-us. I do not throw the bobble out with the bobble-water when I tend to my chores. I have a typewritten list of past—"

"Sheera, you've got to let me handle this my *own* way," said Leon. "I'm the CEO, dammit! You gave me this job, now let me do my—"

"Leon...Leon, dear, calm down." She patted his hand with a cold touch. "I'm afraid talking to Augie won't do any good. I understand he's beyond—"

"You *can't* kill him because of his failing state-of-mind!"

Sheera pouted duck lips. "I'm sorry, Leon...but you need to understand something. It's not only LMI Augie's been mentioning. He's been recounting how he helped to destroy LMI. And he's been dragging your name through it as well. Your *real* name."

Leon stopped. Regrouped. Let rational thought drive.

Dammit.

If Augie exposed Leon, repeated his name in public, everything he'd been working toward would go up in smoke. Right now, his name was hot in Florida. But the room felt hotter, his shirt collar tighter.

From the start, Leon knew there might have to be a few sacrifices made to bring down LMI. To destroy the beast, soldiers had to die.

On the other hand, people wouldn't take Augie seriously, not a senile old man. But as an ex-cop? Who do ex-cops pal out with? Other cops, retired and still working. If Leon's name came up in any of those conversations, flags would be raised. The feds, homeland security, who knew who else would be combing through Montana. Looking for Leon.

And LMI would still be operating to their merry little cold heart's desire. Killing innocent people. Abusing mentally vulnerable people in their pursuit of money.

The big picture painted Augie as not such an innocent himself. A cold-blooded killer. The people he disposed of deserved it, no doubt about it. And, truth be told, Augie was nearly a mirror image of Leon. Would it be hypocritical of Leon to have Augie disposed of?

Leon looked at the other three meeting attendees. All of them appeared anxious to get on with Augie's early retirement, almost gleeful with anticipation.

Was Leon any better than these three cold-hearted killers?

Will the end justify the means?

Yes, dammit to hell…yes.

"Fine, Sheera." Leon's voice ragged out like a smoker's growl. He scooted his chair back. Braced his arms against the table and stared at the floor. Last thing he wanted to see was his delighted coworkers' faces. "Do it. But do it quickly. Don't make him suffer."

"Yey-us, as you wish," said the Amish.

The queen spoke. "Leon, dear…please understand this isn't ultimately your decision. We had already decided on Augie's exit interview." Summers agreed with an "mmm." "I only included you in this meeting out of respect. Letting you know as we move forward. But I'm delighted you're on board with us."

"What do you want me to say, Sheera?" Leon shot up. "I feel great? I just helped to sign a friend's death warrant!"

She held up an imperious hand. "Leon, you're straddling the dangerous line of insubordination. I don't care for insubordination. So crass."

The Amish stood, approached Leon. "Mr. Garber, please know that I am very much looking forward to performing my chores, yey-us." This time he whipped off his straw hat, clutched it in front of him as if courting. "I pride myself on being a hard-working, salt-of-the-earth man and I will not let you down in our future business endeavors."

Summers locked his briefcase, stood. He held his hand out toward Leon, a hand that Leon left hanging.

"You can go now, Leon." Sheera dismissed him with a backward wave. "Tick-tock, you have an organization to run."

Leon left in a hurry. Cold sweat coated him. His stomach bucked. He barely made it to the bathroom in time, a hand clamped to his mouth.

What have I done?

Nanette stood at the kitchen sink, watching through the curtains. Waiting like a needy housewife for her husband to come home.

Damn Leon. Damn him for making me act this way.

But no one ever made Nanette act any way she didn't want to.

Yet, she'd seen Summers drive in this morning. And where he traveled, trouble followed like a storm cloud.

She'd been glued to her vigil for over an hour. Why she couldn't pinpoint, just felt it necessary. Felt it in her bones, as her grandmother used to say.

Sometime around ten AM, Leon shambled out. Like a drunken man, he treaded an uneven path. As he stumbled past her quarters, she whipped open her door.

"Leon?"

"Hm? Nanette. Morning." Very disheveled hair and not in a stylish way. The look of a man at the end of a bender. But Leon didn't drink.

"We need to talk."

His impatient eye roll pissed her off. If she'd been forced into playing the waiting and doting housewife, he'd easily slipped into the role of a patronizing jack-ass of a sexist husband. "What is it, Nanette? I don't have time—"

"Make time. I said we need to talk!"

"Fine." He walked up her sidewalk. "Talk."

"I saw Summers."

"Did you?"

"And was that…an Amish man with him?"

"Guess so."

"What'd they want?"

"Business. Just…business."

"What kind of business?"

"I don't need to tell you every little—"

"Dammit, it's why I'm still here. Asshole! It's what you wanted me to stay for! Now talk. What was the meeting about?" Leon blinked. Hairline bloodshot vessels struck through his glassy eyes. Sorrow—exhaustion?—wrinkled the corners of his eyes, his forehead. But she wouldn't fall for it. Not anymore. "Say something."

He hemmed, hawed, dug a toe into the ground. She'd grown sick of the old "aw, shucks" routine, nothing but diversion. "Nanette...if there's anything important happening, I'll tell you. It was just...business as usual. Another LMI applicant. One Summers recruited. They wanted my blessing. That's all." His gaze darted left; a lie. Something she'd learned during her education with less than trustworthy men.

"Bullshit. What was it really about?"

A deep sigh, a nervous glance over his shoulder. He opened his mouth, closed it again. His shoulders sagged. Retreating again. "Nothing. It's what I said. Just another applicant."

He'd almost told her the truth. But hadn't. He didn't trust her. And that's where her trust ended. "Fine, Leon. Have it your way. I'm done."

"Nanette, don't—"

"Don't what? Put up with your idiocy any longer? It's clear you don't trust me. I'm through dealing with...whatever the hell it is you're going through. I'm leaving. Tonight."

"Wait! Please, Nanette, don't—"

She slammed the door, a nice cathartic moment. The excuses he babbled through the door she'd heard before. Ultimately, though? They didn't mean a damn thing.

Leon didn't feel guilty about taking advantage of the perks that came with being CEO. Why not put the small army of guards wandering around the grounds to good use? During his first month at the ranch, he'd assigned two men the undesirable job of hacking a path through the forest behind the Rasmussen mansion. One where he could enjoy nightly jogs without fear of tripping to death on a deeply embedded root or large rock. His feet had finished the initial work, tamping the dirt down into a nicely smooth trail.

No, enjoying the perks of being LMI's CEO left him guilt-free. Too bad his signing off on Augie's demise didn't.

Usually a jog cleared his mind. Tonight, once he hit his "runner's high," it did nothing but add to his stress.

It didn't help matters Nanette was leaving. He didn't blame her, not really. But he needed her rare ability to chip away at his stone-front to see the man within. Or at least, his potential. He didn't want her to leave, not by a long shot. Still, her choice and he knew better than to try and dissuade her. If he could somehow convince her to stay, she'd regret it later.

Maybe he'd dodge a bullet if she left. *Maybe.* Under absolutely no circumstances could he tell her about his decision to put Augie out to pasture. During their short time together, she'd grown fond of Augie. And Leon just couldn't face Nanette if she uncovered the truth.

Worse, he'd lied to Nanette. And she knew it.

On an upward slope, Leon pushed himself. His calves burned, his feet leaden as he mounted the top of the hill. His knees hurt the most, one of them squelchy sounding. A warning sign from his body. Winded, he bent over, a hand propping him up against a large fir tree's trunk.

Splick!

Inches above his head, splinters flew. He straightened, whirled around the tree trunk. Something whistled by the tree, nearly shaving it.

Spack, spack!

Deep in the woods behind him, flying projectiles lodged into another tree.

Someone shooting at him.

Dammit.

He'd considered the area safe, private property and completely isolated. Even with his aversion to guns, he now regretted the decision to not bring one along.

Crick, snapt...

Footsteps. Carefully landed and coming up the slope.

Stay put? Take my chances and run?

Quick inventory. Ultra bright flashlight. Phone. Water bottle. Not even a syringe, the only time he never carried one.

Frict...

Leaves snapped loudly. Large man, not adept at being stealthy.

An owl hooted. Leon's heart banged, settled.

Easy. Take it easy.

Crunch...

Closer, another step...

Leon peeked around the trunk, then pulled back. Twin red lights approached, devil's eyes. Night goggles. His assassin had the distinct advantage. But one thing Leon'd learned last year about night goggles...sometimes light is the enemy.

Snick...slish...

Only feet away...

Judging by the height of the red beams, the man stood well over six feet. Much taller than Leon. He probably couldn't overpower him, not in a fair fight. But as Cody would say, "Time to go Kamikaze on his ass."

Leon's heart pounded, painful and disturbing. One of his nostrils whistled ever so slightly. He opened his mouth, took in a quiet breath. Held it, afraid of the smallest sound. A knot of a limb prodded into his back. He scooted around it. Slowly, slowly making his way around the large perimeter of the tree. If he timed it perfectly, he'd have the element of surprise. Assuming his stalker hadn't seen him dive behind the tree.

Clickt...snat...

Leon heard the other man's labored breathing. A foot away. One chance. Only one chance. No room for error. Now or never.

Leon leapt out, flicked on his flashlight. The man stood closer than Leon thought, nearly face to face. Leon thrust the brilliant light into his eyes. With a gasp, the man staggered back, his pistol pointed up. A roundabout arm motion and Leon swept the flashlight up into the man's jaw. Flashlight and bone crunched. The assailant wobbled, recovered fast. Leveled the gun in both hands. Before he aimed, Leon dove low. His fist hit the assassin's crotch. Above Leon, the man lurched forward, hands on his genitals. Leon snagged the man's camo covered legs, yanked. But he didn't fall back. Instead he fell on top of Leon. And didn't move.

With some effort, Leon clambered out from beneath the unconscious man. Blood covered the back of his assailant's t-shirt.

What the hell?

Leon dropped in a squat. He scoured the man's back with his light. Snuffed it out when he saw what had happened.

A bullet hole. At least one more shooter.

Leon stayed low, his calf muscles straining.

Ffft...shzzzzz. Spack!

A bullet zipped over his head. Missed by at least a foot. Which meant the second shooter wasn't close. Leon couldn't risk turning the light on again to search for the gun of the fallen man. Dead giveaway. He'd rather make a living getaway.

Leon knew the woods. Better than the assassin, no doubt. He'd escape, try to outrun him. But then what?

Leon wanted the man alive for information.

But he had to move, no time to snag the dead man's goggles. Down on all fours, he lifted to a sprinter's starting position. Took off in a squat, dangerously slow. He risked it, adjusted to full height.

Splick...spat!

Distance. Strive for distance.

Behind Leon, his pursuer trampled across the ground-spread, no longer concerned with covertness. Leon hurtled down the well-worn path. His chest burned, a fuse lit to his heart. A welcome second wind—possibly adrenaline—pushed him harder. He heard a grunt, a thud. Leaves crackled. The man fell.

Perfect.

But Leon didn't dare stay to the path. The man would eventually find him. And once he exited the forest, nothing stood between him and the mansion but empty grassland, making him an easy target. He had to turn the tables, be the tracker.

Ahead, a small fir rose, a familiar one. A thick branch stretched out over the trail. With a quick look back, Leon only saw shadows enveloping darkness. But he heard the assailant back on his feet, panting and cursing. Coming on strong. Leon jumped, missed the branch. Too tall. He stepped back, ran at the tree and hopped up. Grabbed the slender trunk with his arms, wrapped his legs around it. And inched up.

Crish, splick, spack...

Slow going. Too slow. The rough bark raised his T-shirt, scraped his belly. A splinter bit into his palm.

Almost to the overlying branch, just a few more inches...

Footsteps slowed at the crest of the hill. No doubt looking over the lay of the land.

Leon reached the branch. Carefully, he steadied himself, wrapped his hands around the branch and crawled out onto it. His feet dangled openly, his knees barely connected. The branch wobbled.

Crrrkkk...

The branch cracked at the juncture. Just a little. But Leon knew what came next, the law of gravity. If his assailant didn't catch up soon, Leon'd be dropped right into his path, helpless.

Cikkk...

The branch lowered. Still attached. Barely.

Crunch, cunch, chiff...

His target hit the spot. The man duck-walked below Leon, gun up and ready to kill.

Leon dropped. His arm snagged around the man's neck. The weight brought them both crashing down onto the ground-cover.

Chaff!

The branch followed, striking Leon full on the back. The shock jolted him to sit upright. His back throbbed with dull pain. Under him, the gunman thrashed. Leon tore the goggles from the man's head. Then he locked his hands above him, bashed them onto the man's exposed face. The assassin held tightly onto his gun. Jammed it beneath Leon's chin. Leon rolled right. A bullet chuffed into the sky. Leon kept rolling until the fir's trunk stopped him. He thrust his hands across the ground-floor, scrambled to get up before his opponent. Leon's fingers scraped against a smaller, fallen branch. A weapon.

But the assassin proved faster. He staggered toward Leon, the gun at his side. Leon brought the branch up into the man's gut. The assassin doubled over, bounced back a step. Leon kipped up, wound back his arm and rushed the dazed man. With an underhanded swing, Leon slashed the branch at his opponent's face. The branch's full-circle completed and Leon cracked his weapon on top of the man's head. He crumpled to his knees. Then tumbled forward with a *floomph*. Leaves fluttered beside him.

A hysterical giggle escaped Leon. Partly out of disbelief he'd beaten two hit men; partly because a crazed thought raced through his addled brain: *If a man falls in the forest, does anyone hear him?*

Panting and aching, Leon rolled the man over. Made sure he was still alive. Hit him one more time upside the head to make sure he'd stay out a while.

Then he made a call.

"Yo! What's up, old man?"

"Cody, listen to me. I need you to do something. Now. No questions. And for God's sake, don't tell anyone. At the gate if they ask you what—"

"Whoa, whoa, whoa! Slow down. You're givin' me, whaddaya call it, whiplash. The hell's up?"

"Just listen! Come to the forest. Where my running trail starts. Tell the guards you're jogging with me. And—"

"What? Now you want me to go runnin' with you? Cody don't need no exercise, yo! Perfect specimen of male hotness already. I—"

"Goddammit, Cody, for once in your life, do as you're told!"

"A'ight, a'ight. Don't lose your shit. I'll do it already!"

But Leon hung up before Cody had his full say. Sometimes Cody didn't even know why he put up with Garber's crap. Guy was getting some kinda Napoleon complex or something. About time Cody got a raise for all of Leon's drama. More damn drama than a soap opera, yo!

Still, gift horse in the mouth and all that. Cushiest job Cody'd ever have.

At the perimeter of the forest, Cody turned on his flashlight. "Yo, old man! You out here?"

Leon stumbled out of the path and into the light. Looked like crap as he dragged something behind him. A dead guy.

"Day-um, Leon. This kinda exercise I woulda' been up for!"

"Shhh! There could be more in the forest." Leon dropped his bundle. He arched his back and grimaced.

"Why'd you kill this guy anyway?" Cody trotted up to the corpse. "Looks like a hunter, all camoed up and crap."

"Not a hunter. Unless I was the sport of the day. And he's not dead. I intend on keeping him that way."

"*What*? Another dude tried to whack you?"

"Kinda looks that way."

"So why don't you, you know, just off him already?"

Leon sighed. "Because I want to find out who hired him."

"Right."

"Help me get him back to the ranch."

"Jesus, Leon, that's a long haul. Why didn't you let me take one of the sweet rides over?"

"Because they would've never let you out of the gate. Because of what you did last time." He glared at Cody. No respect.

"Whatever. Old news." Although the full story hadn't broken yet. Leon's missing letter. But Cody knew Leon wasn't in the mood to hear it now.

"Let's go. It's not that long a walk."

But to Cody it seemed like miles. Friggin' blue-collar work.

On the way back, Leon surprised him. Even though they had dead weight hobbled around their shoulders, Leon moved like a younger guy. "What's the hurry, yo? Dude looks like he'll be out a while."

"I have unfinished business."

"Like what?"

"For one thing, I need to stop Nanette."

"Stop her from doin' what?"

"Stop her from leaving. I made a mistake not doing it earlier."

"*What*? Can't have enough babes around. *Ever*! She's hot for you, you know. You guys should just bump uglies already, get it over with. Me? I don't see it. But whatever. Love's blind and all that crap."

Suddenly Leon stopped, nearly sending Cody and the

unconscious guy tumbling to the ground. "She tell you this, Cody?"

"What're we, in high school? Jesus, you don't have to be a damn mind reader. Tellin' you straight up, if you don't hit that soon, I will. Just bein' cool and all, tellin' you what's what."

"Good luck with that." Leon laughed. Kinda insulting. Maybe Cody'd show Garber what kinda game he had with the ladies. Just to prove a point. "Anyway, that'll wait. I need to take care of something else…something more urgent."

"You gonna tell me or what?"

"I made a mistake, a huge one. This stays between us, understand?"

"Sure, shit…whatever, my word is solid."

"Make sure it stays solid." Leon paused. Looked at Cody, then up at the moon. "I'm not even sure why I'm telling you this. Guess I need to tell someone. I gave the order to have Augie… disposed of."

"Wait…*what*? Augie? That old crazy-ass guy? Why in hell you do somethin' like that?"

Leon shook his head. Cody wondered if a killing in Leon's future might not be the best therapy for him.

"As I said…a mistake," said Leon. "I thought…Augie's actions would stand in the way of destroying LMI. Guess it doesn't really matter. Sheera was going to do it anyway, with or without my blessing. But…how quickly I agreed to it…" He shook his head as if disgusted with himself, always the lightweight. "I have to stop it. I have an idea to save Augie and satisfy LMI."

"That's just some crazy, effed up shit, Leon."

"Yeah, sound analysis coming from the Denver Decapitator."

Finally, a compliment. Cody grinned, stood a little straighter. "Got that right. Cody knows. The doctor's always in, old man. But what changed your mind, el jefe?"

Leon jerked his chin toward their unconscious passenger. "He did. Someone connected to LMI sent him. And the previous assassin."

"You mean like Sheera?"

"Who else knew about my nightly jogs through the woods?

So…I'm not about to sacrifice Augie for them if they want to do the same to me."

For once, Leon didn't have much to say after that. Cody attributed it to his straight-up stellar shrink work. Maybe he should hang out a shingle or something.

"Kinda sounds like maybe you better, I dunno, get your ducks in a row."

The old man snapped. "Let's just get this guy to the *ranch*, Cody. And I need you ready in twenty."

"Why? What now?"

"We're going back to Miami Beach."

"Kick ass!" Cody pumped his hands into the air. The unconscious man dropped into the dirt.

Clack, ratchet, click…

"Halt!"

Leon stared into an army's worth of gun barrels. The guards stood ready, antsy.

"It's Leon Garber! Lower your weapons! That's an order!"

"You heard the big guy! Get that shit outta my face!" Cody dropped his half of their living parcel. Leon followed, slumped the man to the ground.

The head guard cocked his gun up in the air and looked down at the man at their feet. "We don't have any scheduled visitors on our docket, sir. We—"

"He's my guest. Put the guns away and let us through."

The guard scratched the back of his neck. "I dunno, sir. Strange way to treat a guest. Any unauthorized visitors have to be—"

"He's had too much to drink. You and you!" Leon pointed out two of the closest guards. "Pick him up and follow me."

"Maybe we'd better get Mr. Gaines on the phone. I'm sure he'll—"

"Do *not* call Gaines!" Leon thumped the guard's chest. "I'll handle this."

Clearly unsure of the proper protocol, the guard looked around at his men. They gave him no hope, remained quiet. "Fine, Mr. Garber. As long as you accept full responsibility and let Mrs. Rasmussen and Mr. Gaines know that I objected to it. And my name's McAleister. That's spelled M-c-A-l-e—"

"I know who you are, McAleister! Just do as you're told and you won't get fired." Although Leon felt like firing him on the spot.

"Yes sir!" McAleister alley-ooped his hand. The two men jumped on it and dragged the assassin up between them. The man stirred, lifted his head. Then it drooped to his shoulder.

"Where to, sir?"

"To Nanette's cottage."

Leon hoped she'd welcome him. If he wasn't already too late.

Although Nanette had anticipated the visit earlier, Leon finally showed up, every man predictable as the sun's setting. But when she opened the door, she didn't expect to see an armed circus. With two guards holding up an unconscious man. Strange idea for a last chance at romance.

"What the hell, Leon? What *is* this?"

"Nanette, I have to talk to you."

"Oh, *now* you want to talk. Too late. That ship has sailed. Speaking of which…" She looked at her wristwatch. "…my flight's scheduled to leave in three hours."

"Please, Nanette. I'm begging you. Just give me—"

"Oh, don't beg, Leon. It's so…pedestrian." She reached up, patted his cheek. Power energized. Yet, curiosity absolutely killed. She abandoned her silly flirtatious voice. "What have you done now?"

"Please? Just let me in for a couple of minutes."

"Fine. Whatever. Clock's ticking." She swayed him in with a heavy sigh. Soulful brown eyes always proved her weakness.

Leon turned, called out, "Cody, don't let him out of your sight!"

"I'm on it!" Cody looked around with a self-satisfied grin. His shoulders tossed back, he enjoyed lording over the guards. "I'm in charge now!"

Leon closed the door. He grasped her shoulders, drew her toward him. "Nanette, I—"

"Um, you need to back off *right* now." She whipped her arms up between his, brought them down hard, breaking his hold. "Neanderthals *never* win the day. Not with me."

"I'm sorry. I just…Nanette, I don't want you to leave. I'm sorry I didn't say it earlier, but I need—"

"Oh, need, need, *need*. Neediness is weak. And boring. Besides…" She crossed her arms, tapped a foot. On the defensive. "…you haven't told me *why* you want me to stay. And I can't think of a damn good reason either."

"Besides the obvious reason…"

He stopped. She waited. Opened her eyes wide, held a hand up to her ear. His move.

"I have feelings for you."

"Funny way to show it. You haven't even had time for me, let alone shown any interest."

"I know. I've just been under pressure lately."

"Bla, bla, bla. I wasn't born yesterday. Even if I look it." A seductive smile. On her game again. "Save your crap excuses for the pool bunnies, Leon."

"Nanette, I—"

"Furthermore, I suspect you're here for a reason. Especially with your posse of armed goons outside. You—"

"*Nanette*! I'm trying to save your *life*!"

An argument like that she couldn't ignore. "What're you talking about?"

"That guy out there? The one out cold?" She nodded. "He just tried to kill me. In the forest."

Times like these Nanette wished she hadn't given up smoking years ago, a ghost that still haunted her. Next to Leon, she leaned against the door for support. "I'm sorry to hear that, but what does that have to do with my life?"

"Who do you think hired him?" asked Leon.

Seemed obvious to her, even though Leon'd been clueless until now. "LMI."

"Exactly. So if they're trying to kill me…do you really think they're going to let you board a plane tonight?"

"Suppose not." *Absolutely not.* "Who, Leon? Who in LMI is trying to kill you?"

"I'm not sure. But I intend to find out. With your help."

"And here it comes. What do you want?"

"I have to leave. Tonight. Now. But I need you, along with—" Another knock at the door. Grand Central Station. "That's them. May I?" He gestured toward the door.

"Why the hell not? Seems like I have no say in my life any more anyway. Wouldn't mind having a say about my death, though." She left the support of the door.

Leon opened it. Gus bounded in, arms open wide. Delilah followed.

"The lovely Nanette! Friend Leon! How marvelous to see you both again! Why, I was just talking to Delilah about—"

"Not now, Gus. There's no time. I need your help."

Gustav's two moods hijacked his face: disappointment, then elation. "Of course! I believe there to be some skullduggery amongst us. Especially with the armed armadillo outside." A finger swiped the side of his nose, followed by a wink. "What can I be of your servitude for?"

"I have to go to Florida tonight. With Cody. You're the only other three—"

"Why're you going to Florida?" asked Delilah.

"I hope to save Augie's life."

"Whaaat? Our old friend, Augie, is in trouble?" Stress lines rode Gus' forehead, finally hinting at his true age. "Say no more, friend Leon. I'm your man. Let's go save—"

"No, Gus. I need you to stay here. To guard the man outside who tried to kill me."

"Whaaat?"

"Let Leon finish," said Delilah. She clamped a hand over her lover's mouth.

"I don't have time to get into it now. When I get back, I'll explain everything."

"Promises, promises," said Nanette.

"I will, Nanette. No more lies. But in the meantime...as you three are the only ones I trust, can you please take turns watching over the man outside. He'll be put into a cell. But I'd like for one of you to always be on guard." Gus stood tall, already on patrol. Only thing missing was a salute. "I can't risk having him killed like the last guy."

"Of course! It sounds marvelously intriguing, doesn't it, Delilah?" Delilah shrugged.

Nanette said, "Fine, Leon. Just until you get back. Then we're gonna talk about a way of getting me out of here. Safely."

"Done."

The interchange passed over Gus, but Delilah shot Nanette a puzzled look. Nanette mouthed *later*.

"Oh, one last thing." Leon reached beneath his shirt and into his waistband, pulled out a gun. "I got this from the killer. Whoever stands guard needs it. But keep it hidden. Unless you *absolutely* have to use it."

Gus screamed, "Fabulous!"

Nanette intercepted Gus's reach with her longer arm. "I'll take first watch."

"Of course. Ladies first." Gus bowed, clicked the heels of his shoes. "Please do telephone us when you need relief."

"I will. Maybe you'd better go get some sleep," said Nanette. "We're all going to need it."

"Always the brightest head on your block, Nanette. Good night, my friends."

Delilah scooped her man up. As they closed the door, Nanette heard Gus say, "This is going to be the utmost in excitement, my love!"

"Thank you, Nanette. I mean it. I really appreciate it," Leon said.

"Don't let it go to your head. I'm doing it as much for Augie as I am for you. And myself, of course. Self-preservation's a marvelous motivator. Besides...I'm pretty much trapped here. For now."

"Probably the safest place for you. So they don't hunt you."

"Hasn't stopped them from gunning for you."

"Well...there is that." Leon tried to slip a charming grin in. But her tolerance for charm had long dried up.

"Leon, one last thing...about Augie. How do you know? How's his life in danger?"

"I wish I had time to get into it...but I really don't."

"Whatever. I'm sick of this. When you get back, you're

prioritizing two things." Two accompanying fingers went up. "Telling me the truth. And getting me the hell out of here."

Leon said nothing. Just stared at her. His gaze went from her eyes to her lips, back again. Gently this time, he reached for her. Pulled her close. She let him. But when he bent to kiss her, she turned her head. He finished with a small kiss on her cheek. Possibly a good-bye kiss.

Leon thought that could've gone better. But other things demanded his attention.

When he stepped outside, more guards had amassed. And Gaines had a hand gripped around Leon's would-be assailant, playing tug-of-war with Cody.

Dammit. Who called Gaines?

"Leggo, Gaines! My boy, Leon, put me in charge of the prisoner, yo!"

"Afraid I can't do that, Mr. Spangler. You don't know the first thing about how the system works or interrogation—"

"And you don't know jack about me, lap-dog!" Cody shoved Gaines, a loud thump to his chest. Gaines went flat on his butt. He sat in the yard, growling like a dog.

"Cody, settle down," said Leon. "The situation's under control. Did you let this man out of your sight?"

"Been attached like, whaddaya call 'em, Chinese twins."

Leon didn't bother correcting him. "Good job." He walked over to Gaines, now climbing to his feet. "Gaines, this man's under my care. The only people allowed to enter his cell are me, Cody, Nanette, Gus and Delilah. Do you understand?"

"That's not proper protocol, Mr.—"

"Too bad. It's my protocol."

"Mrs. Rasmussen will not be pleased with—"

"Fine. I'll talk to her about it. But after your mishandling of the last prisoner, I'm not taking any chances."

"I'll just go see what Mrs. Rasmussen has to say about that." Gaines took off at a trot, his hands pasted to his sides, hardly the most efficient running style.

"Yeah, run to Momma, beeyotch!" yelled Cody.

Nanette exited the cottage, carrying a large mug. Steam

roiled off the top of it. She'd thrown on a long gray sweater, good for hiding the gun.

"I'm ready, Leon," she said.

"Good. Nanette, you and Cody take the prisoner to one of the cells. For God's sake, see that a cot is brought in for him. We're not animals. But never let anyone else in the cell unattended."

"Got it."

"Oh, and Cody. Once you've got the prisoner secure and Nanette's on it..." Nanette nodded. "...we're flying out. Along with Gaines."

"Gaines! The hell, Leon? Why you wanna bring that douche along? You said for me to—"

"Cody, stop!" Leon patted the air, for all the good it did. Cody's fluster had skyrocketed. Leon leaned in, whispered, "Gaines is our security blanket."

"What you talkin' 'bout?"

"Gaines is Sheera's favorite employee. Doubtful she'd put a hit on me...or us...when he's around. That's why I want him involved in every step."

Cody smirked, shrugged. "Whatever."

"Alright, get him to the cell. Watch him, Nanette."

"Leon, you don't have to tell me more than once!"

True. And once again, Leon saw that he'd inadvertently insulted Nanette. But after dealing with Cody, reiterating everything several times came naturally. "Sorry, Nanette. Old habits. I've gotta take care of something before we leave, Cody."

"Yo, what you gotta do that's more important than savin' Augie Doggie?"

"Talk to Sheera."

"Gotcha." Cody turned toward the gathered guards, still enjoying his temporary power. "Lissen up, bitches! Clear a path 'cause we're comin' through! Get a cot set up in one of them cells! I'm in charge now!" Nanette cleared her throat. "Well, me and Nanette're callin' the shots."

Cody and Nanette dragged the man between them, Nanette fully up to the chore.

Outside the big house's boardroom door, Leon overheard Gaines whine about Leon's impertinence. For the most part,

Sheera remained quiet. Listening the way predators do.

Leon didn't knock. "Sheera, I need to talk to you."

"So, I understand." Although dressed in her nightgown, her make-up was fully applied. "Seems like you've been a very busy boy, Leon."

Behind her, Gaines snapped to attention, suggestive of past military training.

"If you call dodging bullets busy, yeah, I've been busy as a bee. I need to talk to you. Alone."

She sighed, waved a hand. "Very well, Leave me, Gainesey."

"But, ma'am—"

"I said, leave!" The look she shot him could've peeled paint off walls. Gaines shriveled. On his way out, he left Leon with his usual calling card: half grin, half sneer.

"What the hell're you up to, Leon, darling?"

Without waiting for an invite, Leon saddled up in a seat next to her. "I'm not up to anything. I went for my nightly jog. What I always do. Two armed men tried to kill me."

"Hmmm..." Indecipherable look.

"Sheera...tell me the truth. Did you have anything to do with it?" Not that he expected the truth from her. Lying was standard business behavior for everyone involved with LMI. But he watched her, studied her reaction. Stupid of him. Like reading a store mannequin.

She screeched out a harsh laugh. "You never cease to amaze me! Why on earth would I want anything to happen to my CEO? I have a lot staked in you right now."

Leon wondered if she wanted to pound that stake into his heart. "You can't blame me for asking. Who knows I'm here? And who knows about my nightly runs?"

Again, "Hmmm. Are you suggesting a mole in our ranks? Good help is so hard to find these days."

"Understatement. We need to weed him out, find out who hired him."

"And how do you propose we do that?" Her dancer's leg went high, crossed over a knee. Distracting. Possibly on purpose.

"I brought back one of the gun-men. Alive. He'd better stay that way."

"That's something I'd like as well. But I leave that sort of nasty business up to Gaines. So...drab." She studied her nails, furrowed her brow.

"Gaines isn't the right person for the job." No sense in telling her his suspicions regarding her top-dog. "Besides he's going with me."

"What? Going where?" She lost interest in her nails.

"I'm going to talk to August Schroeder in Miami Beach, ensure his silence. The humane way. I have a mutually satisfactory idea."

Sheera's leg dropped along with her jaw. "Leon...dear... I'm afraid it's too late. The Amish has been dispatched to...well, dispatch of Mr. Schroeder. Such an ugly business, really."

"Dammit, Sheera, call The Amish off! Do it!"

"I'd watch your tone of voice with me if I were you."

He ignored the threat. The threat to Augie's life superseded his own life right now. "Sorry, sorry... But *please* call off the dogs! No one has to die!"

Click, click, click...

Cherry red fingernails tapped the table-top. Casually, she took out a nail-file. Leon nearly wrenched it away from her.

Leon stood, smacked the table-top with his palm. "Listen to me! Call your killer off! Do me this one favor and—"

"What's your plan, Leon?"

Still in the nebulous zone. "I'm putting the final touches on it now." Powerless, Leon stood before her pleading. How she liked all of her servants to attend to her.

"Oh, very well. I've found that keeping one's employees happy makes for a productive work environment." The only time she looked up from her nails was when she said "employee." Keeping him in line. "I'll do you this favor. Just remember it."

"I will. Thank you, Sheera. How do I get a hold of The Amish to—"

Her hand jabbed up. "You take care of that end of things with Mr. Summers. I'd rather not deal with it. Might give me nightmares." She walked toward a desk in the corner, her nightgown billowing behind her. A see-through nightgown. Leon kept his eyes glued to the back of her blond mane of hair.

She rummaged through a desk drawer, plucked out a business card.

"Here's Mr. Summers' number." As Leon reached for it, she withdrew it. Playing games. "Leon, I don't need to tell you to make this a clean operation. No mess. No visibility. Is that understood?"

"Completely."

"It'd better be." She handed him the card. Like magic, a cell phone materialized in her hand. Leon had no idea where she'd been keeping it. Some things are better left unknown. A few barked commands and she ordered one of the company jets ready to go in twenty minutes. "Plane's waiting. Better not tarry! Ta ta for now!"

Leon didn't exchange a farewell, just raced out the door. His stomach curdled. He felt like throwing up, fought it. Didn't have the time.

If he had any time left at all.

Chapter Six

Detective Keats tapped out a pencil solo on her desktop as her coworkers filled coffee cups and snarfed down donuts. Just another day on the job for Miami's finest. She looked across the desk at her new partner, a rookie detective, hardly old enough to shave. Not too long ago, she'd been considered a rookie herself, though, so she didn't hold it against him. Everyone needed a start. Of course, now her reigning title was the "bitch of detectives."

She didn't mind the new title, wore it with pride. Let the others call her names and play their reindeer games, whatever. She'd more than proven herself six months ago. When she'd stumbled onto the bizarre Leon Garber case. The one that nearly killed her.

Sure, commendations were made, backs were patted and higher ups congratulated when she sniffed out a crooked cop in the rat pack: her ex and very dead partner, Arnie Bellup. Once the media lost interest, things pretty much settled back to normal. Still low detective on the totem pole due to her short height, skin color and gender.

She knew it'd play out that way. Men never change, nor do bigots.

Through half-mast eyelids, Keats' partner looked at her, made a point of dropping his gaze to her tapping pencil. Then he sniffed haughtily, oh-so-entitled. How he'd made detective at such a young age came as no surprise: his daddy carried a lotta' weight around the precinct.

So had hers, actually, although everyone seemed to overlook that fact. Boys club and all. Same ol', same ol'.

Still, the kid was definitely a step up from her last partner. At least true detective work and going the extra mile appeared to interest him. And, of course, he hadn't tried to kill her like Bellup had.

On stormy days, Keats still felt her gun wound clawing at her like a cat begging to go outside. She felt it when she exercised, felt it when she rolled over in bed. Mostly it was a good kind of pain. A pain she weathered proudly. Whenever she questioned her skills (perpetuated by the dumb-asses around her), the wound reminded her that she'd uncovered something huge regarding Leon Garber. Something she still didn't understand. Something that bugged like head lice.

"Ramona Keats?"

Keats looked up at the big man. Cop, old school. Tatty suit, hadn't seen an upgrade in a couple of decades. Balding (no, *damn* bald), tired, his face sagged beneath the weight of victims lost on his watch.

"It's *Detective* Ramona Keats. Who're you?"

"I'm Detective Brian Sidarski of the Barton Kansas police. Well, guess I should say I used to be. Retired now. Just not enjoyin' it so much."

"Uh huh. You're in Florida. Shouldn't you be fishing or lounging in a chaise somewhere, drinking mai-tai's like all the other retirees?"

"Not my style. Call me a private detective now. One who's devoted to one case. And I'm my only client."

Typical walk-ins didn't express determination like Sidarski's. He had her attention. "Have a seat."

Keats lifted the open case file folders from the visitor's chair and dropped them on her desk. "What case has you hot and bothered and brought you all the way from Kansas to Miami?"

He sat, lifted his tie, straightened it. Adjusted himself until he molded his heft into the seat. "Know this guy?" Sidarski tossed a photo in front of her. One she'd become intimately familiar with. After all, she'd posted the APB on the subject. Now not only did Sidarski have her attention, he'd earned her devotion.

"Damn straight I do. That's Leon Garber. Although he tried

to pass himself off as Chris Hampton when I ran into him."

Sidarski chuckled. Even that sounded tired. "Fun guy, isn't he?"

"Oh yeah, we had lots of laughs." Not in a sharing mood, not today, she jerked her chin at her partner. "Go get coffee, hit the head, do something. I got this one. No need to drag you off what you're working on."

With an obvious eye roll, he stood. "*What*ever." He stormed off, flocking to the cluster of testosterone.

"Okay, Sidarski. You had me at the photo. What about my boy?"

"First of all, Detective, congrats on unveiling his identity. Good police. You accomplished more than I could when I had the pleasure of meeting him…oh, 'bout a year-and-a-half ago."

"Yeah?" Keats perked up. Compliments came rarely. "Tell me about your play date with Garber."

Sidarski sighed, plucked at his pant leg, almost lost in melancholy. "He got away. But he was knee-deep in dirt. I knew it. Couldn't convince the Feds, though."

"I feel your pain. Had my own share of run-ins with their red-tape bullshit."

"Exactly." Sidarski closed an eye, shot an "attagirl" pointed finger bullet Keats' way. "Anyway, back in Barton, I had a mess of corpses popping up, too many for my nice quiet little suburb. Every time I turned around, Garber—or Owen Gribble, as he was calling himself—"

"Cute."

"Isn't he, though? Garber was connected to the killings. He and his little playmate…" Sidarski struggled, then plucked another photo from his pocket. With a nice dramatic flourish, he flipped it onto the desk. "…Cody Spangler were behind the killings. I just couldn't figure out why. Or how, really. Or, hell, even their real names. Spangler was going by 'Toby Grainger'." He handed the photo to Keats. "Know him?"

Typical grunge kid. Nice looking but stupid eyes. Built, though. "Nope, him I don't know."

"Huh. Sorta figured where one was, the other followed."

"Lovers? I didn't get that impression of Garber. But, hey, my

Gaydar hasn't worked in years. Just ask my last date."

"Tragic. No...not lovers. I think you pegged it when you called my run-in with Garber a 'play-date'. I think he and Spangler were playing some game. One that ended with bodies."

"Pass 'Go', collect a body." Keats considered Sidarski's theory, but it didn't add up. "Garber was a pretty high-strung guy, Sidarski. Not the gaming type, I don't think. Seemed like he wouldn't risk his freedom for something so...high profile like a game. You know he paid me a visit? In the hospital after I'd been shot?"

"No kidding?"

Keats imagined Sidarski didn't have a "kidding" bone in his body. "These lips don't lie. Shakira... You know, the singer? Nothing?" Sidarski shrugged. Keats continued. "Anyway, Garber was clearly shook up. Scared shitless. Guy looked like he'd been through the ringer when I talked to him in the hospital. Only game he mighta been playin' was S&M crap. But here's the weird thing...he handed me a ton of cash to give to a hooker and her kid. Serial numbers were clean. He also told me after twenty-four hours, he'd let me know what was really goin' on. Somethin' about a high-ranking political conspiracy. All that X-Files crap."

Sidarski grinned. "You pulling a doubting Scully here?"

"Hey, no UFO's buzzing my head. I just don't buy into the whole political conspiracy angle."

"Yeah, I don't either. Could be he's delusional. Fooled me, though. He seemed fairly sane." Sidarski rubbed his impressive jowls, a very moist sound. "Okay, you don't believe he's a game-player. Neither one of us believes the political conspiracy. The only thing I believe—no, *know*—is Garber's a cold-blooded killer. I hate when the bad guys get away. Like in the old noir films from the forties."

"Movie buff, Sidarski?"

"Yep. You?"

"Don't have the time. Wish I did. Still haven't seen *Star Wars*. The one from the seventies."

"You're pulling my leg, right?"

"I don't pull, Sidarski. I push. Anyway...I'm still waitin' for

Garber to fulfill his promise." Keats stretched out her arms, hands to the ceiling. "Waiting for that big ol' world Mr. Leon Garber promised me. Where are you, world? Come to mama! Where are *you*, Leon Garber?"

Derisive laughter rose from the cops in the corner. Collins hooted, "Keats, you calling out your voodoo priestess again?"

"Shut up, ass-hat! Before I kick you into the next precinct!"

Juvenile, sure, but it silenced them.

"Nicely done," said Sidarski. "I used to deal with jack-asses like that, too."

"That right? You look just like one of them." She gave him a blatant and totally unnecessary head-to-toe scan. "I mean, no offense or anything, but you look like you'd be right at home in the donut corner."

"Come on, Keats. You're stereotyping. Personally, I don't give a rat's ass about what a detective looks like. As long as they do their job. And do it well."

"Sidarski, this looks like the start of a beautiful relationship."

"Good. Because the only other thing I give a rat's ass about?"

"Global warming?"

"Okay, the only, *only* other thing?"

"Dying of anticipation."

"Catching Leon Garber."

"Let's do it." Keats entwined her fingers, leaned back. Settled in while things got good. "How? Guy's not exactly easy to find. Been stormin' the streets since I got out of my hospital bed, limp and all."

"That's why I'm here."

"Be still, my beating heart."

"Get ready for it to beat faster." Sidarski lowered his voice. "There's a cop bar not far from here. Miami Beach suburb. Old cop, friend of mine, runs it. He says there's a retired salesman, Dale Carter, comes in on occasion."

"I'm thrilled for Dale Carter. What about him?"

"Youth today. So impatient. Anyway, the bar owner knows I got a real mad-on for Garber. So when Carter got loaded one night—guy suffers from Alzheimer's or something—he went on a tirade, said his real name is August Schroeder."

"Augie Schroeder? Retired detective from NYPD? My grandpa knew him, said he was good police."

"That'd be him. But Carter's...Schroeder's, whatever, rant kept growing bigger, a real fish tale. Lots of stuff about a corporation of killers called Like-Minded Individuals. Claimed he helped take 'em down six months ago. And who do you suppose he name-dropped as one of the corporate raiders?"

Keats knew the answer, couldn't wait to hear it. But it was Sidarski's big reveal, very cinematically inclined. Let him bask in his own Hollywood lights for a moment.

"Yep. The one and only, very elusive Leon Garber."

Keats stood, said, "Sidarski, I dunno 'bout you, but suddenly I'm very parched. Let's go hit a bar."

On the plane, Leon held his briefcase close but kept an even closer eye on Gaines. There hadn't been time to pack anything else, but he sure as hell took the time to raid LMI's personal cash coffers, straight from the late Jasper Rasmussen's safe. He'd crammed the briefcase full of as much money, stocks, jewelry as he could. Of course he'd have hell to pay for later but he considered it a CEO bonus.

Cody jabbed a finger toward the briefcase. "Yo, what's up with that? You didn't give me time to pack any of my crap. How come you get to bring stuff?"

"It's not my personal belongings."

Gaines, either feigning sleep or a very light dozer, opened one eye and both ears. Nothing got past him, although Leon certainly wanted to try and keep him in the dark. No doubt he'd run to Sheera if he knew what the briefcase contained.

"Just sayin'."

"Drop it, Cody. I need to try Summers again." On the way to the airport, Leon'd called Summers multiple times. No answer. Possibly ignoring Leon's phone calls. His stomach flip-flopped, the turbulence-tossed flight worsening his nausea. As much as he wanted to speed the flight up, instantly reach his destination, the harsh inevitability of the situation amped up his anxiety.

Before he hit speed dial again, Leon's phone chirped. *Unknown caller.* LMI's typical anonymity.

"Hello?"

"Mr. Garber. It's Mr. Summers. I understand you've been trying to reach me. What can I do for you this evening?"

"Summers! Thank God!"

"I really don't think God has anything to do with—"

"Just shut up and listen! Call off your Amish dog. *Now.* I'm taking care of the Schroeder problem *my* way."

Silence. A click, a whir. The music of LMI electronic ears. "Ah, Mr. Garber, I'm afraid it's too late to—"

"Too *late*? Dammit, is Augie dead already?"

A clipped laugh. *Eh, eh, eh.* "No, Mr. Garber, as of now Mr. Schroeder is still a living member of society."

"Then why's it too late? Call your man off!"

"I'm truly sorry." He sounded anything but. "It's impossible."

"Goddammit, Summers, it's *not* impossible. You contracted him! *Break* the contract. You just said Augie's—"

"Again, I can't work miracles. I have no way of reaching The Amish."

"No way of... What the hell's that mean? Just call him!"

"Mr. Garber, seeing as how this particular business process outsourcer practices the Amish faith, I'm afraid it goes against his beliefs to use a cellular phone."

Leon couldn't believe it. No, he did, having met plenty of strange LMI outsourcers before. "Jesus! How do you get a hold of him?"

"Through a complex, long process utilizing discreetly placed want ads and—"

"Never mind! When's the procedure supposed to happen?" Clammy sweat loosened Leon's grip on the phone. It fell to his lap. Quickly, he snatched it up again. "*When?*"

"Either later tonight or early in the morning. It's up to The Amish' discretion."

"*Where* is the process going to take place?"

Papers rattled. "Mr. Schroeder is currently on a fishing trip. Not far from Miami Beach. The...Seahorse Harbor Marina. He's rented a small bungalow there for the entire week. The locale is a small, relatively isolated—"

"I don't need you to read the brochure! Just give me the address!"

"Ah...do you have Mrs. Rasmussen's approval on this, Mr. Garber?"

"Yes, dammit, the address!"

With a pen trembling over paper, Leon scrawled the address down. "Is the Miami Beach airport the closest one to the marina?"

"Just a moment, please... I see there's a small industrial airport located closer to the shore line. Not too far. I can—"

"Just set it up! We're about an hour-and-a-half out!"

"Fine. Is there anything else I can help you with to—"

Leon hung up, hung his face in his hands.

"What's up, old man?"

Leon sent Gaines front-side to inform the pilot of their new landing destination, then caught Cody up-to-date.

"Well, shit. Hey, maybe this Amish guy will take a horse-buggy, yo. We can beat *that*. We got this by the balls!"

Leon shook his head. Wondered again why he fought so hard for Cody.

Nanette had a helluva time getting the cell key from the head guard. Wouldn't give it up until he got a phone call from the queen bee herself. Their conversation had turned him a ghostly shade of white, Sheera not known for her kind treatment of the help.

Sheera had insisted on the guard staying down there with Nanette. His presence set Nanette on edge. He barely moved, stood like a statue while his gun rested in his arms.

Nanette tried to turn things around, make him feel awkward. Flirted with him. At first, he didn't respond, at least not verbally. But it was all about his nervous tics, his blushes, a little flop sweat, sudden scratching, and finally, a couldn't-be-helped, dog-sloppy grin.

Houston, we have lift off.

Girl had to find her fun somewhere. Sure beat listening to the prisoner's constant screams.

"Let me outta here! Dammit, they're gonna kill me! I don't

wanna die! Not yet! You don't understand! I gotta get outta here!..."

He went on and on and on, finally lapsed into a resigned blubbering.

Nanette leaned the folding chair back against the wall. The gun provided mental comfort at the small of her back, not so much physical comfort. She gave the guard a wink. Uncertain and uncomfortable, he looked away.

Too easy to manipulate.

Then she got mad at herself. Perhaps overreacting, she couldn't help but think Leon'd manipulated her. A little. Claimed her life was in danger. Could be, might not be. Hard to decipher the truth around Leon these days. Plus he'd some gall asking her to do boring watch-dog work and then try to seal the deal with a kiss.

Uh-uh. Not today.

She held onto that small comfort. His shameless ploy failed.

"Please, dear God, lemme outta here! I don't..."

In a way, she felt sorry for the captive man. Then again, he did try to kill Leon. You choose the life, you pay for the fall-out.

The guard checked his watch. Cleared his throat. Avoided looking at Nanette. Because she made him nervous? Or something else? "Um, bathroom break."

"Let it flow, sailor."

He shuffled past her. As he neared the hall's end, he sped up, bladder apparently knock-knock-knocking at his door.

She glanced around the hall, the damn *gloomy* hall. Everything else throughout the compound had been the recipient of a beautification make-over. Not down here in the dungeon, not the bastard step-child of the compound. Cold, damp and sterile. Dull wintry colors of dirty white and grey. Touches of green mold clung to the stone walls. Pale yellow light bulbs dangled from threadbare, hardly up to code wires.

Gloomy.

Hell, she'd rather be back in the cottage, curled up with a nice glass of wine and a good book. But she'd committed to the task.

"Please, have mercy on me... I won't say a word! Swear to

God! Just let me go and I'll…"

Ten minutes and the guard still hadn't returned. Must've been something he ate. Or *not*. Warning signs dinged in her mind. Not full-on gongs, but a distant, subdued tolling.

Actually, she could use a bathroom break herself. Something she hadn't considered when she'd loaded up on coffee. She hated to do it—it'd only been about three hours—but she might have to call in Gus or Delilah to briefly relieve her.

Slowly, she set her chair down on all four legs, no use further agitating her bladder.

Chumph.

The sharp sound lingered, a hollow echo.

The guard returning?

She stood. Listened. Nothing, quiet as a snow-covered country-side.

Clipped to her belt loop, a pair of handcuffs jangled. Something else she had to practically wrest away from the guard. She loosened them. A girl can never be too prepared.

Her bladder pressed with urgency.

Listen to nature.

Gus picked up on the third ring. "Dear Nanette, is it time for me to relieve you?" Unlike her, he sounded giddy at the prospect, always ready to swing into intrigue. He'd be sorely disappointed.

"Sorry to call so early, Gus. But…I really need a powder room break. Just for a few minutes? Then you can go back to sleep."

"Of course, of course, my friend! I shall be at your rescue momentarily!" The phone shuffled, a clunking sound. Then, "Delilah! Delilah, it's time!"

"Thanks, Gus. Appreciate it."

"It is of no skin off my back." He hung up. She imagined him putting on his finest attire for the occasion.

Where the hell is the guard?

The prisoner started up again. "I'll do *anything* you want! I'll give you *money*! Just…"

Chock.

The lights went out. Afterimages of the hall blinked before Nanette. She swayed, set a hand against the wall until her eyes adjusted to the darkness. Total darkness. She took out her phone, turned on the flashlight app. The small rectangle of light only projected a few feet.

"Oh, my God, they're here! They're coming! I *told* you! You're not safe either! They'll—"

"Shut up," she hissed.

The prisoner stopped screaming, but fell into sobbing again. It obscured all other sound. Not that there was any.

"I swear to God if you don't be quiet, I'll just leave you here," she whispered through the small panel set into the door. Abruptly, he stopped, just a few small sniffs.

She strained to listen, cocked her head for a better vantage point.

Deep silence smothered her like the most humid of nights.

A crack.

A door opening slowly? Not good.

She reached behind her, caressed the pistol's butt. Not yet. Best to have her hands free.

She returned to the small door-set panel and whispered, "Listen. Do exactly as I say. Lay on your belly on the cot, hands behind you. Remain quiet. Don't try anything. I'm the only chance you have to live. Understand?"

He said nothing, obeyed her. The way she liked her men. The cot's springs groaned. She flashed the light inside and saw him on the cot.

"I'm coming in. You try anything you're as good as dead. From me or whoever else is after you."

With the handcuffs open, she entered the cell. Perhaps not the brightest idea, but she had to get the prisoner to safety. If safety could be found in the compound. Even better, her captive would provide a nice human shield should things come down to a gun fight.

"I'm going to cuff you now. Then I'll get you out of here."

The man nodded, his beard scratching the sheet.

Shff, shff, shff.

The cuffs slipped around his wrist. She tightened them,

much tighter than she utilized in bedroom games. Showed him who's in charge.

"Now, get up."

She backed away, flashlight pinpointed on the man. With her free hand, she brought the gun out from hiding.

"Wait...stop..."

Tep...tep...tek...

Barely audible, but definite footsteps.

Gus?

Doubtful. He wouldn't take slow, deliberate footsteps. He'd barrel in, hyped for intrigue.

Tap...tek...

Louder.

Tunk...dank...

Coming down the stone stairwell.

"Okay...let's go..." She tried to steady her whisper, but her words stuttered. Her bladder surged. She powered it back, mind over matter. Last thing she wanted to do was die in wet underwear, something her mother had always warned her about.

Her teeth grit down on the phone as she freed both hands. The light illuminated her feet. Not ideal. Close behind the man, she grabbed his bound wrists and rested the gun barrel over his shoulder. And pushed him through the cell door, a four-legged shuffle.

In the hallway, a cool breeze tickled her nose. Someone'd left the upstairs door open. Quietly, she nudged her captive down the hall, one slow step at a time. Painstakingly quiet, except for their terrified breaths.

Choices.

Fire a warning shot? Let the intruder know I'm armed? Or start blasting as soon as I see someone?

Halfway down the hallway, Nanette stopped. And listened again.

Nothing. No more footsteps. Her visitor playing a similar waiting game?

Click.

A familiar, not a friendly sound. A gun's cocked trigger. But no follow-up, not yet.

She continued. One step, shuffle behind, another step, shuffle...

Just around the corner, the stairwell went up, led outside. To freedom.

She took a deep breath, held it.

And shoved her captive to the floor at the foot of the steps.

Zing. Spack!

A bullet dug into the stone wall above the fallen man's head. Blindly, she thrust her gun around the corner, fired. She dared a peek. Two tiny red beams sat atop the dark figure blocking the outside moonlight. Night vision goggles. She hopped into a squat behind her prisoner, pulled him to his knees by his shirt, then fired again.

Chuff, chuff...

The figure yelped. Then turned, clambered up the stairs.

Even though her attacker had long cleared the door, she launched a farewell bullet. A warning not to come back.

Then the lights came back on. Funny how synchronicity works at times. Except...*not.*

She yanked the man to his feet. Sweat flowed from his hairline, his beard. He wasn't the only one in need of a shower.

Outside, footsteps approached. In a hurry, loud and proud.

"Nanette! Hold on, my friend!"

The cavalry.

Delilah stopped at the top of the stairs. Gus rode shotgun in her arms and on her hip.

"You okay, Nanette?" asked Delilah. "We heard gunshots."

Nanette took a deep breath. She relaxed, stumbled onto her captive, knocked him against the wall. "Yeah, all in one piece."

Delilah dropped Gus and they raced down the stairs.

"What happened?" Disappointment drew down Gus's mouth. Bummed out he missed the shooting party, Nanette supposed.

"Someone shut out the lights. Then came gunning for this guy."

"Oh my! But what happened to the guard assigned you?"

"Damn good question, Gus."

Voices rose. Shouts. Soldiers tromped through gravel and approached.

Where the hell were they earlier?

The missing guard rushed down the stairs, eyes glowing wide and white. "Damn. What went on here?"

"You tell me!" Nanette lassoed him by his collar and slung him against the wall. "Where the hell *were* you?"

"Hey, I told you...had to go to the john! And, um, I took a smoke break! Sorry...please don't tell Mrs. Rasmussen!" Smoke smell rolled off his breath, his clothes.

"Whatever." Nanette released him. She looked back at the cell. Disqualified it as a viable option. "Get this guy upstairs," she ordered the guard. "Do something right for once."

"Really, not my fault... I like my job..." The guard muttered as he escorted the prisoner up the steps.

Nanette, Gus and Delilah followed. Closely.

The fresh air recharged Nanette, a nice reprieve after the claustrophobic hallway. Only one option remained, one that didn't tickle her fancy. "Gus, Delilah...I'm gonna have to take this clown to my cottage."

"But...that sounds absolutely horrific, Nanette! I am doubtful he'll make the most charming of houseguests."

"No, but I'm hoping you and Delilah will. It's gonna take all three of us to keep this guy alive. Until *Leon* gets home."

"Of course, Nanette!" Gus clapped his hands.

Delilah said, "Yeah, whatever it takes."

A squadron of guards surrounded them, crowded in. Hands jostled the prisoner, grabbing and pulling like paparazzi. Multiple voices came at Nanette hard, impossible to distinguish. Questions, orders, demands. Someone bumped into her. An intentional shove followed. She spun away from the crowd, twisted, caught her balance. A stampede of legs trapped Gus inside the crowd.

Delilah's voice carried above the rest. "Everybody back the *fuck* off!"

A scream rose. The mass confusion silenced.

The guards dispersed.

At the center, the captive lay on the ground. Foam formed around his mouth, his eyes the color of spoiled milk.

Dead.

A guard dropped to his knees. Gave a cursory inspection, clearly afraid to touch the man. "Yep. Looks just like the last guy. Suicide by cyanide."

"Bullshit!" Nanette stormed off, cutting an angry path through the guards.

Delilah called out, "Nanette! Where you going?"

"To find a damn bathroom!"

Dark and dripping with despair. Just like every other cop bar Sidarski had ever visited. Immediately, he recognized Clemons. Still sporting his ludicrous mullet, the one he'd been so proud of back in his Kansas days. Just now grey and fragile as spider webs.

"If I do declare!" Clemons swiped his hands with a mangy towel, dropped it and jut a hand across the bar. "Sidarski, you ugly son-of-a-bitch! What the hell you doin' in my bar? Maybe you'd better leave before I call the cops."

"Nice to see you too, Clemons." Sidarski shook his hand. He hadn't dried it on the towel nearly enough.

"Who's your little girl-friend?" Clemons leered at Keats with a bush of an eyebrow raised.

Keats swept her jacket back, exposed her holster. "Yeah, I don't think so. I'm Detective Ramona Keats, Miami Police." No extended hand from her; Clemons hadn't met the lowest common denominator of her goodwill.

"Ah. Miami's finest. Read about you last year, darlin'. Nice police."

"Thanks." She nearly smiled. Not quite. But Clemons appeared to have brushed off her shoulder chip.

"So...not a social call?"

"'Fraid not," said Sidarski. "Remember that Dale Carter guy you called me about?"

"Course I do. Strange duck."

"We wanna hear him quack." Keats flipped a photo of August Schroeder on the bar-top. "That Carter?"

"Sure is. A little greyer now, but who isn't?"

"Tell Detective Keats everything you told me." Sidarski settled onto a stool. Could be a long story and his back had been complaining since he landed in Florida.

"Guy was all over the place. After I while, I kinda zoned him out. Just a crazy-ass story about big business hiring out serial killers all over the world. To do their work for them. Take out the competition or something, I guess. Thought he was nuts. Everyone who knew Carter would tell you the same thing. Sometimes the guy couldn't remember how he got to the bar. But when he said Leon Garber helped him demolish this Like-Minded Individuals, I paid attention. I remember Sidarski here..." He nodded toward the large detective. "...saying he wanted to get his hands on him. So...I listened. Once a cop, always a cop."

"Uh-huh. Did he happen to tell you Mr. Garber's current whereabouts?"

"Believe me, I asked him. The bartender, you know, everyone's favorite confidant next to a priest, right?" Keats didn't answer. "But that's when Carter clammed up, just gave me a funny look. Paid his tab and split. Couldn't find his car, though. I had to help him."

"You happen to get the make and plate?" asked Sidarski.

"Yep. Wait..." He looked behind the bar. Yanked a page off a hanging calendar. "Here you go." Schroeder's car deets shared the page with a naked woman sprawled across a car's hood.

Keats rolled her eyes. "Charming."

"Ain't she, though?" Clemons took one last admiring look at the photo before handing it over.

"Anything else you remember?" Keats knocked knuckles on the bar-top. "Anything good?"

"Like I said, his story was a wild one. He said he and his group attacked this Montana ranch outside of Billings. Guns and explosions, the whole nine yards. And Carter said he personally executed the head guy."

"He give a name?"

"Nah. I asked, though. As I said, once I got inquisitive, Carter got squirrely and left."

"You know where he lives?"

"Oh, yeah. Gave him a ride home once. But he ain't there, not now."

"Why? Too busy taking down more killer corporations?"

"Only if fish have incorporated. Last time the guy was in here, said he was gettin' ready for a fishing trip. Seahorse Harbor Marina. He's holed up in a small cottage or something there."

"Yeah, I know where it is," said Keats.

"That's where you'll find him, then. I reckon he's about a couple days into it. Said he wasn't comin' back until he was redder than blood-shot eyes."

"Thanks, Clemons. You've been a big help."

"Yeah? How big?" He tapped his empty tip jar.

Augie Schroeder sunk his line into the water before he sunk into another spell of depression. He knew his mind was failing him, especially his long-term memory. The good news? The spells didn't last long. And he rarely remembered losing his memory. Talk about a Catch-22.

Still, helluva thing to happen to a detective, one who prided himself on worrying details, the kind that don't belong. Closed a lotta cases in his day; closed even more scum-bags' wastes of lives.

The good ol' days.

Anymore, a good day consisted of remembering if he'd had breakfast.

A scarcity of people supplied a good deal of the Seahorse Harbor Marina's allure. For some reason—a wonderfully hidden reason—the marina had never caught on like the other marinas had. Tourists shied away from it. Only folks wandering around these parts were dedicated fishermen like himself and a buncha' rich types who docked their yachts there.

Which suited Augie just fine. Serious fishing tended to be a solitary sport. The fewer people he had to chat up, the less ashamed he felt about his rotting brain. Just him, the fish and his ol' loyal dog, Bruno. He leaned over and scratched behind the Rottweiler's ears. The dog's tongue lolled out, almost as if

Augie's fingers had tickled him. But Bruno never laughed at Augie, no sir, not like people.

At times, he was probably too sensitive regarding his ailment. On better days, he knew this. But that's what pride buys you: not much common sense and a false sense of self value.

He looked out over the horizon. The sun had long ago dropped. A few yachts had set sail earlier. Now unoccupied, the boats eerily floated near the docks. From the vantage point of the dock, he watched the moon's reflection ripple over the water and break into shards of silver. Perfect night for fishing. And forgetting.

Bruno growled, low and definitely threatening.

"Quiet now, boy. Ain't no one out here but us and the fish. Even if they ain't bitin'."

Tap, tap, tep...

Augie shaded his eyes (no real reason, just habit) and looked down the dock. Someone strolled toward him at a leisurely pace. From what he could see, the person carried no fishing gear either. Then again, his eyes weren't what they used to be.

"Evening," said Augie.

"Right beeyoo-tiful evening it is, too, yey-us."

As Gaines drove the rental car, Cody stared at the back of the company man's head, fantasizing about what it'd be like to take his head off. Not that Cody had a thing for beheading men. But Gaines seriously needed an attitude adjustment of some sort.

"Come on! Step on it, yo. Ol' ladies drive faster than you do."

"I'm driving the speed limit, Mr. Spangler. It wouldn't do at all for the local authorities to pull us over at this time, now would it?"

What a dick.

Guy always acted smarter than anyone else in the room. Cody knew better.

Natch, Leon rode shotgun. He always got first choice. Not that Cody really wanted to sit next to Gaines, but he and Leon were equals. Just like last year, he'd been shoved to back-seat status. Story of his life.

"Cody's right, Gaines. Kick it up six or seven miles. No policeman will flag us for that."

"As you say, sir."

The speedometer crawled up another two miles and stayed put.

Leon had a hand pressed on the dashboard, the blood draining from it. For a moment, Cody wondered what would happen if Leon had a heart attack. LMI would probably crown Cody, next in line, as CEO. He'd be hella' good at the top spot, too. Dream big, play bigger.

During the drive, Leon called Augie's home number. Clearly, the guy wasn't home; physically *or* mentally. Old coot was so out-of-touch he didn't own a cell phone. Not even an answering machine. Who *lives* that way?

Leon rocked on his seat like a kid needing to go to the bathroom.

They entered Marina Road, a thin strip of over-water, been there-done that which led to the Seahorse Harbor Marina inlet. Nothing but hard road ahead and wet ocean on the sides.

"Now you can step on it, Gaines," said Leon.

But Gaines' idea of stepping on it didn't amount to much. Not for the first time, Cody thought the dude intentionally dragged his feet. *Literally, yo.*

On the side of the road, a sign read, *Welcome to Beautiful Seahorse Harbor. A Fishing Paradise.*

Even the damn signs bored the hell outta' Cody. Nothing to look at but palm trees and boats. Old man crap. Cody hoped to see some action soon. His hooker fun the other night had just whet his appetite.

Another sign, *Marina: Three Miles.*

"Dammit," Leon huffed. "Faster, Gaines!"

Heart attack waiting to happen, yo.

Keats had her car door open before she wrenched her Dodge Charger into the small cabin's driveway. Best birthday gift ever.

Not that her coworkers had acknowledged her big Three-Oh. Frankly the way she preferred it. But gift-wrapping Leon Garber with handcuffs would truly make her thirtieth a birthday to celebrate. Sidarski would have to wait in line behind her. He'd had more than enough birthdays anyway.

"Hold up, Keats," called Sidarski. "Not as young as I used to be."

"But I'm getting prettier by the minute." At the door, she turned, smiled. "See? Radiant, ain't I?"

"Glowing."

Keats pounded on the door, stepped back. Sidarski caught up.

Next door, an old woman hobbled toward them. A distinct hump rose from her back. "Don't tell me. You're lookin' for Dale."

"Dale Carter, yes, ma'am," answered Keats.

"Popular guy tonight."

Impatient for the woman to finish her long leisurely walk, Keats met her half-way. "Why's he popular?"

"Seems like everyone and their aunt's lookin' for ol' Dale."

"Huh. I'm Detective Keats with the Miami PD, and this is my associate, Brian Sidarski."

"Ma'am." Sidarski nodded.

"Is Dale in some kinda trouble? Don't seem too much like the trouble-makin' kind. Little dotty, though." She tapped her blue-haired head.

"No trouble. We just need to talk to him," said Keats. "Who else has been here?"

"Well...first there was a strange little man. A Mormon or somethin'. I damn near ran him off, thought he was sellin' spooky pamphlets or something. Talked funny, too. But he said he was an old war buddy of Dale's. Then there was this other fella...good-lookin', too. Why if I was a few years younger..." Presumably lost in lust, she licked her lips. "Mm, mm, *mm!*"

"Um...sure." Sidarski whipped out his favorite photo. "Would this be him, ma'am?"

She squinted, adjusted her bifocals. Tapped Leon Garber's photo. "That'd be him alright. Mighty fine lookin'."

Keats and Sidarski exchanged a glance. Child-like anticipation somersaulted in her stomach. Her wound itched. "I take it Dale's not at home. Happen to know where he is?"

"Right as rain, where he goes every night. Down on the Seashore Pier. Fishin' with his damn mutt."

"Seashore Pier, got it." Keats whipped out a notepad. "Can you tell us how to get there?"

"Just go out yonder on Seashore Drive." Her finger wagged in several different directions. "Hang a left, go a couple blocks. Can't miss the sign."

Old school as ever, Sidarski stayed behind and wrapped things up cordially. Keats raced to the car without so much as a goodbye. Grandma always taught her the importance of manners. But surely Grandma would understand this one time.

The man certainly didn't look like any fisherman Augie'd ever seen, anything but. In fact, he looked like he'd just stepped out of a horse-drawn cart, a long way from home and time. Augie's years of avoiding LMI had honed his survivor's instinct. The man just didn't feel right.

Bruno felt the same way. The fur on his back stuck up, his teeth showed with a growl. Carefully, Augie stroked the dog's back. "Quiet now, Bruno," he whispered. "Not yet."

Augie got up on his feet. His arthritic knees snapped with pain. "Help you, friend? You look a long way from home."

The odd man approached, thumbs tucked behind suspender straps. Until he dropped one hand into his jacket pocket.

"Yey-us, if you are August Schroeder, you can be helping me."

The hairs on the back of Augie's neck rose, enough to give Bruno's back a run for the money. "August...August...hmm, ain't no one here by that name. Reckon you got me confused with somebody else. I'm Dale Carter, salesman—"

"I believe there's no mistaking of you-er identity, Mr. Schroeder." The man fiddled in his pocket while he stood outside of arm-swinging distance. He squinted at Bruno, the first sign of sea-salt in his body. "That's a nice pup, yah? Nice pup."

Bruno growled again. Augie let him. "Hold 'til I say so, boy." Augie reached inside his bucket for his filleting knife. "Now I suggest you high-tail it on outta here, friend, before we have a misunderstanding between us. Bruno's already fed up with you. Hope he doesn't feed on you." The knife wasn't long, worthless in anything but a close-up fight. Sharper than a razor's edge, though. Augie twirled it back and forth like a magician, just threatening enough.

The strange man chuckled. Finally plucked out his pocket treasure. A much larger knife. "It's time to terminate you-er contract with LMI, Mr. Schroeder."

"Now, Bruno!"

Bruno tore into a blurry run. His back legs bent, launched him high. The man whirled, one arm out. Knife hand up. His knife plunged down.

"*Ayippp!*" Bruno dropped to the deck.

"Bruno!"

The dog lay still, but answered with a sad whimper.

Still alive.

Augie steadied his feet and jutted his knife out. *Ready.* "Mister, you done made a huge mistake. You don't go messin' with a man's dog."

More guttural than Bruno, Augie growled. And raced toward his opponent...

At the marina gate, a security guard leaned out of his window with a hand of authority raised. "Sorry, folks, marina's closed for the night. Unless you're a boat owner."

Before Gaines said anything, Leon intervened. "I understand, sir. But it's important we find a friend of ours. His daughter's in the hospital. Not doing very well."

"Rules is rules." The guard clicked his lips. "Call him."

Leon unlatched his briefcase, grabbed a handful of cash. The fast way to bypass rules. Gaines glared at Leon as he thrust the money out the window. "He doesn't have a cell phone."

The guard's eyes lit up as he grabbed the bribe. Took his sweet time counting it. "Well...as long as you promise you won't cause any trouble. Can't have any trouble on my watch."

Cody leaned forward. "Yo, no trouble! Just gotta find our buddy. S' like he said…dude's daughter's dying. C'mon, let's do this!"

"Quiet, Cody," said Leon. "Sir, there won't be any trouble."

"Alright, then… I'm trustin' you. Don't let me down." The guard gave Leon a stern look, one weakened by airlessness. Authority that could be bought. "What's your friend's name?"

"Carter. Dale Carter," said Leon.

"Ol' Dale? Sure, I know Dale. Comes down every night when he's vacationing. Fishes like there's no tomorrow. Why, he—"

"Do you know which pier he's on?"

The guard scratched his face. Wasting precious time. "Dale likes to change things up. 'Fraid you're just gonna have to look for—"

"Thanks." As soon as the gate rose, they sped down the drive.

Leon bolted out of the car, hurried toward the marina. Cody bypassed him easily, arms pumping.

"Gettin' kinda slow, old man."

Leon stopped, stared at the length of the marina. Too many piers, too many docked yachts and boats. "Cody…take the other end…check out every dock…"

Cody trotted away as Gaines caught up. Of course it'd make more sense to send Gaines on his own search mission. But the best place for the man was at Leon's side.

Methodically, Leon started at the west end, searched each pier. Something caught his ear, something pitched higher than the tossing waves. From a distance, a low whine. Leon squinted into the darkness. The moonlight spotlighted a huddled figure. Sitting on the next dock.

Leon broke into a sprint and tromped across the loose planks. Out of breath, he slowly approached the man. The way to approach any LMI individual. Frankly, Leon had no idea if Augie would even remember him.

The man didn't move. Just sat silently, hunched over a fishing pole held loosely in his hands. An unmoving mass of fur lay next to him. Only the familiar stock of white, thick hair told Leon he'd found Augie.

Leon reached for Augie's shoulder. "Augie?"

With a jolt, Augie looked up through red-rimmed eyes. "Hmm? Whaddaya want?"

"Augie, thank God we found you..." As Leon set his briefcase down, Gaines' gaze locked upon it. Leon snagged it up again. He sat next to Augie, hung his legs over the dock. "You remember me, Augie?"

Augie straightened, frowned. "Course I do! Leon Garber! Not completely gone round the bend yet, dammit!"

"Of course not. Ah...we need to get you out of here. I'll explain later. But there's someone from LMI looking for you. We have to—"

"Too late." Augie dabbed an eye with his wrist.

"Too late? What're you talking about?"

"Goddamn LMI...damn them. Their guy's already been here."

Leon recognized Bruno's bulk. Hard to forget the dog that had nearly torn them apart six months ago. Bruno raised its head. Released a tiny whimper before lowering back to the deck. In the dark, Leon couldn't be certain, but the dog's black fur appeared matted on its side. Wet with blood.

"What happened, Augie?"

"LMI! That's what happened! They sent their man to kill me. Got Bruno instead! Some freaky Mormon or something."

"Um, Augie...where *is* the man who attacked you?"

Augie croaked out a laugh. "Swimmin' with the fishes." He gestured toward the still water. "Gutted him like a damn fish, too! Even though I had thirty years on him, he still wasn't no match for me! Nosiree! Why, I..."

Dammit. Not exactly part of the plan that's gonna please Sheera.

"Okay, Augie, listen to me...I'm sorry about Bruno. I really am. But we've got to leave before anyone—"

"Only worldly possession I rightly cared about, too, ol' Bruno." The dog whimpered in agreement. "You remember our little throw-down at Rasmussen's ranch? When I got back home, Bruno was waitin' for me at the front door. Nearly starved to death." Augie scratched behind the dog's ear. The dog responded with a scrawny tail-wag. "Had the end of his tail blown off. But still happy as a clam to see me. Ol' Bruno..."

"Yo!" Cody raced down the dock. "You find him? Hey, what's up, old-timer?"

Augie snorted. "Yep, I remember this damn firecracker. Dumb, young and full of—"

"Augie, we've got to go. Before the police, or LMI, send—"

"Now, wait just a damn minute here! I thought you were the new acting chief of LMI! Why'd you send one of your killers after me?"

"I didn't. It's a long story. I'll tell you—"

"Whoa, whoa, whoa! Hold up! What happened to the dog?" Cody fell to his knees beside Bruno. Tenderly stroked its back. "Jesus! Dog's been stabbed or somethin'! We gotta get it some help!"

Leon blew out a long breath and massaged his throbbing temples. Impending headache soon. But the past had taught him arguing with Cody—or Augie, for that matter—led nowhere in a hurry. Gaines smirked at the sitting men, no help whatsoever.

Out in the parking lot, tires screeched. Agitated voices flew across the water. A car idled by the security gate, the guard no doubt giving due diligence with his less than diligent services.

Time to go.

Leon stood. He couldn't see the car's make, too far away.

But Augie's eagle eyes focused in. "Looks to me like an unmarked cop car. Dodge, what they drive." Augie stood, stretched, hands in the small of his back. He looked down at Bruno, rubbed his eyes again. "Don't much cotton spending my golden years in the state pen. But I ain't leavin' Bruno behind either."

"Augie, I'm sorry about Bruno. But, trust me, the dog will only slow us down."

"Oh, hellz to the no, Leon! I'll take the dog!" Cody already had Bruno scooped up in his arms. "I'm with the ol' fart on this one."

Good God. "Fine. But everybody shut up. I need to think."

Still stalled at the security booth, the driver gunned the engine. Growing impatient. And Leon's getaway car sat in the

STUART R. WEST

lot just beyond the booth. No chance to get to it now.

Think, Leon, dammit, think!

Gulls squawked above the marina. Water lapped at the posts beneath Leon, rhythmically thumping to the beat of his heart. But over it all, he heard a different beat: tinny music. Jimmy Buffet.

Several docks down, a lone light flickered in a yacht's window.

Leon whispered in Augie's ear. "Augie...once you told me you wanted to sail around the world. This is your chance."

"As long as my dog goes with me..."

Leon nodded. "Everyone stay low. Follow me." His entourage followed the orders and ran hunched over. Leon's neck ached from the odd position. His leg muscles quivered and he thought he might fall face-forward. Ever the showoff, Cody breezed by them with the sixty-five pound dog in his arms. Gaines lagged behind, practically in a standing tall stroll.

At the foot of the "Second Chancer," Leon raised his voice just enough to be heard over the music. "Ahoy?"

From within the cabin, thumps sounded. A bearded man, sun-burned and possibly in his thirties, popped out from below. He clicked the boom-box on his shoulder off and dully stared at them. He'd either been asleep or nothing rocked his world. "Help you?"

"Hope so. I want to buy your boat."

The man looked at his twenty foot yacht. Shrugged. "Not for sale. Man, it's all I have. Lost my wife, my house, my job, my—"

"Yo, Achy-Breaky, spare us the country song." Cody stepped forward, the wounded dog in his arms. "How much you pay for the boat?"

His fingers flicked at his beard as he mentally calculated the cost. "Seventy-five large. But that was, like, years ago, and—"

"I'll give you 250,000 dollars for it right now. Cash. No questions asked, but you have to leave the boat right now." Leon shook the briefcase. He looked over his shoulder. The car had bypassed the security booth and entered the parking lot. Headlights blinked off. Two car doors slammed.

Again, the man glanced around as if expecting to see a hidden camera. A greedy smile grew beneath his beard. "Well, you guys look like you need the boat more than I do. 300,000 dollars and we'll call it pretty."

"Done." Leon opened the briefcase, counted out wads of 10,000 dollars.

The boat entrepreneur leaned over, whistled. "Man, I shoulda' held out for more."

"You already have enough for a new yacht and a new house. Negotiations are finished."

"Yeah, guess you're right," the man said. "Guess I can call my next boat the 'Third Chancer'."

"Gas in it?"

"Hell, yeah, loaded and good to go."

Voices carried across the marina: a man and woman. The man's voice Leon didn't recognize. But the woman's voice chilled him. *Keats.* The Miami detective who had dogged him six months ago.

Clomp, clump, clump...

Their footsteps grew, amplified by the water, but heart stopping nonetheless.

Leon whispered to the man, "You're gonna have to take us out of here. I promise we'll drop you somewhere safe."

"Hey, just as long as I get my money, it's cool."

"Man of my word." Leon passed an arm-load of bills toward him.

"Let's sail!"

On the dock, Sidarski watched the yacht putter out into the ocean. The boat seemed to have left in a hurry. A coincidence that didn't sit well in his craw. As a matter of fact, coincidences never did, a mythical beast.

"Well, hell, Sidarski." Keats unleashed some prime curses. "Our boy, Garber, can't just vanish. Think he's hiding in one of the boats?" She hooked at thumb out at the marina. "Take us forever to search 'em all. Unless we call in reinforcements."

"You really wanna do that?"

"No. I want this collar all to myself. So bad I can taste it."

"Yeah, me too. Besides, Garber's not the kind to hide. Somehow he slipped by us." Sidarski nodded toward the departing yacht. "You make out the name on that boat?"

"It says...it says 'Second Chancer'. You think Garber's turned sailor?"

Sidarski shrugged. "Got any better ideas?"

"Alright. Let's go see what that damn rent-a-cop has to say about the yacht."

"Lead the way. But...it might take me a while to catch up. Not used to the fast life of pursuing killers." Sidarski patted his ever-growing stomach. Sweat drenched him. The pain in his chest scared him. Either his heart-burn had sky-rocketed to astronomical acidic levels or something even worse lay in hiding. But he hated doctors, feared what they might tell him. Out of sight, out of mind. Of course the excitement of the chase probably had something to do with his current symptoms. Or maybe it was the let-down of defeat. So close, yet so not.

Once Sidarski reached Keats' car, he practically collapsed against it. Caught his breath and joined Keats at the security booth.

"Second Chance's cap is a guy name of Troy Miller. Dead-beat. Lives on his boat." The security guard nodded proudly, more compliant than their earlier encounter. "Always ready to help my fellow law men. Um, and women."

"The boat took off pretty late," said Sidarski. "He do that often?"

"Yep. Pretty much every night."

Keats asked Sidarski, "Whaddaya thinking?"

"I think it's time to call the coast guard."

"Well...that's about the best I can do," said Troy. He mopped his forehead, stepped back and appraised his work. Bruno'd put up a struggle through the kitchen sink surgery, but thumped his tail now. "Like I told you guys...I'm just an ex med student. Sewed the dog up best I could. You gotta watch for infection. I've got some antibiotics, but...I mean, you won't tell anyone I have 'em, right?"

Leon laughed. "No, Troy. Your secret's safe."

If only you knew our secrets.

Throughout the procedure, Augie'd held onto Bruno, their heads pressed together so hard, Leon thought they might fuse. "Why, ol' Bruno seems to be doin' better already! Ain't you, boy?" Augie clapped a hand on Troy's back, knocked him forward. "Can't thank you enough, Doc!"

"Um, not a doctor. I'm—"

"You're a damn life-saver, that's what you are!"

"We're, ah, not out of the danger zone yet. We'll have to—"

"Ah, you take that ol' Negative Nancy attitude elsewhere, son! I ain't havin' none of it!"

"Hell, yeah!" Cody pumped a fist. During the stitching, he'd remained quiet, practically holding his breath. "Dog's gonna be all right! Damn, doc!"

"Again...*not* a doctor."

Gaines tapped Leon's shoulder. "A word, Mr. Garber?"

Leon gestured toward the cabin door, let Gaines lead the way. Turning his back on the man seemed like a very bad business decision.

Up-board, Leon blinked into the sunlight. They'd sailed all night long, none of them sleeping. "What is it, Gaines?"

"Sir, about your expenditures..."

Leon knew it'd come eventually. Gaines watched LMI's money like it came out of his wallet. "What about them? I know a lot was spent. But sometimes, a CEO has to make financial decisions to—"

"I *must* voice my outrage over the purchase of this yacht for a third of a million dollars." Hardly outraged, Gaines' tone remained cold, robotic.

"I know you don't value human life. But to me, it was worth it. A necessary expenditure to keep LMI's visibility low."

"And then...then..." Gaines sputtered. His face radiated angry heat. "Paying off the coast guard last night! That's just unheard of!"

"Would you rather be sitting in jail?"

Gaines zipped his lips, drained them of pigment.

"I thought not."

"What if the coast guard should stop us again?" asked Gaines.

Leon shrugged. "We'll see what happens. But now we're well on our way to Key West. Augie and Troy will drop us off. We'll grab LMI's jet there. Don't worry, Gaines. We'll have you back in Mrs. Rasmussen's arms before you know it."

"I've *never* felt her touch! You're being...highly *disrespectful*! I'm going to *tell* her what you said." Gaines turned away, gripped the yacht's rail. Under his breath, he muttered, "Mrs. Rasmussen's *not* going to like this. Not one bit."

Of course she wouldn't. It wasn't ideal for Leon either. Once they got home, he'd have a lot of explaining to do.

Down in the cabin, Leon pulled Augie aside. "Augie, while Gaines isn't here I want to give you something." The briefcase a lot lighter, Leon yanked it up. "There's more than enough here to start over. Just...go far away. Live in the Caribbean, maybe. But please...you have to remain quiet about LMI, about me, about your real name. Get a new identity."

"Ah, Leon, you don't have to worry about me. I can keep a secret." *No you can't.* "This is a life I've dreamed of. And Cap Troy here...he's decided to go with me. Watch after Bruno. Cruise the world. Ain't that right, Troy?"

Troy said, "Why not? I mean...it's not like I got anything else going on."

"You and me both, Doc!" Augie smacked him on the back again.

Troy winced. "Okay, ground rules...that's gotta stop."

"Whatever you say, doc, whatever you say!"

"*Not* a doctor."

"Besides Doc Troy here knows how to navigate the waters. And sail under the radar."

"Yeah...I, ah, I've had experience." He nodded toward a couple cases of medical supplies against the wall. Troy might not be a doctor, but apparently his hidden talents ran deep. Leon just hoped his past trespasses wouldn't resurrect Augie's idea of justice.

For the first time since they'd left Montana, Leon allowed himself to relax. He sat down, closed his eyes. And thought of Nanette. Sheera wasn't the only one he had to explain things to.

"Aw, shit." Keats tossed her cell-phone up on the dash. It clacked like dice against the windshield. She really had to watch how she treated her phone. It didn't thrill her sergeant how he had to keep replacing them.

"Let me guess." Sidarski sighed, locked his fingers across his belly. Prepared for disappointment. "They couldn't find the 'Second Chancer'."

"Guessed it in one. May as well've sailed off into the Bermuda Triangle."

"Maybe it did. Solve our problem easily enough."

"How in hell can one guy be so lucky? He keeps slippin' away like a shadow."

"Been thinkin' of nothing else for a year-and-a-half. He's either the luckiest guy on the planet or he's got supernatural powers." Sidarski wiggled his fingers, tried to emulate a Theremin sting. The humor blew over Keats' head. Only cop he'd met more serious than him.

"So what now?"

"Well…" Sidarski tried to cross an ankle over his knee, gave up. Cars weren't built to accommodate big men. "You remember my pal, Clemons, yeah?"

"How could I forget a charmer like him?"

"Right. But remember what he said about Carter-slash-Schroeder braggin' about how they took apart some Montana ranch? Outside of Billings, Montana?"

Keats tossed her head back into the rest. *Stupid.* She should've thought of it herself. "Gotcha."

"You got vacation time, Keats?"

With nowhere to go and no one to visit, she had scads of vacation time wasting away. "You know something? I hear Montana's beautiful this time of year."

Chapter Seven

T *hree days.*

Not a word from Leon in three days. Radio silence ever since he'd warned Nanette her life may be in danger. Not a call, text, postcard; not a goddamn peep. And she'd hung her life out on the line for him. Getting shot at didn't exactly fill her heart with joy.

And three long days later, Leon comes home. Heads straight for the cottage where he squirreled Skeeter away. To make matters worse? Bastard had a suntan. A suntan, for God's sake. A gloriously golden Florida-born tan that would make George Hamilton envious. While she dodged bullets with a full bladder in a dank basement, he saturated himself with beach bunnies and Florida skin cancer.

Oh, hell no!

She dashed out of her cottage, broke into a sprint. Didn't slow until she reached Skeeter's cottage. Leon had his hand up, knuckles ready to rap on the door.

"Yeah. Hello to you too, *Leon*."

Leon turned. Bags pushed up his glassy eyes, hardly the look of someone returning from a vacation. Unless he'd been on a bender. But she knew Leon didn't drink, she knew Leon. Thought she did at least. Suddenly, she realized she didn't like him much these days.

"Nanette, believe me, you were my next stop."

"I think I merit much more than a second stop on your itinerary. Especially after what happened."

"What're you talking about?"

A breeze swept by them. She stepped away, out of Leon's

back-draft. He smelled like fish gone bad.

"You don't know?" He shook his head. "Your little pal? The one who tried to shoot you? He's dead."

"No…" Leon stumbled back, the way a drunk would. If not for the cottage wall, he would've toppled over. "How'd it happen?"

"*Not* my fault. I did everything I could to—"

"I'm not blaming you. Just, please…what happened?"

The more she told him, the more lines etched across his forehead. "Dammit." Not angry. Just oddly disappointed.

"We did everything we could. But these damn guards…" She fluttered a hand through the air. "…they swarmed us. Crowded the prisoner. One of them obviously killed him. Fast-acting poison's my guess."

"Yeah. I've seen it before. I need to have a long talk with Sheera—"

"Enjoy it, Leon. God knows you've been talking to her more than me."

"Nanette, don't—"

"Save it." Her hands went up, an emotional blockade. "I want outta here. You told me you'd see to it. I want results. I'm tired of sitting around this…this camp of killers!"

"Okay…okay. I'll see what I can do."

"Do more than just 'see' about it. *Do* it!"

"I will. First I have to—"

"We're not finished here yet. What happened to Augie? What happened in Florida?"

Leon stared down at the grass, avoided eye contact. *Chicken.* "Tell me!"

His recap played out worse than Nanette had imagined. But he withheld something. She had to know the full truth, her worst suspicion. Even if she didn't want to.

"Leon…who ordered the hit on Augie?"

"It's complicated. LMI has—"

"Don't give me that teenage social media crap! *Who* ordered the hit? And why?"

Long hesitation. Never a good sign. "Sheera did."

"*Sheera*? Why?"

"Because Augie was losing it. Talking about what we did to LMI six months ago. Name-dropping everyone he could remember. In a cop bar and who knows where else."

"Huh." Sheera's call sounded reasonable, a hard decision in a worse situation. Suddenly, Nanette hated herself for thinking like LMI. LMI was *far* from sound. "That's crap. Why didn't they bring Augie here? To keep an eye on him? Every other killer in the country's here!"

"I really doubt he would've gone for that. Doesn't matter. Everything's fine now. Augie's safe. He's gone to—"

"So help me, God, if you say 'he's gone to a better place,' I'll gut you right here!"

He laughed, a nice, honest laugh. Condescending, though. "He's safely tucked away in the Caribbean. Or will soon be."

"You telling me the truth?"

"Scout's honor."

"Right. Like you were ever a scout."

"Watch me start a campfire with two twigs. He's safe."

"Leon...did you know about the hit? Before it was sanctioned?" The question she'd danced around. But when you're the only dancer on the floor, sometimes you had no choice but to take the lead.

This time he locked his eyes on hers, the way things used to be. Truth time. "No. That's why I stopped it."

What she wanted to hear. Unless, he'd accomplished the fine art of lying to her, no easy task.

But he was a company man now, after all.

"Dude! Why're we talkin' outside?" Skeeter shaded his eyes and looked up, Chicken Little in a faded T-shirt.

"It's a nice day out." Whenever Leon talked to Skeeter, he felt his own paranoia levels ranked at a normal level.

"I guess..." Skeeter sneezed. "Sorry, allergies."

"Did you send the money like I asked you to? To Bart and Sheila Shoemaker?"

"Yeah, dude, of course! Wired it to an untraceable account."

"And you sent the note along with it?"

"Um, yeah, but...I'm not big on threats. I don't wanna know

anything about it, but I'm just not cool with—"

"Skeeter, what threats? There weren't any threats. Don't worry." The note he'd instructed Skeeter to post with the money read, *Mr. and Mrs. Shoemaker: Ricky's had a bad life with his mother. Please take him in as family. He has nowhere else to go. The money I've sent will more than cover his upbringing. As long as you treat him with the kindness, respect and love he deserves, you will continue to receive a monthly allowance. To be used for Ricky only. We'll be following Ricky's progress closely. Any breaking of this agreement will result in termination of our agreement. You don't say a word, we won't say a word. All up-board. A Friend.*

LMI's legal team couldn't have put together a finer piece of saying nothing while implying everything.

"Leon, it still seemed kinda…I dunno, sketchy."

"It's not sketchy. It—"

"Dude, I don't wanna know!" Skeeter's hands waved in front of Leon, seeking absolution.

If only Leon could erase his sins so easily. He felt like LMI had dragged him down into a deep, dark hole, one he might not be able to climb out of.

"What about the other things I asked you to look into?"

"Yeah, about that…the board members are cagey. I mean, I hacked into some of their personal email accounts. No easy task, you know. They talk around in circles, never going anywhere. But, reading between the lines, they're up to something."

"How so?"

"Your name gets tossed around a lot."

"What're they saying?"

"Your methodology is…unorthodox. Not conducive to keeping LMI's business practice in the black. Some of them have said you're, um…a liability. But you know how they talk, dude."

"Yeah, I'm painfully aware. Did they mention any plans about business process outsourcing?"

At the mention of LMI's code-name for their stable of assassins, Skeeter's face leeched white. "Leon, dude! What're you all up in? I mean, did I sign up with the losing team or what? Are they gonna *off* me?"

"Not that I'm aware of."

"*Aware* of'! Hardly reassuring!"

"Take it easy, Skeeter. I have every reason to believe you're still considered an important asset to the company. You're in no danger. But did any of the board members mention business process outsourcing regarding me? Or any of our allies?"

"No, dude. At least not in so many words. Someone tossed around an exit strategy plan. But not in direct mention of your name. And—"

"Can you put this correspondence onto a flash-drive for me?"

"Already done." Skeeter dug deep into his jeans pocket and pulled out a "My Little Pony" flash-drive. All the shades of embarrassment rolled his color back. "Um...that's not *really* my flash-drive. Belongs to someone else."

"Of course. Anything else?" A little friendly prodding, the way to handle Skeeter. At times, he could be as addled as Augie. Leon imagined a life-time in front of a computer screen could do that to a person.

"Yeah. There's one guy they're keeping outta the loop. They only include him in basic, boring business talk."

Interesting. "Who?"

"Kaito Takihiro. He's the—"

"The Japanese LMI affiliate. I've met him. You figure out why he's unpopular with the cool kids?"

"Seems to be the only one who's willing to back you. For now at least. And from what I gather...he kinda wants to completely get out of the whole political end of things. Take LMI into more..." Finger quotes. "...'legit areas' of commerce."

Sheera's speech about putting LMI's political ambitions to rest had been a lie. No surprise, really. Unless Sheera didn't get invited to the big boy table either. Probably unnecessary, but Leon dropped his voice to a whisper, "Skeeter, what about Sheera? Is she involved in these talks?"

"Quit *whispering*," exclaimed Skeeter. "You're *seriously* creeping me out!"

"Sorry. Regular indoor voice now. Better?"

Skeeter twitched, nervous tics jumped over his eyelids. He scratched his arm, his chin, his ankle. It was all Leon could do to not start itching himself. "I just don't *know* about all this, Leon! Not what I signed up for."

"I know. But…I promise it'll be over soon. You'll come out just fine." *I hope.* "In the meantime, keep doing what you're doing. And, um…well, just keep doing it. Thanks."

"Whatever, Leon. Steaks aren't worth this." Skeeter closed his door. From within, a chain lock scrabbled against the woodwork. Leon even thought he heard a chair dragged across the floor and wedged up beneath the doorknob.

Maybe not such a bad strategy.

Nanette turned the chaise around, faced it toward the sun. If Leon could work on his tan, she may as well do the same. Sure beat sitting around in a cottage waiting to die. By far, these had been the strangest months of her life. And she'd lived through quite a few.

But now, as she lived in the lap of luxury, death was on its way.

"Yo, mamacita! What's up, what's up?"

Nanette sighed. She couldn't even catch any downtime at the pool. Of course she knew better than to expect peace and quiet. Cody could always be found one of two places: poolside or playing with the guard dogs down in the kennel. Predictable as time.

For one blissful moment, she shut her eyes and attempted to make Cody and the rest of her LMI world vanish.

She heard fast bare feet slap onto pavement. Cody hollered, cannonballed into the pool. A mini typhoon of water soaked Nanette.

"Damn it!"

Cody broke the water's surface. He slapped his hands like flippers and emulated a poor dolphin's whistle. "King of the ocean!"

King of the idiots, more like. "Put your fins away, fish-boy. Unless you wanna get speared."

Impervious to her threat, Cody glanced toward the endlessly frolicking bimbos, hoping to catch their attention. They weren't biting.

Cody swam to the edge of the pool, draped a muscular arm over the ledge. "Join me, yo."

"No need to now." Nanette shook her hands, water droplets flying. "Feel like I've already taken the plunge."

With one easy motion, Cody hopped out of the pool. He stood in front of her and pulled back his hair. Formed a muscle. Always on. But she had to admit, he looked good. Water glistened on the smooth curvature of his muscles.

"Dayum, girl, you're just like your man..." He jerked his chin toward the mansion. "...never any fun. Maybe you oughta, you know, lighten up, have some kicks or somethin'."

"You're blocking my sunlight."

He took that as an invite.

Grnnndddd...

After dragging another lounge chair next to hers, he plopped down onto it. Like a dog, probably where he learned the move, he rapidly shook his head. More water flipped onto her.

"*Stop* it."

"You can't stop the Cody, baby, he's—"

"Shouldn't be talking about himself in the third person."

"See? S'what I'm sayin'. No fun."

"More fun than you could ever handle, little boy."

"What? I invented fun! Give me a spin, you'll never wanna get off! You know what they call me? They call me..."

So tiresome. Yet. At least he paid attention to her. Tiresomely so, but still. Did a girl's pride wonders. She let him ramble on, the way she always did. One thing he had right: you can't stop him.

But something he said bugged. It hooked her like a fishing lure.

"He's *not* my man, you know."

Abruptly, Cody's endless tirade ended. "What?"

"You called Leon 'my man'."

"S'what I hear. You know...you're his woman."

Nanette shot up in the lounge chair, whipped off her sunglasses. "Um, no. Just...no. I'll never be *any* man's woman. I'm not someone to be kept in waiting by the so-called bigger, stronger sex! I'm not a helpless little damsel in distress waiting for my knight in shining armor to...ah, forget it!" She leaned back. Pointless preaching to a caveman.

In a surprisingly tender voice, all bluster buried, Cody said, "Hey, Nanette. Damn. Sorry, girl. Didn't mean nothin' by it. I just thought...well, you know what I thought. Ain't goin' there again."

"Good call." They sat in silence for a while, the way Nanette liked it. The way Cody didn't like.

Cody. He'd been hitting on her for six months. Relentless. Kinda cute in his never say never, but hopeless, advances. Too young for her. But, really, she'd mounted her sexual peak. And he definitely looked like he might be climbing right behind her.

In the past, she'd always rejected him, a tedious game of tug 'n war. Although she'd never felt more tugged.

But that was all crap, pure justification for lustful motives. She knew the real reason she kept rejecting him. Absolutely nothing to do with Cody. Once again, she abhorred herself for falling into the hand-wringing position Leon'd boxed her into.

"Cody?"

"Yo."

"If you think Leon and I are an item, why do you hit on me?"

"Cause you're *hawt.* Duh."

"But...Leon's your friend, right?"

"Guess so. I mean, we don't exactly have sleepovers or anything, but...yeah, we're chill."

"Then why hit on me?"

"Hey! All fun and games, baby! I wouldn't break the bro code! No way!"

"So you're just doing this...for fun?"

"Hellz yeah. So fuckin' boring around here."

"For once, we agree." She thought about Cody, considered a meaningless quick fling. Just as quickly discarded the notion as preposterous. A disaster waiting to happen. Then fantasized about it. Just a little. Then again, she'd break the young stallion before he could be properly trained.

But why couldn't she have a little fun? She owed Leon nothing. "You know, Cody...you'd never be able to handle me."

Like she knew he would, he pulled the bridle. "*What*? That's wack! Yo, baby, I'd be too much man for you! I could…"

So predictable, so easy to manipulate. She'd missed her games.

"Prove it." She rolled off her chaise and straight onto Cody. Grabbed his ears, violently forced her lips onto his. At first he hesitated. Mumbled something, tossed his arms about like a drowning man. Temptation took him. His hands explored her back, his fingers dragged through her hair. To keep him in line, she playfully bit his lower lip, just a nibble. She released him and stood. Watched him gasp, his chest heave. He held his arms out, waiting, longing for her. She lowered her gaze. A tent had pitched in his trunks.

She leaned over, drew a finger down his wet chest. Heat roiled off his body. He grabbed for her hand and she jerked it away. "Ah, ah, ah. Patience."

"Damn, baby…" Panting like a dog.

"Told you I was too much for you."

"Yeah, right! Come on, gimme some sugar!"

"What about Leon?" She grinned, gave him a coy look.

"Oh…right." The tower in his shorts leaned, shrank. "Bro code."

"But there is no bro code to break, Cody. I told you we're not a couple."

Disappointed eyes sparked again. "You sure 'bout that?"

"Oh, I'm sure." She dragged another finger down his chest. Made sure to jab a nipple with her sharpest fingernail, one she filed more than the others. He yipped. She left, added an extra wiggle. Brazen, but undeniably fun. She turned around, peek-a-booed over her shoulder. "Coming?"

"Hellz, yeah!"

He caught up to her, dropped an arm around her shoulders. Between her fingers, she pinched his arm up, dropped it like trash. Added an exaggerated pout. "Ah, ah, ah…do what teacher tells you to do."

"Dayum! Role playing!"

Or *something* like that. This was a mistake, no doubt about it. For a few moments, she thought she'd go through with it. But she'd end up using Cody to get to Leon. A game she didn't want to play. She had no intention of seeing this disaster through to the end. But Cody could use a little lesson in humility. And of course she desired a little fun. Hell, she felt entitled to some fun.

And a little fun never hurt anyone.

Did it?

"Sheera, I have to talk to you!" Leon stood in the doorway, tried to temper his exhausted anger. Hard to do when he'd lost two would-be assassins under Sheera's watch. And Gaines'.

As expected, Gaines had beaten him to the punch. He ignored Leon's bullish entrance and whispered into Sheera's surgically altered ear.

"Just the man we were discussing." Sheera gestured toward the end of the table. "Really, darling, you need to learn to knock, perhaps make an appointment."

"This is urgent."

"Well, despite your rather abrupt and rude entry, I'm glad you're here. I have something I need to discuss with you as well."

It could go either way. Leon'd prepared the best he could to defend his latest actions. A trying, dangerous battle lay ahead, for sure. Particularly on little sleep. But he wouldn't be ramrodded.

He sat across from Gaines at Sheera's side. "Great. Let's talk. Just the two of us."

Sheera shook her head, used to it by now. "Gaines, give us the room please."

Gaines stood, straightened his crisp jacket. Honestly, Leon didn't know how Gaines did it. He appeared showered and rested, the recipient of a lovely siesta. Unaffected by their three day, sleepless trip. On the way out the door, he paused by Leon. Sniffed. May as well've urinated to mark his territory.

"What the hell, Sheera? I go away and the man I put in my friends' care is murdered?"

"Leon, dear, perhaps it should be your friends you should be directing your ire to."

"That's not true and you know it. One of your guards tried to kill Nanette, then killed—"

Her hand went up, the imperious queen in charge. "That has not been proven. We don't know that's true."

"The hell we don't!"

"Again...how do you know you can trust your darling Nanette? Or the charming little man and his...interesting mate?"

Leon's addled mind circled the drain, made him question his allies. But he wouldn't go there, fall into Sheera's ploy. Divide and conquer. "I absolutely trust them. Unlike your guards. And...you."

Her mouth formed an "O," a stretch in every imaginable way. It looked painful. "Why, Leon! You wound me!" In her best southern belle routine, a hand fluttered to her breast. "You know you can trust me. Why, I've taken great measures to place you in your position. Against others' judgment, mind you."

"I've heard it before. I'd like to see proof."

"What do you want from me? I've done everything in my power to give you what you need. Which brings up the real point of our meeting..."

She did it again. Master of railroading Leon's train of thought. "Wait a minute... We haven't settled the issue of the two men's deaths yet!"

She leaned forward, so close Leon smelled mint on her breath. Her overpowering perfume brought moisture to his blinking eyes. Face to face, her plastic encased eyes narrowed to one. "I told you I'm looking into the possibility of a spy amongst Gaines' guards. I will not have you doubt my decisions. I'm not fond of having my methods questioned. I am your boss."

"I know you are!" Leon scooted back, uncomfortable with her breach of private lines. "But you say you're looking into the guards...what about Gaines? I don't trust him."

"Preposterous. He's one of the few people I trust. His loyalty knows no limits."

Of course Leon wanted to remind her how loyal Gaines had been to her late husband. Until he switched sides to Sheera's team. No sense in rocking the boat, though. Even if it did have a leak in it.

"I know you trust Gaines. I don't," said Leon. "Please…just do me this one favor? Look into him?"

Her red nails tapped over the table-top, detailing the time passed.

Tic, tic, tic…

One eye flinched, just a hair. Finally, "Our last meeting had you asking me for one last favor. I granted you that. Now…" She picked up a stack of papers. Licked a finger, went to the second sheet. "We need to talk about your out-of-control spending."

Uh-oh. "I know my expenditures appear—"

"Astronomical."

"I wouldn't say that exactly."

"Oh?" She struggled to raise a thin, blonde eyebrow. It didn't fly high. "I see you've had your little friend, Skeeter…" She wrinkled her nose. "…set up an on-going financial allowance for a…Ricky Shoemaker. Please explain." She sat back, satisfied with herself, and dared Leon to present his case.

"Um, yeah…about that. I meant to tell you about it. It…just trust me, it's been implemented to keep LMI's complete market invisibility intact. A situation came up that required a quiet solution, one that a well-placed budget could—"

"Situation, Leon? What kind of situation?"

"Ah…let's call it a clean-up situation. One that couldn't be avoided. But I've taken care of—"

"Oh, *really* now?" Again, she licked a finger, a cat cleaning its fur. Flicked to another sheet. "Might this situation have something to do with…a Billings prostitute having an unfortunate accident?" Puppy-dog eyes and pouty lips. "An accident involving a decapitation?" She tapped a lip. "Now… where have I heard about this type of accident before?"

Crap.

"Okay, fine…I meant to tell you about this, too, but—"

"Darling, if you ever told me all the things you've meant to, you'd never get anything else done. And you ask me to trust you. Tsk, tsk, tsk'"

"In my defense…things have been kinda fast-paced around here lately."

"Undoubtedly. But how can you possibly defend your psychotic little protégé's excursion?"

"Sheera, in our line of work..." She giggled, rolled her eyes. "Fine. As you know, most like-minded individuals feel an overpowering need at times. A scratch that has to be itched before it turns infectious. I caught Cody's scratch early, made a few safe adjustments. Applied the salve, if you will."

"Cute."

"I made sure Cody acted with the utmost caution, cleaned up thoroughly, left no clues behind. Without my intervention, Cody would've acted on his own and brought unwanted attention upon LMI. And to your ranch, Sheera."

"Hmm. Not a very strong defense, Leon." Which he knew. "This smacks of the work of the Denver Decapitator. That won't do at all."

"But, the Decapitator always took the bodies and disposed of them. Cody didn't. He—"

"So you're telling me this will look like your garden variety psychopathic decapitation."

Humiliated, chastised and more than a little embarrassed, Leon nodded.

"Regardless of how careful you were, Leon, this is 300,000 dollars—so far—of LMI's capitol that shouldn't have been spent. In fact, the entire event should've never transpired. All to take care of your little sociopathic pet. He's becoming a liability."

Unfortunately...that's true.

"That is *not* true. Cody's proven his value and worth to me time and time again. He's...he's my Gaines! He—"

"Yeah, yeah, yeah, he completes you. Leon, darling...I've said it before, I'll remind you again. If you can't keep your mad dog on a leash, he'll need to be put down."

"He's leashed."

"Remains to be seen." Lick, flick, stare. "Oh, and here's another little item on the expenditures list. Your little Florida excursion...minus all travel expenses...has tallied up to nearly...three-quarter of a million dollars! I can't *wait* to hear your explanation."

"I'm sorry, but I can't accept the sole blame for this. If it hadn't been for your inability to call off the Amish business process outsourcer, then—"

"Again, you forget who you're talking to. As fond as I am of you, do not take my kindness for granted. Are you blaming me for this outlandish expenditure?"

"No, no, no…not at all, I'm just—"

"Need I remind you that you made the ultimate decision on August Schroeder's fate? Frankly, I saw it in your eyes, Leon. You couldn't wait to dispose of your friend." She smiled, all the teeth of a piano.

"I did *not*." But Leon doubted himself, his motives. He knew Sheera was playing him, worming her way into his mind. Yet he'd made the call. The corporate LMI way, the way that came natural these days.

"Say what you will, Leon. But this is on you. Another expenditure that could've been avoided."

"Come on, Sheera. Let's not forget why you hired me. We share the same goals. I'm *trying* my best to put LMI into the black. I'm—"

"By spending nearly a million dollars?"

"I know how much money LMI's sitting on. How much *you're* sitting on. Billions. Hellooo! Ex-accountant here, remember? You need to look at the big picture, the long-term goals. Not the small picture."

"So, you've handled the August Schroeder situation?"

"No one will ever see or hear from him again. You have my word." *Fingers crossed.*

"And what of The Amish?"

"He's…been taken care of."

She sighed, picked up a pen. Ripped a line across a sheet of paper. "Honestly, Leon, you really need to quit wasting company resources. What does this make…five business process outsourcers you've disposed of?"

"Um…" *Yes.* "Just remember, Sheera, to make money you have to spend money. Some eggs need to be broken."

"Just not *your* eggs. Regardless of how pretty a picture you paint, the two situations could've been resolved much easier. Much quieter. Much cheaper."

The deaths of Cody and Augie.

"Sheera, how can you put a price on people's lives?"

Her shriek of laughter filled the room, drove nails into his head. Window-panes rattled. Eventually she settled, caught her breath. Leon knew it'd been a stupid question, but he had to ask it nonetheless. If for nothing else, to consider what kind of answer he would've given.

Sheera wiped tears from her eyes. "Dear Leon…if you truly have to ask such a silly question, then you're the wrong man for this job."

Cody felt a little odd, maybe a little uncomfortable over the whole deal. A weird sensation. Every time he thought of Leon, though, lust sort of shoved Leon aside. Besides, as Nanette said, she wasn't Leon's squeeze. Leon'd said the same thing. *Pretty much.*

No big deal, brah!

Yeah, he'd never broken the bro code before. And he *still* wasn't breaking it. That's what he kept telling himself. Hell, whenever auto-pilot kicked in, his little big man did all the driving anyway. Totally out of his control, a defense that'd hold up in court, yo.

And it'd been months since he'd bedded down a babe. The two weird chicks at the pool only had eyes for one another. Whatever.

He watched Nanette's backside as she led him to her cabin. Coming onto him. Asking for it. Hot, completely.

Whaddaya call it…consenting adults. Yo, your honor, I rest my case!

No way he'd pass up an opportunity like this. And when opportunity knocks, body bits knock next.

Nanette opened her door, ducked inside faster than a jack-rabbit. She left the door ajar.

Cody entered, locked the door behind him. If he had a "Do not disturb" sign, he would've hung it.

The girl could move, nowhere to be seen.

From the bedroom, "Codyyy, I'm waiting!"

Some damn!

He kicked off a sandal, hobbled on a foot, struggled with the next. Time to get it on. Before she changed her mind. It'd been six months of playing their game, six months of her blowing him off. He heard the clock ticking, sick of the cock blocking.

The swimming trunks came off next. He kicked them off his foot.

Flap.

They slapped onto the sofa with a satisfying and wet noise.

"Where are you, Codyyyy?"

His fingertips trembled around the door-knob. Almost afraid to touch it and wake up from a dream.

Get it together, yo! She's just a chick!

He opened the door. Nanette lay in bed, her wet bikini a thin glove on her body. She'd folded the covers back. Talk about moving fast. He needed to catch up. As he trotted across the room, she giggled. He sprang onto the mattress, rolled on top of her, the hell with getting wet. He couldn't wait any longer. He dove in for a kiss, the sloppier and furious the better. She stopped him with a surprisingly steely finger pressed into his chest.

"Ah, ah, ah! Not so fast, tiger."

"Whaddaya talkin' 'bout, baby? You was just callin' for me like a three-alarm fire. Fireman's here, hose and all!"

She chuckled again. Rolled out from beneath him. Landed on her feet next to the bed like a cat. A very hot and human cat. Tanned, muscular legs. Perfect pert breasts. Best of all? No stretch marks. Not that he'd thought she'd ever had kids. Otherwise he wouldn't be here now. And she'd be somewhere different, somewhere very deep and dark.

"C'mon, baby! You're killin' me!" He reached for her, wiggled his fingers.

"Shhh." She pressed a finger to his lips. "For once, just be quiet. Let me do all the talking."

"Whatever you say, ba—"

Her hand clamped over his mouth. She liked to play. *Cool*. Cody could play with the best of them. King of playahs.

Delicate as a faun, she pranced across the room. Scrounged

around for something in her dresser drawer. As she came back, her hands stayed behind her back. Smiling, smoldering style.

"What's up? Thought we're playin'?"

"Oh, we're playing alright, Cody. My rules." From behind her back, she whipped out two pairs of hand-cuffs. Fur-lined.

Cody'd never experimented with cuffs before. Been curious though. Call him "cuff curious."

"Alright, baby! Bring it! Whadda ya into, some kinda kinky crap?"

"You'll see. Put your hands up next to the bedposts."

Cody obliged, gave his muscles an extra flex. He rippled his belly, showed off his six-pack, something he didn't do for just anyone.

"Ooh, hot. I like that." Nanette flicked at his ribs, strummed his body's guitar. Then she locked one of his hands to the post, then the other. Kinda tight, maybe too tight.

Cody shook the bed-post. The cuffs rattled. He felt like freakin' King Kong. He gave a Tarzan yell. "Me Tarzan, you—"

Again, her palm slapped over his mouth. "Cody, what'd I tell you about your noise? You don't speak unless I say so. Got it?"

"Just tryin' to get into the game, yo. I—"

The slap wasn't hard, didn't sting. But it surprised him. "What the *hell*?"

The second slap to his other cheek hurt a little bit more. His cheeks felt on-fire, not really in a good way.

"Again…silence is golden. Got it?"

Her sudden stern appearance didn't do much for him. Dr. Nanette and Ms. Hyde: hot school girl and mean-ass schoolmarm. Regardless, he was all in. "Cody Junior" agreed.

"Just to make sure you understand the rules of the game, Cody…" Hop, skip, jump to her dresser again. Cody wondered just what the hell she had in there. And where she got it. Maybe Gaines had gone to the sex shop for her. "Here's something to ensure you abide by my rules."

"Whoa!" She dangled a leather strap in front of him. That didn't bug him too much. But the red ball in the middle kinda did. "Whoa, baby, hold on a minute! I dunno 'bout that!"

"Shh, shh, shh." Her face fell into a playful sulk. Not nearly as sexy as earlier. "I thought you wanted to play with me? Change your mind? Sooo disappointing. I knew you wouldn't be able to handle me. Just knew it."

Well, hell, Cody never backed down from anything. 'Specially when his manhood was on the line. "Show me what you got!"

Lightning-fast, she grabbed a handful of his hair, yanked his head up. The band slipped around his head, the ball stuffed into his mouth. He panicked, not that he'd ever show it. Hard to breathe. Cody worked around it, bit into the ball and hyperventilated through his nose. Partially from arousal, mostly from danger. A killer combo, yo.

"There we go." She stood back. With elbow in hand, the other hand tapped her jaw. "Something's missing..."

Jesus. What now?

Still, he stood fully erect. Patiently waiting to have something done about it. He watched her race back to the dresser.

Crap.

Cody didn't like the look of her newest toy. Nanette held the purple whip up, studied it. Whisked it through the air. A mop's worth of purple rubber strands snapped at the end of the pole.

Wssh-spack!

"I think this will do nicely." She smiled at him although it seemed as genuine as a plastic Halloween mask. "One of my favorites. You should feel honored."

When she cracked the whip again, Cody yelped.

"Ah fink ah duh!" *I think I'm done!*

His junk agreed, wilted like a rain-drenched flower.

"Cody, I didn't quite get what you said. But...sounded to me like 'you can't wait.'"

"Nuh, nuh! Leh muh ah!" *No, no! Let me go!*

"That's the spirit." Her grin stretched wide, wicked and hungry. She kissed his chest, set his nipples tingling. Maybe it wasn't all bad. Until she started cracking the whip closer.

The strands brushed over his chest, ants on parade. Arousal dampened. Cody felt himself shriveling to an embarrassing size. *Uncool.*

The leather felt cold. Ice cubes. Yet sweat started leaking from places it never had before.

Nanette pulled back the whip, the strands hanging down behind her. "You ready for this, Cody? Yep, I think you are. I guess you can keep up with me after all. Wait! One more thing!"

Dammit! How much worse can it get?

Cody shut his eyes so hard, his teeth hurt. He listened to her bound across the room, the grind of the dresser drawer open. Silence. He opened one eye, then the other.

"Been waiting to try this baby on somebody." She stared at the beast in her hand. The rubber, spiked sex toy wiggled back and forth, some kind of monstrous, mutated caterpillar.

Some kind of hell, no!

A crucial second caught on the edge of time. Terror built from his gut, filled his bladder. He imagined what she had planned, where the toy would go, how painful it would be. He closed his eyes. Clenched down hard on the ball. He had no idea the chick was this nuts. Dayum, Leon never said a word about it.

"Last chance, Cody...can you keep up with me?"

"Nuh! Don wah tuh nah moh, oh!" *No! Don't want to no more, yo!*

"What was that, Cody? Say it again?"

"Cah kee uh, oh! Leh muh gah!" *Can't keep up, yo! Let me go!*

First time for everything. Cody had never passed up a hottie. But this was outta his wheelhouse. Sure as hell didn't want to be mentally scarred for life.

"Oh, my. I think I heard defeat. Here...let's just find out what you're trying to say."

Gently, she set the whip and toy next to Cody where he stared at the objects in horror. She undid his gag.

Cody spit the ball out. "Jesus Christ, Nanette! Let me up! I don't—"

"Say it."

"Say *what*?"

"Say you can't keep up with me."

Cody hated giving in. He really did. He rattled the cuffs, tried to loosen them. Thrashed around in the bed. Growled, ashamed as hell.

"Well, if you're gonna act this way, we'll just go back to the toys."

"No! Goddamn! Fine, I can't keep up with you."

She leaned over, a hand cupped around her ear. "I'm sorry. Can you say that a little louder?"

"I can't keep *up* with you!"

"Thought so." She laughed. Pulled out keys from who knows where. "Here you go."

As soon as she released his wrists, Cody rolled out of bed. The sheet came with him. Immediately, he wrapped it around his waist, humiliated. He massaged his wrists. "Damn, girl… this the kinda kinky shit you and Leon get all up in?"

"None of your business." She strapped on a robe, clenched it tight.

"What the hell's this all about anyway?"

She shrugged. Fluffed her hair out from the robe's collar. Back to straight up normal, damn near ready for a Wall Street meeting. "Girl's gotta have her fun where she can get it."

"Yeah, I get that." *Not really.* "So, you like, never wanted to get sloppy with me? Every chick does, yo! The Cody, he don't—"

"Cody, just…stop. No, I wasn't going to go through with it." Her eyes narrowed. "Well, maybe I thought about it a little…" She pinched a small space between her fingers. Which made Cody's genitals shrink just a little bit more.

"So you was playin' me?"

"Oh, look who's talking. Get over yourself. You know, you're not the only 'playah' on the ranch."

"Yeah, whatevs. You know, like you said, I'm just gettin' my kicks where—"

"Well, get 'em somewhere else from now on, cowboy. I'm not your toy. You've been bird-dogging me our entire time here. Thought I'd teach you a lesson."

Cody stared at her, wondered what the hell kinda lesson he was supposed to take from this.

Never go to bed with a kinky babe?

"You're trippin'. All this just ain't my bag."

"Yeah, I've seen your bag." Again she pinched her fingers together, squinted between them. And laughed.

"Stop doin' that with your fingers already! Fun-time's dunzo! I gotta bounce."

Cody hurried from the room. Quickly jumped into his swimsuit. Thankfully, his golden tan covered his red glow of shame. Still, maybe Nanette had a point. Damned if he knew what it was, though. He'd work on it, though. If he ever got any spare time.

She followed him into the living room.

"A'ight, I won't hit on you no more. Didn't mean to, you know...make you feel like crap or anything."

She smiled, genuinely. No flirt or mischief or scary sex weapons in sight. "Thanks, appreciate that. We outsiders have to stick together. As equals."

"Yeah, it's cool, it's cool, baby. I get it. Just, you know, do me a favor, yo?"

"Name it."

"I'll quit houndin' you...even though I still don't get why any chick would want me to stop, but—"

"Get to the point."

"I'll stop hittin' on you...if you keep this just between us. I mean, especially to Leon. But, you know, also to every other hottie. Or dude, too."

"Fine." Her fingers twisted in front of her lips, tossed away a faux key. "I don't kiss and tell."

"Yo, I did kiss pretty hot, though, right? I mean, I'm kinda a big deal. All the chicks say that I'm—"

"Bye, Cody!" She pushed him toward the door, tossed him out. Slammed it.

Worse, he heard laughter behind the door.

Dayum. That chick be whack, yo.

On his way toward his cabin, Leon cursed about how badly the meeting went. The ground beneath him wasn't just shaky, it felt absolutely full-on earthquake. Basically Sheera'd implied he was becoming an LMI liability. Whenever dealing with LMI, true threats were always hard to discern over probationary threats. Either way, it could've gone better. Immensely better.

But now, he needed sleep. More than anything. Suddenly, a

shadow merged with his. Sleep would have to wait a bit longer.

"Um...Leon?"

Skeeter. It had to be important for him to venture this far out of his bunker.

"Hi, Skeeter. You find out anything else about the board members?"

"Dude, shhh! We're outside!"

"Well, yeah...be kinda hard to put 'bugs' outside. Other than mosquitoes and the like."

"What? Dammit, so you're sayin' my place is *bugged*?"

Oh, for God's sake. "No, Skeeter, that's not what I meant. Guess I was just making a bad joke." *A very bad one, lost on its audience.*

"You'd tell me, right, if you knew anything about—"

"Of course I would. What can I do for you?"

"I...uh, I don't know how to tell you this, Leon...but you've been cool to me in the past...and I thought you might wanna know. But, dude, it might not be anything! Really, dude! It could just be—"

"What the hell is it?" Sleep seemed so close, yet impossibly far away.

"Um...it's about Nanette. Nanette and Cody. Now don't kill the messenger! But...I have it on good authority that they..."

The more Skeeter told Leon about Nanette and Cody's secret tryst, the less he wanted to hear.

Betrayal. A two-pronged betrayal.

He pushed Skeeter aside. Calmly threw up in the flower garden.

"Jesus, dude! You okay? I mean, can I do anything for you or what?"

"Just leave, please."

"Yeah, sure, whatever you say."

Leon barely made it inside. He fell to his knees, gave in to all fours. He curled up, too emotionally—physically—weak to make it to bed.

And sleep still never came.

"Jesus, Sidarski, how many times you gonna go to the

bathroom?"

Sidarski stumbled past the person in the aisle seat, banged into her knees, muttered an apology, then dropped into the seat next to Keats. "Damn heart-burn. Keep thinking I can do something about it in the john, but...no luck."

"Yeah, TMI." Keats closed her eyes, pushed her seat back. How she could sleep in an airplane completely baffled Sidarski. Not only were the seats and leg room impossibly confined, there was the pesky, ongoing threat of terrorism. He always played "spot the air marshal" to pass the time, hone his skills and calm his nerves.

His chest burned as if a tanning booth had crisped his innards. Whenever he thought of Leon Garber, the pain persisted longer. A human thermometer of discomfort. Only effective antacid? Arresting Garber. A dream he vowed to make happen.

Always a nervous flyer—especially now—Sidarski opened his iPad. A long-shot at best, he searched the Billings, Montana news for any possible shoot-outs that may've occurred within the last year at an isolated ranch. He came up blank.

Then he scanned recent crime news. Lots of DUI notices and domestic disturbance incidents, humanity in its flawed flow of life. His eyes glazed over, his eyelids grew heavy. Maybe he could sleep on a plane for once. He was ready to pack it in when something he saw jerked him awake. Something all too familiar. And very exciting. The first sign they weren't pursuing a wild goose.

"Huh. Interesting."

Keats kept her eyes shut, but said, "What? Your fave boy band getting' back together?"

"No. Something much worse." He nudged Keats and handed her his iPad. "Check it out."

"'Local Woman Found Decapitated,'" read Keats. "Sidarski, weird things excite you."

"I'm an excitable boy. Just keep reading."

As Keats read, the woman next to Sidarski gave him an odd look, leaned her head in to listen.

"Sorry, ma'am. It's business related." Sidarski stared her

down, until she scooted as far away as possible. Which really wasn't very far.

"Okay. Yeah, it's horrible." She flipped the device back to him. "But how's this factor into our boy?"

"The method of murder. Ring any bells?"

"Not exactly sleigh-bells."

"The Denver Decapitator. His M.O."

"Right. I got that. Still don't think it's Garber."

Sidarski's flight neighbor gasped. She fled from her seat, sought safety elsewhere. Sidarski embraced his new freedom, whipped up the arm rest, sprawled out into the recently abandoned seat.

"It's not Garber. But the other kid I told you about? I think that's our man outta Denver."

"No shit?"

"No shit."

"Alright, Sidarski...maybe you better tell me the full story."

Sidarski stood, head tilted beneath the overhead bin. "This might take a while."

"I love a good story."

Sometime during the early hours of morning, Leon dozed off. He woke, snorted, and panicked for a moment until he recognized his surroundings. When he sat up, something jagged in his back. His left arm hurt. He welcomed the pain. Anything to dull his feelings.

Honestly, he didn't know what to do. Confront Nanette first, then kick Cody out. *No.* Have Cody beaten, then confront Nanette.

Or just let it lay. Sleeping bear and all.

He tried to look at the situation objectively, an impossible task. He had no hold over Nanette. She was an independent woman, fiercely so. And they weren't exactly exclusive. But he'd always hoped she'd be a part of his long-term plans. As soon as he wrapped up his LMI stint. He thought he'd made that abundantly clear to Nanette.

Really, could he ask her to wait around for something that may not ever happen?

But to sleep with *Cody*, of all people. One of the few people he considered a friend. And Cody knew how Leon felt about Nanette.

Poke the bear? Or let it hibernate?

His head—his profound sense of loss—hurt too much to lend the problem the logic it demanded.

The pounding on the front door added to his tired misery.

"Gaines."

"Mr. Garber. Your presence is requested by Mrs. Rasmussen."

"Of course it is."

Gaines stared at Leon. "I believe she wants to see you now, sir."

"Be there when I feel like it." Leon closed the door. Seconds later, Gaines began tapping again. Let him wait. Let Sheera wait. Let everyone wait.

Like Nanette.

Maybe that's what he needed. A task. Away from the ranch. Far, far away from Nanette.

Neither the shower nor coffee alleviated Leon's headache or his exhaustion. He lurched down the sidewalk, cut through the grass. He passed Nanette's cottage. Wondered what exactly was going on inside. His gut muscles tightened at the imagery. For a moment, he thought he'd be sick again.

He couldn't help but glance over at Cody's cottage as well. The one he'd supplied to his traitorous ally.

Bastard. After everything I've done for him...

Leon hauled himself up the main stairwell. He pushed open the boardroom door, no salutations this morning. His back caught again as he lowered himself into his customary seat. And he glared at Sheera and Gaines.

Sheera glanced at her watch, a set of diamonds dangling from it, teenage bling. "Took your time, didn't you?"

"Yes."

Gaines shot his master a blatant *told you so* look.

"And, dear Leon, you look like absolute hell, if you don't mind my saying so."

"I don't mind." In fact, he didn't care much about anything. A dangerous mind-set, particularly when his life had been targeted.

Bring 'em on...

"I see." Sheera stared down at the paperwork in front of her. "I have an important chore for you, darling."

"Fine."

"I need you to pick up Kaito Takihiro in a few hours. From the Billings Crowne Plaza Hotel. He's the—"

"Japanese LMI affiliate. I know."

"Of course you do." Her smile appeared even more plastic than usual. Unable to hold Leon's gaze, her eyes flitted toward Gaines. Something seemed off.

"Why am I going? Why not just send a car for him like you usually do for visitors?"

"This is a matter of respect for Mr. Takihiro. Surely, I thought you'd understand how important it is to abide by Japanese customs."

"I suppose."

"And as you're the CEO of LMI, I'm afraid anyone less than you would offend Mr. Takihiro's sensibilities. We wouldn't want that now."

"Of course 'we' wouldn't."

One of her eyebrows arched. He'd succeeded in getting quite a rise out of her today. "You're to pick up Mr. Takihiro at 2:00 in front of the Crowne Plaza where he'll be waiting for you. He'll have his attaché with him."

"What do I do with him?"

She flourished her hand, model style. Barked a laugh. "Why, wine and dine him, of course! Then bring him back here when you're done schmoozing."

"Uh huh." Dulled and emotionless, Leon sat in a haze. Absolutely uncaring about a schmooze fest.

"Well?"

"Well what?"

"Off you go. You might want to...ah, dress a little nicer."

Leon looked down at his jeans and t-shirt. In the past, he'd prided himself on dressing the part, being the part. He shrugged. "Fine. Gaines, when will you have the car ready?"

"I'm afraid I'll not be joining you on this venture, Mr. Garber."

"What?" *Definitely* wrong. Rarely had Sheera ever let Leon out of Gaines' sight. "May I ask why?"

"No, you may not." Her mouth set into a nondescript straight line. "I'm just kidding you, darling!" She laughed, giving the approval for Gaines to join her. "Gainsey is needed here. With me. Boring financial matters that I wouldn't want to bother you with. But do take your little sidekick with you." She fluttered heavily ringed fingers.

"Ah…I'd rather not."

Apparently, this brightened Sheera's day. Her mouth curled up before her implanted cheekbones forced it back down. "Why, whatever is the matter between you and your protégé?"

"Nothing. I'd just rather go alone."

"I'm afraid that's not a request, Leon. It's an order. Don't forget that—"

"You're the boss. You don't need to constantly remind me."

"Then perhaps you'd better start treating me that way, hmm?"

"I just don't understand…if this is about 'courting' Mr. Takahiri, why in the world do you think Cody'd be a good peace ambassador?"

"It's time your minion became civilized. Teach him some manners. Lift a pinky, dab your mouth with a napkin, whatever." She shot a sly look to Gaines. "Consider it…a trial by fire."

"Heh." That one snippet of sound out of Gaines, a chuckle interrupted, chilled Leon. The temperature bottomed out around him. Sheera shot Gaines a look, sharper than a sword.

"As a matter of fact, Leon darling, please feel free to take the rest of your entourage with you. I understand the little man can be quite enchanting. And your vixen, Nanette, is not without her charms, I suppose."

"I'll have my hands full with Cody." The last thing Leon wanted to do was take a trip with Nanette. Cody was bad enough.

Sheera tipped her head, smiled. "Suit yourself. Now, go. Ta ta, for now." Again, she wiggled her fingers at Leon, but she buried her head deep within her paperwork. Dismissed.

And why did Leon have a feeling this was his much feared, not totally unexpected LMI exit interview?

Chapter Eight

Trees, rocks and mountains as far as the eye could see. Of course Keats was used to trees, plenty of those in Miami, just of a different sort. Not so many mountains. She'd heard Montana called "big sky country." For good reason. The vast expanse of sky made her feel small, their hunt for Garber futile. Give her civilization any day, criminals flocked to buildings. So did rats. Montana may as well've been an alien landscape.

"Damn." That's about all she said on their drive to the Billings Police Department. Sidarski just nodded at her assessment and focused on the road in their rental.

She almost cheered when they reached the center of Billings. Tall buildings penetrated the low cloud cover; cars zipped by with horns rudely harping; people scurried through downtown, eyes glued to their phones. Blessed civilization.

Keats thought the countless "Bomb Squad" trucks filling the Billings PD parking lot looked like overkill. The Miami PD had a couple at their disposal; nothing like these behemoths. Bulky, ominously threatening and less than covert. She wondered what kind of crime they had in Montana.

"What's up with that, Sidarski?" She pointed toward the line-up. "Billings get a lotta bomb threats?"

"Who knows? If our perps are here, yeah, probably."

It took a while to bypass the desk jockey. But with Keats' aggression and Sidarski's bulldog can-do, they made it in to see the detective who mattered.

A wiry man with a wispy mustache, Bob Dawbins juggled his coffee cup between his hands as if it scalded them. "Have a seat, have a seat."

Keats and Sidarski obliged. Dawbins dropped the cup, wagged a hand.

"So...you're Keats? As in Keats from the Miami PD? The one whose partner tried to off her?"

She nodded. "My claim to fame."

"Bellup, right?"

"Late and not so great."

"Yeah. I knew Arnie." Dawbins bent forward, blew on his coffee. With his head down, he tilted the cup to his lips. "Went to the Academy with Arnie back in the day. He sucked even then. Jack-ass."

Keats knew they wouldn't encounter any problems after that, mutual enemy established.

"Anyway, enough reminiscing. Sidarski, don't know you."

"Retired thirty-two year vet from the Barton, Kansas police."

"Barton? Never heard of it."

"No one has."

"You a detective?"

"Yeah. Or, I was." Sidarski's eyes pulled down, obviously ashamed.

"Retired, huh? Full pension?"

"Yep."

Dawbins smiled. "Glad to see someone made it."

Keats' patience stretched, nearly snapped. Every second counted. "Listen, Dawbins, what can you tell us about this Shoemaker beheading?"

Dawbins coughed on a fresh sip of coffee. He swallowed it quickly, fanned his mouth. *Surprise.* "Whoa. Didn't see that one coming. You guys are both far from home. Why in hell you wanna know about a local hooker who got with the wrong john?"

"A hooker?" Sidarski sat forward. His folding chair complained with a screech. "Also a mother, right? Young kids?"

"You read about that in the paper or something?"

"No. Online."

"Yeah, she had one kid. Apparently not parent-of-the-year either."

"Abusive, right?"

"Nailed it. How'd you know?"

"Lucky guess."

"Bullshit. You wanna know what I got? You give me what you know. This damn case is big...it's got the top politicos freaking out, putting pressure on the boys in blue." Keats cleared her throat. "Um, and the girl cops, too."

"Ahem!"

"Christ. 'Women.' Everyone's involved from the damn media to back-slapping would-be White House wonders. So, I've gotta solve this thing. If you can help, great. I'll pitch you the ball. But if not...I'm taking my ball and going home."

"Dammit. You boys and your balls. Fine, I'll pitch first," said Keats. "I'm lookin' for a guy name of Leon Garber. Know him?" She scooted the well-worn photo across the desk.

"No. Should I?"

"Depends. My buddy here..." She inclined her head toward Sidarski. "...he thinks he might be in alliance with a guy who... perpetrated some similar incidents to your beheading."

"Similar? Like...chopping off some broad's head?"

Keats let that one slide. Sliding into home base topped her to-do list. "Yeah..." Keats slipped Sidarski a look: *How much you wanna tell him*?

Close to a whisper, Sidarski said, "The Denver Decapitator."

The color drained from Dawbins' face. The chair made a loud *squonk* when he sat back, an angry crow call. "The Denver... Oh, good Christ! I don't wanna deal with—"

"Fine," said Keats, "we will."

"What?"

"We'll bring him in. We'll do our job." Sidarski nodded.

Dawbins inhaled deeply as if preparing to dive into water, blew it out. Keats glanced at her watch. Finally, he calmed. "This is...this is gonna be a shitstorm."

"Welcome to our world," said Sidarski.

"Yeah, thanks. No...no, dammit. I'll do my job. But tell me everything you can about this..." A hand went up beside Dawbins' mouth as he stage whispered, "...Denver Decapitator."

Sidarski leaned forward to tell his tale, literally on the edge of his seat. Keats feared his chair might tip. It didn't surprise her Sidarski omitted details. Hardly a surprise, either, that Dawbins didn't follow up with the obvious questions. A lame cop, frightened of his shadow and clearly lazy.

Sidarski finished his saga, nearly out of breath. So was Dawbins. Keats fairly expected them to light up with a post-tale smoke.

"So you think this Decapitator is here in Billings?"

"Not sure. But the M.O. is pretty close to what I dealt with back in Kansas. Could be Spangler just pulled a hit and run. Maybe gone by now."

Relief visibly lowered Dawbins' shoulders. "Best thing for everyone," he muttered. "So this *kid* is...the guy?" He wagged the photo of Cody Spangler. With a grunt, Sidarski reached over and snatched back his prized possession.

"Presumed to be. At least by me," said Sidarski.

"Uh huh." Dawbins started swinging in his chair.

Crrrkkk...zkkkk...crrrkkkk...

Suddenly he stopped, the wheels of justice grinding to a halt. "And...you think he might be gone now?"

Keats sighed, wondered if they'd ever get back on the road. "Maybe. Maybe not. But we need to find him. Right now, we're your best hope, Dawbins. Now, there's another little matter we're following up on...have there been any shootings, any reported injuries, excessive property damage to a Montana ranch located around here?"

Dawbins stopped his seat-swing, grimaced. Ready to pack up his toys again. "Whaddaya talkin' about?"

"Just like I said, do you know about any such dust-ups?"

The detective's eyes shifted left, shuttled right. Keats watched the lump in his throat slowly plunge. Easier to read than a coloring book. He knew something. "I haven't heard of anything like that, no, ma'am."

First time he brought out old-fashioned manners, an obvious giveaway.

"Fine," said Keats. "Can you give me the addresses of the more prosperous ranch owners in a...oh, fifty mile radius?"

He pressed his lips together like a pissed-off librarian. "Afraid not. Below my pay grade."

"What?" Keats jumped to her feet, ready to vault across the desk. "You're so goddamn afraid to go find a killer, you can't do a little leg-work?"

Sidarski sighed, reached over and patted Keats' arm. "Sit down, Keats. We're not done yet."

"Get your damn hand off me, Sidarski! Thought you were better than that condescending bullshit!"

"Please, Keats. Sit."

She sat, glared at her new nemesis. Just like home, after all.

"Now, Dawbins," said Sidarski, "I thought you were ready to play ball."

"I am. I was."

"Uh huh. How'd you like to crack this case? Be a gold star for you."

Keats shot Sidarski a look. Her case, dammit.

"That's what I'm tryin' to do," said Dawbins.

"Yeah, right," huffed Keats.

"Maybe I have more information to lighten your burden. Make it easier." Sidarski winked at the cop. "But, remember... quid pro quo. Anything else you can tell us?"

"Well..." Dawbins peered around to see if anyone was watching. Rollers groaned when he opened a desk drawer. He dangled an evidence bag in front of Sidarski, far from Keats. Even though wrinkled, she could read the note in the bag.

Better than Omaha steaks.

Do it right, clean & discreetly.

Do not use your regular handiwork.

Clean up.

No mistakes.

Old Man

The note meant nothing to Keats. But to Sidarski, clearly it was better than sex. He loosened his tie. Cleared his throat. Wiped his forehead. "Hot in here. So...you found this note at the crime scene?"

"Yep. Wadded up into a little ball, scuttled off into a corner. Been wracking my brain trying to make some sense of it. Mean anything to you?"

"No, can't say that it does." Sidarski drew a palm across his forehead. Probably the first time he'd been on the other side of sweating a suspect. "What about you, Keats?"

"I got nothin'. Maybe it was a letter from the dead girl's pimp. Or her father." She barely suppressed a grin.

Dawbins bit down on a well-chewed pencil, affording Keats' bullshit some serious consideration. "Yeah, maybe..."

"Okay, thanks, Dawbins. We better get goin'." Sidarski suddenly stood, wobbled a bit.

"Yeah, thanks, you're a real prince among detectives," added Keats.

"Hey, wait!" said Dawbins. "You said you had info for me!"

Sidarski didn't hear him, or pretended not to. Determined, he strode toward the elevator. Keats shrugged. "Sometimes when you play ball, you gotta play dirty, Dawbins. Besides... pretty damn sure you're not tellin' us everything about the ranch incident."

Dawbins stood, opened his mouth, closed it. Dumbfounded.

Gotcha. The dumb fish are always the ones who chomp at the worm. Now just to reel him in.

Keats caught up to her partner. "Hurry up, Sidarski," whispered Keats.

"What? Why?"

"I got a live one here."

In the stairwell, Sidarski fanned himself with his hat. "Dawbins?"

"Yeah. Pretty sure he's coming after us. Ready to talk."

Sidarski nodded. "Go on. I need a short breather. Meet you outside in front of the station."

Excited, Keats zipped down the stairwell, blew out the doors and into the welcome sunlight.

As expected, Dawbins barreled out the door. He brushed by Keats in silence. Over his shoulder, he said, "Walk with me."

Keats hurried to match his frenzied pace.

"What's goin' on, Dawbins?"

Dawbins surveyed the area in every direction. "Look...this didn't come from me. Understood?"

"My lips are sealed."

"There was a strange report six, maybe seven, months back.

Something about gunshots and explosions reported at a ranch, say thirty miles from here." Dawbins wouldn't look at her, spoke out of the corner of his mouth.

"You got my attention."

He said nothing until they crossed the street and entered a small park, the kind all quaint towns have located in the center of town.

"Well...I offered to go check it out. I mean, it's not really under our jurisdiction, but we're the closest thing to it. The ranch is pretty much in a no man's land. But through default, it falls on us."

"Dawbins, can we slow down? This cloak and dagger crap's a little much." Keats looked around. No one but an old woman on a bench. "Your fellow cops aren't anywhere to be seen."

"Fine." He hurried to a bench buried deep within the park. He sat down, sweatier than a fat man in a sauna. Probably the best work-out he'd had in years. Yet he still wouldn't look at Keats.

"Dawbins, hello! I'm over here." Keats sat next to him. "What's got your feathers in a dander anyway?"

"You don't get it. This ranch...the people who own it... they're untouchable. My boss put the kibosh on me. Told me to let it be. It's not the first time."

"Okay...why?"

He tossed his hands up. "Don't know for sure. But there're rumors...rumors that our department's in the ranch-owner's pocket. Along with the city. Hell, most of outlying Montana."

"So. Your mysterious benefactor buys a buncha tickets to the annual policeman's ball. Big deal. What's—"

"Dammit! You just don't get it!"

"'Spose not."

"It's big. Bigger than the Billings P.D. It's not the first time we've been shut down from investigating the ranch's owner. If it's enough to scare my bosses, the mayor, everyone...it sure as hell scares me."

"So why tell me then?"

"Because, contrary to what you might believe, I'm good police."

"Okay."

"Or at least I'd like to be. Some day. Away from here."

Aha. "And you don't think you can while being under the thumb of these ranchers?"

"No. That's why I need to solve this decapitation case. To get outta here."

"Fine. Do these mysterious ranch-owners have a name?"

"Rasmussen."

"Hang on." Keats reached into her jacket pocket and pulled out a note-pad. Old school, she knew, but at least it never needed charging. "Alright. Spell it." He did. "Got a first name?"

"The person's name on the lease is Sheera Rasmussen. That's all I know."

"How about an address?"

"Hell, I'm not even sure they have one. I can tell you how to get there, though. Only place out there for miles around."

"Fire away."

After he gave her directions, Dawbins said, "Remember... you never talked to me. Forget my name."

"Who're you?"

"Gotta get back before I'm missed."

Keats doubted that'd be a problem. "Thanks, Dawbins. This might be what we're looking for."

Dawbins stood. "You think she's tied into my beheading? Sheera Rasmussen?"

"Nah. Sidarski's just looking to collect on a debt."

"Hey, now wait a minute! You guys said if I told you what I know, you'd share more info to help me close this case."

"We will. When we find out more."

"But you said—"

"We lied. Somethin' I'm sure you know a little bit about."

"Goddammit! I'm putting my neck on the line here!"

"Simmah down. Tell you what...as soon as we find out something solid, you'll be the first person we call. That work for you?"

"Fine. But you'd better damn well come through!" He plucked out a business card, tossed it at her feet.

"You can get fined, you know, for littering."

"Just call me!"

Keats watched him hustle off in a stiff-legged gait, gaze locked down at the ground. Sidarski entered the park, said something to Dawbins as they passed. Dawbins ignored the larger cop.

Sidarski spotted Keats and collapsed next to her. "Damn, Keats...give this old man a break."

"What, you miss geriatric aerobics this week? Maybe shuffleboard?"

"Funny."

"So all my friends tell me."

"Uh-huh. What'd you find out?"

Keats filled him in. "Now, how 'bout you tell me what got you all hot and heated when you saw that lil' note Dawbins flashed around. And shouldn't that be, I dunno, locked up in evidence or somethin'?"

"Yeah, probably. But Dawbins' ineptitude is our gain. The note was signed 'Old Man.'"

"I can read. Big deal."

"When Spangler was in Leavenworth for pulling a candy-ass carjacking, he received a note. Very low-key, no giveaways. Other than it was postmarked from Florida. And signed 'Old Man.'"

"Well, damn and hallelujah, Sidarski. Let's saddle up and mosey on down to the ranch!"

"Yee-haw."

"Where the hell we goin', old man?"

Leon gripped the steering wheel tighter, ignored Cody's incessant babbling. And how he'd betrayed Leon. He had bigger issues to contend with.

"I already told you, we're picking up the Japanese LMI affiliate. Now shut *up*."

"Jesus, uptight much?"

Leon wanted to backhand him. Slap him like the petulant child he is. Not abuse in this case, far from it. Call it well-deserved payback. But not while driving. Safety first.

"Just tryin' to, whaddaya call it, make some conversation, yo."

One forty-five. They didn't have much time to reach Billings.
Trial by fire.

That's what Sheera'd said. Ordinarily, Leon wouldn't have given it any more thought. Just Sheera being cute again. Except for Gaines' little snicker. An inside joke chuckle. And besides the fact that Gaines never laughed, his chuckle had angered Sheera. All which bothered Leon.

Trial by fire.

And now, driving on a fool's errand, stuck in a car with the last person on earth he wanted to travel with, he couldn't focus. Strike that. The *second* last person he'd want to be stuck in a car with.

"How 'bout some tunes? Maybe I can find some of that jazz shit you like." Cody turned on the radio, fiddled with the dial.

"Turn it off!" Leon punched the power button.

"Whoa! Chill the hell out, already! Day-um! Just tryin' to lighten the mood!"

"I told you I need quiet to think!"

"Think about what?"

"Get this through your thick skull, Cody...Gaines isn't with us."

"Yeah, I know, right? Kick-ass. Party-time!" He raised his hands, patted the sky. "You oughta' be celebratin', you know? Don't got that creepy dude all up in your grill for a change."

"How stupid are you?"

"I ain't stupid, old man," growled Cody.

"Could've fooled me."

Cody smacked the windshield with an open palm. "The hell's *up* with you, Leon? All this time, you ain't said jack! I'm just tryin' to kill time! And you're dissin' me like—"

"Shut the hell up! Since when has Gaines never gone with us? Think about *that* for a minute! If your pea-brain can fathom such an idea!"

"*You* shut up! I can, um, fathom—"

"Gaines is Sheera's golden child. Her watch-dog. The only reason Sheera wouldn't send him along with us? Do the math, Cody. You need a calculator?"

"What the hell? Ain't no thang. Nothin' to get your panties

in a bunch over! And maybe you better start showin' me a lil' respect, yo! Callin' me names and shit. Maybe I need to—"

Leon took his eyes off the road, stared down Cody. Intentionally jerked the car into the on-coming lane, then wrenched it back. "Yeah? What're you gonna do?"

"Dammit! Watch what you're doin'!"

"Why, Cody? Since when did you care about what happens to you? Or to me? You've never shown any—"

"The hell's your problem? The other day Nanette tol' me you was—"

All Leon needed to hear. Blood throbbed at his temples at Cody's mention of Nanette. A mother-lode of a headache dumped on him.

"Shut up, shut up, shut the *hell* up!" Leon cut sharp onto a small dirt road leading into the woods. Instead of slowing, he pressed down on the gas. They careened down the narrow road, the tires dipping into sunken tread tracks and bounding back up. Seatbeltless, Cody banged his head onto the dash, then bounced into the ceiling.

"What're you *doin'*, old man? Slow *down*, dammit!"

Nearly delirious, Leon grinned. His teeth snapped together tightly, biting through anger. He drove even faster into the woods.

"You *don't* talk about her to me, you little bastard!"

"Whoa! What? The hell you—"

"You never know when to shut up! You don't even know how to be human, goddamn you!"

"Jesus Christ, Leon! Is this about Nanette? I didn't—"

"I told you not to talk about her!" Leon pulled the wheel right. The car lifted over a fallen tree limb, crunched down. He buzzed the gas, entered a clearing and spun into a donut. Pedal to the floor, he targeted a large fir tree.

Cody shrieked. Scrambled for his seat belt.

Leon slammed the brake a few feet from the tree and braced himself against the steering wheel. Not as lucky, Cody smashed his cheek into the windshield than crunched back into his seat.

Leon jumped out of the car and shook out of his suit jacket.

"Come on, you little shit! Come *on!* For once, let's see you make good on your threats! Be a goddamn man for the first time in your life!"

Clearly dazed, Cody opened his door and wobbled out. With a hand against his cheek, he said, "Yo, I dunno what you think happened between me and Nanette, but—"

After flinging his jacket onto the car hood, Leon rushed Cody. With an arm pulled back, he launched. A solid fist impacted Cody's face. A very cathartic punch.

"Uff." Cody went down.

"I told you! Don't mention her—"

"Fer Christ's sake, Leon! You know you can't take me!" Cody hopped up, shook off his stupor. He rolled back his shoulders. Danced a little, his usual warm-up that made Leon hate him even more.

Leon decided to skip the ballyhoo and get directly to the main event. An uppercut sliced Cody below the chin. Non-stop, Leon double-fist pummeled Cody's belly.

Cody staggered back, wind milled his arms. His back hit the car and he crashed onto the hood. Fists coiled, he bounced back up.

"You're crazy, old man! Thought you'd learned your lesson by now! I've beat the shit outta you more times than I can—"

"And you never shut up!" Leon grabbed Cody's throat and drove him back. He pulled Cody's head up and banged it onto the car's hood. Satisfyingly crunchy. He did it again until Cody's head dented the hood. "Everything I've done for you! Everything! And you—"

Cody jut his arms up and knocked Leon's grip loose. His head bashed into Leon's.

Stunned, Leon swiveled. A dip in the ground caught his foot. He worked with the momentum, twisted in a circle, and delivered a roundhouse punch.

Cody blocked it. Hammered his fist into the side of Leon's skull. "You want some a' *that*? Huh, old man? Think you can *take* me?"

Leon dropped to his knees. Stabilized himself. Stared into Cody's crotch, an easy target. "You mean like you *took* Nanette?" Clasped fists together, Leon punched the target.

"Ooooff!"

Cody fell back on his rear and cupped his wounded pride. His mouth formed a painful looking "O" of anguish.

That's just a little of the hurt I feel!

Leon climbed to his feet, rushed around behind Cody. He grabbed his hoodie—always the damned hoodie!—and pulled. Muscles fully strained, Leon dragged Cody through the dirt and worked up to a jog. The small, solid *thud* Cody's head made when it met the fir tree put a smile on Leon's face.

"God *damn!*"

"God damn *you*, Cody!" Breathless, Leon wavered. Hoped Cody would stay down. A foolish thought. Cody whipped his legs up and kicked Leon's stomach. Leon stumbled back. A fallen branch tripped him.

"*Aghh.*"

Leon stuck his elbows out behind him to soften the landing. The collision jarred his arms and stabbed pain into his lower back. An unsettling, very human crack sounded frighteningly loud.

Faster than Leon could recover, Cody ran toward him. Leaves crackled at his feet.

Crackle, shfffle, slish…

Cody hefted a leg up, obviously aiming for Leon's chest. Leon rolled. Cody's foot came down hard on the dirt.

"*Shit!*"

Cody folded down onto one knee. Leon sat up, grabbed the treacherous fallen limb and swung it onto Cody's back. Cody reached out, snagged it between his hands. Both now on their knees, the limb separated them. Leon tugged. Cody pulled harder. Leon let go. Cody flumped back into the dirt.

Leon scrambled up. On one foot, he hobbled toward Cody. Lifted a foot and kicked him in the side.

"That's for what you *did* to me!" Kicked him again. "*That's* for sleeping with— *Oof!*"

Leon saw the branch coming but couldn't stop it. His neck took the blow. He twirled, managed to keep his hands up even though tiny lights blinked in his vision. A fist slammed into his gut.

"You *can't* take me, old man! Never could, never will!"

"Then I'll...die trying!"

"Just give it up already!" *Crack*. Cody punched Leon in the face. Leon fell on his back. Cody straddled him. *Thwack*. "You had enough yet, old man?" Cody held up a threatening fist.

"No." Leon grabbed a handful of dirt, slung it into Cody's face.

"Dammit! Uncool!" Cody clawed fingers across his eyes. Leon bucked, tossed Cody onto his side. He brought his legs up and sliced them onto Cody's shoulder. The impact delivered pain into Leon's legs. Synapses responded in his spine. He scrunched up on his bottom, scissored his legs around Cody's neck and clamped them together tight.

"Fightin' like a damn girl, yo!"

"You've got no honor! No loyalty!" Leon squeezed his legs tighter.

Cody lifted a hand, hammered a blow to Leon's crotch.

"*Uff!*"

Nausea coursed through Leon, surged into his stomach. He curled into a ball, attempting to stave off the sickness. He barely felt Cody's foot kicking into his back.

"Dammit, Leon, if you'd just *stop,* I'll tell you what the hell *happened!* I *didn't* have sex with Nanette!"

Another lie. Something Leon'd grown accustomed to. But what if Cody, for once in his life, was telling the truth? Leon'd dangerously flew off the handle, not giving Cody a chance to explain his actions. Then again, could he trust Cody, believe a word out of his mouth? Could he trust anyone?

Leon spat blood into the dirt. "I'm pretty sure I've had enough now."

"Jesus." Cody dropped on his knees. Dirt wafted up like smoke from an extinguished fire. "'Bout damn time. I didn't want to have to beat you senseless, old man." He panted through his words. Of course Cody'd never admit it, but it sounded like he'd had enough, too.

"Don't call me 'old man.'"

Cody laughed. "All this shit and that's what you take away? Get a clue."

"Fine. Why don't you...start clueing me in." Leon sat up and crawled toward a tree. With his back against the tree for support, he cradled a rib. Another broken rib, something he'd gotten used to. Still, the physical pain felt inconsequential compared with his grief. "You say you want to explain, Cody? Start."

Cody kicked his feet out, planted his bottom in the dirt. "A'ight, check it, yo. Yeah, I'd been hittin' on Nanette. You blame me? Chick's on fire." He looked at Leon for corroboration. Leon glared at him. Not the best way to begin a story. "Anyway, just did it 'cause I'm bored. Nothin' goin' on at 'Rancho de Psycho'. Just playin', that's all, just playin'."

"You could've 'played' with anyone else, Cody. Not—"

"Hey, she tole me you guys wasn't a thang. 'Bout a hundred times. Still…I tried to be cool, yo. I knew you were still hot for her. Like a friggin' school crush or somethin'." When Cody grinned, blood dribbled from a split lip. *Good.* At least Leon had managed one lucky punch.

"Coming from the kid who still acts like he's in high school."

"Whatever, old man. I—"

"Don't call me 'old man'!"

"Chill, Leon! Gonna get your blood pressure up or somethin'. Anyway…I knew she was still hung up on you."

"Then why'd you keep chasing her?"

Cody shrugged, winced. He rubbed a shoulder, rotated an arm like a man rowing a boat. "Thought nothin' would ever come from it. Like I said, just playin'. But…at the pool yesterday, she started mackin' on me and shit. Surprised the hell outta me. So she invites me back to her crib. I didn't wanna go, Leon. Really, I tried to fight it. Bro code and all, ya know?"

"I know. You don't, apparently."

"Hey, I'm only human."

"That's up for debate."

Cody dismissed Leon with a hand wave. "So I go after her. In her cottage, she's comin' on strong, teasin' me." He looked down, a brief human moment of shame. "We kissed a little bit more. I mean, I'm hard to resist."

"Yeah. Who in their right mind could possibly resist you?"

"I know, right? Then the chick hand-cuffs me! Starts freakin' out, bringin' out gags and whips and…and other crap. I'm thinkin', 'what the hell?'"

Despite his pain, Leon grinned. "She does like her toys."

"You know about that kinky side of hers? And you never tole me? What's up with that?"

"Hardly your business."

"Hey, she made it my business. She's, like, all freaky and ready to whip hell outta' me! Laughing and havin' a good ol' time. I just wanted outta there. Yo, you can have her."

"I don't think anyone can 'have' Nanette."

"S' what I'm sayin'! I'm tryin' to scream through the gag, get her to let me go. And she's just laughin' her ass off. Finally, she uncuffed me and I got the hell outta there."

Cody paused. Leon watched him carefully, looking for signs of lies: a shifty glance to the left, stutters, nervous laughter. But he seemed sincere, at least as sincere as Cody could possibly be. Leon knew better than anyone the way Nanette rolled. Life's a game to her, men mere pawns to manipulate. Or kill. Oddly enough, the thought renewed hope.

"And that's all that happened?"

"All that happened, yo. That's one freaky chick. Leon...she wasn't gonna bump uglies with me. No way."

"Maybe. Maybe not."

Exasperated, Cody raised his hands, slapped them down onto his jeans. "One thing the Cody knows about is chicks. She was playin' me, Leon! Kept her swimsuit on the whole time. Tryin' to teach me a lesson or somethin'."

"How do you *know* this?"

"She *tole* me, that's how! It was never 'bout me. It was all about you. She still digs you."

"Did she say that?"

"Dammit, Leon! I don't want in the middle of this crap."

"Looks to me like you pretty much put yourself there."

Cody sighed. "Whatever. I'm out. Look...you want her? Do somethin' 'bout it. Quit blowin' her off. Your fault."

"My fault for your kissing—"

"Really, Leon? *Really*? Just man up already! Get your head outta LMI's ass and—"

"I'm trying. Believe me."

"Nanette don't think so. Me neither."

This argument again. So tiresome.

"I've explained to you before…and to Nanette, I'm trying to bring LMI down. Once and for all. It takes time. It takes—"

"Try harder, yo! Nanette thinks you like it. Got a real jonz for being the big LMI dawg."

And that's what it was really all about. Not only did Nanette humiliate Cody to make him back down, but Nanette's message for Leon stood out clearly: *Pay attention or you're going to lose me.* Mission accomplished. She now had Leon's full attention.

"Nothing matters to me more than taking down LMI. I mean to see it through to the end."

"Well, hell, boss…just make sure you don't take everyone down with you, know what I'm sayin'?"

Leon did. And coming from such a ridiculous source, it made sense. More than time to step up his end-game.

If he had time to do so.

Two eighteen P.M. Eighteen minutes late to pick up Takihiro.

Trial by fire.

Sheera's words drifted back like the remnants of a nearly forgotten dream.

"We gotta go, Cody. We're late." With his back braced against the tree, Leon climbed into a squat, then stood. A rib caught, painful and tender.

Cody rushed over, extended a hand. "Damn, Leon, sorry. I didn't mean to give you the smack-down of a life-time."

Leon batted his hand away. "I'll manage." Things didn't seem nearly as dire regarding Nanette and Cody. Still, he wasn't quite ready to forgive, not completely.

He needed to get his mind back in the game, though. A distracted mind is a sloppy—ultimately dangerous—mind.

"Have it your way. Just tryin' to help."

"Yeah. You've helped enough."

Cody grinned, nodded.

Besides Leon's possibly cracked rib, his temples throbbed. Parts of his body felt either numb or on fire.

Still, Leon felt elated. Maybe it was the beating making him loopy. More than likely it was the hope that things with Nanette weren't completely finished.

As they walked toward the car, Cody attempted to strut in his usual cocky manner. Leon took a small bit of satisfaction as he watched Cody favor one foot over the other.

"So...Nanette whipped you?" Leon couldn't hide his smirk.

"She didn't. But she was goin' to. Man, that wasn't all she was gonna do, either. But...never mind that crap. Chick's wack!"

Leon's smile faded as they neared the car.

I'm afraid I'll not be joining you on this venture, Mr. Garber.

Gaines' words. Uncustomary words.

Leon put his arm out in front of Cody, stopped. Just ahead, the car ticked, metal parts settling. Or something else?

"Stop, Cody."

"Thought you said we was late."

"Just...wait."

Do take your little sidekick with you.

Sheera'd been adamant about Cody joining Leon. Another first.

...take the rest of your entourage with you.

Killing a lot of birds with one stone? Sheera ridding everyone she considered a threat?

"Yo, let's get this show on the road already!"

"Shut up for a minute!"

Sunlight gleamed off the car's hood. A sizzling sound wormed into Leon's ears, bacon in a frying pan. Or warning signals.

Something Gaines had said, back when the first assassin had attempted to kill Leon. What was it? Something about the car...

...had anyone touched the car, it would've self-detonated. We have a very elaborate security system.

Leon looked at the keys in his hand, jangled them.

"Cody...get back."

"What?"

"Just follow me." Leon back-tracked and entered the brush. He stood behind the largest fir tree in the woods, yanked Cody beside him.

"Playin' hide and seek?"

"I'm being careful. Something you could learn a lesson about."

From around the tree, Leon stuck his arm out, pressed the automatic start button.

"The hell? Everyone wants to teach me lessons all a sudden."

Chunk.

The car unlocked, beeped, started. Silence.

Tik…tik…tik…

Maybe nothing more than paranoia. Perhaps a forest creature fleeing over ground cover. But Leon heard the ticking, growing louder than a street-worker chiseling pavement.

…tik…tik…

The sound stopped. Overhead, a bird cawed.

Flump.

Brammm!

The hood lifted, spun in the air. A second explosion flung it into a tree. Flames rolled out the car windows. On fire, a bird flew before snuffing out in the dirt.

Badammm!

The gas tank ignited. Metal screeched. Mechanical moans. Fire licked at the car's exterior, peeling the paint. The body folded in. Smoke curled into the sky. Even from a distance, the heat blew hotter than a windy August day.

"Holy shit!" Cody roared with laughter. "Ka-boom!" His fingers shot out from his temples and spread imaginary debris. He laughed again, nearly doubled over.

"Cody…in what *possible* way is this *funny*?"

Chapter Nine

As only one person called Nanette's burner phone, the caller's identity came as no surprise. She considered letting Leon dangle in the wind, much like he'd left her over the past months. Then again, maybe he'd found out about her little game with Cody. Could be interesting.

"What do you want, Leon?"

"Nanette, listen, there's not much time." Very worried tone. Okay, more than interesting. "You have to—"

"Leon, this is getting old. How many times do I have to tell you no one tells me what to do? No one puts baby in a corner." She smiled, very much in her element.

"LMI wants to put baby in a box. The six feet under kind." He rattled the words out quickly, his fear nearly palpable through the phone.

"I'm listening."

"I can't go into details now. I'm sure my phone's tapped. Go get—"

"I need more info."

"Sheera just tried to blow us up."

Nanette sat—more like fell—on a chair and tweaked back the curtain to look outside. "You sure about this?"

"Positive. Your life's in danger. All of ours is. Grab Gus, Delilah and Skeeter and get the hell out of there. Don't pack. Just do it. You'll need to get a car, maybe some guns from the armory and—"

"I know what I'm doing."

"Nanette...the one thing I'd never doubt is your resourcefulness."

The way to a girl's heart. "Fine. I'm on it. Where will you be?"

"Not sure. But I'm dumping my phone after I hang up. I'll contact you as soon as I can."

"Consider me gone."

"And, Nanette? Please...be careful." The old Leon, come home again.

"I always am."

The tide had turned, in more ways than one. For the first time in months, she felt alive, ready for something—anything—to happen. And now that LMI had shown their true colors again, she sensed the change in Leon. He'd awakened from his corporate nightmare, one that had threatened to obliterate him.

Outside Nanette's cottage, everything looked normal. A few guards patrolled the perimeter of the surrounding wall, several on the gate. Hardly the death-threatening portrait Leon had painted. But LMI always wore sheep's clothing.

Rather than use her phone, she strode toward Gus and Delilah's cottage before breaking into a near sprint. Excitement motivated her, adrenaline spiked it. An odd time to realize how much she'd missed her old life, dancing on the edge, never knowing which way she might fall. But at least it'd never been boring.

Last time she felt this way was when they'd fought their way into Rasmussen's compound. Now they had to fight their way out.

Sounds fun.

With a face-wide grin, she knocked on Gus and Delilah's door.

A half-mile down the highway, small country houses started popping up within the woods, a sign Billings wasn't far. It didn't take long at all for Cody to spot a car he could work with. Several old junkers sat in front of a one-story cottage, just ripe for the picking. About damn time, too. Cody'd banged up his left foot in his scuffle with Leon.

Well, calling it a scuffle seemed too charitable. More like a one-sided blood-bath. Leon'd definitely received the worse end of the throw-down. His fault, though, yo. Nobody beats Cody in a fight, straight up.

"Chill your heels while I get us some wheels." Crouched down in the woods, Cody peered through the bushes at the house.

"Cody, now more than ever it's important to stay together."

"You'll just slow me down, old man. I'll zip back and pick you up." Every second counted. LMI'd put a target on their back and Cody wanted to open up a huge can of whup-ass. In a squat, he scuttled toward the house.

From the back of the house, a dog ripped out a non-stop barking tirade. Cody dropped behind a pick-up truck, his eyes on the front door. The sounds of a television drifted out from behind the screen door. A studio audience clapped, canned laughter abruptly stopped. Someone was home, but not aware of him. Yet. He'd have to move fast.

He considered the pick-up, ditched the idea. Fairly rusted through, the truck sat amidst overgrown grass. Probably hadn't been on the road in some time.

But the Impala, now that showed promise. He'd always wanted to ride one of 'em, ride it hard. Especially a vintage model like this. A cherry '66 Chevy.

The dog roared on. For a moment, it struck Cody the owners might mistreat the animal. He considered sneaking a look. No doubt Leon would throw a fit, though. Maybe some other time.

He abandoned his squat walk; too much effort, way too uncool. Still low, he raced to the Impala. Didn't stop until his shoulder banged into the door.

Clumph.

Damn. That one hurt all the way up into his nose. Apparently Leon got lucky, did some damage to his shoulder.

Dick.

Whatever. He'd probably have done the same thing if he'd been in Leon's shoes. The old man could carry a grudge. Unpredictable as hell, he could snap at a moment. Pretty unbalanced guy, really.

Slowly, Cody rose, peeked inside the car. No keys, no luck. Have to do it the hard way. He gripped the door handle. Unlocked.

Eeeeerunch. The door opened with a song of rust.

Shit.

In the woods, Leon shifted from one foot to the other. A nervous spectacle and hardly helpful. Dude needed to seriously chill out. Cody patted the air: *Simmah down, I got this.*

Cody held the door in place. His heart hammered. In small increments he opened the door, ensuring it'd settle into silence. Head down, he slipped into the driver's seat.

Okay, older model, no locking mechanisms.

With an open palm, he slapped the steering column cover. Did it again to no effect. He pounded his fist onto it until his hand couldn't feel anything.

Stubborn.

The dog kicked into hyper hysteria, louder and closer sounding. He glanced above the dash. Still no one at the door. But the TV had been turned off.

Move it!

On the floorboard lay a screwdriver, small enough to work. Not ideal, but he'd stolen a car using the method before. Fifty-fifty chance, though. He had one chance to get it right. Be better if he had a hammer or something to pound it in. But, hey, go with the flow.

With the tip of the screwdriver hovering over the keyhole, he took a deep breath and whacked the handle with his palm. The tip slipped, scraped sideways. His palm stung, redder than blood.

Dammit!

Another look at the door. Whoever was home still hadn't noticed him. The dog sure did, though.

He grit his teeth, braced himself.

Thwack!

The tip slid in. Not far enough. He pumped his arms, took several breaths. With a power surge, he hammered his palm down. The blade drove all the way in, breaking the locking pins.

I still got it, yo!

One final step.

"Come on, baby, treat me right," he whispered.

He twisted the tool's handle. Stepped on the gas.

Wugga, wugga, wugga...

"Come on, come on, come on!"

Wugga...wugga...wugga...

The engine slowed. A gasoline odor permeated the car. Flooded. It'd take a few minutes, minutes he didn't have. Unless the car owner was a deaf, little ol' lady.

His gaze glued to the door, he drummed his fingers over the steering wheel.

Behind a tree, Leon threw a hissy fit, his hands up in the air: *what're you doing?*

Some people gots no patience.

The gas gauge read a little less than half-full, not the problem. But in his experience, once flooded, cars tended to stay that way. At least the newer models.

"A'ight, let's do this."

He twisted the screwdriver again.

Wugga, wugga, wugga, wugga, wugga...froom!

"Son-of-bitch, *yeah! That's* what I'm talkin' about!" He whacked the front dash, reviving the pain in his palm. Along with his adrenaline rush, he gunned the engine. Felt good, sounded powerful.

Voom, va-brooommm....ba-roooommm...

"*Hey!* What the *hell* you doin'?"

Not a deaf old biddy. In the now open doorway, a slob in a wife-beater scratched his whiskers. A *big* slob. At the top of his whiskey damaged voice, he yelled, "Get the *hell* outta my car, *goddammit!*"

"Shit!" Cody dropped the gear into reverse, slammed down the pedal. Too much, too fast. The Impala lurched backward. Grass spat up from the tires.

Grnchhh!

He collided into the pick-up truck.

"Whoa!"

He shoved the gear into drive. Floored the gas, hoped the bumper hadn't lodged onto the truck. The car tugged, tires spun. Metal sizzled. The man disappeared, probably calling Five-O.

Worse. The home-owner barreled out of the house, baseball bat in hand. Faster than he looked.

Flimp. Zzzzzz…

Like a sling-shot, the Impala loosened. Cody rocketed through the yard, straight toward the angry man. Hard left he rolled the steering wheel. The man dove in the opposite direction and landed in the gravel. Back on his feet in no time.

Cody tamed the metal beast and braked. Wrenched the steering wheel to the left and shot out of the yard. Not quite fast enough. The man ran directly behind Cody, bat held high. Cody punched the gas pedal again. A cloud of smoke belched out of the tail-pipe followed by a gunshot-like *pop*. The car shot forward.

In the rearview mirror, Cody saw "Mighty Casey" swinging his bat in an angry figure eight.

Cody laughed, high on the thrill of it all.

"Yeah, baby!"

Ahead, Leon's pale face struck Cody as even more hilarious. With mad driving skills, Cody raced right up to the woods. Showing off. At the last minute, he braked and swung the car around in a perfect donut. After the car's front end wagged to a stop, the back end edged close to Leon.

Cody leaned over, popped open the door. "Piece o' cake, old man!"

Cake looked like the last thing on Leon's mind as he crawled in. Pasty white, his hands shook. He steadied them against the dash.

"Seen a ghost or what?"

Cody floored it and bounced Leon across the seat.

"Can't you do *anything* without drawing attention to yourself?"

"No." Which reminded Cody of one last piece of business. He whipped the wheel again, pulled a U-turn in the grass. Headed straight back toward the pissed off man as his fat fingers jabbed buttons on his phone.

"Cody…stop! What the *hell* are you doing?"

"Got somethin' I needs to say."

"Don't—"

"Hang on, Leon!"

Cody raced the car close to his target, hit the brakes and turned at the last minute. The man sought cover behind the pick-up truck. Cody leaned out his window, said, "Yo! Treat your dog decent! Got it? Or I'll be back. And pissed."

Nothing.

Cody raised his voice to a throat-straining scream. "I said, 'got it?'"

The man couldn't be seen, his voice small. "Um...okay, got it."

"Cool."

Cody pulled away slowly, pointed his fingers toward his eyes, giving the dog-owner something to remember him by. Then he stomped the gas pedal until they hit the highway. And he didn't slow, leveled out at seventy-five miles per hour. The car drove like a beauty. Real solid piece of work, yo.

The old man didn't look so good, though, practically holding his breath and looking like he could mess himself.

"Hey, it's all good, Leon!" Cody smiled. Hit the ceiling and whooped. Even the pain reinvigorated him.

"Nothing about that was good! Your stupidity put us at risk! You—"

"Whoa, whoa, whoa! Chill! And knock off the insults. Seriously. Just takin' care of bidness. Somethin' I thought you'd understand, seeing as how you're Mr. Big Bidness yourself."

Leon's fingers finally loosened on the dash. He strapped himself in, just a lap belt, no shoulder attachment. "What you did was reckless, stupid, attention-grabbing, risky—"

"Know somethin', old man? I don't wanna hear your crap about 'risk.' Seems to me you're the one put us at risk, what with LMI gunnin' for us again. Ain't me they wanna whack. Except for, you know, whaddaya call it? By proxy or somethin'."

Leon didn't have anything to say about that.

Served!

Frankly, Nanette appreciated the opportunity to do what she did best. Nanette's education of male manipulation had more than made up for her student loans of suffering.

Before she entered the garage, she fluffed her hair. Daubed her lips one last time with her lipstick, then kissed her compact mirror.

Showtime!

Busy waxing one of the numerous cars, the guard snapped to attention when he noticed Nanette. Clearly flustered. "Um, ma'am...you're not supposed to be in here without permission from Mrs. Rasmussen or Mr. Gaines."

"Now, now, Mr...." She strolled up to him, lifted his name-tag, and then flicked it back. "...Mr. Holloway. Do I look like a threat to you? Or to your lovely collection of automobiles?" With her hands clasped beneath her chin, she swayed her hips. Blinked, wide-eyed and innocent. Overkill, of course, but men were helpless when confronted with her ludicrous "what, little ol' me?" persona.

He flagged nervous hands, slapped them to his sides. "Of course not, ma'am. But orders are—"

"I'm not a 'ma'am,' you know." Her finger zipped up the front of his suit jacket. "That's for grandmothers. I'm just..." She waited a beat, stringing him along. "...Nanette."

"I know who you are, ma..., pardon me, Nanette." He afforded her a smile, just the smallest one. But one that practically screamed, *I'm hooked.* " But, I'm afraid I'll have to escort you—"

"Escort me? How...*nice.* It's not every day a woman gets escorted by such a handsome, strong man." Part of her couldn't stand it. But the other part—her devilish side—couldn't resist. Neither could the guard.

He rubbed the back of his neck, smiled at his feet. "It'd be my pleasure. Another time, another place. But I have my rules to—"

"Mr. Holloway, I'm just exploring. Doing a little walkabout. It gets so...lonely in my cottage at times. I just don't know what to do with myself during those long hours." No holds barred, she leaned over the car hood. Ran her hand up and down the waxed veneer. "Mmmm...smooth. Strong. Put together solidly." She straightened, turned. Gave him an up and down inventory with her eyes. "I see that's not the only thing like that here."

He stuttered, at a loss for words. She wandered over to the

work-bench. Her fingers walked across various tools, settled on a large wrench. She held it up, said, "Big tool." Finished larger than life with a sultry smile.

"Okay…okay, if we're doing this, the least you can do is call me Grant." His grin grew as he walked toward her. With his jacket now around his shoulders, his arms straight-jacketed, Nanette swung the wrench. An upper-jaw cut. Grant spun. Still on his feet, but unsteady.

"Whoops. I'm sorry, Grant. My hand slipped." Her fingers flew to her mouth.

"The hell? What…what…" As he shook off his daze, he grappled for a shoulder-strapped radio.

"Ah, ah, ah, Grant." Quickly, Nanette plucked the radio out of its harness. "We can't have that." She set it down on the work-bench behind her.

He stomped toward her. "Bitch! I'm gonna—"

"Never call a woman 'bitch' again." This time the wrench impacted solidly on his temple, enough to topple him forward. Nanette whirled, just in time. Grant collided with the table, his already wounded chin absorbing a second blow. He slithered down, his key ring jangling on his belt loop. "And here I thought you were an old-fashioned gentleman."

On the floor, Grant moaned. His head wagged as if trying to stave off unconsciousness. "Now, Grant, I'm feeling a tad clumsy today. I'd hate to have another unfortunate wrench accident. After you've been so accommodating and all. I need you to roll over on your stomach."

"Gonna…kill you!"

Nanette raised the wrench and knelt. "No way to talk to a lady."

"Okay! Jesus…" With a bit of effort, Grant rolled over.

Nanette grabbed her hand-cuffs out of her purse and hooked his hands together. Cinched them tight.

"Ow, dammit! That hurts!"

"Hurts so good, you mean. Quit complaining, Grant. I used the fur-lined ones." After expanding the range on another pair of cuffs, she bound his ankles. "Such big feet you have." For the final touch, she removed the leather gag and ball from her purse. He panicked, struggled, but one shake of the wrench and he caved. The way they always did when confronted with her toys. "Look at you, all trussed up and ready to eat like a turkey. Happy holidays, Grant." She patted his cheek.

"*Nnfff, nnf ooh raht!*"

"My, such language. You kiss your mother with that mouth?"

She'd probably spent too much time playing with the guard, more time than she had to spare. But you just can't take the flirt out of a playful girl.

Decision time.

The Beemer parked closest to the exit, a no brainer. Not a bad car to start her new life with.

She just hoped the others were faring as well.

Marvelous. Simply marvelous.

In all honesty, this was the true reason Gus and Delilah had decided to visit Leon. Where Leon went, trouble and excitement always followed. Not disappointing so far.

Heavily guarded, the armory was located in one of the cottage's basements, one Gus hadn't visited yet. But the floor plan appeared to be identical to the prison cottage. Not a problem. On recon, Delilah had skipped off ahead of them to get the lay of the land and sneak into the building from another entrance.

Five minutes later, Gus and Skeeter followed. Gus had his doubts about Skeeter, however. He didn't think he had the fortitude for "shock and awe." On the other hand, based upon his pallid color, he'd mastered the "shock" aspect quite well.

As they entered the building, Skeeter whispered, "I don't know about this, dude, I don't know. Maybe I should just, you know, stand guard outside or something."

"Friend Skeeter!" Gus stopped on the stairwell to face Skeeter. "You need to trust me! I imagine if you were standing outside the building, you might call more attention upon our little party."

"Some party."

"Yes, I know, it's absolutely splendid, isn't it?" Unable to contain his glee, Gus clapped his hands. Skeeter jumped. "Now, stick with me and it shall all be…easy-pleasy."

"Um…'peezy.'"

"Ho! I so love your quaint American slang terms. El-oh-el!"

Skeeter groaned. "Not what I signed up for."

"Just follow my lead, my friend."

At the bottom of the stairwell, Gus opened the door leading into the hallway. Half-way down the hall, a guard snapped to attention. "Halt! Do you have authorization to be down here?"

"My dear friend…" Gus spread his hands, a sign of truce. "…I'm afraid we do not. We are here to negotiate."

The guard drew his pistol from within his jacket, cocked it. Held it up with both hands, just like in the American movies Gus loved. "Stop right there! I'm giving you one warning. Do not approach. Turn around…*now*."

"Oooh, this is thrilling." Undeterred, Gus strolled forward. Skeeter attempted to blend into the shadows behind him. "But I'm afraid time is of the utmost consideration. We would like to appropriate some of your fabulous guns, if you don't mind."

"Yeah, that's *not* gonna happen." The guard broke out a grin once he clearly saw his two visitors. Relaxed his stance and lowered the gun. His mistake. "What…a midget and a computer geek are gonna overpower me?" The guard's laughter echoed throughout the hallway.

"Um…I'm not a geek."

"Hush now, friend Skeeter, let me tackle our terms and conditions." To the guard, Gus said, "I would very much hope it doesn't have to come to our over-powering you, kind sir. Please just let us pass into the armory and we'll be gone in lickety-splat." Gus snapped his fingers. He'd always wanted to do that in such a moment, very hip.

"This is gotta be a joke, right?" The guard looked over Gus's head, past Skeeter. "Someone put you up to this?"

"Oh, dear." Gus' smile faded. "Sir, it is true many people find me to be quite amusing. I'm very popular at parties. 'Take my wife if you would like to, please!' However, it would be a mistake on your behalf if you were to laugh at the lovely Delilah. I'm afraid she doesn't have much of a sense of humor."

"Says you." Behind the guard, Delilah stepped out of the

shadows. She grabbed his gun hand, wrenched it behind his back. A kitchen knife went to the guard's throat. "I can kill with comedy," she whispered into the stunned guard's ear.

"What the *hell?* What're you *doing?* You can't get away with this!"

"Oh, but I'm afraid we will, sir." Gus reached behind the guard, grabbed for the gun. The guard held tight.

"Drop the gun," said Delilah. "Do it or I'll cut your throat. Kinda want to, anyway."

The guard's knees locked together, stubborn and unyielding. Delilah jabbed the knife's tip into the flesh beneath his chin. Several drops fell, not life-endangering. Yet.

"I don't like this, dude, don't like this at all. This isn't—"

"Quiet, Skeeter," said Delilah, "you've been working for killers for years, you know."

Skeeter said nothing, just turned to face the wall with a hand over his mouth.

"Now. You're gonna drop the gun and help us. Or I'll take your head as a trophy." The guard struggled and Delilah danced along behind him.

"Sir, I would advise you to comply with Delilah's demands. Unlike me, she does not do the kidding around."

The guard's eyes closed. He nodded, loosened the gun. Gus scooped it away.

"Fabulous! Now, sir, if you would be kind enough to enter your hand into this delightful security coded system, we can be on our way."

"I can't do that! Mrs. Rasmussen will fire me! I—"

"My, my." Gus shook his head, tsked. "I understand the economy isn't what it once was and employment is hard to come by in these troubled times. But I would believe your health is more important. Otherwise...I'm afraid Delilah will take your hand."

Delilah nodded. The leather collar of her jacket rumpled.

"Fine." The guard held up his hands, walked toward the security pad next to the door.

"One moment, sir. How many guards inside?"

"Ah...one."

His hesitation smelled of deceit. Which made it all the more exciting. "I see. Be ready, Delilah, my love." Gus pointed the gun toward the opposite side of the door. Naturally, Delilah didn't truly need his stage gesture; everything they did was of one mind. She hugged the wall. "Now, Skeeter, my friend...you, hmm...just go back down the hall and wait. I'm afraid you may not have the constitution for what follows."

Skeeter high-tailed it away, more than happy to comply.

The guard said, "Now, wait a minute! I'm cooperating. You can't kill me!"

"But we can, sir, indeed we can! But I kid, I kid...you perform your duty and we'll all get through this unscathed."

The guard paused, then placed his hand over the device.

"One moment, sir, as I situate myself." With gun in hand, Gus stood behind the guard. "Now, please, do as they say on the TV and spread them."

"What?"

"Please spread your legs. Oh! I see the confusion. Not to worry, dear boy, I am not of a perverted persuasion."

Delilah grinned, stifled a chuckle.

The guard scooted out one leg, then another. Placed his hand in the device. The red light snapped to green. A buzz emanated from the box. The door clicked and opened a couple of inches.

"Go on, my friend, enter."

With a finger looped around the guard's belt-loop, Gus stuck close, attempting to match the guard's bow-legged stride. No easy chore.

Another guard, seated at a desk, said, "What's up, Harry? Haven't heard anything about a weapons order."

"Ah...Mr. Gaines...he called, said, um...he needed guns."

Quiet. Almost *too* quiet. Gus nearly giggled at the film quote playing out on his mind's big screen.

"I didn't hear anything about that."

"It's...an emergency."

Gus squatted, just a hair, to peer between the guard's legs. Suddenly, the seated guard popped out of his chair. The chair scraped back across the cement floor into the wall. Something rattled. Then a click. The new guard had his gun out and up.

"You're acting weird, Harry. I'm calling Gaines."

"They're *behind* me, oh my *God*, they've got my gun! *Shoot* 'em!" The guard squirmed trying to get out of Gus' hold.

So much for the diplomatic approach. Between the wriggling guard's legs, Gus fired upward.

Crick! Cack!

The first bullet pinged off the metal desk, ricocheted into the room. Gus held tight, using his hostage as a shield. The second bullet bounced off a metal wall and rebounded into his human barrier. The guard groaned, fell forward and pulled Gus with him. Gus plopped down onto his back, flipped the gun up. Pulled the trigger.

Snak!

The bullet knifed into the room guard's chest. He flew back into the wall with a resounding *thump*.

Gus rolled off the still breathing original guard. "A pity, my friend. We could've done this without a mammoth production."

Delilah bounded into the room. At a run, she dropped a hand on the desk, vaulted over, and landed in a crouch. She came up, the dead guard's gun in hand.

From the hallway, "Oh, my God, not what I signed up for, not one bit. This is, like, crazy shit! I don't wanna—"

A green bulb flashed above an adjoining door. A loud buzz accompanied it. The door *snakked* open. Another one of the endless armed suits appeared, dropped to a knee with gun leveled at them. Delilah didn't hesitate. Three bullets burst into his body. Silently, he went down. Smoke filled the small room. Perforated metal ticked. A folder slid off the desk.

Spat.

Gus whispered, "Do you think that's all of them?"

Delilah shrugged. Before Gus could respond, she hopped over the downed guard by the desk, leap-frogged over the one in the doorway and disappeared into the adjoining room.

Bang. Spack. Bing.

Seconds later, she reappeared. Smoke curled off her gun. "That's all of them."

Gus' love for his soul mate swelled. Constantly, he couldn't believe his luck in having this dark goddess of death in his life. But, alas, romance would have to wait.

"Wonderful, my darling!"

Delilah grinned. "Come on, Gus. We hit the jackpot. And Nanette's waiting."

More riches than a bank's vault dazzled Gus. Fabulous guns and weapons of such mysterious magnitude and glorious gleaming metal, Gus could only imagine the destruction them capable of. He stood in awe, practically heard trumpets blare. Until Delilah brought him back down to earth. As she always did. His rock.

"Gus, just grab some. We've got to go!"

Gus swept up as many as he could carry. Delilah took off her jacket and filled it with boxes of ammunition. When finished, she carried it over her back in a bundle like Krampus.

In the outer room, Delilah stepped over the still breathing original guard. "What do you want to do with him, Gus?"

"Oh, I don't know. I rather like him. Can we let this one live? Just this one time? Please?"

Delilah rolled her eyes, wagged her head. "You know I can't resist when you beg. Fine, let's roll."

"Come on, come on, come on!" Nanette craned her head, checked the rearview mirror, watched for the first sign of anything askew. She doubted the guard in the garage would be making any fast getaway, but it was just a matter of time before someone found him.

The BMW hummed at a nice comforting level, nearly lulling her into a sense of false security. The armory crew still hadn't surfaced. And the gunfire she'd heard—faint, but definitely gunshots—didn't exactly settle her nerves. The compound guards obviously didn't hear it, though, as they continued to patrol the wall and the gate. Which posed another problem: how to get past the gate?

"Damn it." As she reached for her phone, the armory building door opened. Delilah ran out first, carrying a bundle for once not her lover. Gus raced out next, arms full of rifles. Not exactly the most inconspicuous of sights. Skeeter brought up the rear, his laptop cradled to his chest like a child's teddy bear. Looked like he needed the comfort. White as snow, he kept his head down and stared at his feet as he stumbled along.

Delilah jumped into the passenger side, Gus and Skeeter in the back. "Hey, Nanette." She smiled, small but mischievous. And troubling.

Uh-oh.

Before they buckled in, Nanette shoved the Beemer in gear. "Ready?"

"Absolutely," answered Gus.

"How'd it go?"

"Splendidly!"

Yeah, I'll bet. Nanette had learned Gus' idea of "splendid" usually defined trouble. But there'd be plenty of time to get the low-down later. At least Nanette hoped there would be.

Nanette's first inclination to gun the car and speed the hell out of there seemed hasty. So far, their coup hadn't raised any flags. None she knew about. Slow and steady, she ambled toward the gate.

As expected, two guards stood in front of the gate. One had a hand up.

"Halt!"

"Want me to shoot him, Nanette?" At some point, Delilah had locked and loaded a pistol, now resting in her lap.

"No! Hang on a minute…let's try and make it out quietly." As Nanette slowed the car, she glanced in the rear-view mirror. Tree limbs of gun barrels stuck up from Gus' lap. "Stash the guns!"

"Oh, right as rain!" Gus trunked them down onto the floorboard. Delilah dragged her leather jacket over her gun, kept a hand underneath.

Nanette rolled down her window half-way. "Just going on a trip into town. Supply run."

The guard bent down, looked inside. His hand rested on his unsnapped gun holster, not a welcome sight. "All four of you?" Nanette nodded. "I assume you have Mrs. Rasmussen's or Mr. Gaines' approval?"

Nanette gave him an orbital eye-roll. "We don't need

permission. From anyone. Personal errand for Mr. Garber. You know him, right? Your boss?"

"Righhht." As soon as the guard smiled, a sardonically framed smile, Nanette knew she'd made a mistake. Leon's company status had already fallen. "Why don't you just step out of the car, nice and easy? I'll give Mr. Gaines a call. If everything's kosher, we'll have you on your way."

"Look...we don't have time for this. Just let us go and we'll make sure you don't get in trouble."

"Trouble? I like trouble. Get out."

Gus leaned forward. "Sir, I can most definitely give you assurance that everything is as kosher as pig-meat. Why, we—"

"Um, pork's not kosher," Skeeter peeped.

"I never could keep that straight, I'm afraid," continued Gus. "At any rate, I've had quite the trying day. My legs are with ultimate pain. I must be seen by a surgeon."

Oh, good God.

"Quiet, Gus, let me handle this," Nanette said.

"I told you once...I'm not telling you again. Get out of the car." The guard backed up, gun now in hand.

A click sounded from beneath Delilah's jacket. The jacket pitched up where her hand hid. Trigger happy. Nanette shot Delilah a quick glance, mouthed *no*. Time to pull out the charm, the gambit she should've started with. She rolled the window all the way down, better to ensnare him.

"Why, Mr....Matthews." She twirled a lock of her hair, giggled. Delilah groaned. "Do I look like I'd lie to you? A big, handsome man such as yourself should know better than to think I could ever pull anything over on you." Zip, her fingers sped up his chest. "Tell you what...just open that little gate and tonight, I'll bring you something...*special.*" She sealed the deal with a wink, a small alluring promise.

The guard smirked, arrogantly cocked his head to the side. "You gonna try that shit on me? On *me*? Really don't think my boyfriend would be too happy about it."

Great. Plan B. Whatever the hell that is.

"Oops. My bad, Mr. Matthews. Tell you what we'll do. I'll just turn around, go see Mr. Gaines and have him call you back. That sound fair? It'll cover your ass and ours."

Matthews glanced at the other two guards, one in front of the gate, the other sticking his head out the security booth. And came back grinning. "Don't think so. Out. Now!" Another two steps back, his gun pointed at Nanette.

"Oh, put that silly thing away, Matthews, before you hurt someone." Nanette didn't give him a chance to respond. She clunked the gear into reverse, started backing up.

Matthews dropped in a crouch, legs splayed, gun up. "Stop! Or I'll shoot!"

Nanette continued on her backward trajectory. She gave Matthews a little wave, called out the window, "Be right back!"

"Now what?" asked Delilah.

"Now...I suppose we do it your way. But only fire if they do first."

"Splendid! I've been absolutely dying to try out one of these fine pieces of killing machinery!" Gus prepped a rifle.

Skeeter hunkered down in the seat. "We're all gonna die, dude, we're gonna die. Dammit, I shoulda just stayed in my—"

"None of us are going to die! Not if I can help it." Big words. But Nanette really had nothing to back them up with. Except full-on dive-bombing. "Hang on, everyone. Here we go." She stopped the car. Put it into park. Revved the engine. "Seat belts on."

A commotion rose behind them. From the big house, armed guards filed outside, Gaines amongst them. Headed their way. Armed men behind and in front of them, trapped in the middle. Poor odds. Nanette loved a challenge.

She brought the lever into drive, stomped on the gas. Instead of heading toward the gate, she whipped right into the yard.

"What're you doing?" screamed Skeeter.

Nanette ignored him. Bullets whiffed behind them, plucked up large chunks of grass.

Spack.

A bullet cracked into the back wind-shield. A jag of lightning scrawled across it.

Nanette pulled a donut. No reason. Just it seemed like the

last thing they'd expect. And maybe she could draw the guards away from the gate.

"Alright, guys...*fire.*"

The moment Gus and Delilah had been waiting for. Delilah took aim and shot out of her window.

Nanette cranked the wheel hard left. Delilah slammed into her, then hopped back.

Zing. Crunch. Bing. Ting...

Bullets spackled the BMW's body. Nanette pulled another donut in the reverse direction. At high speed, the car tilted, bomped back down to the ground.

The guards behind them spread out. Some sought shelter. Finally, Gus finagled the barrel of his semi-automatic out the back window and spread a sheet of wildly dispersed bullets.

Yet the men at the gate held their post.

Dammit. Now we do things the rough way.

No other choice. Nanette sped out of the grass, turned the wheel without slowing. Set up a straight course into the gate. Maybe she could bluff the immovable guards, a game of chicken. Doubtful.

They sped toward the gate. Dust bloomed behind them, a valuable smoke screen.

Crack. Tinkle...

The back windshield shattered. Glass shards flew inside. A sliver bit into Nanette's neck. Skeeter screamed.

"Just stay down, Skeeter!" Nanette knew he'd be the most vital component to their survival. If they survived round one.

Gus took advantage of the newly opened back windshield and levered his gun over the seat. Non-stop fire erupted from his automatic. His small body rattled with it.

Delilah turned, closed an eye, fired over Skeeter's head.

"Jesus! Dude!"

The gate zipped toward them, stolid. Impenetrable. Last time, they'd barely managed to take it down with an SUV. And it had totaled the vehicle.

In for a dime...

"Shoot them!" Nanette jutted her chin toward the gate's guards. Delilah leaned out her window, so far Nanette thought she'd fall out. And blazed an arc of bullets. The guards scattered, left and right. Still, they had to get through the gate.

Stop? Get out, run into the booth?

No. She didn't have the security codes, didn't have the time to torture it out of one of the guards.

Only one way. If not, they'd die. Simple. Go down trying.

Even though Nanette had the pedal floored, she pressed her foot down until it hurt. Trees flashed by in a blur. A large group of guards amassed behind them and opened fire.

One hundred feet, fifty feet...

"Everyone hold on! Brace yourselves!" Nanette barely heard her own screams over the hailstorm of bullets. Didn't matter. More than likely, this would be their farewell.

The iron bars loomed in front of her. Close. Closer. Fatally close.

On the other side of the gate, a limousine screeched to a halt. Nanette slammed on the brakes. The car skidded, turned. The back end clanged into the gate. The chest strap cut into Nanette's chest, her lap, before it yanked her back down. Twin thumps bumped into the back seat. Rifles clattered forward and shuffled onto the mantle.

The dust around the limo dissipated. Out of the thinning cloud, the limo's occupant strode forward. A man in a chauffer's uniform sporting dark sunglasses and wielding a formidable looking weapon. A bazooka.

"Move," he said and waved Nanette aside.

Nanette didn't bother straightening the car. She punched the gas. The Beemer tore into the yard. The passenger side rode the wall. Sparks fired up. Skeeter screamed again.

Screeeeeeeee...thump...reeeee...

"*Aaaaahhhhh! We're goin' to die, dude, I just know it! I know it...*"

To Nanette's left, guards dropped down on their bellies, firing indiscriminately. Bullets ripped up the wall, rained down plaster pieces.

Brammm! Clang! Renckkkk....cling, clang...

The bazooka explosion behind them lifted the back-end

of the Beemer and propelled them forward. Nanette's heart thrashed out a frenetic drum solo. The car twisted in the grass. The front end scraped across the wall.

Grnnnnnchhhh...

She braked. The back end completed the journey, slammed them into the wall. The car bucked, staggered, and then pitched the occupants forward. Smoke billowed out from beneath the trashed hood.

Dizzy, Nanette shook her head. "Everybody out!"

Easier said than done. A shrill pitch drilled her ears. She opened her door, undid the seat belt. When she stepped out, the ground shifted beneath her feet. Disoriented, she fell, half on the ground, half in the car. Bullets zipped through the windowless car.

"Nanette, catch!" The gun Delilah tossed to her landed close, but so far away.

Gus jumped out. With a gun nearly as large as him, he laid down a sweeping round of fire.

A hand reached down to Nanette. A gloved hand. "Let's go."

Nanette grabbed the chauffer's hand. Easily, he yanked her up. He multi-tasked with an automatic he'd traded in for the bazooka.

As Gus raced toward the exit, Delilah circled him protectively, firing her pistol. The chauffer practically dragged Nanette, yet kept pace beside Skeeter, his laptop over his head. Bullets drew a chalk line in the wall's plaster.

The gate passage lay in ruins. Chunks of the wall had been vaporized. One of the gates lay in a crumpled pile several hundred feet away. The other gate sat in front of the limo.

First to reach the opening, Gus and Delilah laid down constant bullet coverage.

The limo door opened. The chauffeur shoved Nanette. Startled, she tumbled inside. No surprise at the limo's occupant.

The Man with the Shoebox. Aka, Bartholomew...something.

He smiled his shark's smile, held out a helping hand. All the while stroking his constant companion, his mystery shoebox, anchored on one knee.

"Ah, Ms. Nanette. We meet again. Looks like I'm right in time."

"Oh, *hell*, yes!" All she could muster. Bartholomew's smile faltered a bit. Probably didn't like hearing women curse. Good up-breeding and all that.

Everything seemed so surreal, Nanette almost forgot about the chaos outside. "I've gotta help the others!" She reached for the door. Bartholomew grabbed her wrist, pulled her back.

"Everything's under control now, my dear. Tommy...well he's even better equipped for battle than the first Tommy."

Apparently, the Man with the Shoebox had a thing about naming all of his chauffeurs Tommy. Or only hired guys named Tommy.

Helpless, Nanette watched out the window. Skeeter clambered inside. Still screaming his lungs out. Gus and Delilah followed. The chauffeur, Tommy, raced around to the driver's side. Stopped. Then from within his jacket pocket, he extracted a grenade. Service with a smile, he tossed it inside the compound.

"Go, Tommy," ordered Bartholomew.

"Yes, sir."

Faster than gunfire, Tommy had the car in gear before the explosion went off.

Brmmm!

Nanette thought the Beemer had speed. The limo must've had a rocket strapped under its hood. They flew down the road, the speedometer reaching one hundred, one hundred and ten and climbing.

An industrial chimney's worth of dust clouds obscured everything behind them.

"Well, that was certainly fun, wasn't it?" Bartholomew favored Nanette with a wink, then leaned forward. "Any followers, Tommy?"

"Not that I can see, sir."

Nanette felt ragged as a sliced tin can. Her eyes watered, her ears rang. Dust coated her throat, blood matted her hair (from whom she had no idea). Yet her nerves jangled, a loud, stomping full-on Dixieland band. Nervously, she looked behind her, waiting for the inevitable LMI followers.

"Don't worry," said Bartholomew. "I'm sure Tommy left everyone far behind. Isn't that right, Tommy?"

"Yes, sir." Tommy half-turned, smiled at his gold star for the day.

Finally, Nanette sat back. And breathed. Deeply.

Everything'd happened so fast, she hadn't had time to question it.

Honestly, she thought she'd never see the Man with the Shoebox again. The curiously creepy, elegantly eerie, mysteriously murderous serial killer who took his victims' feet. A woman loves mystery in a man. But he was one mystery she'd just as soon not unravel. However, she'd love a peek into his shoebox.

"Bartholomew...what're you doing here? Not that I'm ungrateful, but...how'd you know we needed help?"

Bartholomew stared at his shoebox. Shifted it to his other knee. Nudged it a bit, just so. "That was just a fortunate, remarkable stroke of fate for you, Nanette. Actually, I came seeking retribution. Against your lover, Leon Garber." His cold gaze captured Nanette, one of the very few men capable of doing so.

"Um, first of all..." She extended her forefinger. "...Leon's *not* my 'lover.' Second—"

"Be that as it may, dear, would you mind telling me why Leon's attempting to have me killed?"

Oh, boy.

Chapter Ten

Not the most ideal situation, of course, but Leon didn't have any choice. His broken rib impeded his driving abilities, abilities Cody had proven adept at in the past. Still, a white-knuckled ride with a hot-head behind the wheel of a hot car didn't exactly add to Leon's sense of well-being.

"Slow down, Cody."

"Yes, Dad."

Cody slowed, but as they pulled into Billings' city limits, he kicked the speed up again. Leon really knew better than to try and teach an old dog new tricks.

"You know...seems like ol' times. I mean, you and me. On the run again. From LMI dicks." Fire burned in Cody's eyes.

"You have a strange sense of nostalgia. And I said slow down."

"You know we're already late, right? Thought you wanted to hurry and pick up this Tomato-Hero guy."

"Takihiro. And please get his name right."

"Day-um. We just escaped another, whaddaya call it, near-death experience and you're all about gettin' this guy's name right. Whatever."

"We don't need any more enemies. We need allies."

"And you think this Tacky...Tuckimojo...this Japanese guy's gonna side with us?"

Earlier the notion made sense. Talking it out, though, did seem like grasping at straws. "No idea. But LMI set the car-bomb to explode a good twenty minutes after the designated time to pick up Takihiro. And I know the rest of LMI's board members were siding against him. He's probably our best bet now."

"Yeah? How's that?"

"He might be able to give us inside info about LMI. So we can finish this."

Cody banged the steering wheel. "Yeah, baby! Thass what I'm talkin' about! About damn time we gots down to bidness."

Business. Leon was tired of LMI "business," fed up. Then again, numerous death attempts might sour even the most stalwart corporate soldier. For once Cody was right. *It's about time,* he'd said. Maybe all of this had been Leon's fault, putting Cody, Nanette and the rest at risk. Had he taken a faster course in completing his mission, things might not have reached such disastrous levels. All the more reason to end it. Once and for all.

"So, you're the big dawg at LMI, right? Why's Sheera trying to whack you alluva' sudden?"

"Who knows? But LMI loves playing their games." He forced a grin. "Welcome to the world of corporate America, Cody."

"You can have it, brah."

As they reached downtown, Leon ordered Cody to obey the speed limits. Like spitting in the wind. Already, the stolen car set them at risk. Once they hit town, they probably should've ditched it. But Takihiro wouldn't wait forever. At 2:45, they pulled onto Crowne Plaza drive.

"Stop the car, Cody."

"What? We're not at the hotel doors, yo."

"Just do it without arguing for once."

At the curb, Leon got out. Looked around. Suits hurried down the sidewalk, luggage tugged behind them. A few tourists, decked out in shorts and Hawaiian shirts, snapped their phones at everything in sight. Nothing out of the ordinary.

Except for the giant, Japanese man standing by the curb. Wide and tall as a rich man's Christmas tree, clearly Takihiro's attaché. Stolid-faced, he glanced at his watch, his only show of impatience. His suitcase was large, too, bulging at the sides. Very important contents, no doubt, since he kept it in his hand at all times.

Leon approached the man.

The attaché glared at Leon, his mouth set in a grim slip of annoyance. From what Leon had gathered, the Japanese prided themselves on punctuality. Hopefully, not punching.

Leon extended a hand, an initial engagement into a peace treaty.

The man stared, didn't move. Peace negotiations had already broken down.

"Ah, I'm Leon Garber with LMI. I assume you're Mr. Takihiro's..." Leon didn't want to insult the man further by crowning him something he might not be.

The big man tapped his phone, spoke a few stilted Japanese words. Replaced it into his pocket and continued to gawk at Leon. Several uncomfortable minutes later, Mr. Takihiro walked out of the revolving doors, clearly none too happy either.

"You're late, Mr. Garber."

Leon bowed. Too little, too late. "Mr. Takihiro, my sincerest apologies. But I assure you I have good reason. We have much to talk about."

Takihiro grimaced at Leon's dirt-stained and torn suit. Then he noticed the panic on Leon's face. "Very well, let us go."

Leon waved Cody up. Cody revved the engine. Rubber marked the street behind him while the tires squealed.

Dammit!

Cody jerked to a halt, all grins and metal music blaring. Takihiro studied the car, hesitated getting in. Not exactly the chariot he'd expected.

Leon opened the back door, invited Takihiro inside.

Kak!....splick...shngle, dingle...

Leon knew the sound all too well.

He dropped behind the car. Screams erupted along the drive. One of the hotel's front windows shattered. Small glass pebbles snowed onto the sidewalk.

Gunfire. Again.

The large man shoved Leon out of his way and rushed to his boss' aid. A man ran past the car, yanking two children nearly off their feet. Another bullet shaved the top of the Impala. One very brave, very stupid lurker had his phone up, capturing the excitement. Hell's tourist trap.

"Leon, get the hell inside already!" With his arm hanging out the window, Cody banged the car door.

Takihiro's man hunkered down next to Leon. Casually, he opened his suitcase on the sidewalk and began assembling parts.

He glanced at Leon, calmly said, "The 3D printed firearm. Gets through customs."

Leon crawled to the back passenger door, reached for the handle. Another shot pocked the top of the Impala's roof then cracked into the hotel's mason wall.

"Jesus!"

"Get in, dammit!" Cody gunned the engine.

Leon crawled in, then crawled over Takihiro. No time for diplomacy. He looked out the window. The crowd had thinned. No sign of their assailant. Another bullet plunked into the Impala's front fender.

"Takihiro, get your man in here!" screamed Leon.

Outside the car, the attaché methodically assembled his rifle. He shouted a one syllable word, stood. Balanced the gun on the roof and fired at the building across the street. Another bullet chocked into the sidewalk beside him. A sniper. Somewhere high, shooting low.

Once Leon climbed off Takihiro, the ambassador lowered in his seat. Apparently comfortably assured of his bodyguard's pressure under fire.

Leon jerked the window down, yelled, "Get in! You're putting Takihiro's life at risk!"

That did the trick. Leon knew it would. "*Hai!*" the attaché roared.

The large man jerked the door open and slid in, squeezing Leon into the middle. Takihiro brushed his shoulder as if Leon had sullied him.

"Go, Cody!"

Main Street, already jam-packed with early rush hour traffic, intersected the end of the hotel surrounded drive. The last of the on-lookers had dispersed, seeking cover inside the hotel. Cody tore out, recklessly whipped the Impala toward the main drag. Sirens cried in the distance, growing louder. On Main Street, a Cadillac screeched to a stop and blocked their exit. A blonde, tall woman jumped out from the driver's side. Flashed a brilliantly white smile. And leveled a gun over the car roof.

"Oh, hell no!" Cody flumped an elbow over the seat, dropped the gear into reverse. A bullet cracked the windshield. Cody sped up. Barely in control, the car wagged back and forth in reverse.

A nearly identical looking blond man ran out from the hotel across the drive, rifle gripped in hand. He saddled up next to the woman behind the Cadillac, hoisted the rifle up. Both of them voguing.

"Futago." Takihiro said it matter-of-factly, the way he said everything.

"What?" screamed Leon.

"Ah...twins. 'The Doublemint Twins.' Not good."

Cody took his eye off the road for a split second, eyeballed Takihiro. "No shit!"

Takihiro confirmed with a nod. "No shit."

Behind them, bullets hit the parking garage wall.

Spik...spack...

The twins jumped into their Caddy, backed up, pulled into the hotel avenue. Coming at them. The male twin leaned out the passenger window, a pistol in his fist.

Leon tore his attention away from their pursuers and looked back. The parking garage wall approached fast. Cody'd miscalculated as they careened toward it at a dangerous speed.

"Cody! Look out!"

"Know what I'm doin', old man!"

He punched the brakes. Tires wailed. Cody spun the steering wheel, corrected course. They backed into the garage entrance, crashed through the wooden gate. Yellow and black wood soared up, clattered down onto the windshield.

Cody slowed. Still too uncontrolled, too fast to take the winding curves in reverse. But Cody jockeyed the steering wheel with expertise, a gaming joy-stick his training. The constant screech of tires followed them as they wound their way upward. The walls narrowed. Leon felt them closing in, burying him in a dark, cement tomb. Sparks flew off the tail end as the Impala grazed the wall.

Cody hooted. "Yeah, baby! You don't jack with the Cody!"

Leon's stomach threatened to expel its contents. He couldn't see the Caddy behind them, but heard it storming up the ramp.

"Straighten the car out, Cody! Straighten it out!"

"They're still too close!"

Cody bypassed the second level, continued their hellish backward ride up the ramp.

"Day-um! Kicking ass!"

Cody's grin looked unhinged. Crazed enjoyment. He added more speed, the devil in the detail.

Screeeeeeeee....

Metal embraced concrete. A shower of embers sparked beside them. On the third landing, Cody sped down the long parking alley. Slammed on the brakes. Cranked the wheel. And sent them into a tailspin.

Rrrrrrrr...crunk!

The Impala didn't clear the turn. It's front fender hooked onto a parked car's back bumper and forced them to a rapid, bouncing stop. Takihiro rolled into Leon, Leon into the bigger man.

Cody laughed. "Day-um!"

"*Deteke!*"

Leon didn't understand the word, but the intent rang clear. Belying his size, the large man exited fast, his plastic rifle up over the roof in no time. Leon and Takihiro followed. Still giggling, Cody hopped out next.

"Cody, dammit! This isn't a game! We need another car. Now!"

Cody's grin dropped. His pupils were dilated, then quickly swam back to normal. Focus ruled his mind again. With a nod, he jogged off.

The Caddy exited the ramp, growling straight at them. The engine grew louder, deafening in the graveyard of the garage. Twin headlights of eyes turned the grill into a metallic grimace. Behind the windshield, two perfect sets of teeth gleamed.

"Hayaku!" Takihiro's man gestured for them to leave.

Takihiro bowed, said, "Thank you, Goro."

No time to stand on ceremony, Leon grabbed Takihiro by the arm, yanked him away.

Tires shrieked to a halt. The Caddy revved the engine, a

challenge to Goro. Goro met the challenge with a cascade of bullets. The twins returned fire.

Throughout the garage, metal chunked and glass tinkled. Dust rose from bullet-ridden cement pillars. Leon hunkered down, then pushed Takihiro ahead as they duck-walked, weaving in between parked cars.

A car door opened, then another.

From a distance, "I think we got him." Clipped, over-enunciated English.

"Just to make sure, sister."

Where the hell are you, Cody?

The Caddy's doors shut.

Tumph. Dimp.

The Caddy's engine grumbled, mounted into a monstrous bellow. Tires squealed until lift-off.

Rrrrrrrrrr... Spang, whumph, crckkk... Tsssssssss...

Metal crashed, ripped and died in a slow whine.

Leon poked his head up. The twins had rammed their car into the Impala. No sign of Goro. Or Cody. Behind the Cadillac's wheels, the female appeared slumped over while her brother shook his head, clearly dazed but not out.

Dammit.

Hidden between two cars, Leon wrenched Takihiro close to him. Held his finger up to his lips. And listened.

Glass popped, fell. Something hissed. Metal loosened.

Clunk, rattle...

A fender clattered to the floor. From outside, sirens grew louder.

Click...runchhh!

A car door opened. Followed by another.

Tik...tek...tak...

Footsteps. Uneven, unsteady, but footsteps. Soon joined by a second pair.

The twins back on the hunt.

The acoustics of the garage made it hard to pinpoint their exact location. The footfalls echoed above Leon, next to him, beneath him.

Ahead sat the elevator. Leon gestured for Takihiro to follow him.

They waddled to the end of the car coverage. A risk, but their only shot. One mad dash to the elevators, possible freedom. Better yet, the stairwell next to it.

Leon looked at Takihiro. Impassive as Buster Keaton.

Another gun-blast froze Leon. Above them a bulb snuffed out.

Like a tiger, a car snarled; ferocious and coming on strong. Headlights glowed at the end of the lane. Leon bolted up, strained to see the driver. Prayed for Cody. Anyone other than the twins.

The car wrenched to a stop. Dark blue Mustang. *Cody.*

"Yo, let's go already!" Cody gunned the engine again.

Gunfire boomed.

Cody popped the door open, pulled his seat up. "Let's go!"

Leon shoved Takihiro into the back-seat, then jumped in after him.

"Get us out of here!"

"We cannot leave Goro behind. Not without knowing his fate."

Leon understood. Completely. But, now, Takihiro was his main concern, a possible way out of his situation.

"Mr. Takihiro...I'm sorry. Goro's probably dead. Now, let's—"

"Then I'm not going. Open the door."

"Goddammit, we can't risk it! What good is it if we *all* die?"

"Honor, Mr. Garber."

Honor. Something Leon worried he'd lost recently. Or if he'd ever had any. In the past, Leon wouldn't have left any of his people behind. At least he'd like to think he wouldn't.

Against all logic, everything that made sense, Leon said, "You heard the man, Cody. Turn around. We're going back."

"Jesus Christ, you gotta be kidding me! We can't—"

"Just do as I say!"

Fump!

Leon jumped. A boulder landed on their trunk, shook the car. No, not a boulder. Goro leaned on the trunk, clearly hurt.

His hand squealed on the car's back windshield, a bloody trail drawn from his fingers. Then he stood tall, straightened his jacket. Calmly, he limped toward the passenger door and fell inside. He dropped his plastic weapon into his lap.

Takihiro said, "Hai. Now we can go." He nudged his finger several times toward Cody.

"Go slowly, Cody. No more attention."

"Slow my ass! Cops are comin'. No way I'm goin' back to prison."

In the distance, an engine started.

Rrr...rrrr...rrrr...voom!

A surge of gas, a punch of brakes. Once again, the twins had rejoined the party.

"You win, Cody. Just get us the hell outta' here. Find a different exit."

Already at home in the Mustang, Cody zipped the car down the alley, then stopped. Two arrows pointed in separate directions.

"Go right."

Sirens blazed, intensely loud in the garage. Nearly on top of them. Cody followed the floor-painted arrows until they wound down to the basement. Leon heard nothing, just the incessant cries of police vehicles.

The exit Cody found led out to Werner Avenue, a major street running parallel to Main. *Salvation.*

Yet another barrier gate blocked the exit. Cody pulled up short, inches from the gate.

"Yo, anybody got validation?"

The booth sat empty, no doubt locked. Leon didn't see any sign of metal teeth in the ground, though, a bit of good luck for a change.

"Damn it," said Leon. "We break through it, an alarm will go off."

"What the hell we 'sposed to do then?"

Goro opened his car door, walked to the gate. Dropped in a squat, grunted, then yanked on the gate. Stubborn at first, it cracked, then lifted. Goro pushed it all the way up, got back in the car. And closed his eyes.

"Goddamn Sumo wrestler," said Cody as he pealed out. Despite Goro's efforts, a bell clanged behind them.

After the darkness of the garage, the sudden sunlight stung Leon's eyes. Over on Main Street, a chorus of sirens peaked into a symphony of disorder. Otherwise, a typically busy Billings afternoon: commuters intermingling with shoppers on Werner Avenue.

"Be careful, Cody."

"Leon, I got this by the balls!"

Leon doubted that. But, truth be told, they wouldn't have gotten this far without Cody. Plain and simple, Leon couldn't believe their luck had held out this long.

Lady Luck can be a fickle mistress, though.

Several cop cars zipped by them, cherries spinning red and blue. In the oncoming lane, a Caddy, front end damaged, slowed. The driver waved. Miss blond beauty pageant showing off her toothy, dentist bought smile.

Leon unleashed the beast again. "Step on it, Cody!"

Cody took to the order with gusto. Jack-rabbit fast, he brought the car from thirty-five to fifty. In the middle of Werner, the Caddy yanked a U-turn. Horns blasted, voices shouted. Another collision of metal banged out behind them. Yet the Caddy remained unscathed, a two-car wreck in its wake. The Caddy swam after them like a shark on wheels.

"This totally rocks!"

Takihiro's eyebrows rose as he glanced at Leon. Expressive for him.

Goro, so tall he had to contort his head sideways, picked up his rifle.

Uninhibited, Cody laughed. In the right lane, he darted in front of a car. Dodged back left and cut off a van. The Caddy shadowed them, filling the tight pockets Cody evacuated.

"Cody, we've gotta lose 'em!"

"Duh."

Ahead, a light turned red. Cody didn't look, lost in full-on tunnel vision. Against all odds, he applied more gas. Barreled through the light. A car blasted toward them. At the last moment, it pulled into a swerve. Cody slipped the Mustang right, left again, barely missed an on-coming car. Leon braced a hand against the ceiling, one on Cody's seat. Little protection from the human pin-ball machine they were stuck in.

The Caddy picked up speed, blew through the light as well. At the next intersection, a sign read *One Way*, arrow pointing left.

"Cody...don't go down the—"

Too late. Cody's usual problem.

Cody cut the turn sharp. The three back-seat passengers slid right.

Tmp, flmp, bmp.

Cody barreled into the street. Parked cars filled the right side, barely wide enough for a car to pass safely on the other. Hipsters lounged outside on a coffee shop terrace and watched the Mustang speed down the road. A hand-holding couple stalled mid-street, then the man pulled his companion safely to the sidewalk. Closely behind, the Caddy entered the street, closing the gap at a rapid pace.

A Volkswagen rolled into the end of the street. Coming at them, horn blasting out one, long, hysterical note. Headlights flashed. On the sidewalk, screams rose. Egged on, Cody grinned, leaned into it.

"Jesus, Cody, look out!"

Cody whipped left. The car lifted over the curb. It bounced onto the sidewalk, came down with a solid crunch. The Volkswagen swerved right, bashed into a parked car.

Doomph!

A store-front potted plant lifted, exploded onto the street. Cody aimed the car between two poles holding up a store's awning. Missed.

"Cody, get us—"

Pangggg!

The right pole went up like a javelin. The awning cover flapped across the windshield. Driving blind, Cody didn't panic, maintained high speed. The Mustang crashed into an object, then another. An artificial sound, not the dull thud of human bodies Leon dreaded. Leon looked back, saw only a couple tables strewn across the sidewalk. A more sensible crowd than at the hotel, everyone had fled indoors.

The awning flew away, unveiling two people ahead. Spoonfuls of yogurt lingered close to their mouths. Completely paralyzed.

"Cody! Get over!" Leon lunged forward to wrest control of the wheel. Cody yanked the steering wheel hard right before Leon came close. The car slalomed off the sidewalk. The back-end snapped like a whip. Leon flew back into his seat.

Scrump!

The Mustang fed off the parked car they side-swiped, then released. Cody rolled the wheel left, then right, overcompensating until he centered the runaway beast.

Leon looked back. The Caddy swerved around the stalled Volkswagen, two wheels up on the sidewalk, two in the street. And behind the windshield, sat two very happy twins.

One hundred feet away, Main Street opened up. Sirens mounted. Red and blue lights alit on the surrounding buildings. Police cars crowded the street.

The cops or the stop sign didn't slow Cody. Without looking right, he took the turn at breathless speed. Leon dug his fingers into the upholstery until he punctured it. The car lifted off the left tires. When it landed, the Mustang swerved. Expertly, Cody rolled the steering wheel both directions until the car straightened.

The Caddy did the same thing, now almost glued to them.

Police officers filled the Southbound side of the street, redirecting traffic, most of them occupied. Except for the intrepid cop who joined the high-speed parade, quickly clipping away the distance.

On-coming traffic sat at a stand-still, bumper to bumper. A few lookie-loo's hopped out, strained on tip-toes to watch the commotion. A car pulled a U-turn to leave the log-jam. More cars joined it.

Goro rolled down his window. Tried to maneuver the gun outside.

Leon grabbed his arm. "No! Goro, don't! You might hit a bystander!"

Goro stared at his employer. Takihiro shook his head. The

large man sat back and watched America zip by his window.

The Caddy nearly tagged the Mustang's bumper. Then it pulled into the next lane and caught up, matching their speed.

"Faster, Cody!"

"What? You don't think I'm tryin'?"

Neck and neck, they raced down Main Street, a cat and mouse game.

Two commuters trapped the cop between them, one in front, one next to him. The cop laid on the horn, blasted the drivers aside. Quickly, he maneuvered into the left lane directly behind the Mustang.

Dammit.

The female twin smiled, flirty with her lashes. The rush of wind blew back her long hair. She tucked it behind an ear. Next to her, her brother brought his rifle up, laid it across his sister's chest. The barrel protruded out the window. Aimed at Cody.

"Whoa!" Instinct drove Cody as sure as he drove the car. He tapped the brakes, then immediately sped up. The cop car nearly tagged them, rebounded into a tire-burning swerve. He stopped, then thrust the car into hot pursuit again.

An intersection lay ahead. The cop switched lanes, lined up behind the Caddy. Undoubtedly due to the gun out the window.

Leon wanted to cheer, thought Lady Luck might jinx them again.

"Right, Cody, turn right!"

"On it!"

Just when Leon thought they couldn't possibly go any faster, Cody nailed the pedal to the floor. They flew past the stalled line of cars and whipped into the cross-street. The Mustang lifted onto two wheels. It plopped down and slung them even faster.

Leon saw the cop's taillights vanishing. And he hoped like hell the cop would catch the twins.

Like coils ready to spring through an old mattress, Leon's muscles tensed. Impossible to unwind.

"Cody, don't stop until we're out of Billing's city limit."

Vigilantly, Leon kept a look-out. So far no sign of any more police vehicles. Absolutely no battered Caddy.

Yet he still couldn't relax.

If Takihiro felt the same way, he didn't show it. With his eyes shut, Leon thought he'd fallen asleep. His eyes opened and fixed on Leon. "You said we have much to talk about. Well?"

"Hmm. Don't imagine you see that every day in the woods of Montana." Sidarski tapped the brakes and watched the speeding limo zip past them and vanish in a broccoli head of dust.

"Mm-hm. Wanna go after it?" said Keats

"Depends. You get the numbers?"

Keats tapped her head. "Stored it away in my portable file cabinet. Lookin' up hits now on the iPad."

"We've seen what? Only five, maybe six cars this far out. None of 'em in the limo's league. Maybe a friend of the elusive Sheera Rasmussen?"

"Now you're just being optimistic."

"Keep hope alive." A fireball ignited in Sidarski's gut, though, hardly a sign of hope. Either his body had just sent him a *told you so* or an ulcer. He didn't care for either prospect. Especially if it meant he'd let someone connected to Rasmussen slip by him.

"Nope. No hits. Don't mean anything, though."

"Why don't you give your new BFF, Dawbins, a call? Tell him to look out for the limo? Let him know it could be a lead in his case." Sidarski knew Dawbins would jump at the chance, particularly since a BOLO would pretty much bring the guy to Dawbin's desk.

Keats called Dawbins, shouted and argued her way through the mostly one-sided conversation. How she conducted most of her interviews. She got results, though, no denying that.

They turned onto the two mile stretch of gravel road leading to the Rasmussen ranch, Sidarski saw smoke lazing in the sky or thought he did, at least. His eyes weren't as eagle-like as they'd once been. He asked Keats to confirm.

"Smoke."

Sidarski rolled down the window, took a big whiff, swallowed a mouthful of dust. "*Yaaachoo*! Excuse me. Allergies. But I love the smell of napalm in the morning." He looked at

Keats, grinned, waited for acknowledgement.

"The hell you talkin' about?"

"Oh, c'mon, Keats, I know you're a movie philistine, but that's a quote from *Apocalypse Now*. Duvall?"

"Christ, last movie I saw was...*Old Yeller*. Hated the ending."

"Why? Make you cry?"

"Hardly. Just didn't see the point of the film. Sit through it all just to have the dog die. Whatever. What do you smell?"

"Gunpowder...something burning...something else I can't place."

"Look at bloodhound Sidarski, sniffing out crime. Damn!"

They rolled up to the remains of a gated entranceway. Parts of the wall had been blasted into piles of rubble. Most of the gate lay in a twisted pile of black metal.

"Looks like we're a little late to the party," said Keats.

Sidarski slowed to a crawl, tallied up the damage. Tiny holes—clearly of the bullet-causing variety—pocked portions of the outside wall.

"No gate, open invite. Right?"

Sidarski edged the car into the destroyed entrance. Two men, packing obvious heat beneath their jackets, jogged toward them.

"Welcome wagon."

"Let's make new friends."

Sidarski lowered the window. Cautiously, one of the men approached, hand inside his jacket.

"Can I help you, sir?"

Quicker than the eye could follow, Sidarski flashed his P.I. license. It didn't open any legal doors, but as long as you did it with authority it didn't matter. "Sidarski, Barton Police." He didn't bother mentioning "Kansas." A life-long barrage of jokes about Dorothy and Toto cured him of that.

Keats added solid back-up. "Detective Keats, Miami Beach Police Department. We'd like to speak with Mrs. Rasmussen, please."

"May I ask what this is about?"

"Nope. But we'll let Mrs. Rasmussen know."

The man straightened, cracked his neck for show. "I know

you're out of your jurisdiction. So why don't you just turn your car around and head on back where you came from? Next time, bring a warrant." He walked fingers through the air, an annoying trait if Sidarski'd ever seen one. He knew a few bad cops who wouldn't balk at breaking those fingers. "And good luck with that."

Keats leaned across Sidarski. *Fireworks!* "Listen, jackass. You've been watching too many TV shows and obviously don't know anything about Montana's ordinances! Montana allows cross-state territorial arrests. Now, unless you want me to arrest your ass for obstructing justice, I suggest you get your boss mama on the phone right now and tell her we're coming in. Tell her I want coffee."

Which, of course, was all bullshit. Keats slipped Sidarski a covert shrug, smirked: *You gotta break a few eggs...*

"Ah... Hold on a minute." The guard trotted away while the other guard gaped dumbly at them.

A minute later, he reappeared, visibly shaken with phone in hand. "Fine. Mrs. Rasmussen will allow you a few minutes. But we'll need to escort you."

"Great," said Keats. "I always wanted to be a debutante at the ball."

Slowly, Sidarski tapped the gas pedal, brake, gas, repeat, while he followed the two walking men.

"Nice place," said Keats.

"Crime pays."

Keats pointed out the miniature architectural duplicates of the main ranch. The number of armed guards interested Sidarski more, though. They hustled along urgently, spoke into earpieces. Putting out fires. Or maybe they'd just put out a helluva fire based on the pungent smoke still lingering in the air.

Near the front door, Keats nudged Sidarski, jerked her chin toward the stone-work of the house. More bullet-holes. "Design by Capone," she whispered.

Other guards joined the entourage as they shuffled them inside the house and up a winding stairwell.

"You sure know how to make a girl feel wanted, fellas."

Keats sounded anything but flirtatious.

The lead guard knocked on a door.

"Come in."

At the end of a long table lounged a Barbie doll reject. Sidarski imagined she could file a meaty law-suit based on her cartoonish surgical alterations.

"Good evening." Her mouth barely moved. But her eyes were certainly busy, checking them out head to toe. "I'm Sheera Rasmussen. Now, why in the world would a Miami and Kansas cop want to talk to me?"

"Detective Sidarski, ma'am. And this is—"

"Keats. Detective Ramona Keats." Keats sat down across from a suited man, nearly as stiff as the woman of the house. "Nice digs, Mrs. Rasmussen. Although, apparently not everyone agrees."

Mrs. Rasmussen raised her eyebrows, a true struggle. "Why on earth would you say that?"

"Looks like someone blew up your entryway and shot up the place."

"Nonsense! We're just doing some remodeling. Out with the old, in with the new." Her hands fluttered nearly as fast as her eyelashes. "And I insist my guards keep up-to-date with their target practice. Two birds, one stone."

"Uh-huh," said Sidarski. "You use your house for target practice?"

"Yes, well, I'm afraid the skeet targets sometimes get away from us."

"I'll bet. You mind my asking what it is you do, Mrs. Rasmussen? To afford such an estate?"

"It had belonged to my dear sweet, late husband, Jasper. He'd made his fortune in real estate and oil, a true entrepreneur."

"Why all the armed guards? Real estate a dangerous business these days?"

Mrs. Rasmussen tittered. "You'd be surprised, Detective. My husband had been somewhat ruthless in his dealings, accumulating as many of his competitors' holdings and businesses as he could. Some people don't deal with loss very well." She offered a strained smile.

"Yeah, I see you're all torn up over your husband's passing," muttered Keats.

"Did you say something?"

"Nothin'. Just thinkin' out loud." Keats typed something onto Sidarski's iPad. "You said Jasper Rasmussen. Hm."

"Why 'hm,' Detective?"

"Can't find any mention of him anywhere. Funny. For such a big wheel businessman, you'd think he'd have a high internet profile. Or something."

"You'd think so. But dear Jasper valued his privacy. Worked in the shadows, a silent businessman of sorts." She dabbed an artificially manufactured tear away. "Poor, dear Jasper."

"How did your husband die, Mrs. Rasmussen?"

"He was very ill. And quite elderly. He went peacefully. In his sleep."

Sidarski noticed Mrs. Rasmussen's sidekick's foot jerk. Then he scratched an ear, his solitary movement thus far. "I'm sorry... who are you?" asked Sidarski.

"Mr. Gaines." No first name, no further explanation given as if he'd said it all.

"Again...I'm finding no obits on your husband, Mrs. Rasmussen," said Keats. "Odd."

"Isn't it, though? As I said, Detectives..." Her hands spread, nothing to hide. "...Jasper was a private man. He had no living relatives...no friends, really. We held a small, personal gathering."

"Where's he buried?"

"Excuse me?"

"Where's your husband buried, ma'am?" Sidarski leaned forward, unleashing his inner bulldog. Something smelled wrong.

"Why...at his family mausoleum, of course. In Billings. I'm afraid you've upset me, Detectives. Dredging up sad memories." She sobbed into her hands and her blond head bobbed.

Gaines interjected. "I'm afraid I'll have to ask you to leave now, Detectives. As you can see, Mrs. Rasmussen is in a very vulnerable place."

"Apparently not as vulnerable as her late husband," Keats mumbled.

"I'm sorry?" Gaines whipped off his glasses, ready to defend his queen's honor.

Keats ignored him. "We understand there was quite a shoot-up here six months ago. Care to explain that?"

"What *are* you talking about?" Fast as a whip, Mrs. Rasmussen dried up. Sidarski imagined she might make a great actress. Probably where her husband had recruited her.

"There were reports of gunfire and explosions coming from your ranch some time ago. Just wondered what that was all about."

"Oh. Oh, my. How could I have forgotten? That was shortly after my beloved husband passed away. After his memoriam, we held a fireworks display. In Jasper's honor. The way he would've loved it."

"I'll bet," said Sidarski. "Seems like there's an awful lot of gunplay going on around here."

"I don't much care for your insinuation, Detective. I've explained everything I've needed to. And I can assure you we're well within the zoning ordinances for firework displays. As you can see…" Again, her hands went wide. "…we're pretty much on our own out here anyway."

"That you are. Did you have any visitors earlier today? Someone in a limo?"

"Of course not. I don't pay my renovators that well!" Mrs. Rasmussen and her shadow shared a giggle.

Sidarski sighed. They were getting nowhere and now faced a hostile suspect. Old-fashioned grilling wouldn't thaw Mrs. Rasmussen. She hardly felt the heat.

As a last ditch effort, he pulled out his two favorite photos. "Mrs. Rasmussen, do you know this man? Or the other one?" Garber was up first, followed by Spangler, a one-two pitch. He watched her face closely, hoped she'd swing.

If she had wrinkles on her forehead, surely they would've folded due to the lengthy consideration she gave the photos. "I'm afraid not. Should I know them? Were they business associates of Jasper?"

"I'm hoping you can tell us."

"I never had much interest in Jasper's business dealings,

Detective. But, I can tell you, no, I've never seen either man."
She glanced at Gaines. Gaines angled to see the photos, then
shook his head.

"You're certain about that?"

"Oh, my, yes. Couple of handsome men like this I'd definitely
remember." Beneath her bulging cheeks, she smiled.

Sidarski slipped her a card with his cell-phone number.
"Fine. If you should happen to remember anything, please give
me a call."

Mrs. Rasmussen disregarded the card as if it offended her
delicate sensibilities, nodded at her sidekick to pick it up. "Of
course. Anything I can do to help local law enforcement. Oh
my...I nearly forgot. You're not 'local,' are you?" Another awful
grin.

"Thanks for the reminder."

"Now, I've a very busy day ahead of me. I must say goodbye."

Sidarski rose, tucked in his constantly betraying shirt-tail.

Keats remained seated. "Dunno what you're not telling us,
Mrs. Rasmussen, but...I'll find out."

"Oh, good luck with that, dear. Nothing I'm hiding but my
beauty tips. And I'll take those with me to the grave."

"Amen to that," spat Keats.

"Let's go, Keats." Sidarski nudged Keats' shoulder.

She shrugged him away. "I think you know Garber and
Spangler. And clearly there's something goin' on around here.
Bullet holes don't lie. If I have to, I'll come back with the full
Billings force."

"Again...good luck." Mrs. Rasmussen tittered. "You have
my blessings. In the meantime...ta-ta." She looked down at
the paperwork before her, dismissed them with a fly-shooing
gesture.

"Come on, Keats."

Keats growled, kicked back her chair as she stood.

"Picked the wrong cop to play with. So...ta-ta, girlfriend.
For now."

The guards who'd lingered behind them rushed forward,
grabbed Keats by the shoulders.

"Get offa me, dammit! I'm goin'!"

Keats huffed out first, the guards and Sidarski following. Mrs. Rasmussen's taunting laughter reached them all the way to the first level.

As the guards hurried the detectives out the front door, they remained silent. So did the detectives. As before, Sidarski drove slowly behind two walking men. This time more guards joined the march, beside them and behind them. A heavily armed parade.

Sidarski waited until they left the compound before he asked the question on his mind. "What? You tryin' to put a target on our backs, Keats?"

"Pretty much, yeah. We ain't getting' nothin' from Rasmussen any other way. Let them come after us. I'm ready."

Sidarski thought about it. Although the prospect of putting his life at risk seemed like a hell of a way to spend his retirement, he agreed. "Fine. I was gettin' kinda bored anyway. The Rasmussen widow's lying. She knows our boys."

"Yeah, I got that, too. Although hard as hell to tell behind her granite face."

Sidarski chuckled. "Pretty extensive work, yeah?"

"Friggin' Mount Everest. Anyway…guess we wait until Rasmussen calls our bluff. The Billings PD ain't gonna lift a finger to help. Dawbins—and Lady Macbeth—pretty much made that evident."

"You really think waiting's the best course of action? Could lead to a whole lotta nothin'."

"Got any better ideas?"

Although the idea sounded less than appealing, particularly to Sidarski's back, he did. "Yeah. You like campin', Keats?"

On edge, Bartholomew paid careful attention to the car they'd just blown by. "Tommy?"

"Sir?"

"I don't like the way that car slowed down back there. I believe it's time for another license plate change."

"On it, sir." Immediately, Tommy hooked a right onto a small dirt road and circled around. He hopped out. The trunk opened and the sound of an electric drill buzzed at the back of the limo.

"Bartholomew," said Nanette, "Leon didn't try to—"

"My dear comrade, Bartholomew!" Gus bellowed. "How wonderful to see you again!" With obvious pained effort, Gus rose from the facing bench seat, and pumped Bartholomew's hand. Exhausted by the effort, he crawled into Delilah's lap. His eyes closed while she stroked his hair. She nodded toward their host on wheels.

"Delilah. Gus." Bartholomew acknowledged them with a gentlemanly doff of his hat. "It's nice to see you both again. Particularly you, Delilah, after your last close call."

"I'm hard to kill," she said.

"Truer words. And, good afternoon to you, Mr.....ah, Skeeter." Bartholomew faltered over Skeeter's name as if he found using a nick-name undignified. "We've spoken on the phone before."

Skeeter took it all in slowly. He blinked like a newborn, questioning babe. He glanced at Bartholomew, down at the shoe-box, back at the man again. Enlightenment nearly blew out his eyes. "Jumpin' Jesus! You're the friggin' Man with the Shoe-Box! Oh my God, oh my God, we're all gonna die! I just knew it, I knew—"

"Ah! I see my reputation precedes me." Bartholomew flashed large ivory teeth, embracing his notoriety. "I believe we have some things to discuss later, Mr. Skeeter."

"Oh man, I don't want any part of this!" Skeeter squeezed his laptop tight, closed his eyes. Suddenly, he cupped a hand over his mouth, bucked forward and gagged.

"Tsk. So uncouth. Mr. Skeeter, please do take it outside. Leather interior is very hard to clean."

More than happy to oblige, Skeeter bailed out like a parachutist. Next to the car, he dropped to his knees and threw up. Tommy hovered over him, shook his head with bemused disgust.

Remarkably, Gus and Delilah had fallen asleep. Just Bartholomew and Nanette. She had little time to save Leon's life. Impatient as a driver suffering road-rage, The Man with the Shoe-Box didn't like to wait.

"Bartholomew, I can assure you Leon had nothing to do—"

A gloved finger jutted up, silencing her. "Nanette, you know how fond I am of you, I'm sure."

No, not really. And I'm not sure I want to know.

"But to be honest, I'm not even certain if I can trust you, let alone Mr. Garber."

"I understand…no, I don't. Not really. Look, all of us worked together last year. We had each other's backs. I don't know what happened to you, but Leon had—"

"He had someone from LMI try to kill me. *Twice*. Once…I can forgive." He gave a half-shrug, tapped his shoebox. "We're only human, after all. People make mistakes. Twice? Unforgiveable."

"But I know for a fact, Leon didn't—"

"Do you honestly, Nanette? How well do you truly know Mr. Garber?"

A question Nanette had been asking herself a lot lately. Which led to a more troublesome question: Had she ever truly known Leon? Had he played her the way she had with men for most of her career? The answer seemed clear. And it troubled her. No, it pissed her off. Still, she couldn't sign off on Leon's death decree, not just yet. "I know Leon well enough to know he'd never send someone to kill you. He's an honorable man."

"Ah, honor. So hard to define, so much harder to achieve. I must say I had my doubts last year when Mr. Garber accepted the position of CEO of LMI. It seemed rather contrary to our goal of destroying LMI."

"But that's why he took the job. And he had no choice."

"Be that as it may, what has he accomplished toward said goals? Absolutely nothing."

Agreed. "That's not necessarily true, Bartholomew."

"My, ah, inside source tells me differently."

Of course. Bartholomew had more eyes than a scallop. "What's your source said?"

"That Mr. Garber's fully embraced the mantle of LMI's CEO. Along with everything that comes with it. He decides who dies, who LMI's enemies are. Of which I'm proudly one." He sniffed, held out his hand and admired his manicured fingernails. "Hence, Mr. Garber is directly responsible for ordering my demise. But like our friend, Delilah…" He nodded at the snoozing woman. "…I'm extremely hard to kill."

"I get that, I do. But…LMI's trying to kill Leon, too. And you saw what they tried to do to us!"

"And what makes you think Mr. Garber isn't lying about his, ah, life expectancy chances? How can you possibly know he isn't the one who ordered your demise?"

"Because I trust him." *Sort of. Mostly. A little?*

The Man with the Shoe-Box turned in his seat, his treasure riding with him. He dropped a paternal hand on her knee. Nanette nearly jumped as if a snake had encircled her neck. "My dear…my dear, naïve Nanette…"

Ordinarily, she'd slap a man for talking down to her in such a condescending manner. But she wanted to hear him out. He spoke with confidence, perhaps the truth. Plus, you don't slap the Man with the Shoe-Box, a pretty smart rule of life.

With a jaw-stretching grin, he continued. "You realize Mr. Garber attempted to have our friend, August Schroeder, murdered."

"That's *absolutely* not true."

"How can you be sure of the truth, dear?"

"Because Leon told me what happened! He saved Augie's life!"

"Did he? LMI is nothing if not a player of games. Games built on lies, deceit…death."

Nanette couldn't think about it, didn't want to think about it. Leon would never send someone after one of their allies.

But…but…

A worm of doubt inched through her thoughts.

Maybe Leon's been lying to me since the beginning. About everything.

"Leon's not like that. Trust me…I know." Her words sounded rock-solid. But her delivery lagged. Clouds of ignorance parted, rays of awakening poked through. "What proof do *you* have that Leon did that to Augie?"

He tipped his hat back. Laughed. Something he didn't do often. Nanette imagined the Grim Reaper sounded the same way upon sealing a contract. "Because my source, who I stand by completely, told me so."

Worse than a gut-punch. She thought she might join Skeeter outside, tell him to scoot over. "Who…who's your source?"

"I'm afraid I can't divulge that information, dear. But I trust him. Educated him fully before sending him into the trenches, so to speak. Not that it matters. You wouldn't know him. He's an expert at blending into the background. And his Intel is solid."

Out of control thoughts ambushed her. The car spun, her stomach chased after it. Confusion, anger, betrayal swirled into a merry-go-round of dread. Leon'd played her. His worst crime.

Still. She held on. To the one thread she could grasp. Even if doubt had entered her mind, she trusted herself. The one person she always relied on. And her intuition regarding Leon couldn't be dismissed out of hand. "Fine, Bartholomew. But we're going to find Leon. And give him a chance to explain."

"Of course. I'd have it no other way. I do so enjoy a good interrogation." After Nanette witnessed one of his "interrogations" last year, he may as well have said "torture."

"I mean it, Bartholomew. Leon gets a fair trial."

Bartholomew breathed in deeply, let it out slowly. "I've always been a push-over for beautiful young women. We'll play it your way. For now. But…I'll be the jury and judge. Not to mention executioner."

If Leon truly tried to have Augie killed, she might want the job herself. Or maybe not. A hung jury. She left the thought hanging, didn't want to give Leon any more of her time.

Apparently satisfied, Bartholomew rolled down the window, leaned out. "Tommy?"

"Sir?"

"Find anything on your phone?"

"Yes sir." Tommy trotted to the window. "A shoot-out in front of the Billings Crowne Plaza hotel and in the parking garage. A stolen car reported. High speed chase through downtown involving the stolen car."

"I see your Leon's been a very, very busy boy, Nanette," said Bartholomew. "Very well, Tommy, take us into town." He rolled up the window, then stopped. "Ah, Mr. Skeeter?"

"Um, yeah?" Skeeter wiped his T-Shirt sleeve over his mouth, mopped his forehead.

"Are you about finished? Tick-tock. Time's fleeting. We must be on our way."

One look at the Man with the Shoe-Box and Skeeter's flesh turned even whiter. "Not yet!" He leaned over and continued to expunge his lunch.

"Oh dear." Bartholomew shook his head, a grandmotherly smile hiding the man behind it.

"And that's when you and Goro joined us, Mr. Takihiro." Leon waited and hoped Mr. Takihiro would fill in the blanks. But his face looked blank as well.

"I see."

"Yo, this sumo guy's bleeding all over the front seat!" Cody wheeled the car into the World-Mart parking lot.

"Quiet, Cody."

Goro hadn't moved for a while, slumped over with his face pressed up against the window.

"Think he's dead. Just sayin'."

Leon didn't need a corpse on his hands in addition to everything else. Already they had cops combing the area for them.

"Mr. Takihiro, through default, we're now allies. LMI wants you eliminated as well."

"It would appear that way."

"Why do they want to kill you?"

"Unlike the rest of the board members, I backed you and your ideology. I wanted out of the political arena, an ugly business. I'm first and foremost a businessman. Money matters more than power. The others disagree. Apparently, I made a very poor business decision." He offered a small shrug.

"Just pull into a spot over there, Cody." Leon gestured toward the back of the parking lot. "Mr. Takihiro, I appreciate your siding with me. It—"

"Merely a business decision, Mr. Garber. Nothing more."

"Be that as it may, we have a common enemy. These two twins. Who are they?"

"The Doublemint Twins. LMI's remaining best business process outsourcers. You've eliminated most of the others."

"Yeah. Um—"

"They're extremely dangerous. Swedish twins, both expert marksmen."

"Great."

"Yes. Great."

"So…what next? Any suggestions how we can fix this mess?"

"I've considered changing alliances. No offence, Mr. Garber, but I could possibly save myself by going forth to LMI, explain how I made a huge mistake."

"Mr. Takihiro, you and I both know LMI doesn't forgive. Just not in their playbook. But maybe we can use you to—"

"I'm not interested in being your pawn. You've already put me at great risk."

"That's LMI's doing, *not* mine."

"A matter of perspective."

"When you deal with LMI, matters of perspective can get you killed."

"Perhaps you're right."

"Dude," said Cody, "I'm tellin' you the big guy's dead!" He prodded Goro with his fore-finger.

"Dammit, just…deal with it! Mr. Takihiro, the only way for us to survive is to take the battle to LMI. There's no other way out."

"Perhaps, but very risky and stupid."

"You could be our way in."

Takihiro shook his head. "LMI wants me dead. I won't be able to get anywhere near them."

"We don't have a choice."

Takihiro paused, considered his words for a lengthy time. "There's the summit tomorrow. If I go, make good—"

"Summit? What summit?"

"Mr. Garber, as the CEO of LMI, I expect you to be apprised of—"

"The only thing LMI's interested in apprising me of is my death. Tell me about the summit."

"Mrs. Rasmussen has called a summit, involving all of the board members, stock-holders and investors. Tomorrow. In Washington D.C. But before I agree to your…cowboy tactics, can you assure me my safety?"

Absolutely not. "I'll do everything in my power to do so. You have my word."

"Not very comforting."

"We live in uncomfortable times."

"Hai. After I gain you access to the summit, I leave. What do you propose to do once you're at the meeting?"

Damn fine question. "Not sure yet. But I'm working it out."

"Work competently and quickly, Mr. Garber. I don't believe you know what you're going up against."

Probably not. But the meeting screamed golden opportunity. All the LMI heads, the big dogs, under one roof at the same time. His one and only chance to bring them to their knees and stick a fork into LMI. End game.

"We're all taking chances, Mr. Takihiro. Okay, I have to get us some burner phones and we need to get rid of the car. You good, Cody?"

"Beyond gooder, I'm great, yo! But whadda' I do with the dead guy?" Cody nudged Goro to no effect.

"Good God… Just deal with it. Don't leave him anywhere where he can be found quickly."

"No! Goro died an honorable death," said Takihiro. "His body goes with us until we can give him a proper burial."

Not the time for an argument. Bad enough Leon had to leave Cody unattended with the Japanese delegate. Who knew what he might say? Or incite?

"Fine. Put him in the trunk of the new car. Without witnesses."

"Duh. I'm, like, a professional and everything, yo."

Takihiro groaned and closed his eyes. What Leon felt like doing. "Pick me up in front of the store in five minutes."

With three burner phones in a bag, Leon exited the store, his head down, collar up. An old Corolla raced up, Cody behind the wheel. Takihiro sat in the back, his fingers dug into the back of Cody's seat and braced for anything. The passenger seat sat empty.

Leon slid in. "Go, Cody. Carefully."

Never one to obey orders, Cody left a black-marked signature on the pavement.

"Slow down, dammit! What'd you do with Goro?"

Cody hitched a thumb behind him. "In the trunk. Dude musta' weighed a thousand pounds. Takifuji was no help. All up in his grievin' I guess."

"Show a little respect, Cody." Leon activated his phone. His fingers shook over the key-pad, alternately fearing and anticipating who might answer. Only one way to find out.

"Leon." Nanette's voice sounded dry and raspy, a husk of her usual self.

"Nanette! Thank God you're alright! Did everybody get out? How did—"

"Everyone's fine. We need to meet. Immediately."

"Um...okay. Where?"

"We're in Billings. Heard about the damage you left in your wake. Can you meet us at the Mountview Cemetery in thirty minutes?"

Leon plugged the address into his phone, searched for the directions. "Yeah. Yeah, I think so. Nanette, I'm relieved you're—"

A small click on Nanette's end terminated the call. Clearly something was wrong. In many ways, he dreaded this confrontation more than the pending LMI showdown. And wondered if the cemetery locale had been chosen for a good reason.

Located on a mountain and surrounded by a forest's worth of trees, Mountview Cemetery provided a perfect place for a covert meeting, nothing but ghosts and bodies bearing witness. Nanette wondered how many more might be added before the end of the meeting.

Parked deep within the cemetery, the limo's occupants sat in silence. Bartholomew picked at his fingernails with a long, slender knife, humming. She hoped she'd get a chance to talk with Leon before Bartholomew decided to use the knife on Leon. Or maybe she'd grab it and deliver the killing blow. Still undecided.

A clunker of a Corolla tooled into the cemetery and approached them. Nanette exited the limo, folded her arms and leaned against the car. Waiting.

Behind the wheel, she spotted Cody. Before the car stopped completely, the back door flew open. Leon rolled out and jogged toward her, loping like an excited dog.

"Nanette! I'm really glad you're okay!"

She sprinted toward him. Stupidly, he opened his arms, awaiting a hug. Not today. Anger propelled her faster. She brought her arm back.

"I'm happy to see—"

Bumph.

Leon never saw it coming. Her fist exploded onto his jaw. He buckled back, waved his arms in a losing battle with gravity. He tumbled down.

"Gah!" He sat up in the grass, massaged his jaw. "Why is everyone *hitting* me today?"

Nanette stood over him, her legs straddled. "Save your bullshit, Leon! Tell me the truth and I mean the *entire* truth for a change!"

Cody left the Corolla, laughing. "Day-um!"

"What're you talking about, Nanette? I—"

"Did you order Augie's death?"

"What? No, of course I—"

Timp!

A quick kick to Leon's ribs didn't quite pay for his lie. But it felt good. For him not so much.

"What'd I say about your bullshit, Leon? Bartholomew said you ordered Augie's death!"

"Bartholomew? He's here, too? No, Nanette...I did *not*—"

"The truth!" On her haunches, she grabbed Leon's collar, shook him. "No more half-truths, half-lies. Anything! You look me in the eye and tell me the *truth*, dammit!"

Leon grimaced. Shaded his guilty eyes against the late-afternoon sun. "It seemed like the only way to maintain our cover. To end LMI. Augie posed a threat to our operation. But a short while later I came to my senses. I tried to get Sheera to call it off. I—"

"He was our friend, Leon! You don't kill friends! Is he dead now? Was your story about sending him away a cover-up?"

"Of course not! He's alive and well!"

"Yo, Nanette, it's true." Cody stepped forward. "Guy's livin' the sea-life now. Friggin' Popeye."

Nanette looked up at Cody. Him, she believed. Too dumb to lie convincingly. With a growl, she released Leon. But not before giving him an extra shove. "For you to even consider killing Augie is *despicable*, Leon! What *happened* to you?"

"It was the only way...the only way for me to bring LMI down. I couldn't risk Augie jeopardizing everything by talking. Not yet. Not until I—"

"That doesn't even make sense! I'm sick of your 'everything for the mission' attitude! You haven't done *anything* to destroy LMI! You've just been enjoying playing the whole big-shot CEO position!"

"That's...not true. Well, maybe I did a little. But not anymore. Trust me. No one wants to see LMI destroyed more than I do. And I saved Augie's life."

"After you meant to have him killed!"

"It's the truth." Dumbfounded, Leon shut up. Maybe too scared to say anything else. Just sat on the ground like a chastised child. *Good boy.*

Cody silently nodded in corroboration.

Slowly, Nanette's anger lifted. But what she felt now was worse: *disappointment.* She hadn't realized it until now, but she'd respected Leon. Hard to find respect in a man's world. She no longer felt the urge to throttle him, yet she couldn't look at him either. Disgusted, she stood, walked away. Paced. She had a lot to think about.

But Bartholomew still had quite a bit to say.

"Hello, Leon." Slowly, Bartholomew strolled up, shoebox beneath one arm, knife in his other gloved hand. Casual as a cat. He knelt.

"Bartholomew. Didn't think I'd see you again."

"Why's that? Because you tried to have me killed?" The knife-tip lashed out, found Leon's throat, pressed in on his skin.

"No, *what*? I did *not*—"

"Shh, shh, shh." Soft as a mother's comforting whisper. Carefully he placed the shoebox on Leon's chest and held a fingertip to Leon's lips. "I understand differently. My source tells me you most certainly did put an elimination order on me, Leon." He tipped his head, grinned. "Unfortunately for you, you didn't try hard enough."

"You've got to believe me! I didn't—"

"Quiet, Leon. You're disturbing the dead. So, tell me...why would you do such a thing? Weren't we allies?"

"We were! We are! I swear on my mother's grave I had nothing to do with the attempt on your life! I haven't even heard about it! I knew they were discussing you as a potential liability, but—"

"Ah, now we get to the truth. I never had you pegged as a liar, Leon. But...people change some times. Especially when corrupted by power."

"Fine. Whatever. Clearly, you're not going to listen to me. Go ahead, cut my throat. I'm sick and tired of being attacked by friends and enemies. But if you kill me...you'll never destroy LMI. And I have the means to do so."

Bartholomew pulled back the knife, just a bit.

Behind them, Gus said, "Friend Bartholomew! I'm sure Leon would do no such thing! Why he's a wonderful human being! Noble and—"

"Ah, Gustav, I'm afraid that's where you're wrong. How much do we truly know about Leon Garber? LMI has a way of twisting everyone they associate with. Leon's working as a double-spy."

"Sure, that sounds right," said Leon. "That's why I tried to have myself killed three times now. It's all an elaborate cover-up."

"You survived all three attempts, of course."

"I give up."

Truly, that's what Nanette should do regarding Leon: give up. But, God help her, she believed him. She didn't know why either. He certainly hadn't earned her trust. Call her a fool for love or at least the unattainable dream.

"Let him go, Bartholomew. He didn't do it," said Nanette.

"You weren't so certain a few minutes ago, my dear."

"I know. But I am now. I think he made some mistakes. But he's right. He wouldn't put three hits on himself."

"Nanette, have you asked yourself why LMI didn't dispose of Leon earlier? Why wouldn't they when they had him right under their collective thumbs?"

Frustrated, Nanette slapped her hips. "I don't know! LMI likes to play their damn games! I'm betting this has been fun for Sheera and her cronies. Or maybe they were hedging their bets…seeing if they could truly bring Leon over. He was an effective CEO."

"An elaborate game, you're suggesting?"

"I'm just throwing things out, Bartholomew. God only knows Sheera's bored, looking for fun. And…maybe Leon posed her biggest challenge. She wanted to tame a wild bronco." A swing, a big one. But Nanette had long ago given up on making sense of LMI's business practices.

Mainly she wanted to give Leon the benefit of the doubt. Honestly, just now, she saw a little sincerity come back in his eyes.

"LMI are the bad guys here, Bartholomew. Not Leon."

Bartholomew chopped the knife down into the dirt next to Leon's head. He winced. Nanette grinned. She still thought he was owed a little payback.

Bartholomew stood, brushed his hands, retrieved his shoebox. "Fine. For now. Leon, I don't believe you. Certainly don't trust you. But apparently you've earned the goodwill of everyone else. I must say, Nanette, you sadden me. I didn't exactly have you pegged as a…ah, pushover."

The words burned. Deeply. More than anything she wanted to grab the knife and make the Man with the Shoebox eat his words. No one called her a "pushover." Particularly regarding a man. But she knew better than to attack. Things were hairy enough. After this was all over, though, she had some serious self-examination to attend to.

Nanette carefully managed her words. "I'm *not* a pushover. I just believe Leon."

"Well…glad someone does." Leon climbed to his feet. White-faced and sweating, he looked around at his spectators. "Before we continue…anyone else wanna take a swing at me? Hold me at knife-point? No?"

No one responded, although Delilah performed a little odd and edgy jig. Probably seriously considering Leon's offer.

"Fine. Can we go destroy LMI now?"

"I'm curious as to how you propose we do that," said Bartholomew. "One of the other reasons I've decided to let you live. For—"

"Yeah, yeah. For now. I get it. But, frankly, we're all living on borrowed time."

The Corolla's back door crunched open. A Japanese man stepped out.

"Ah! Mr. Takihiro!" Bartholomew gave a bow. Takihiro returned it. "It's been years since we've had the pleasure."

Of course, Bartholomew knew him. He knew everyone, it seemed. For a man living and killing in the shadows, he certainly wasn't afraid of the limelight. Nanette wondered how many presidents he'd wined and dined over the years.

"Will you be joining our visit with LMI?"

Takihiro looked at Leon. "I would rather not. But I may not have a choice."

"Spoken like the gambling man I know you to be! Let's adjourn to the limo to make final—"

Tump. Bump-bamp!

Cody yipped. "What the hell, yo? That a ghost or what?"

Tump-tump!

Leon shook his head. "Dammit, Cody, did you even check to see if Goro was dead?"

"Hey, don't go gettin' all high and mighty with me, chief! You tol' me to dump him in the trunk!"

Leon trotted toward the Corolla, pulled the inside trunk lever.

A large Japanese man crawled out of the trunk. He straightened, bowed. "Hai!"

"God damn Terminator," said Cody.

"Marvelous!" screamed Gus. "The more the merrier!" Delilah gathered her lover up and scurried back to the limo where Skeeter had remained.

"So tell me, Leon, of this miraculous plan of yours to destroy LMI." Bartholomew had fallen in step with Leon, nothing but the best of buds on a stroll.

"There's a meeting with the board members, the—"

"Yes, yes, I know all about the summit." Bartholomew waved his free hand. "Washington D.C. I already have a plan of my own in motion. But what of your plan, Leon?"

Leon paused, toed the gravel. "Skeeter and I are working that out. I need a little more time, that's all." Which meant he had no plan. Back to lying again.

"That tells me absolutely nothing."

"What about your plan, Bartholomew? Why do you expect me to explain everything while you're holding yours in check?"

"Let's understand something. The onus is on you to win back my trust. Not the other way around. I owe you absolutely nothing."

"Fine. As I said...I need to work more with Skeeter. Right now I suggest we head to Washington D.C. and—"

"Already set in motion. My private jet's awaiting our arrival."

"Good. But I can't stress this enough...we can't have our plans running at cross-hairs. Something's bound to go wrong if we do. Bartholomew...what exactly do you have planned?"

"Very well. I intend on killing each and every person at the LMI meeting."

Cody whooped. "Day-um! You're one sadistic, devious sum-bitch!"

"Why, thank you, Mr. Spangler." He grinned, late afternoon sunlight gleaming off his white grill. "That's exactly what my parents called me...before I took their feet." Despite the heat, a chill ran down Nanette's spine. Bartholomew glanced down at his shoebox, tapped it as if knocking on wood for good luck.

Bartholomew's plan frightened her. And judging on how pale Leon looked, she wasn't alone.

Chapter Eleven

"Damn, Sidarski, no one ever told me it gets so cold out here at night. Turn on the heat." For hours, they'd been sitting in the rental car about a quarter of a mile from the compound, a tree providing meager concealment. Given Sidarski's weak eyesight, Keats snagged binocular duty. Her arms ached from holding up the unwieldy binoculars. Coffee pushed at her bladder. Her feet grew numb from the cold, brittle night. Watching a whole lot of nothing had grown tiresome. All in all, Keats decided she hated camping.

Sidarski started the car, flipped on the heater. "Florida weather's spoiled you, Keats. Try surviving a Kansas winter."

"No thanks. How long you wanna keep this up tonight?"

"As long as it takes. Can't see we have any other option. We're kinda on our own here."

"The way I always roll." She'd rather roll with something concrete. But as her Grandma used to say, "Good things come to those who wait." Of course, Grams had never been on a boring stake-out either. "Sidarski, you think we might be barking up the wrong tree?"

"No." Neither did she. But it always helped to have validation. "I can feel it, Keats. Our boy, Garber's gonna be ours. One way or the other."

"Uh-oh."

"What's up?"

"We got action." Keats recognized the grotesquely hour-glassed shape of Mrs. Rasmussen as she left the house. Her loyal servant, Gaines, escorted her into a Town Car. "Big Momma's on the move. Lil' Twig's with her."

"Nice code names."

"Had some time to work 'em out. They're pulling out. Coming this way."

"Strange time for a drive. It's goin' on ten o'clock."

Keats watched as the Town Car left the grounds and ambled onto the gravel road. "Back up a bit. Their headlights might sweep over us."

Sidarski draped a big arm over the back-seat and reversed. Then he dropped the gear into drive, foot on the brake. "Here we go."

In no hurry the Town Car cruised past them; a driver in the front, Rasmussen and Gaines relaxed in the back.

"Jesus, hope I can drive with the headlights off."

"All you're gonna do is eat up grass if you leave the road, Sidarski."

"Not keepin' it very green."

"Oh, don't even go there."

Sidarski still hadn't budged. Keats nearly jammed her foot on top of his. "The hell you waitin' for? We're gonna lose 'em!"

"We don't wanna be seen. Besides we're the only two cars out here. Even with my eyes, I can spot them." Sidarski pulled out, moved at a snail's pace.

Once the Town Car exited the gravel road, it slipped into a more populated cross road. Finally, Sidarski flipped on the headlights. "Thank God."

After an uneventful thirty-five mile trip, they entered civilization again. On the outskirts of Billings, they followed the Town Car into a small industrial private airport.

"Ah! Mrs. Rasmussen's taking a trip. Wonder where to this time of night? Kinda cloak and daggery, sorta like a Bond flick."

"Everything's a movie to you, Sidarski."

"Hey, shoot for the stars."

They hung back, killed the headlights in the parking lot. Keats jumped out and watched the entourage approach a small hangar. Thirty minutes later, a small jet rumbled out of the hangar. Keats noted all the pertinent details.

"Big Momma has flown the coop. I repeat, she's flown the coop."

Sidarski started the car. "Let's go find out what nest she's landing in."

Inside the hangar, a short man in an even shorter jacket stopped them. "Sorry, folks, private property." He tapped away at his phone. "No more flights scheduled out of here tonight. I'm afraid I'll have to ask you to leave."

Keats flipped open her badge, quickly put it away. "That's okay. We're just curious as to where Mrs. Rasmussen flew to."

"I'm sorry." He gave them a smarmy smile. "Not without a warrant."

Sidarski sighed, reached into his pocket. Plucked a twenty dollar bill from his wallet. "Here's my warrant."

Greedily, the man grabbed it. "Feels a little light, if you know what I mean."

"Oh, for God's sake." Thoroughly disgusted, Keats tapped a foot, gave her partner a long look.

Sidarski again reached into his wallet, pulled out two more twenties. "Feel about right now?"

"I think so." After consulting his phone, he said, "Reaston Industrial Airport, D.C. Flight number 1602. Due in at around 11:20."

"Thanks," said Sidarski.

"Hey, always glad to be a friend to the law."

"Yeah, some pal," said Keats.

On their way back to the car, Keats said, "Sidarski, no wonder you're always broke. I'm sick of buying you coffee."

"Consider it an investment. Buying my way to Heaven."

"Let me know how that works out for you. Who you callin'?"

"Detective friend in Washington. Owes me a favor."

"Damn, you got friends on the force everywhere."

"Comes with being nice. You should try it some time, Keats."

"I squandered my nice genes in grade school."

A few minutes later, Sidarski arranged coverage for Mrs. Rasmussen's D.C. arrival. "Boom. Easy peasy. Looks like our tour of America continues, Keats."

During their flight, Leon avoided Bartholomew. The man frightened him, no sense in getting shish-kabobbed. Bartholomew settled into his chair, one knee majestically and arrogantly up, high ruler over the small cabin of his private jet. Leon caught him glowering at him. He'd have to remain alert, even amongst his "allies."

Bartholomew wasn't the only person Leon avoided. Not that it proved hard. Nanette ignored him. Although she closed her eyes, Leon knew she didn't sleep. Just chose not to deal with him in the easiest manner. Maybe time would dull some of her sharp edge. Even though time felt like an endangered concept in Leon's life.

Much too nervous to be of any help, Skeeter waved Leon away. Soon, though, Leon needed to sit down with him, work out the rest of their seat-of-the-pants plan.

One thing above all others stuck in Leon's mind. He couldn't get over the look in Bartholomew's eyes when he said he wanted to kill LMI's board members and affiliates. Cold and grey as the knife he was so fond of.

No doubt they all deserved death. But Leon worried about collateral damage.

Once they landed, Bartholomew set them up in a ritzy hotel, their group occupying one of the top floors. As they parted ways for the night, Leon watched Nanette enter her room. Not a single glance back his way.

Not that he expected to, but Leon couldn't sleep. A morass of thoughts and questions mucked up his mind. Finally, he tossed away common sense and aligned with his gut. His gut hadn't led him anywhere decent lately. But actions speak louder than words, so he'd been told.

He had to know. Had to explain himself to Nanette. Perhaps even beg for forgiveness.

Leon knocked lightly at first. Maintained an incessant, yet polite beat. Finally, he pounded. Another door opened behind him. One eyeball peeked out, then a small fist with a thumb up. Little help, but nice to have Gus in his corner.

The door opened, chain-lock securely in place. "Go away, Leon. It's late."

"Sorry. Um…seems like I've been saying that a lot to you lately, Nanette."

"Broken record."

Leon looked up and down the hallway, felt vulnerable, particularly emotionally. "Please let me in. Just for a little bit. I...I just want to talk."

She said nothing. But she shut the door, reopened it. *Actions speak louder than words.*

"Okay, so *now* you want to talk. After months of badgering you to open up to me." She cinched her bathrobe closed. She may've opened the door, but her body language definitely shut him out. "What? Are you afraid Bartholomew's gonna kill you? Looking to me for help?"

"No! Well, yeah...guess I am afraid of Bartholomew. Who wouldn't be?" He smiled, a wasted effort. "But that's not why I'm here."

"I'm tired. I want to go to bed. Very much alone. Make this fast." She swung her head, snapped her freshly wet hair against her back. Sat down on a chair.

Leon sat on the sofa. "I apologize. For everything. I know I haven't included you in any LMI related—"

"Anything."

"You're right. Anything. I guess...it's because I sorta got lost along the way."

"Ya think?"

"I know. Now I do. Took me a while to realize it. But running a corporation, even one like LMI...it reminded me of my past life. When I was a corporate contender, working for the big boys. It made me feel alive again. I got into it. Enjoyed calling the shots, the—"

"Fatal shots?"

"That's not fair. True, I considered doing something... permanent about Augie, but—"

"How could you, Leon? Really, just answer that. Honestly."

"I...don't know. Honestly."

"Funny word coming from you."

"I know. But...bottom line is I didn't have Augie killed. For a short time it seemed like the easiest way out of the situation. So I could move on with my plan—"

"Oh, bullshit, Leon. You've been falling back on that for too long now."

"Maybe I have. But no more. One way or another, it all ends. Tomorrow."

"You're really not telling me anything new. I've heard it all before. And it means nothing. Just words."

"But now I—"

"Was it worth it, Leon? Giving up everything for LMI?"

"What did I give up?"

"Me, for one thing, dammit! Me!" Nanette jumped up and paced in front of Leon. "And your soul. They took your soul. And you let them."

Leon stood, wanting to be seen, heard. "I don't think I ever had a soul to give! You give me too much credit! I'm just—"

She stopped in front of him. "Then what about me? How do you feel about me?"

"I love you!"

She sealed it with a slap.

He rubbed his cheek. "Are you going to start punching me again?"

"Yes!" The second slap didn't sting nearly as much, his cheek already numb. "You don't get to say you love me!"

"It's true. And you wanted an answer."

"You don't even know what love is. You just admitted you don't have a soul!" She brought her hand back again for a third slap. The corner of her mouth curled up in a sadistic grin.

Leon grabbed her wrist, held it high. "If feelings for you are what it means to have a soul, then...I guess I have one. I love you. I do."

"More words. Show, don't tell!"

He couldn't argue with that. He grabbed her shoulders. She fought, squirmed in his grasp. She loosened one hand and swung. Leon dodged left. Her fingernails scratched his cheek. "Stop it, dammit!" Frustrated, confused and completely aroused, he pulled her closer. Their lips met and he powered through a rough kiss. But not without passion. Instead of relaxing into a natural flow, she struggled. Her knee came up, hit his thigh. A close call. He yanked back. Her teeth caught his lip, drawing first blood.

With a grin, she smeared the blood from her lips with the

back of her hand. A carnivore, relishing the taste. And just like a panther, she pounced onto him. Nanette's legs wrapped around him, he stumbled back. She clawed at his chest, his face. Then kissed him. They crashed onto the sofa. He tried to roll and position her beneath him. She had a different idea. Locked in their embrace, she clenched her legs tight and pulled him to the floor. The coffee table up-ended. A magazine fluttered up.

Leon shoved the table out of the way, then returned a hand to her back, the other to her neck. Fingernails scratched his back, a freshly vibrant pain. Still on top of him, she pecked at his face with fleeting, teasing kisses. She nibbled at his lower lip. Her head rose and she laughed, a slap to his chest punctuation to every outburst. He sat up, pinned her against the sofa. Face to face, they kissed, her breath hot and stirred. Violent passion flowed into tenderness as their lips explored, became reacquainted.

He remembered how she'd felt, her smell, her taste. Truth be told, he never forgot. Like riding a bike, sometimes you never forget.

"I love you, Nanette," he said between kisses.

"Damn you. I love you, too."

During their night of love-making, Nanette had almost forgotten why they were in Washington. Not quite, but almost. Late into the night, they'd finally dozed off into each other's arms for a couple of hours.

The sunrise announced the morning. Still on the living room floor, Nanette shook Leon awake. Lightly, he snored, then snorted, something she'd see about changing in the future. If they had a future.

"What? Is it time?" Leon leaned against her, his shoulder comfortably warm.

"No. But we still have unfinished business."

"We finished several times last night."

"Cute. And shut up. What does this make us, Leon?"

"Thought we pretty much said it all last night."

"You're not getting off that easy. Where do we go from here?"

"Assuming we survive today...I'd like to explore our future

together. It's gonna be tough. I bring a lot of baggage with me."

"Yeah, you're not the only one packing heavily. Duh."

"Sometimes...sometimes I forget who we are. Maybe I'd like to start over. No more killing."

"That'd be nice. Maybe. I'll have to think about that part. But, you know...the way you treated me the last six months really sucked."

"I know. I'm sorry."

"You don't even know what you're sorry about. Like all men, you're just saying that to quickly end the uncomfortable conversation."

"I'm not all men. And that's not true."

"Just shut up and listen. You say you'd like to forget who we are. That might be all good and dandy for you. But...I never want to forget who I am."

"Doubt that's possible."

"But you were leading me that way. How you treated me."

"I never meant to—"

"It's not always about you, Leon."

"I know. But, honestly...I didn't see you giving me a lot of support over the last six months either."

"You're kidding, right? Have you already reverted back to idiotic caveman Leon? First of all, you didn't *let* me support you. You pushed me away. Dick. More importantly, though, you think I'm just a female crutch used to support the big he-man in her life? That I exist as nothing but your accessory?"

"Course not." Leon yawned, hardly the reaction she wanted. Had her hand not been so sore, she would've slapped him again. But that might've led to more hate/love sex. Her hand wasn't the only part of her body that suffered battle wounds.

"But I responded to your actions, reverted back to a helpless baby bird. Just waiting to be noticed. Pining away like a stupid little girl hopelessly in love."

"I can't control how you respond. Again, I'm sorry, but it wasn't my intention to—"

Whack.

"Ow." Too tired to argue, Leon accepted his punishment and settled back against the couch.

"Never, ever, *ever* use the 'control' word on me again, Leon."

"Agreed."

"And, again, it's not all about you. I'm not your support group. We're equals. I expect to be treated as such, no matter my gender or how we act in the bedroom."

He smiled. "Okay."

"And *honesty*. In every way. If we're truly going to make this work, it has to be the only way."

"I'll try. Really, I will. But, you know it'll be tough."

"I know. It is for me, too."

Through the curtain, they watched Washington wake up. The sun rose, cars plugged the streets, horns blasted annoyance. A new day awakened old fears.

"Nanette, I'd like you to come with me. To talk to Skeeter about what I want to do. Open book policy."

"Let's turn the page together."

"Okay…Bartholomew worries me. What he's planning."

"Me, too," she said thoughtfully. "That's why we have to present him with a viable alternate plan. What you have going with Skeeter…will it work?"

"I honestly don't know."

"Guess we'll find out."

We. It sounded so different, an alien word rolling off her tongue.

"Nanette…I really do want to quit killing after this. After what we have to do this afternoon. I'm serious about that. Ever since…I dunno, Cody killed my dad, I just haven't had the lust for it."

"Maybe that's because you've found somewhere else to focus that lust."

"Maybe so."

"We'll see what happens."

Tenderly, he kissed her. She didn't even care about her morning breath. Neither did he. "I really do love you, you know."

"I know. Me, too. Now, let's shower. We have an evil corporation of serial killers to topple."

Cody felt awesome. Good night's sleep, kick-ass day ahead. He couldn't wait to put some caps in LMI's collective ass. And no one even noticed his snagging the semi-automatic from Shoe-Box's gun collection on the plane. Guy had enough guns, wouldn't notice one missing.

He slipped on his hoodie and it smelled like ass. Kinda ripe. What the hell, he wouldn't go into combat without his good luck hoodie. It'd kept him alive all these years. Everyone would just have to deal.

Right now, he felt like he could eat his weight in food. With breakfast on his mind, he left the room.

Down the hall, the door to Nanette's room opened. Hand-in-hand, the old man and Nanette strolled out.

"Whoa! 'Bout damn time, yo!"

Leon's face flushed. They broke contact, tried to play it cool. Cody figured he'd have some fun with it. Give back a little to the old man.

"Morning, Cody." Nanette grinned, the look of someone who'd been bumpin' bits all night long. Totally unlike Leon, who looked like he was sitting on a stick.

"Up high, Leon!" Cody held out a fist. Leon left him hanging.

"Ah, Cody, I'd appreciate your discretion about this."

"Who me? Discreet's my middle name. Quit worryin', old man! Just happy like a pig in slop you finally got it on."

"You're not living up to your middle name very well."

"Chill, chill. It's all cool. I knew you guys would do it. The Codester helped you along. S'what I do. Helpin' out. An angel from Heaven or somethin'."

"Um, no."

"Hey, wanna get some chow?"

"We would, but we have to meet with Skeeter." Nanette gave him one of those sad, pacifying smiles. Never liked those.

"Business shit?" It kinda pissed Cody off they didn't tell him about the meet and greet. After all, the second big cheese gig at LMI didn't come easily.

"Yes, business," said Leon.

Nanette nudged Leon, gave him a stern look. He sighed, said, "Cody, you want to come along? You're part of the plan, too."

Nanette added, "Part of the family. Dysfunctional as all get out."

"Hey, I don't know 'bout no dysfunction, but hellz yeah, I'm there!"

Cody'd never been part of a family. Not really. Never thought he would, chalked family up to greeting card junk. But today just kept getting better.

They played "knock-knock" at Skeeter's door for at least five minutes. Skeeter kept asking "who's there," Leon kept answering. Finally Skeeter freed the locks and opened up. Seriously not cut out for this kind of business.

Twitchier than a tweeker, Skeeter eyeballed Cody.

"Um, dude, what's he doing here?"

"Important part of the team, beeyotch. Why are you here?"

"Boys, go back to your corners. We're all on the same side," said Nanette.

In front of the balcony windows, they sat at a table.

Always straight-up business, Leon said, "Skeeter, how'd you do with getting everything together?"

Skeeter took a pile of papers off a printer, stacked them, fingered through them, stacked them again. "Dude! I was up all night working on it. But...it's pretty thorough. Everyone's accounted for."

"And you have the electronic documents set to go out when I asked?"

"Scheduled a mass cyber e-bomb. Boom!" Skeeter floated his hands up. "Course they won't know who sent 'em."

"Everything's been redacted properly?"

"No need to. None of us was mentioned. Not once."

"Not even me?" asked Leon.

"Sorry, dude, but...I really don't think they cared that much about you."

Nanette smirked, nodded her head. Freaky as she was on their play date, Cody still dug her. Maybe she's who Leon needs to get his head out of his ass.

"What about the bank accounts?"

"Set to go elsewhere at the designated time."

"Offshore, too?"

"Dude, I'm thorough."

"Course you are, Skeeter. Meant no disrespect."

Huh. He gets Leon's respect.

Cody let it go. Too good a mood to be spoiled.

But this wasn't Cody's thang. No action, all boring cyber talk. Bla, bla, bla. His stomach growled. "Can I order some room service, already? Gotta get my protein and carbs in." His flexed muscle went unnoticed, everyone too wrapped up in the pencil-necked geek.

"Fine, Cody. Order up something for everyone," said Leon.

"Of course I assume you took your share, Skeeter."

"Oh yeah, just waitin' for me. But..." Skeeter lost the luster of cyber-king. Looked like he was ready to cry. "...what if I'm not alive to spend it? What's the point?"

Wimp.

"I understand," said Leon. "Our, ah, meeting could be very dangerous."

"Dude! Don't tell me! I don't wanna know! Really, I don't! As a matter of fact—and don't hate on me for this—but I was kinda hopin' to bow out today."

Leon looked at Nanette. Then Cody. Cody shrugged. Frankly, firing Skeeter's ass sounded cool to Cody. "Yo, afraid of a little killin', Skeeter?"

"No, no, no...yes! Dude, don't even tell me about it!" When he shut his eyes and clapped his hands over his ears, he looked like one of those monkeys who didn't want to hear anything bad. "After that shoot-out at the Rasmussen ranch...I can't go through that again, Leon. *Please.* No more!"

"But you ain't even passed our initiation yet," said Cody.

"Initiation? What...initiation?"

"You gotta pop someone's ass, Skeeter. Bang!" Cody pulled a mock gun trigger. Skeeter jumped.

"Noooo... Leon, dude, tell me that's not true."

"Enough, Cody. No, Skeeter, it's not true. Cody's just got a...sick sense of humor. To tell you the truth, I've kind of been expecting this. And it's fine. You've done me a great favor. Good work. Couldn't have done it without you."

"Omaha Steaks?"

"I'll throw in baked potatoes."

Skeeter grinned, practically salivating. *Amateur.* "Cool, cool, cool. Just...don't thank me yet, Leon. It's not over."

"No one knows that better than I do." Leon stood, stuck his hand out. "But thank you for everything. No matter how it turns out. Just promise me...you'll go far. I mean, both distance wise and with your future."

"Already on it, dude. Ticket bought for the Cayman Islands."

"And you have enough cash?"

"Dude! The world's my bank."

After the mutual appreciation society wrapped up their love fest, Leon said, "Oh, before you go, Skeeter, one last favor?"

"Um, how dangerous is it?"

"Not dangerous. Can you get me a Miami Florida police detective's cell phone number? Name's Ramona Keaton."

"Easy as pie."

Cody never understood how easy pie was exactly, but Leon's request seemed bat-shit crazy. "The hell, Leon? That Florida cop who about nailed you? Why you wanna go callin' her? You gonna send her Omaha Steaks, too?"

"Just the last part of the plan, Cody. And I'm going to make good on an old debt."

"Well, isn't that interesting?" asked Keats as they walked out of the Washburn Hotel's lobby.

"Very. Sure would like to see who's on Mrs. Rasmussen's guest list," said Sidarski.

Keats felt alive despite the lack of sleep she'd had over the past forty-eight hours. On the hunt. Adrenaline energized her stronger than a double dose of fear. On the other hand, Sidarski looked like death warmed over. Pretty much smelled that way, too.

"We got time to kill, Sidarski. You wanna check into a hotel, get a couple hours of shut-eye? Maybe a shower?"

Sidarski laughed. "Yeah, I don't think I can afford the Washburn. Crime pays. Crime-fighting doesn't."

"Ain't that the truth." Keats looked up at the tall luxury hotel Mrs. Rasmussen had checked into. Easily overtowering most of the other buildings lining Embassy Row, the hotel stood out like a giant tombstone, memorializing the rich and idle. She imagined one of the smaller rooms cost more than a month of her paycheck.

"Couldn't sleep anyway," said Sidarski, "now that we're closing in on Garber. My spidey-senses are tinglin'."

Keats still thought Sidarski was leaping before looking, but the big cop had good instincts. He didn't make it that far on the force without having the right stuff. Still, he looked tired, ruddy-faced. Unhealthy. A heart attack stuffed into a cheap suit. But, if he was anything like her, she knew he wouldn't let it go.

"I hear ya," said Keats.

"Course you do. You're sitting right next to me." Sidarski started the rental car, drove across the street and edged into a parallel spot. "And now we wait."

"Again. So...the clerk fessed up to Mrs. Rasmussen renting out the second floor ballroom at 4:00. Your wallet feeling a little lighter yet?"

"Nothing's free. Especially since I'm no longer a working cop. And you're wildly outta your jurisdiction."

"Doesn't matter. I'm gettin' Garber."

"Race you there."

Just the walk to the car had winded Sidarski. Mouth-breathing as if his nose had stopped up, he cranked the air on. Sweat poured down his face.

"Don't think you're in any condition to run a foot-race."

"Probably not. But nailing Garber's gonna go a long way in curing my heart-burn."

"The doctor has spoken. Whydaya suppose Rasmussen's rented the ballroom?"

"No clue. But I'd sure like to find out. And I can't wait to see who arrives for the big to-do. Got my eyes peeled for two particular guests."

Keats' cell-phone buzzed. Odd. Practically no one called her but work and they knew not to call her on vacation. Blocked caller's ID. She expected no less.

"Keats."

"Good morning, Detective."

The caller's voice sent an electric charge through her body.

Immediately, she turned off the radio, pointed at the phone. Sidarski mouthed, "What?" She waved him down, focused on the call. No way she'd let him go now.

"Mr. Garber. Long time, no hear."

Sidarski sputtered on his coffee, spilled it in his lap. Smoke rose, but he ignored the burn. He leaned closer, listened.

"I told you you'd hear from me again, Detective. I keep my word. How's your gun wound healing?"

"Not bad. But I still have a major pain-in-the-ass. I'm talkin' to him now." Ordinarily, talk like this might alienate someone. Not Garber. Sometimes Keats thought he enjoyed baiting her. Besides, he called her. Clearly he wanted something.

"Ouch. Maybe you can get a doctor to prescribe something for you. But since you sound combative, I'll take it you made a full recovery."

"Where are you, Garber?"

"Here, there. I get around. But enough about me. I've just sent you a large, encrypted file." As if to corroborate Garber's promise, her phone dinged.

Caller unknown. *A gift from your old ally*, it read. Smiley face emoticon. *Cute.* A paperclip symbol was attached.

"Just got it. What's in the file?"

"Now that would be telling. Have patience, though. At 4:30 this afternoon, Eastern time, the file will become unencrypted. That's Miami time."

Interesting. Garber still thinks I'm in Miami.

Next to her, Sidarski grew agitated and shifted in his seat. It absolutely killed him not to be in on the action. She hoped it wouldn't become a literal prophecy.

"This is all really exciting, Garber, but...why should a file bring sunshine into my life? I'd much rather, oh, I dunno, meet with you over coffee, talk about old times...maybe arrest you."

"That sounds like a nice offer, but I'll have to pass. The last time we talked, do you remember that? Maybe you were too out of it, but—"

"Oh, I remember it all right. Your little hospital bed visit."

"Hey, I didn't get a chance to thank you for bringing my money to the boy and his mother."

"I live to serve. Back to the file."

"I promised you a big bust, one that'd really put some medals in your drawer. It's time to follow-up on that promise. Call in the Feds, Detective, before you read the file. Set them up to raid the Washburn Hotel in Washington D.C. Second floor ballroom, 4:45 this afternoon. You'll find the largest collection of killers, extortionists, corporate thieves, white collar criminals—"

"And I'm just supposed to take your word on this? From a known killer?"

"I'm not really a *known* killer. But, unfortunately, this is the way our arrangement has to be. For now. Just trust me."

"Trust? You gotta be kiddin' me. Why would I ever trust you?"

A pause. Apparently Garber didn't have a good answer. "In this world...sometimes that's all we have, I suppose."

"You live in a world of fairy princesses and unicorns?"

"No, they give me cooties. But it's a lovely sentiment. Regardless, if you follow my instructions, this will be well worth your time. Frankly, it'd be worth the world's time to have these people behind bars."

"How 'bout we talk this over some more? Set up a private meet? Make sure it's as sweet as you say it is."

Garber sighed. "I'm not part of the package deal. But, as I promised last time, Leon Garber will cease to exist after today. For good."

"Ah, this cryptic bullshit again. How's this supposed to earn my trust?"

"I didn't lie to you six months ago. Not about my money. Or my intentions."

"What *are* your intentions?"

"Like so many of us, Detective, I'm an explorer...still trying to discover who I am."

"Bla, bla, bla. Let me help you figure that out."

"No. I'll call my therapist. Now, are you going to do as I recommend? I thought I'd give you first dibs. I mean, if not...I'll call some Fed to follow-up."

Another long silence, Garber dangling the carrot in front of her. And damn if she didn't want to snap at it. On the other hand, if this ended up hinky, she could lose her badge. But Grandma always said, *seize the day.* "This sounds sketchy, Garber. I'd be going out on a limb here. Big time."

"I realize that. But ask yourself…what would I have to gain from setting you up? Why would I even call you?"

"To get me off your case."

"I suppose there is that. But I know you and Detective Sidarski aren't going to give—"

"How you know about Sidarski?"

"Hm?"

"How'd you know I'm working with Sidarski?"

She swore she heard him swallow. He screwed up. Somewhere he'd seen them. Sidarski hit it bang-on. They're close. "Let's just say I have my sources."

"Yeah, right. Garber, I don't trust you. But last time I went out on a limb for you, no one got hurt falling off it. Still, you have a nasty habit of leaving bodies behind."

"None of them my doing."

"So you say."

"Again, Detective…*trust.*"

"Because you're so damn honest."

"Thank you."

"If I call in the Feds…there gonna be another blood bath?"

Another silence bugged Keats. Silence trumps truth in all cases. "Not if I can help it."

"The hell's that supposed to mean? Either this'll go down nice and easy or you tell me the goddamn truth, Garber! Is anyone's life at risk? I need to know!"

"No." Short, snippy, falsely confident. Absolutely lying.

"Anyone dies outta this, I'll personally inject you on death row."

"That's why I called you, Detective. I expect nothing but your best. Same with Detective Sidarski. If you leave now, you just might make it to D.C. in time to lead the brigade. Smile pretty for the cameras."

"I just might be closer than you think." *Boom! Microphone drop!* Keats smiled, basked in her moment.

A shuffling sound, a few thumps. Heavy breathing. When

Garber spoke again, his words flew urgently. "Listen to me, Detective, it's crucial you and the Feds arrive at 4:45. Not a minute earlier. Or later. Timing's everything. For my plan to work accordingly, you have to—"

"Don't tell me how to do my job. In case you forgot, you're a wanted murderer. The hell you think this is? *Let's Make a Deal?*"

"I just... I'd like to avoid any bloodshed at any cost. That's why it has to be 4:45. Please, *listen* to me. I—"

Keats slapped the phone off. "Yeah! That's what I'm talkin' bout!"

Horrified, Sidarski's mouth hung open. "You hung up on him? The hell, Keats? We needed to hear everything he had to say! Dammit!"

"Ah, chill. Garber wants to say anything else, he knows my number. This is all very...interesting."

"Yeah, interesting." Sidarski rolled his window down, stuck his head out the window and panted like a dog. "Dammit." He shook a couple tablets loose from a well-used stomach acid relief bottle. Chomped down and grimaced at the taste. "I heard most of that. Garber wants us to bust up Mrs. Rasmussen's little tea party? Why?"

"Didn't say. Just said the file he sent me would explain it all. A file we can't read until 4:30. Fifteen minutes before the big bust."

"I don't get it. All this mystery crap. Love the films, hate mystery in real life. You think Garber's on the level?"

Keats kicked her feet up on the dash and thought about it. "He's up to somethin'. As always, he's not tellin' the whole story."

"That's a given."

"It's time to roll the dice, Sidarski, shoot some craps. Money down. Whaddaya wanna do?"

"What if he's telling us the truth? What if we can take down someone—something—bigger than Garber and his playmate Spangler? Decisions, decisions..."

"Oh hell, you goin' soft on me? Guy's a sociopathic liar! You buyin' into his bullshit?"

"I dunno. Unless he's setting these other party members

up…and that seems far-fetched. But as he said, what would he gain from it?"

"I can't believe this," Keats huffed. "If he's lyin', we're gonna have hell to pay. Lose my badge, maybe worse. Besides what would we tell the Feds? There's no proof."

"I get that. And fifteen minutes between reading the mystery file and having the Feds come crashing in doesn't give us a lotta' time. So…" Sidarski scratched his thin mustache which made Keats itchy all over. "So, we don't call the Feds. We finish it alone. And I don't care about being a hero, Keats. You can take all the credit."

Now that really pissed her off. "What? You think that's why I'm all up in this? For the mornin' glory? Same as you, I gotta pending date with our boy, Garber!"

Sidarski's head retracted, hands went up. "Sorry, sorry. No offense meant. I'm glad we're on the same team, that's all."

"Yeah, Wonder Twin powers unite."

"What, you don't like movies, but watch crappy cartoons?"

"Stick on topic, Sidarski. So…we're agreed. No Feds. Could get dangerous."

"The way it always is with Garber."

Keats grinned, excited again. "No doubt. And we're probably in over our heads."

"Go down with glory or go home." Sidarski held his hand high. Keats smacked it.

"And I'll bet you a year's worth of donuts, Garber's on Mrs. Rasmussen's guest list. Or maybe he'll crash the party. His plan sounds pretty precise. He's still all about self-preservation. Could be we can have the cake and eat it, too."

"Yep, what I was thinkin'. You ready to party?"

Stoked, Keats offered Sidarski another high-five and united their Wonder Twin powers.

"Well…that could've gone better." Leon stared at his phone, wondering if he'd just made a huge mistake. He'd certainly been making a lot of bone-headed moves lately.

"You think she'll go along with it?" Nanette placed a steady hand on his arm. A nice feeling, his anchor. Pity he hadn't taken her into his confidence earlier.

"No clue. But I think Keats and Sidarski are already here. In D.C."

"What? How? We didn't even find out about the LMI meeting until late yesterday."

"They're both smart cops." Leon'd been kidding himself. He thought he stood a chance of succeeding while he and his friends skated away scot-free. But delusion is an insidious disease. "Nanette, you don't have to do this. We could get arrested. Or maybe..."

For a second, Leon thought she might slap him again. But her eyes softened. "I know the risks I'm taking, Leon. I'm all in."

"I appreciate it, Nanette."

"Don't go getting all sentimental on me now. We've got work to do."

Already late due to preparations, Leon knocked on Bartholomew's door. Tommy, dressed in a red button-down shirt, blue tie and collarless white jacket, opened the door. Caterer's clothing. He ushered them inside.

Again, Bartholomew had set up digs in the hotel's nicest suite. In front of open French doors, he sat at a lavishly decorated table. He held up an impaled sausage on a fork by way of greeting. A slow grin grew as he took his time finishing his breakfast. Best sausage in town, obviously. Finally, he said, "Good morning. You look...not so well rested. Please join me." Carefully, he brought his shoe-box closer to him as if wary of thieves. "Have you had breakfast?"

"Yes, thanks." They sat down next to him.

"So. Big day. I understand you've been busy this morning, Leon..." Leon thought it a good sign—a sign he might be off Bartholomew's killing list—he'd been promoted to Leon instead of "Mr. Garber." Until Bartholomew finished his line of inquiry. "...so tell me, who exactly have you been phoning this morning?"

How in the hell did he know that?

Leon knew Bartholomew couldn't have bugged his cell phone; it hadn't left his person. Could've cloned it, though. Then he remembered who'd set the hotel rooms up in the first place. Better to be honest than face Bartholomew's wrath again.

"I called a detective I knew from the past. Part of my plan."

Bartholomew arched an eyebrow. "Detective Keats? Your, ah, 'friend' from last year?" A fishing expedition, his way of testing Leon.

"That's right."

"Do you think that's wise?" He dabbed a cloth napkin over his lips. "I have absolutely no intention of going to prison."

"Neither do I."

"Then why involve the police?" Bartholomew picked up a serrated knife, grinned at this reflection in the blade. Self-consciously, Leon moved a little farther away.

"I know I'm taking a chance here, but—"

"That involves me." The knife twisted in his hand, back and forth, floating like a magician's wand. Leon didn't want to see it disappear inside his throat.

"You don't have to go, Bartholomew. I have this under control."

"Oh, really?" He placed the knife down. Leon breathed a little easier. "Control like you've had over everything else?"

Nanette interjected. "Bartholomew, Leon's made some mistakes, sure, but his plan—"

"Oh, plan, plan, *plan!*" He flicked the knife up again, struck it down into the table. The handle wobbled like a punching bag. "That's all I've heard is the word 'plan!' Now's the time to explain this glorious plan of yours."

During Leon's detailed break-down, Bartholomew dug into a covered container on a portable heater. At times the French Toast captured his attention more than Leon, clear skepticism and wry amusement his only response.

"I see. And, tell me, do you honestly believe this will work?"

Fifty-fifty. "Absolutely."

"Mm-hm. What do you think, Tommy? Does this sound like a solid plan to you?"

Tommy rushed toward the table, looking every bit the over-zealous waiter. "Not for me to say, boss."

"Tommy's a well-mannered sort, not the type to scoff at ill-fated and half-cocked ideas. I so value his judgment...when he speaks it." Bartholomew narrowed his eyes. Leon imagined

Tommy would have to stay after class and Leon didn't envy him one iota. "Leon, have you given any thought as to how you're going to keep this room full of merciless bastards sitting still for your grand unveiling? Honestly, I'd thought better of your skill-set. You do realize every LMI delegate will have armed bodyguards." Not a question; a fact delivered from the mountain on high.

"Of course. I assume you brought a suitcase full of weapons." Leon jagged a thumb back at the over-stuffed suitcase by the closet. "Never leave home without 'em."

Bartholomew didn't share Leon's half-hearted grin. "Always best to be prepared."

"I agree."

"And how will you mount this full-frontal attack?"

Leon hadn't worried that part through yet. Perhaps naively, he thought he'd rely on the LMI board members' not wanting to personally dirty their hands. Stupidly, he realized once you corner a dog—no matter how well-mannered—it's going to bite back. "The old shock and awe routine. Worked out well for us in the past, not to mention a couple presidents."

The Man with the Shoe-Box snorted. "That's the kind of blind arrogance that can get everyone killed. Pathetic, really."

Worse than being in the Principal's office, Leon may as well have been spanked. A loud banging at the door set his heart thundering.

"Ah. There's the answer to your problem, Leon." Bartholomew nodded toward Tommy. "Tommy, please show our guests in."

Cody bounded in first, wearing the same catering suit Tommy had on. He'd also shaved, snipped his hair short. He spun around, stopped on an unsteady foot and waved his arms, "ta-da" style. "Not bad, right? Gots me a future in the food and service industry."

Truthfully, he did look very different. But not nearly as unrecognizable as the young woman who followed him in. Exasperated, Leon wondered where Cody'd picked her up. With hunched over shoulders, an embarrassed, melt-into-the-room gait, she shuffled toward them. Her jacket, tie and blouse matched the men's, but she wore a black apron tied over checkered slacks. Not until she leaned up against the wall and kicked a leg up on a chair, did Leon recognize her.

"Delilah?"

"Not a word! Not a damn word!" Without her trademark powder-white make-up, she appeared as any other young, pretty woman. A touch of pink highlighted her cheeks, giving her an uncustomary Midwest girl-next-door glow.

Nanette threw a hand over her mouth, but her eyes gave away her smile.

Not to be outdone, Gustav paraded in behind them, dressed to the nines in a tuxedo. "While the lovely Delilah thinks otherwise, I believe she looks to be absolutely beautiful! The apple of my eye! A vision of—"

"Stop it, Gus," she snapped.

Wisely, he did, and assumed a position of folded arms solidarity next to her.

"There's your means of entry, Leon," said Bartholomew. "After all, I've had the owner of the catering service in my pocket for some time now. I've assured him a very solid financial future." He leaned back, sighed. "Of course, he has no idea what I've planned."

"Yeah, about that. What exactly are you—"

"Enough about me, Leon. If you remember, you're trying to win me over. In trust and your..." He sniffed, haughtier than a zealot. "...*plan*. What else can you tell me?"

"With your weapons and our team on the inside, I can make them listen. And if that fails...did you get what I asked for last night?"

"Of course. Tommy." Bartholomew snapped his fingers. Faster than Leon could track, Tommy plopped a briefcase down in front of Leon.

Leon opened it. Two dozen hypodermic needles of Azaperone, ready for use, gleamed under a beam of sunlight. Nothing ever looked more beautiful to Leon. Home again. Could be a problem injecting a roomful of people under fire, though.

"Good. Okay, clearly the board members all know me, so

I can't just walk in as a waiter. The others may pass, but..."
He glanced at Gustav. "...no offense, Gustav, but you'd be a
giveaway."

"Yes, I suppose I am rather renowned in certain social
circles." Gus took a bow. "But I am here to be of service,
naturally."

"I've devised another way for Gustav to gain entry," said
Bartholomew.

"Splendid!" Gus nestled in front of Delilah. She wrapped
her hands around his neck and swayed him like a child.

"Now, Leon, I'm going in with you," said Bartholomew.

"Not that I wouldn't welcome your help, but I don't think
it's necessary—"

"You're hardly in a position to deem what you 'think' is
necessary. I'm going in."

"Why?"

"You have no right to ask me that. But...since I'm in a
particularly giving mood today, I'll answer. I want my betrayers
to know who destroyed them. They chose the wrong person to
anger. They need to be made aware of it. Before the end."

Leon didn't care for the way Bartholomew emphasized "the
end." Something was definitely cooking in Bartholomew's pot
and Leon didn't want to end up in the mix. "Fair's fair. I showed
you mine, now how about telling us your plan?"

Bartholomew's hand shot up. "We're still talking about you,
Leon. So impatient. Is this the sum of your plan? Tell me...what
part will Mr. Skeeter play in it?"

Uh-oh. "Um...Skeeter won't be...ah..." Leon looked to
Nanette for support. Bartholomew seemed to have a soft spot
for her. Or at least a less thorny one.

She stepped up. "Skeeter's not one for violence. You know
that. Frankly, he'd be a liability."

"So you sent him home. And without my blessing, I might
add," said Bartholomew.

"Yes. But who made you our priest, Bartholomew?" asked
Nanette. "We don't need your blessing."

"Ah, but you do, my dear. I'm financing this little jaunt.
And I'm risking my life on Leon's misguided attempt. Like it or

not, I'm the leader of our adventure. I should've been consulted regarding your dismissal of Mr. Skeeter. Not that I necessarily disagree with your reasoning, but I wasn't finished with his talents yet."

"Apparently you already knew about Skeeter," said Nanette. "So, why the games? We're supposed to be allies."

"Oh, I know everything that transpired last night." He smiled warmly at Nanette, not so much at Leon. Half a blessing. "And I must say it was an interesting night all around. Gustav and Delilah would've given our new love-birds a run for their money based on the sound of events."

"*What?*" Anger uncovered the hidden Delilah. "*Very* uncool."

Never phased, Gus piped in. "Friend Bartholomew! How simply decadent! Did you happen to take corresponding video? We would love a copy for our own collection!"

Hard to believe, but Bartholomew appeared suddenly uncomfortable. He averted his eyes. "Afraid not. Only audio. And Mr. Spangler, Heaven only knows what you were up to in your room last night. I believe I'd rather not know."

"What? Wait...*what?*" Cody barreled forward, fists curled. Leon hoped he wouldn't have to pull him off Bartholomew. It'd be a dead-heat for the knife. "You recorded us? That's just wack! Get your rocks off that way or what?"

"Oh settle down, Mr. Spangler. You're so tiresome. I can assure you the recordings weren't made out of malice or with blackmail in mind. I just like to know who I can trust. And who I can't." The last sentence he aimed at Leon.

"That's just fine and dandy, Bartholomew," said Leon. "But we're supposed to be a team. We don't know what you have planned."

"Because I'm not sure what I'm going to do yet. Are you done detailing your rather haphazard plan yet?" He looked at his watch. "I'm afraid it's getting late in the day."

With their lives at risk, Leon hardly thought their situation merited Bartholomew's cavalier attitude. "We'll need a lot of luck on our side, of course. But I think we can do this, Bartholomew. I truly do. A sound and safe way to ensure the end of LMI. We also have the added strength of Goro to—"

Bartholomew sucked in air through clenched teeth. "No, I'm afraid not."

"What?"

"Goro and Mr. Takihiro are no longer a part of the team."

"What'd you do? The *truth*." Leon didn't have to ask the question, not really. Cold sweat beaded across his forehead. His stomach roiled. LMI's reach tainted all involved.

"I can safely say Mr. Takihiro and Goro no longer represent a threat to us."

"A threat? Takihiro was prepared to help us!"

"Oh, wake up. Do you really think the LMI board members would welcome Takihiro back into the fold? After attempting to kill him? Takihiro would've jeopardized our entire operation."

"I'm afraid he might be right, friend Leon," said Gus, sad puppy eyes big and round.

"That doesn't matter! Bartholomew, you expected me to tell you about Skeeter. I expect the same from you! You made a decision that—"

"That possibly saved all of our lives. Sexual gymnastics weren't the only thing I overheard last night. Takihiro and Goro were planning on fleeing. They sought asylum with the Japanese consulate, turning evidence against us for safe sanctum. All of it spoken in Japanese, of course. Now, my Japanese is a little rusty these days, but I knew enough to understand the gist of things."

Leon bolted up from the table. "That's not the point! You chose to get rid of Takihiro and Goro without—"

"Leon, sit down." Nanette grabbed his arm. "Bartholomew may be right. If Takihiro was turning on us…we'd never get a chance to bring LMI down."

Common sense sided with Nanette, but not Leon's gut. It felt like a stab of betrayal.

"Yo, old man, listen to your woman. Ain't no way 'round it." The voice of reason from Cody. Clearly, they outnumbered Leon.

Leon sat down, regained his composure. Tried to, at least. His voice tremulous, he said, "What'd you do to them,

Bartholomew? We have a right to know."

"Again with your rights. This isn't a democracy. I made an executive decision, that's all."

Spoken like a true corporate man. Perhaps Bartholomew had set his sights on leadership of LMI, the new regime. "Fine. But once this is done, *we're* also done. No more. I want no more part of you, of *this*. Of...any of it."

"Dear me. Here I thought this was the start of a beautiful relationship. Alas, I have so few friends any more. Living ones, that is." Bartholomew smiled as he tapped his shoe-box. "Be that as it may, Mr. Takihiro and his manservant didn't suffer. I'm not inhuman, after all."

Beg to differ.

"As a matter of fact, if it helps put your mind at ease, we did Goro a favor. He was near death's door anyway. And he's certainly no stranger to riding in car trunks. Isn't that right, Tommy?" Bartholomew giggled, a *tk-tk-tk* insectoid sound. "I apologize, my friends. A rare moment of uninhibited mirth. It won't happen again." Clearly humiliated, he dropped a shroud of seriousness over his joviality. "I just don't know what's come over me today."

"Good one, boss," Tommy tossed off.

"Back to business. Let's finalize, synchronize our watches as they do in the movies. Prepare for the final showdown. We have little time left."

Things felt far from final, though. Bartholomew acted cagey, purposefully so. When it came right down to it, Leon didn't want him at his back. "Bartholomew, we're going to try this my way."

Bartholomew hesitated, mentally rolling his dice. "We'll see how things proceed. But if they go south...my back-up plan is in place."

"Once and for all, Bartholomew, *what* are you planning? You're not the only one putting their neck on the line today," said Leon.

"Yes, of course you're right." Bartholomew sat up on the edge of his seat, lowered his voice like a child with a secret. "I'm going to blow up the second floor of the Washburn Hotel."

Even if he wanted to, Leon couldn't say anything.

Jesus Christ!

Cody knew a little something somethin' about bat-shit crazy. It followed him around like a love-starved puppy. But damn if the Man in the Shoe-box hadn't climbed 'round the bend. Planned on blasting the second floor of a hotel. Cody didn't know much about architecture, didn't really care too much about the people on the upper floors of the building, but some of them might be travelling with pets. Definitely not cool.

Leon fled the room, whiter than a Klans-man. Guy had the weakest stomach out of anyone Cody knew. Really didn't understand how he made it in their business this long. His woman, Nanette, chased after him. Not much she could do, really. If a guy's hurling, whaddaya gonna do? Hold his hand?

Gus and Delilah gathered around Shoe-box, asked about their roles. Excited, even.

One of these days, Cody thought he might look into some, you know, normal pals.

Out in the hallway, Leon stood against the wall. Nanette cooed sweet somethings into his ear. Pacified him like a mother. Not that Cody knew anything about the warm caress of a mother.

"Yo, Leon, we can't let that guy blow—"

Leon straightened, held a finger to his lips. Always the parent. Motioned for Cody to follow the couple into the stairwell at the end of the hall.

Cody looked up, down, saw they were alone. "He's gonna kill everyone in that damn hotel, yo! Be like 9/11 all over again!"

"Keep your voice down. Bartholomew's got ears everywhere."

"But his brain's missin'! We can't let him do this."

"I'm going to make sure it doesn't happen. By whatever means necessary."

The old man Cody knew came roaring back: Leon the lion. Color filled his cheeks, fireworks ignited his eyes. Taking charge and kinda crazy doing it. But, damn, if Cody wouldn't follow this Leon to the end. "You say the word, Leon. And..." *Thwack!*

Cody's fist smacked into his palm with the sound of a bear trap closing. "...I'll take the crazy bastard out."

Leon clapped a hand on Cody's shoulder, the way a good leader might. "Cody, I appreciate that. Let's hope it doesn't come to it. But if it does..." He didn't issue the order. Just nodded. Still kinda lacking a back-bone where it counted. But his intent rang out loud and clear.

Cody reached around to his back and touched the nice killing metal tucked securely away.

At first, Nanette hated the results. A blonde woman—as light-haired as blondes are supposed to be light-headed—stared back at her in the mirror. She frowned at her reflection. Then decided she could make it work.

As she walked out of the hotel bathroom, Leon's jaw practically unhinged. "Wow. You look...different."

She smiled, fluffed her still wet hair. "Different good? Or different bad?"

"You could never look bad." He walked toward her, arms open.

She pushed him away. "No time for that, tiger. And if you're getting any notions about sleeping with a blonde, don't get too attached." Shamelessly, she leaned in with puckered, Betty Boop lips. When he responded, she twirled away. Funny how she'd regained her flirting powers, their loss only temporary.

"Pity," said Leon. "It'd be like having two girl-friends."

"Ew-wooo, I'm your girlfriend. Woo-woo-oooooh." She paraded around the room, twirling a hand like a band-leader, singing her silly taunts. Anything to avoid thinking about what they were walking into. Completely ridiculous.

Just like the entire notion of entering into a relationship. Maybe that's why she jumped in. She knew a built-in safety net lay beneath her. Too bad it was only six feet under her.

"Yeah, when you put it that way, it does sound kinda juvenile, doesn't it?" Leon grinned. A nice counter-point to his grim demeanor of late. But like her, he hid behind mindless flirtation. Particularly with the revelation of Bartholomew's crazed plan.

"Nothing juvenile about me, Leon. I'm all woman."

"Truer words..."

Flirting, for God's sake, on the brink of disaster.

"Nanette, not even your mother would recognize you now."

"Doubt she ever recognized me." At the mention of her mother, her flirtatious manner dried up and crumbled away. It reminded her how much she and Leon didn't know about one another.

Absolutely crazy she thought they could make a go of it. But then again...isn't love supposed to be uninhibited? Crazy in a good way?

She shook her head. Dropped her emotional anchor down deep. No time for such foolishness.

"You okay?" asked Leon. This time she welcomed his embrace.

"Yeah. Just thinking. About what we have to do. About the possible outcome."

"Me too."

"Even Cody seems scared," said Nanette.

"Yeah. Nothing scares him. If he's scared..."

"Right."

"You, um...are you worried about Cody, Nanette?"

"Of course I am! Wait...wait..." She backed up, thumped a finger onto Leon's chest. "Don't tell me you're jealous of Cody." Flattered as she was, she couldn't believe it. It made everything seem silly again. Like love. And there it came again—the "L" word—round and round and...

Head straight, eyes on the prize!

But she couldn't disregard Leon's adorable behavior. He stammered. His cheeks flowered red. Absolutely endearing. "Maybe a little bit. You don't...um, still like him, do you?"

"Oh my God! You *are* jealous! Leon...don't be ridiculous. I never had a thing for Cody. Sure I like him...yeah, he's kinda hot." Leon winced. "But he's just a kid. He's not you."

She said it. Realized the truth to it. She needed to work on letting her emotions reign more often instead of calculating everything before she said or did it. *Different!*

"And only you're you, Nanette." He kissed her. Nice, warm, soft. Tender.

She broke it off. "I can't be distracted now, Leon. We have to get ready. We'll have plenty of time to pick this up after today."

Slowly, he nodded. With eyes large and slightly moist, he solemnly said, "You're right. We will."

But she could tell neither one of them believed it.

Chapter Twelve

Good Christ, Sidarski's stomach burned. He tapped out two more antacid tablets and swallowed them whole. Couldn't stand the taste any more. Of course his doctor had read him the riot act about his living on burritos, coffee and antacid. *Just the nature of the job*, he'd said in his defense.

He swung the binoculars up again, scanned the hotel's front left to right. Nothing unusual. Businessmen, tourists, hipsters, screaming bag ladies and daredevil bicyclists weaving between them all at top speed. No sign of Garber or foul play.

Admittedly, Sidarski and Keats were spread thin, David versus Goliath. With Keats watching the back of the hotel and Sidarski stationed out front, they couldn't possibly catch everything. Maybe they should've called the Feds. Sure, they'd both agreed not to call them. And the Billings PD wouldn't be any help if Dawbins represented Billings' finest. But Sidarski wondered if hubris had played a part in his decision, his desire to finish the job he'd started a couple years ago driving his ego. Hubris had taken a bite out of his backside in the past, a painful lesson. A lesson he'd clearly forgotten.

Be that as it may, Sidarski knew things were finally coming to a head. One way or another. In the second floor ballroom of the Washburn Hotel.

"Excuse me, sir?"

Sidarski nearly yelped. Coffee sloshed over the side of his Styrofoam cup. She'd taken him by surprise, appeared out of nowhere. Sloppy police work on his part.

"Can I help you?"

A looker, no doubt about it. Tall, slender, long blond hair.

Sharp, exquisite features. Blazing blue eyes. Dressed in a smart business suit, legs up to her chin.

"I believe I'm lost. I wonder if you could help me."

Odd. He placed her accent as Swedish, possibly Norwegian. A tourist.

"Ah, I'm not from around here, miss. I'm sure I can't—"

"Oh, but you must try. Here...let me find the address I'm looking for." She dug into her purse.

Her hand came out with a small canister.

Tsss.

"Aghhh! Dammit!" The pepper spray burned. Blinded, Sidarski dug into his suit jacket, grappling for his gun.

"Ah, ah. Let's have none of that."

Through blurred eyes, he made out a gun in her hand, a small pistol.

Stupid, rookie mistake.

"Please hand over your weapon. Very slowly. Two fingers."

Had Sidarski still been on the force, he would've never complied. He'd have defended the badge to the end. But now? Defending his life took precedence. And as a fifty year veteran, he'd learned to choose his challenges. Especially while so close to nabbing Garber and Spangler. He plucked out his gun as instructed and handed it to her. Quickly, she tucked it into her purse.

"Thank you very much. Now, please scoot over."

Sidarski did. She jumped in next to him. Fire scorched his eyes, unleashed a well of tears. Cautiously he reached into his other pocket for a handkerchief.

"No, no. Hands up."

"Just a handkerchief, lady. See?" Slowly he pulled it out, waved it like a white flag of surrender. "Lady, if you're trying to roll me, I'm afraid you got the wrong guy. I'm broker than America."

He could tell she wasn't a petty thief. Much too professional in action and dress. Perhaps connected to Garber. His cop's instinct told him to play along. He just had to gain control of the situation. With handkerchief in hand, he dabbed his eyes which didn't dam the flow of tears. "Dammit. You did a real number on me."

"You'll live. Maybe. If you cooperate."

"Cooperate? I told you I don't have any money!"

"Are you here with Leon Garber?"

Bingo. "Leon who?"

"I believe you heard me the first time."

"Lady, I heard 'Leon,' nothing else! I got other things on my mind!" He pulled the hanky away, blinked swollen eyes at her.

She studied him. "I saw you watching the hotel. Why are you here? Who are you looking for?"

"Christ sake, I'm just a P.I.! On a divorce case. Watchin' a wayward husband! Here...I'll show you my I.D." He held one hand up. "I'm just gonna get my wallet, 'kay?" He hefted a butt cheek, slid his wallet out. Took some work with his blurred vision, but finally loosened his private investigator's identification. "See?"

She grabbed it. "You're a long way from home, Mr. See... Say... I'm sorry, but my English is sometimes challenged by names such as these."

"Sidarski. And, yeah, the guy I'm watchin' travels a lot." Sidarski shrugged. "I get to see a lot of the country. Now...what about this Leon guy? You lookin' for him? I might be able to take on two jobs at once if—"

"You ask too many questions."

"I'm a curious guy. But what say you—"

"Very well, Mr. Seedarski. Forget you saw me."

"Lady, I can't see anything right now! I couldn't pick you out of—"

"Good."

A flash of flesh, her trailing sleeve. A stabbing blow to his temple, followed by a blast to the back of his head.

Lights out.

If Nanette looked unidentifiable, she thought Delilah had mastered a chameleon-like change. Or rather, Delilah had simply reverted to her origins before the make-up, the faux-hawk, the leather and spider web veined leggings had whisked her away to the dark side.

As Delilah maneuvered the catering van through busy

Washington streets with expertise, she still exuded her regular
self-confidence.

"Not that it's any of my business, but Gus won't let it go,"
said Delilah. She gave Nanette a sideways glance, clearly
uncomfortable with the topic. That made two of them. "He
wants to know if you and Leon...you know..." She shrugged.

"You're right, it's none of anybody's business except our
own."

"Yeah, it's what I told Gus. But you know him..."

"It's bad enough Bartholomew listened in on us last night."
Nanette still couldn't believe it. No, actually it seemed like a
natural thing for The Man with the Shoe-Box. Call him a less
benevolent Santa Claus. *He sees you when you're making love. He
knows when you're awake...*

"I hear ya. Creepy."

Since Delilah cornered the marketplace of "creepy," that
said a lot. "Yeah, it is creepy. Not to mention his plan to bomb
the hotel."

Another shrug. "Shit happens." Delilah left it at that, no sweat
off her leather shoulders. Nanette thought her own upbringing
was hellish. She wondered what could've possibly happened to
Delilah to render her so cold and uncaring. Or maybe she used
indifference as a defense mechanism, something Nanette knew
a little bit about.

"Just hope we're not caught in the shit-storm," mumbled
Nanette.

Delilah maneuvered the van around the back of the hotel.
Knots twisted in Nanette's stomach. Too many loose ends
hadn't even been considered, let alone tied off. Hotel security
seemed an after-thought while everyone deliberated over the
destruction of LMI.

The engine still running, Delilah stopped in front of a
serrated, two vehicle-width garage door. "Ready, Nanette?"

"No. But we're going to do this anyway, right?"

"Yeah." Delilah grinned, primed for battle. She hooted the
horn.

A red light above the garage door flashed to green. The door
ground up on mechanical tracks. Two men in suits, sunglasses,

ear radios—the entire Rasmussen ranch chic look—crawled out from beneath the door before it'd fully opened. One scurried to Delilah's side, the other toward Nanette.

"We're here for the Delaware Room banquet," said Delilah. "Dolores Catering."

The guard jerked his chin in a self-important matter. "Paperwork?"

Fully prepared, Delilah handed him the falsified papers. Insane as Bartholomew is, he's always thorough.

The security guard took the papers, ran a finger through them, nodded with significantly extended lips. Nanette doubted Sheera Rasmussen's goons were trained in catering.

The other guard hung his arms over Nanette's open window. Flashed a swamp-green smoker's grin. "Hey there, sweet thang. How 'bout you cater a little somethin' for me later?"

Good God. Even when she wasn't on, men treated Nanette like a sex object. "Don't think so. Back off."

"Whoa! Feisty!"

"Yeah and I bite, too."

"I like that. I like that a lot."

She didn't intend to flirt. But clearly that's how the guard took it. She wondered if flirting had become such an ingrained part of her personality, she didn't even realize when she did it anymore. A problem for another time.

"I've got work to do. Let us get to it."

"Okay," yelled the guard on Delilah's side. He twirled his finger around. "Open the van. Mrs. Rasmussen wants everything inspected."

Crap. Cody and Gus were stashed in the back, snuggled up to a few military-grade weapons. She hoped they wouldn't have to resort to the guns. At least not this soon.

Quickly, Nanette glanced around. Behind them traffic hurried along the street. A few people sauntered down the sidewalk. They couldn't win the battle in the open, not without onlookers. The door opened onto a large garage with industrial sized boxes filling metal racks. *Perfect.*

"That's fine," said Nanette as she hopped out of the van, "but we gotta get the van outta' this heat. Check it out in the garage."

"Missy, surely you got your food refrigerated in the van."

Anger boiled. *Missy.* Not just one of Nanette's pet peeves, but a major meltdown trigger word. Through gritted teeth, she forced a smile. "My name's not 'Missy.' Of course the food's refrigerated. But Mrs. Rasmussen made it clear she wants everything perfect. Even the slightest heat could taint the food. If you want to give Mrs. Rasmussen botulism, I'll be sure and let her know it was your decision."

His grin sagged, cockiness neutered. "Fine. *Missy.*" He hissed it with a spitting sibilant S, hardly threatening sounding.

Delilah moved the van inside. Nanette followed on foot. Inside the garage, she punched the button to lower the door.

One of the guards said, "Hey, what're you doing?"

"Keeping the heat out. Duh."

Delilah left the cab, joined Nanette and the two guards at the back of the van.

"First we gotta search you ladies." The tip of his tongue dipped out. Nanette planned on making him eat it.

She said, "Union rules say—"

"Gotta do what I'm paid to do. You know. Union rules." He grabbed Nanette by the waist, spun her roughly to face the van. "Spread 'em." Nanette shut her eyes as the guard's hands wrapped around her ankles, then crept up. He lingered over her thighs. A quick grab at her groin, a painful grope of her butt. Then his hands inched upward. She felt totally violated, seethed with anger. Her teeth clamped down, near breaking point. *Bastard.*

He finished, stood back. Mopped his forehead like he'd had a work-out. Nanette spun around, ready to rip into him. Not yet. She held onto her anger, savored it, let it build as a weapon.

Bad as it'd been for Nanette, though, Delilah had a worse time tolerating it.

"Get the *fuck* offa' me!"

The guard took great pleasure in his intrusive pat-down, a sick smile pasted on his face. Delilah kicked a foot back. The guard stepped back, still smiling. Delilah spun, fists up.

"Oooh, a bad-ass! You gonna pull some catering karate on me?"

"I'm gonna serve you up some shit!" Delilah bounced on her

heels, ready to strike. Nanette caught her eye, shook her head. Delilah hissed like a cat, but lowered her fists.

The guard laughed. "Whatever. Couple dykes. But they're not packin' heat. Okay, open the van up."

"Waste of time, dickhead. It's just food and junk," said Delilah. "Catering crap."

"Then there's nothing to worry about."

"Look," said Nanette, "we're just caterers. We just want to do our job." A last chance effort to keep things from getting messy. But things in her world rarely ended up clean. Truth of the matter, she hoped things would get messy.

"Just open the damn van!"

"Fine. But Mrs. Rasmussen won't like it if we're late." Nanette tapped on the door three times, a warning. Purposefully, she dropped the keys, bought a little time. The guard behind her stepped closer, so close she could smell his body odor. Delilah inched behind the other guard.

The key slipped in. The lock unleashed. Nanette grabbed both handles, turned them in opposite directions with a glaring *rnchhh*. She took a deep breath. Yanked open the doors and freed the animal.

"Yo!" Cody leaped out, hooked one of the guards around the neck. They hit the cement floor, Cody on top.

Delilah tossed a strangle-hold around the other guard's neck and pulled him back toward her. His hand vanished into his jacket. Out zipped a silencer-equipped gun. A wild shot chuffed above him. The bullet zinged and cracked into a box. White powder spat out from the hole, spilling to the ground.

"Jesus Christ," screamed Delilah's captive. His arms flailed for freedom. His weight advantage tumbled them back into a shelf. Boxes wobbled above them. Delilah and the guard hit the floor. Several boxes crashed on top of them. Winded, Delilah released her neck-hold. The guard jumped to his feet, swung his gun toward Delilah. Delilah rolled away and kept rolling like an experienced gymnast.

Pfft. Pfft. Spak. Crik.

Bullets cracked the cement next to Delilah. On her knees, she dove behind a storage rack.

Nanette grabbed the closest box in the van, pulled out a plastic baggy containing a hypodermic. Her hands shook as she freed the needle. She raced toward the gun-holding guard, a vein of hatred bulging on her forehead. She jammed the needle into his neck. She swept his feet out from beneath him with a well-aimed kick, added a shove.

Cody straddled the other guard, riding him hard. The guard bucked. Cody held onto his throat like a saddle-horn. He battered the guard's face. The gun dropped from the guard's hand.

Nanette tapped Cody's shoulder. "Let me finish him, Cody."

"You wanna piece of this? Be my guest." Cody hopped off, spirits high. He danced around, shadow-boxing invisible opponents. Warmed up and ready to go.

"This is for groping me." Nanette delivered a foot into the downed man's groin.

"Oof!" He rolled over, cupped his damaged area.

"And this is for calling me 'missy.' Never, *ever* call a woman 'missy' again. Show some manners." She brought her leg up as high as it'd go, landed a solid foot onto his face. The resulting crack was anything but lady-like. Extremely satisfying, though.

Gus had just managed to get down from the back of the van. "Oh, dear, it appears I've missed out on all the fun."

"You'll get your chance for fun, Gus," said Nanette. "Got a syringe handy?"

"Indeed I do, my dear!" He opened his tuxedo jacket, displayed a line of syringes in his pocket like a street peddler. "Would you like the honor?" He held a syringe out to Nanette.

"Why, thank you, Gus. Always the gentlemen." She jammed the needle into the guard's neck, wiggled it about, ensuring it'd bruise later. "Nighty night."

Gus ran over to Delilah, out from hiding and on her feet. "Delilah, my love! Are you fine? Anything hurt?"

Delilah picked him up, hugged him. "Just my pride."

"We can't have any of that." Gus' feet kicked until Delilah dropped him. His forehead rippled with fret. He pulled a gun from his deep pockets and raced toward the unconscious guard who had violated his lover.

Nanette stopped him. "No, Gus, we need to go. I know it sucks. But they're out. They'll be that way for hours. Remember the big picture."

Gus sighed. "Indeed. Very well, lead on."

Which bothered Nanette. In no certain way did she want leadership responsibility. But it'd fallen on her. Even though she didn't have a say in the manner. "Okay, Cody, help me get these asshats into the back of the van. We'll lock 'em in there."

Cody made short work of it, unable to keep from showing off a bit. Can't ever take the boy out of the man. He slapped his hands together, job well done. "Let's get this party started, yo."

With the hotel's blueprints committed to memory, Nanette led her team through a basement corridor, up a flight of steps and into the kitchen. Bartholomew's man, Tommy, had been sent ahead to take care of the kitchen staff. Based on the few people in the kitchen, Nanette tried not to dwell on what "taking care of" meant. A nervous chef paced behind a man and woman working the stoves. Several waitresses sat huddled together at a small table. All of them had their eyes locked onto the floor: out of sight, out of mind. In the middle of it all, Tommy sat on top of a large stainless steel table, one leg propped up, the other dangling. Casually, he scratched his chin with the barrel of a gun.

"'Bout time you got here," he said.

His prisoners said nothing, maintained their floor-watching vigil. Nanette hoped their wise discretion would save their lives.

"Unfashionably late, that's me," said Nanette. "We had a minor problem."

Alert, Tommy jumped off the table. "What happened?"

"Nothing we couldn't take care of. Let's do this."

"Yeah, baby," Cody hooted, "let's go kick some LMI ass, yo!"

"Um, Cody..." Nanette approached him, mentally strapped on her kid gloves and gently placed a hand on his chest. She knew he wouldn't like what she had to tell him. "You have to stay here. For now."

"What? Like hell I am! I'm a' gonna—"

"Cody, listen to me. Sheera knows you. Probably everyone in the ballroom does. You're ah..." Slightly sexy smile, sway the head just so. "...notorious."

Cody's eyes grew round and proud. "Damn straight, yo. Once you go Cody, you never—"

"And we need someone to watch the kitchen staff. Until 4:10. Then you come in. Ready to go."

"A'ight, a'ight. Sucks bein' outta the action, but whatever." He sulked away, head hung low. Still just a little boy. In a hella hunk of a package.

"You'll get your action, Cody. Just wait until it's time, cool?"

"Already said whatever. Just save some for me."

"I think there'll be plenty to go around."

As they prepared for the final showdown—today's menu: death!—Nanette glanced back at Cody. He'd taken up Tommy's vacated spot, flat on his back on the table. A muscular arm draped over his eyes. He could've been asleep.

Part of her wanted to slap him into full attention. A nurturing side wanted to cradle him in her arms, tell him everything would be okay.

If only she had someone to do the same for her now.

His money and resources apparently endless, Bartholomew had traded in his limo for something slightly less flashy: a Town Car. Just the two of them, Leon knew the ride would be unnerving. But it also might allow him a chance to feel the Man with the Shoebox out. Talk some sense into him.

Leon still hadn't learned anything about naivety.

Of course, sprawled out across the car's back seat made it tough to present a powerful argument. "Bartholomew, you're giving my plan a shot first, right?"

"I'm tired of discussing this, Leon." Cautious as a student driver, Bartholomew drove slower than the posted speed limit. Obviously unused to driving himself. "I've already told you I'm game to see what happens." He adjusted his mirror. Leon caught his eyes' reflection. "Possibly."

Possibly. As cryptic and full of understated menace as ever. Almost as if he couldn't wait to set off his explosives, a new toy he'd yet to use, in the Washburn. Cody, the later years. Only richer, more intelligent. Clearly educated. Okay, maybe not so much Cody from any year. More like an alien being.

"Possibly. What's that supposed to mean? We agreed to—"

"Enough. I have back-up contingencies in case something should go wrong. The realistic nature of warfare."

"Bartholomew, have you considered the others in the hotel? The innocent lives that will be lost through structural damage? The whole building will come down!"

"Oh, who's 'innocent,' Leon? Are any of us truly innocent? Why, even the Good Book says we are all born with sin."

Arguing the Bible with Bartholomew seemed like a ludicrous dead-end, one Leon couldn't believe Bartholomew started driving down. Leon lacked the proper knowledge. Besides, he had other things to contend with rather than get bogged down in a theological debate. "You're just making excuses."

"Don't presume to know what I'm thinking."

"I didn't mean to offend. But a lot of those people are—"

"Collateral damage." His shoulders hitched up. "From day one, I thought we were after the same thing: the complete eradification of LMI. That's what we're doing. No, it's not ideal if some people get caught in the cross-fire. But this is war, Leon. You should understand that better than anyone. After all...it was your philosophy while you ran LMI."

He spoke the truth, of course. The painful truth. But Leon knew, should he live through this, he'd never let that philosophy lead him astray again.

"But I think my plan will work. Without collateral damage."

Bartholomew shrugged. "We'll see. Now stay down...we're entering the hotel parking garage."

Truthfully, Leon didn't know if his plan would work or not. Now that the impending encounter grew closer, doubt wheedled into his mind. But he had to try. And if the Man with the Shoe-Box intended to blow up the second floor, Leon would stop him.

The car slowed. Bartholomew turned off the ignition. "It's time..."

Parked on a bench across the street from the hotel's back entrance, Keats watched the catering van pull to a stop. Nothing appeared out of the ordinary; two women in the front, a "Dolores

Catering Services" logo emblazoned across the van's body. But then two goons stormed out, the kind Mrs. Rasmussen bred like bunnies at her compound. Clearly packing guns within their suit jackets.

The van pulled inside a garage. She didn't recognize the two women, but Keats didn't socialize either. It's what—or who— rode in the back that really piqued her interest.

As the garage door lowered, Keats crossed the street. She stood outside and listened.

She couldn't make out the words, but the intensity came through clear. Voices rose into shouts. A heavy thump. Scuffling. Metal cracked. A man's yowl.

Something was going down now. Time to socialize sooner than she wanted to.

She stepped back several feet, pulled out her phone. Quickly she dialed Sidarski.

"Dammit, Sidarski, answer your phone! Something's happening at the back dock. Two muscles fighting a couple of women. Or something. Hit me back!"

She cursed, paced back and forth. Helluva time for Sidarski to take a bathroom break. Unless something had happened to him, that old paranoia kicking in again. Funny how paranoia had been a constant shadow since her shooting. But she didn't want to go in alone. Learned her lesson earlier after a hard recuperative time in the hospital.

She called Sidarski again. And again, her messages growing shorter and more imperative.

Shit.

Maybe she should go around, look for Sidarski. Then again, if lives were endangered, she had an obligation to investigate.

After a less intense muffled conversation, the garage's occupants fell silent. Keats checked out the garage door, no external button. Next to the garage entry sat a loading dock with more garage doors, these ones with handles.

She hopped onto the ledge, rolled to her feet. Drew her gun. The door opened with an intrusive screech. No one in the garage, not that she could see. She hurried down the steps to the parked catering van.

One more look around, then she stepped to the back of the van. In a squat, gun up in her free hand, she opened one of the doors. Inside were the two suited men, out. Or dead.

She holstered her gun, hoisted a foot up on the back bumper.

An arm wrapped around her neck.

"Oh my, you appear to be in the wrong place." A strong accent hindered his enunciation. His clean pine scent, not unlike a car freshener, overwhelmed her nose.

She grabbed his arm for leverage, ran her feet up the opposite closed van door. Bent her legs and thrust hard. A phantom—or reopened—wound tore at her side where she'd been shot before. The man faltered back, carrying Keats by the neck. He grunted as they crashed to the floor, Keats' landing softened by his body. She popped back a fist, connected with his nose. She heard cartilage tear. Her elbow jabbed into her attacker's side. She needed her gun, but couldn't risk going for it yet. Not with his strong arm choking the life out of her. She struggled, kicked, tried to unravel their bundle of wriggling limbs.

She brought her head forward, bashed it back into his face. The second time did the trick. His arms fell to the floor. He hissed, settled like a deflating tire.

Keats rolled forward, landed in a squat. She turned, yanked out her gun, held it on him.

The blonde man tented a hand over his nose. "You broke my noathe. My *perfect* noathe!"

"Accidents happen. Who're you?"

"Ah, that would be telling." He smiled, an unlikely reaction for someone in his position. Until she realized the stupid mistake she'd made. She'd remained too close.

Fast as a whip, he swept his feet beneath hers. She fell back, firing off a shot into the ceiling.

Tunk!

Her head hit the van. The gun spun away across the floor. She wobbled, her arms rotating like propellers. On his feet, the man came toward her. Still smiling like a damn cover model. Punched her in the face.

"Whoops." He shoved her into the van. Darkness dropped over her as the doors shut.

Helluva way to treat the second most important person at LMI.

Cody groused about his kitchen duty stint.

Something the military punishes you with, yo!

The small kitchen staff seemed kinda freaked over the whole deal. Some of the women cried. The men's eyes never left the food in their hands, chopping vegetables and kale and junk he didn't recognize. It's not like they needed babysitting.

Behind him, a door opened. Instinct kicked Cody into gear. He rolled off the metal table, squeezed between two food shelves, his back against the wall.

Good thing he did, but he'd expect no differently with his incredible luck.

The blonde killer, one of LMI's Doublemint Twins, strolled in, his gun drawing him forward.

A woman released a weak scream and hunkered in closer to her partner at the back table.

"Shhh, I'm not going to hurt you." He held a handkerchief over his nose. Blood speckled his chin. "Not if you kindly stop your ruckus."

The woman geared up for another scream, but her friend pulled her in tight for a hug, effectively muffling it.

"Now. Tell me who else has been in here."

Cody hugged the wall, willed himself smaller. The gun at his back pinched his flesh. A sign if he'd ever seen one.

The blond man breezed by the frightened women. He stopped behind a chef, who pretended he hadn't seen Blondie's entrance.

"You. Please face me."

The chef turned, gaze glued on his feet.

"Eyes up here, please." Blondie gestured the gun toward his eyes.

Unwillingly, the chef finally raised his head.

"Who's been in here?"

The chef looked over the twin's shoulder, stared at Cody.

Crap. Dude's gonna give me up.

Cody reached for his gun, thought better of it. Partially because of the noise the report would make. But mostly, because just out of arm's reach, a meat axe hung on a hook. Swaying. Calling to him. Reminding him of old times, better times. He hadn't cut into flesh in, like, a really long time. He imagined the sharp slice, the tough yet liquid-like entry into flesh. The resultant blood. Hair prickled the back of his neck, kinda a nice, goosey feeling.

"Speak up, sir. I can't understand a word you're saying."

The chef mumbled, a prayer maybe. Again, his eyes gravitated toward Cody, then back to the blond.

Cody stepped forward, arm outstretched, hand raised for the axe.

Closer, closer... Almost got it!

"What is it you're looking at, friend?"

Perched on the edge of the shelf, the can may as well've been invisible. Until Cody's shoulder nudged it. The can dropped, almost in slow motion.

Bang.

The tell-tale can rolled across the floor like a smoke-bomb tossed through a window.

The blond twirled, gun up.

Cody took two giant steps, grabbed the axe handle. Forgot to pull it up off the hook. The axe yanked him back.

"Shit!"

Pfft. Splack.

Cody spun, axe handle still in hand, contorted in a painful and awkward way. A bullet whiffed by his cheek, close enough he felt a breeze. He hopped up, loosened the axe. And jumped, all in.

The axe came down, a perfect landing. With ecstatic ease, the axe sliced through the man's wrist. His hand fell along with the gun.

"Yeah, baby! That's what I'm talkin' 'bout!"

Screams rose, the appreciation of a crowd. No one screamed louder than Blondie. He cradled his wrist between his knees. Blood raced down his pant-leg, possibly a little urine, too. Cody didn't let up. One perfect thrust sliced off the man's ear. A couple of hearty swings to the chest opened him up like a piñata.

Warm blood spattered Cody's face, a cleansing sensation,

nearly Baptismal in euphoria. Oblivious to the kitchen staff's howls, Cody finished the job. And delighted in doing so.

A slight dizziness—a very pleasant dizziness—streamed through his body. He shuddered. Goose bumps rode his arms. Fully content, he turned, and noticed the kitchen staff's eyes upon him.

"What? Saved your lives, yo!"

Just the start, though. Warrior blood strengthened him. A near sexual rush set him on-fire.

Now more than ever, he had to get to the big party.

Nanette used the kitchen chef appropriated key-card to open the service elevator. Like a military commando, Tommy jumped in first, flicked his eyes left, right, gave them a silent *all clear*. Nanette held the door open while Delilah rolled the sheet-draped serving cart inside.

Nanette pressed the second floor button and the doors rolled close with a breathless *whmph*.

"You ready, Delilah?" asked Nanette.

She hitched a shoulder up, smirked. "Guess so."

Tommy said nothing during the eternal journey to the second floor, just stared blankly at his co-conspirators.

The elevator dinged. The doors pulled back.

At the end of the long hallway sat the ballroom. Guarded by two more of Sheera's men. Not unexpected, but Nanette hoped all hell would stay at the devil's home until the appropriate time.

The wheels on the cart squeaked as they approached, round and round and squeak, *reech, squeek*. The longest prison mile had nothing on their trek. The guards stood at attention, backs as stiff as their upper lips. Interrogation mode.

"Stop." One of the guards held up an unnecessary hand. "Gotta search you. And the cart."

"Oh, for... We're caterers. You wanna taste test the food for poison, too?"

The guards shared an uncomfortable look, one that said *this is above my pay grade*. "No, that's not necessary."

"Look, the food's getting cold. I'm sure your boss won't be thrilled if you keep us from serving." The gambit hadn't worked out so well the first time Nanette tried it, but ever the optimist, she held onto hope.

"Just following orders." The talkative guard lifted the cover from the large centerpiece serving dish, then replaced it. He hitched up his trouser legs and knelt. He swept the sheet up from the lower portion of the cart.

"Hello!" Gus shot out a hand and buzzed the guard a good one in the cheek with his stun gun. The man jerked, flopped about on the floor. His grey slacks darkened, the urine stain spread.

"What the *hell*?" The other guard dug his hand into his jacket pocket. Delilah nailed him in the throat with her stun gun. He flopped back onto a table, desperately trying to grasp the table's edge on his way down. His fingers didn't work, just stubbed at the air. The table overturned and banged on top of him.

Nanette's heart pounded. She listened. Watched the closed doors intently to see if they'd attracted attention. Silently, they waited in the hallway, counting down the crucial seconds perched on the edge of disaster.

Finally, Nanette nodded. She grabbed the exposed guard's legs, Delilah took his arms and they dragged him behind another clothed table. Delilah did most of the heavy lifting. Nanette's muscles quaked as her half of the man dragged the floor. As an afterthought, Delilah swept off the table-cloth and covered him with it.

They wouldn't be out too long, even at the stun gun's full charge. Gus was more than happy to top off the guards' momentary slumber with a dose of Azaperone.

Absolutely beaming, Gus crawled back into his hiding place. They entered the ballroom.

Several tables comprised a U-shape, fourteen people sat around it. Like a Queen, Sheera dominated the center spot, Gaines at her elbow. She shrieked, downright giddy in conversation with her neighbor. A prison line-up of some of the largest, scariest thugs Nanette had ever seen stood behind the seated royalty. No doubt all of them bearing firearms.

Clearly outnumbered, Nanette didn't like their odds.

Particularly since all they had were non-lethal weapons, something Leon had insisted on. She questioned his decision-making ability, wished she had something that'd deliver instantaneous death. They'd have to work fast, efficiently, hit everyone at once as a cohesive unit. Her team a couple of sanity-challenged serial killers and a chauffeur. The odds just lowered.

Sheera raised heavily mascaraed eyes. "Ah, the food's here! Perfect."

Nanette didn't like the way Gaines stared at her as if she comprised the main course. His brow wrinkled. He looked at her through squinty eyes, confusion fluttered his lids. As much as possible, she kept her head down, concentrated on ladling out soup. From what she could see, the LMI board members were weaponless. Probably no need to carry guns with their armed bodyguards standing closely by. Their biggest obstacle.

As planned, Tommy worked his way to the Northeast corner. Delilah planted herself on the other side of the room. Two minutes to go until 4:15, the time to strike.

Now it depended on Leon. Timing was crucial.

She prayed to a God she hadn't believed in for a very long time that Leon wouldn't let her down. Again and for the final time.

In the parking garage, Bartholomew pulled his fedora low. Their chins glued to their chests, they walked quickly toward the elevators.

Leon gave it one last shot. "Bartholomew, don't go forward with the explosion. We—"

Bartholomew responded with a finger over his cadaverous grin: *Dead men tell no tales.*

As they waited for the elevator, the Man with the Shoe-Box finally broke his silence. "Chewing gum?" He held out a pack, a foiled piece sticking out.

"Ah, no. I'm good."

Before they entered the elevator, Bartholomew again lowered his fedora. From his pocket, he withdrew a small can of spray paint, reached up and covered the security camera lens. "Always keep them guessing. No need to take chances now."

Which, of course, was what they were doing: one big last Hail Mary of a chance. Leon gave his briefcase a little shake, his secret weapon. He hoped it'd be enough.

Muzak droned overhead, everything else calm and quiet. Deceptively so. Sweat drizzled Leon's forehead, rolled down his chest. He swallowed, a dry lump that refused to go down.

A *ding* announced their second floor arrival. Leon's shoulders jerked. The doors slid open. Unnatural silence flowed over them. Not what Leon had expected. The hallway sat empty and quiet as a church. Only an upended table next to the ballroom suggested his plan had begun.

With his hand trembling over the ballroom's door, Leon snatched it back. Checked his watch. 4:14. One minute to go.

Then heart-stopping shouts roared out from behind the closed doors...

Keats woke disoriented, the mother of all headaches embracing her. Memory caught up, smacked her upside the head. Reminded her how stupid she was for getting locked inside the van.

She pulled out her phone, squinted at the blue light, glad she had bars. She hadn't been out long, still time to get back into the thick of things. No way she'd sit this one out.

Another call to Sidarski yielded the same aggravating non-results. Something had happened to him. He was too good a cop to be sloughing off now.

She gritted her teeth, tamed her pride. Time to call in reinforcements.

"Hotel security."

Gaines turned up his chin, watched every move Nanette made. She willed her shaking hand to steady as she ladled soup into his cup. She couldn't help but look, just a quick glance to meet his eyes. She gave him an innocuous smile, one meant to disarm.

It didn't work.

He snaked out a fist, coiled it around her wrist.

"Why, hello there, Nanette." He grinned, a proud *got you* look.

"What? Oh, dear." Sheera dabbed her pouting lips with a

napkin, an unfortunate interruption to her dinner plans.

Time to do it.

Nanette yanked her arm, but Gaines' grip didn't let up. She dumped her ladle of steaming soup into his lap. He yelped, released her. From beneath her apron, she grabbed her stun gun, jacked it onto the back of his neck. Zapped him. His hands waved at the side as if trying to fly. Beneath the table, his legs kicked. He flopped forward into his empty soup bowl. The porcelain cracked beneath his forehead. He bolted back, flinging him and his chair down to the floor. Blood streaked across his forehead. His glasses had broken in half. The two halves dangled from his ears.

A flurry of shouts and screams bombarded Nanette in languages she didn't understand. But the international language of panic ruled.

Nanette turned, nailed the chest of the closest bodyguard. She dropped into a squat, twirled with one leg out, punched the stun gun into another guard's stomach.

Gus sprang out from beneath the cart. He double-fisted electric shock prods, better for his short arm length. His natural target: the guards' groins. His high-pitched giggle stood out over the chaos as he raced a circle around the room, maniacally enjoying his handiwork.

Delilah got off one shot before a bodyguard grabbed her from behind, both arms around her waist. She dropped her stun gun. The guard lifted her up. Her feet kicked the table, knocked over a bottle of wine. She bent her knees, pulled her feet in and stomped down onto the bodyguard's foot. He pushed her forward onto the table. Her hand landed on a steak-knife. In one nearly balletic move, she grabbed it, used the continuing momentum of her fall and spun. The knife thunked into the guard's throat. Blood spurted from between his fingers, arcing high and splattering the white table-cloth. More screams arose.

A bullet whizzed over Nanette's head, cracked the window behind her. Broken glass cascaded down. Tommy punched the gun-toting guard, stunned him on the way down.

Half of the body-guards were decommissioned. The others had silencer-outfitted guns out, wagging them about, attempting to pinpoint their constantly shifting targets. Nanette and her team stayed on the move, part of the plan. A staccato of whiffs flew. Bullets crossed, a few hitting LMI bodyguards. Lit candles flew up like projectiles. Dinner ware danced and dinged. Another window shattered. Most of the board members had crawled beneath the table, seeking desperate shelter.

Gleefully, Gus continued his low-aim trajectory, now sporting a shotgun loaded with electro-shock projectiles. For every bodyguard he incapacitated, he carefully reloaded, did it again. Oblivious to the bullets flying overhead, he walked about freely, unseen and ignored.

In the confusion, Nanette had lost her stun gun. She rolled under the table.

Come on, Leon, dammit!

She found herself face-to-face with the improbable, immovable face of Sheera.

"You bitch! You're ruining everything!"

"Gee, sorry about your party." Nanette pulled back, threw a fist into Sheera's face, aiming to cause some serious damage. Sheera gave as good as she got. She launched a powerhouse punch, crunched it onto Nanette's cheek. Nanette twisted, banged her head beneath the table top. Momentarily dazed, she swung out blindly, ineffectively. Her knuckles grazed wood. Sheera grabbed Nanette's hair. Nanette's senses cleared. She banged her forehead into Sheera's. Sheera flopped out wiry but muscular arms and embraced Nanette. They tumbled out from beneath the draping tablecloth and into the room. Bullets whizzed by overhead.

"Ladies and gentlemen, *enough!*" Bartholomew's shout demanded attention, stronger than his usual hushed baritone. "We've come here to discuss business. If you'd like to live, I suggest you all lay down your firearms."

To prove his point, he fired numerous lethal bullets into the ceiling, a weapon no one had counted on him bringing.

Leon looked over the chaos, searching for his team.

Smoke drifted, the odor of cordite so strong he could taste it. Glass tinkled. Objects snapped. A chair collapsed. Those still standing froze, stunned, questioning faces seeking answers. A surreal sensation after the preceding bedlam.

Behind Leon, the door snapped open. Cody, red-faced and wide-eyed, stood in the doorway panting. "Did I miss everything?"

"Well, well, the gang's all here." Sheera popped up from the floor, dusted her hands. Straightened her torn dress. Patted her hair. One cheek drooped lower than the other. "What's the meaning of this, Leon?"

"It's beyond time to stop your games, Sheera. None of us have the time." Leon nodded at Nanette and Delilah. Gus stood on the table, a cowlick sticking up on his head, double armed with a shotgun and a baton. He hopped down. Quickly, Leon's team circled the room, administering Azaperone into the recovering bodyguards' necks. Gus played doctor to the few conscious bodyguards.

"Everyone under the tables, come out," Leon ordered.

A slow exodus, the board members complied. Their egos had taken a blow since Leon's last meeting with them, timid shadows of their blustery previous incarnations.

A level playing ground now: the refugees against LMI's board members.

Leon dropped his briefcase onto the table. He shook his head at Bartholomew, gestured for him to put his gun away.

Bartholomew ignored him, swiveled his weapon around the room. Leon didn't want another firefight on their hands, but he realized the gun captivated his audience's attention.

Bartholomew said, "Everyone in this room had a hand in trying to kill me. So, ladies and gentlemen, I'm here to return the favor." He doffed his fedora, bowed. "Had you left me alone, things wouldn't have come to this. I certainly hope you've learned your lesson. Tommy?" Tommy nodded. "I believe you know what to do." Another nod, not an enthusiastic one either.

It troubled Leon, but time was short before the police arrived. "Sheera, why'd you do it? Try to have us killed?"

"Simple, dear Leon. It became obvious you weren't a company man. You refused to toe the line." She shrugged. "Just a business decision, surely you understand."

"Then why didn't you just fire me?"

She laughed harshly, a braying donkey. "Killing *is* how LMI fires employees."

"Your days of 'firing' people are over. In this briefcase, I hold documentation on every one of you, of all the things you've been up to over the past years. As a failsafe, I've sent out emails containing copies of the same documentation to journalists and government agencies around the world to be delivered at 5:00. I have a viral email that will counteract it and destroy the messages before they're read. If, and *only* if, my team is alive to deliver the email. Now, should you or your people decide to come at me afterword...or any of my friends," he gestured toward his team, "the information will be released again."

"This is preposterous!" shouted Senta Rosen.

"Maybe it is. But it's not as preposterous as my life's been with LMI. Everything you do is preposterous. Oh, and there's more. I currently have access to all of your bank accounts, no matter if hidden, off-shore, whatever. To sweeten the deal, I can hack into your accounts immediately. Send your blood money to charities."

A buzz built around the table, several "oohs" and cries of anguish. Hitting them where it hurt.

"How do we know you're not bluffing, Mr. Garber?" asked Sheera.

Leon tossed the briefcase her way. It landed on the table in front of her. "Have a look yourself."

She nodded at Gaines, always up for her dirty work. Gaines discarded his broken glasses. Through narrowed eyes, he clicked the case open, rifled through papers. Held them close to his face. "Ah...I'm afraid he appears to be telling the truth, Mrs. Rasmussen."

Sheera sighed. She tapped a foot, said, "And if we leave you alone...what assurance do we have you'll do likewise? I'm not exactly comfortable with your holding this information over us."

"Too bad. I'm not exactly comfortable with you trying to have me killed. It's a chance you'll just have to take, Sheera."

"Very well. Shall we put it to a board vote?"

At first, Leon thought a cat had entered the room. The growl started low, grew. Gaines' lips pulled back, his teeth bared. His fists curled, uncurled, curled again. His shoulders heaved up and down. Nostrils flared big as quarters. Crimson poured into his cheeks, his forehead.

Uh-oh.

"I won't let you do this to Mrs. *Rasmussen!*" His tone rose with each word, crashed into a crescendo. He darted a hand into his jacket, yanked out a gun. He rushed toward Leon, madly firing.

A bullet bit deep into Leon. He twirled a complete 180, remained on his feet. Then shock knocked at his senses. Pain opened the door and delivered him into a ball on the floor.

"Oh, my God!" Nanette ran to Leon's side. "Leon, get up. Dammit, don't you do this to me! Get up!"

Cody lunged for Gaines, grabbed him by the throat. Cody never let go as they plummeted into a table. He punched the man repeatedly. Bits of flesh and blood trailed his fists. Gaines gasped, hissed out a dying breath. Afraid, confused, the crowd watched but did nothing. A few of the board members looked antsy, ready to make a break for it. But the coven of cowards stayed put.

Nanette turned her attention back to Leon. The blood beneath him continued to pool out. Half-lucid, she tried to remember how to treat gun wounds. She seemed to recall—hazy, though, like a dream—you shouldn't move gunshot victims. She'd never had a reason to test the theory before, always on the administering end of pain. But she had to do something. Carefully, she cradled Leon, leaned him forward. The bullet had torn through his side, exited out his back. From her limited knowledge of human anatomy, vital organs had gone unharmed. Still...the hell with not moving him. She knew Leon'd rather die than live in prison.

"Leon? Leon? You hear me? We've got to go!"

He opened his eyes, grunted. "Yeah...okay." His words slurred, drugged sounding.

"Can you walk?"

"Think so."

It took him a while to crawl to his feet, even with Nanette and Delilah's assistance. Upon his first step, his lips spread in a painful grimace.

Gus stood over Gaines body, exclaimed, "Friend Cody, you've made quite a mess there."

Cody's eyes were heavily lidded, completely out of it. He gazed out over the terrified gathering, but didn't truly see them. Nanette didn't know who'd be harder to get out of there: Leon or Cody. "Cody? We've got to *go*."

"Fine. Run away with your little rag-tag gang," said Sheera. "We'll see how far you'll get. Just remember...I had nothing to do with Gaines' actions. He acted independently."

"He never did anything independently," snapped Nanette. "Delilah, help me get Leon out of here." Delilah braced Leon's arm over her shoulder, Nanette took the other one.

Bartholomew stood in the room's shadows, lording over Tommy. Whispering to him. The Man with the Shoebox pinched off his glove, shook his chauffeur's hand. He turned toward Nanette. With a smile, said, "Let's be on our way."

"Remember our deal, Sheera," said Nanette on the way out.

Still stupefied, Cody stumbled after them with the tired and content look of a man who'd gorged himself on a satisfyingly full meal.

They exited the ballroom and Nanette closed the doors behind them.

"Oh, one last thing," said Bartholomew. Then he locked the ballroom doors.

"Wait...what about Tommy?"

Bartholomew gave a sad shake of his head. "I'm afraid Tommy's staying behind. To ensure this ends properly."

Nanette didn't like the sound of it. Fear spread through her. But distant sirens superseded all fear.

Leon moved slowly, pushed to his limits. Inside the service elevator, he broke away from Nanette and Delilah and leaned up against the elevator wall. "Bartholomew, what's Tommy doing?"

"Don't worry about Tommy. I've made sure his family will be well taken care of." He brandished his gun in a near threatening gesture.

"It's not Tommy I'm worried about. Tell me!"

"It doesn't concern you any longer. You had your fun. Let's just—"

Leon thrust off the wall, grabbed Bartholomew's gun. Bartholomew held on, their arms stretched overhead, the gun a baton worth fighting for. Leon banged their entwined hands against the elevator door. Bartholomew dropped the gun. It skated across the floor, stopped at Nanette's feet. She snatched it up. Locked her arms, grabbed her right wrist with her left hand and pointed it at Bartholomew.

"Talk," she said.

Bartholomew stared down the barrel, then glared into Nanette's eyes. "You've just made a huge mistake. I don't much care for being on the dangerous end of a gun."

"Tell us!" demanded Leon.

"Very well. Tommy's agreed to stay behind to ensure everyone stays in place."

"Until what? The bomb goes off?"

"Tommy has the remote. The only way to make sure the job is completed. I'm a stickler for seeing things through to the end, you know."

"Jesus Christ!" said Leon. "You can't do that!"

"Oh, settle down, Leon. Do you really think your threat of incriminating evidence is going to stop LMI from coming for you? For us?"

"It's not just a threat! I lied! Something LMI knows a little bit about. As soon as we hit the road, I'm releasing the emails. And, as of now, thanks to Skeeter, their accounts have already been drained and dispersed to worldwide charities. *That's* the way you hurt them!"

"Hm. I can appreciate your point."

"Call off your man! No one else dies! I'm sick of the death! The only way to hurt them is through their money and freedom!"

"Again, I'm not very happy to have my hand forced. But... fine. I always did think you were too much of a bleeding heart, Leon." With a heavy sigh, as heavy as his downturned eyebrows, Bartholomew clicked away at his phone. "Afraid he's not answering."

"Try again! Leave a message!"

The elevator doors opened into the parking garage. Half-heartedly, Bartholomew tried Tommy's number again. Kicked into voice-mail. "Tommy, it's me. Call it off. Change of plans." He shrugged, powered his phone off. "I tried."

Midway to Bartholomew's car, Leon stopped. "I've got to go back."

"What? Leon, you can't!" Nanette faced him, hands on his chest. "You can barely walk! You can't—"

"I'll do it." Cody stepped forward, eyes now clear.

"Cody, no, you—"

"Leon, chill! I can do this, yo! I got it by the balls!"

"Don't Cody! You won't make it before the police—"

Too late. Cody dashed back to the elevator, gun waving in his hand. Before the doors closed, he smiled, cock-sure and certain of his invulnerability. "See ya on the other side, yo!"

As the doors closed, Leon collapsed against Nanette. Whether out of weakness or sorrow, she had no idea.

Big deal. Storm into the ballroom, cap Tommy's ass before he blows everything sky-high, get out and ride off into the sunset.

Cody'd already taken out tons of LMI jackasses. What's one more?

It's called "taking one for the team." Besides, God—Buddha, fate, Elvis, whatever—always kept an eye out for him.

Full-throttle, he tore down the hallway. Outside, sirens whined louder, Five-O closing in.

Fly like a lightning bug, don't get jarred.

A hand on the knob, his other on the gun, he unlocked the doors. Then kicked them open. Probably not necessary but a way cool entrance.

"I'm back, bitches!"

Startled, Tommy swung his gun Cody's way. Gasps spread around the room.

"Yo, numb nuts, answer your damn phone! Your boss called off the big ka-boom." Cody tossed fingers out from his temples.

"I don't think so," Tommy said. "He'd never do that. Done deal."

Slowly, Cody walked toward him, his gun up in the air, TV style. "Just check your damn phone! And gimme the remote."

"You want it hot-shot? Come and get it." He reached into his pocket, plucked out a device smaller than a phone. Taunted Cody with it.

Cody could never resist a challenge. A fair one. He tossed the gun at Tommy. The chauffeur flinched. Cody saw his opening, dove in.

Humiliated didn't even begin to describe how Keats felt. As soon as hotel security opened the catering van doors, she blew by them without looking back.

"Come on!" she yelled. "Call 911. There's all kindsa hell breaking loose on the second floor."

According to the indicator, the elevator appeared stalled on the fifth floor. "Dammit, hurry up!" Frustrated, Keats growled. She raced toward the stairwell, bypassed the panicked security team. She mounted the stairs, two at a time. On the second floor landing, she paused, opened the door a crack. Looked down the hallway. Voices came from inside the ballroom, loud and frightened.

Time to collect my dues, Garber.

A ding behind her back jolted her. She turned, gun up. The elevator doors flumped open. Sweating and ruddy-faced, Sidarski ran out, two men in blue behind him.

"Keats! Got your message."

"Yeah, where you been? Hot dog run?"

"Something like that. Let's do this." He jerked his chin down the hallway. Keats couldn't help but notice his grin, one he couldn't lick.

A uniform said, "What in the hell's goin' on here?" His hand wavered over his holstered pistol. Keats doubted it'd remain that way for long.

"We're after some serious perps. Serial killer types."

"Jesus..." The cop's face went white.

"Just follow us. Keep your voices low." Keats patted the air, hoped they'd take the hint. Close to the walls, they made their way down the hallway, clearing open doorways they passed. At the end of the hall, a mass of people screamed in unison.

One last nod from Sidarski. Keats shoved the doors open and dropped low.

"*Freeze!*"

The Man with the Shoebox's chauffeur pulled out strength Cody didn't know he had. Arms like iron rods, he wrapped Cody into a bear-hug. Cody worked his fists up between their touching chests and punched out. The remote flew up, head over end. It dropped to the carpet. So did Cody, waiting for the Big Bang.

Nothing happened. But he had to get to the remote before Tommy.

He brought a fist up into Tommy's groin. Cheating, but what the hell. Tommy groaned, hunched over. Cody clawed his way across the carpet. Tommy jumped on his legs.

Two feet away, two lousy feet.

Like a frog, Tommy leapt. He came down on Cody's back, knocked the wind out of Cody. He cleared Cody, scrambled for the remote.

The doors cracked open. An outbreak of activity jumbled into the room.

"*Freeze!*"

Shit. Five-O.

"Hold up, yo! This dude's tryna' blow the hotel to hell!" Cody jumped to his feet.

"Put your hands up and freeze! Don't make a move!"

Cody shot a look at Tommy. The remote lay inches from him. "You don't get it, yo! I'm tryin' to save your asses!"

"I said don't move!"

Tommy grabbed the remote. Sat up, carefully turned it around in his hand. Cody looked at the cops, the big pain-in-the-ass Kansas cop with them. Then back at Tommy.

No other choice.

The way he'd always wanted to go out. Like Butch and Sundance from the DVD Leon'd sent him.

"Live fast, die bad-ass!" Cody jumped, landed on Tommy, then properly clocked him in the head. Snatched up the remote.

Bullets ripped through the room, zigzagged into his body.

Pulses of painful energy jerked him like a punk-rock slam-dancer. One last defiant gesture, he held up the remote like the Statue of Liberty. Followed it with a middle finger salute, all his own.

"Eat it, yo!" Probably not the best last words he could've come up with. But ones that would no doubt immortalize him.

The gunfire rattled all the way down into the parking garage. In the backseat of the car, Leon tensed. Closed his eyes. He knew what it meant.

Cody.

Stupid, damn, crazy kid.

"Oh, my." Bartholomew's eyes filled the car's mirror. "Sounds like the situation ended how you wanted it to, Leon. No explosion."

Leon said nothing. Forced his tears inward. He'd mourn Cody later.

Nanette leaned her shoulder next to his. "Doing all right?"

"Fine."

Anything but…not Cody…

They'd been through so much together.

"Dear, dear me. Are they *ever* going to learn?" Bartholomew slowed the car. Barring their path to the exit, the blonde female twin boldly stepped in front of them, gun firm in both hands. Bartholomew sighed. She fired. The windshield split, shattered. The bullet passed between Leon and Nanette and buried into the back upholstery.

"Here we go."

The tires squealed as Bartholomew kept the car in neutral. The back end shimmied back and forth. Bartholomew dropped the gear and floored the gas.

Floomph!

The twin flew up, blond hair parachuting behind her. She landed, crumpled into a disfigured store window dummy. An arm twisted unnaturally behind her, hand up and obscenely waving at them.

"Smashing hit, friend Bartholomew," cried out Gustav.

"Shh, Gus." Delilah favored him with a loving smile. "You're bad."

"Aren't I, though?"

At the exit, the guard stuck his head out the booth, stared at them through the broken windshield. Bartholomew handed him a validated pass. "Vandals," said Bartholomew rather snootily. "Honestly, you should beef up your security."

Unbelievably, they made it out past the growing cordon of police cars and ambulances. Washington D.C.'s finest had more on their mind than a broken windshield.

"Turn on the radio, Bartholomew," said Leon.

News updates came in slowly at first, mere teases and rumors and guesses regarding the Washburn Hotel ruckus.

They drove in silence, far away from the destruction left behind. Finally the news had more of a story to report.

"Two men died in a shoot-out with the police. No names of the suspected terrorists known at this time. Stay tuned to—"

"That's enough."

Quietly reverent for a change, Bartholomew turned the radio off.

"Oh...Cody..." This time, Leon didn't care if anyone saw him cry. He released the floodgates.

He already missed his friend.

The jet landed at a small, private airport in Los Angeles. Where Leon decided to part ways with Bartholomew. The Man with the Shoe-Box didn't ask questions either; in fact he didn't say a word during the flight. Just stared out his chair side window. Leon hated to think about what was churning in his mind.

Gustav and Delilah decided to explore L.A. as well before taking off for other regions. On his way down the aisle of the idling airplane, Gus stopped, hugged Leon around the waist. Leon flinched under the small man's hug, still smarting from his patched up bullet wound.

"Friend Leon! The lovely Nanette! It is time once again that we bid you adieu!"

"So long, Gus, Delilah."

Ever mannerly, Gus bowed. "Always glad to be of the service to you, my friends. In case you ever have another adventure awaiting you, we'll be there."

Leon stole a look at a grinning Delilah. "I think our

adventure days are behind us, Gus."

"God, I hope so," said Nanette. "Take care of yourselves."

"Always. The world awaits us!" Gus spread his hands wide as he left the plane, welcoming the world to his peculiar sensibilities.

Delilah just said, "Later." And followed Gus off.

"You ready?" asked Leon.

Nanette nodded.

"Not so fast," said Bartholomew. He didn't move from his seat, waited for them to approach him. With tented hands, he took his time and appraised them fully before speaking. "As I said, I'm not accustomed to having a gun waved in my face. And I'm afraid I tend to hold a grudge." *Tap-tap-tap* on his shoebox. "The next time we meet, I—"

"No offense, Bartholomew," said Leon. "But I doubt there'll be a next time. We're going far after one more stop."

"You interrupted me. I don't care for that either." Leon nodded, coughed over a dry gulp. "Pray that we don't meet another time. If we do…I believe it'll be on opposite sides of the battle lines." He stared at them, unblinking. "But for now, be on your way. Live life while you can."

"Goodbye Bartholomew." Leon held his hand out. It went ignored.

As they took their last step off the plane, the engine rumbled. Leon felt the Man with the Shoe-Box's anger from the ground, a primordial force.

Keats walked Sidarski toward his airline gate. "Well, how'd you enjoy your vacation, Sidarski?"

He laughed, hollow as an empty can. "It had its ups and downs."

"Ah, don't be such a sour-puss about everything. One of your perps ended up dead, shot by some overzealous cops."

"Yeah. But he's now being proclaimed a hero in the press. He was no friggin' hero."

Keats linked her arm inside of Sidarski's. A gesture of camaraderie but also meant to steer him on board his flight. Frankly, the guy's cynicism wore her down. "Hey, the evidence didn't lie. Of course it didn't help that all of those Like-Minded Individual big-wigs dummied up."

"With lawyers in tow."

"They'll get 'em. Eventually. It's outta our hands now."

At the gate, Sidarski stopped. "Keats, it still bugs me that Garber's out there."

"Tricky fish, ain't he?"

"Yeah, the one who keeps getting away."

"Don't let it eat you up. Karma's got a way of stabbing back. In the meantime, my best advice to you is to quit your Ahabbing. Go buy a yacht, a Russian mail-order wife, a movie theatre, whatever. Live your retirement."

"We'll see what happens. Are you done hunting our boy?"

Keats smiled. "Remains to be seen." She stuck out her hand. "So long, Sidarski. It's been real."

"After everything we've been through, I'd say a hug's in order." He opened his arms. She caved.

"Be still my beating heart, Sidarski. 'Til next time."

As she watched him board, she noticed how much older he appeared. He walked with a limp, his shoulders hunched. Damn Garber chewed up everyone who came near him.

Her phone chirped. Caller unknown. Someone she'd been expecting.

"Keats."

"Hi, Detective. Nice job rounding up the Like-Minded Individuals board members."

"Garber. Wondered if I'd hear from you again."

"Yeah, well, what can I say? Without you, I'm nothing."

"Show me. Let's meet for beers, eat some nachos, laugh about old times."

"I would but my social calendar's full at the moment."

"Uh huh. You left us quite a cluster to unravel, you know."

"I have complete confidence you're up to the challenge."

"Flatterer. But I've got nothin' to do with it any more. Now it's in the hands of the Feds, the CIA, Social Security...I think even the Postal Service wanna put their stamp on the matter."

"Funny."

"I'm a funny person."

"My files are very complete, though. Even the most bumbling of bureaucrats can't botch this one up."

"We'll see."

"Detective, I wanted to thank you for telling everyone that Cody Spangler died a hero. He would've liked that, I think. He—"

"Didn't do it as a favor to you, Garber."

"Fine. But he was a hero. He stopped the bombing."

"A bomb placed by you?"

"What? No! Never. Regardless, I'm retiring from my... business."

"What exactly is your business?"

"I correct wrongs. Like you, Detective."

"Hardly think we're on the same team."

"Think what you will. But you'll never hear from me again. And I definitely will be on the right side of the law from here on out."

"And that's supposed to make me feel better?"

"No. You'll probably need a good hug for that."

"Now who's the funny one?"

"What can I say? A sense of humor makes the world go round. So...are you still coming after me?"

"Always. As you said, what am I without you?"

"Nice sentiment. Truly. But you won't find me."

"We'll see."

"I suppose we will. So long, Detective."

"Sooner than you think, Garber."

Garber ended the call. Keats' excitement mounted again. On the hunt.

She probably should consider cross-stitching or something a little less exciting.

Nah.

"Feel better?"

"Like a million bucks."

"Honestly, Leon," Nanette pulled off her sunglasses, "I don't know why you called her. You practically baited her. You thrive on adrenaline?"

"Hardly."

"And, hellooo! Flirting with her?"

"You're the only one I'll ever flirt with. She's just a…work colleague."

"Yeah, I bet it makes office parties interesting."

"Very." Leon looked down at his iPad. "Turn here."

She signaled, turned the car onto the street. Mansions sat back behind trees and on top of pampered lawns, neighborhood of the wealthy.

"I just like everything wrapped up nice and pretty, Nanette. You know that. I don't think I could put this chapter of our lives behind us without calling Keats."

"Still…you're asking for trouble."

"Nanette, I think I've had my fair share of trouble. I'm just looking forward to a lifetime spent getting to know you."

She smiled, held an open palm out over the console. He took her hand, gave it a squeeze.

"Maybe you won't like what you'll find out about me, Leon."

He sighed. "Look when it comes to baggage, we may as well hire a full-time airport baggage handler. It's a two-way street…as someone once told me. Ahem."

"Smart words. *Very* smart person."

"Very. Oh! Take another turn here."

At the last minute, she cut sharp. "Sorry. Give a girl some warning next time."

"So. I've been thinking about our future. I've always wanted to see Canada."

She wrinkled her nose. "Too cold. I was thinking somewhere a bit warmer."

"Like what, Florida? Too humid, too many bugs. Too many Keats."

"Hey, she's *your* BFF."

"I don't care where we settle as long as it's far away. And as long as we have a cozy cottage, two and a half children, and a white picket fence, of course. You can't start a life without a—"

"Wait, hold up! Whoever said anything about kids?"

Leon smiled. "I'm kidding. I don't think we're, ah, the most genetically appropriate parent material out there." He gave her hand another squeeze.

"Don't scare me like that." She drove on, air from the open window blowing back her returned to normal black hair. "So this is retirement. Leon, you know how lucky we are? We get to retire at a younger age."

"You'll always be eternally young in my eyes."

Nanette rolled her eyes. "Good Gawd."

"Hey, this is the house."

Nanette rolled into the long driveway. The three floor mansion had lights burning in most windows, not exactly a greens-keeper. "Nice place."

"Maybe we can buy it." They got out of the car. "So...I guess we agree children are out of the picture."

"Way out of the picture," said Nanette. Hand in hand, they strolled the length of the driveway until they reached the double-set doors. "Maybe a pet, though. You like pets, Leon?"

"You a dog or cat person?" Leon rang the doorbell.

"Depends on what kinda mood I'm in. I love the feistiness and independence of cats—"

"Hmm. Wonder why?" asked Leon.

"But sometimes I'm in the mood for a dog's sloppy, completely devoted love. But that's why I keep you around."

"Bark," said Leon. In a silly mood, Leon leaned down and licked her cheek.

"Gross!" Nanette wiped the offensive saliva away, but giggled anyway.

"All right. Game face on." Leon furrowed his brow, turned his eyebrows down, frowned the worst pumpkin face he could imagine.

Nanette snorted, said, "Seriously, get it together."

"Okay, okay. Man, it takes him a long time to answer. Wonder if he's home."

"With all the lights on, somebody's gotta be home." Nanette pressed the doorbell again. Leon followed with a tug of the gold-embossed, lion's head knocker.

"In all seriousness, Nanette, this *is* our last operation. We definitely agree on that, right? I don't want to be led any longer by death and I'm sick of it following us around." He took her hand, held it to his heart. "Nothing's felt more right to me than this. You and me together? We'll make a new life of it. No looking back."

"No looking back." On tiptoes, she stretched up to kiss him. "We may as well enjoy it, though. One last hurrah." Leon smiled, nodded. Kissed her again. The door opened, broke their kiss. Embarrassment planted roses on Leon's cheeks. Nanette chuckled.

A young Asian man in a dapper three-piece suit stared at them. "Yes?"

"Hi. We're the neighborhood welcoming committee." From her purse, Nanette whipped out a stun gun and zapped him. He fell, writhing, laying half in the doorway. "I gotta admit, Leon...a little bit of me will miss this."

Leon watched the wriggling man. "Maybe me too. Just a bit. But it's time we tried other things. Better things. Together."

"Kenny? What's..." Mr. Summers, LMI's procurer of the damned, stopped behind his fallen manservant. Quietly, he pulled off his bifocals. Folded them, precisely so. "Mr. Garber. Nanette. I suppose I should be...surprised by your visit. But I'm not, to be quite honest."

"Just business, Mr. Summers. Surely, you understand," said Leon, echoing Sheera's words.

"I do. Will you be, ah...conducting your business here? Or are we going out?"

"We'd rather do it elsewhere if you don't mind."

"Of course. Less messy that way. You two were always very professional, I must say."

"Thanks."

"One favor, though...would you see that my cat gets taken care of? It's the only thing I have in this world." A small tabby wrangled around his pajama clad legs.

"Of course." Nanette bent down, lured the cat into her arms. She picked it up, scratched it behind the ears.

"I'd appreciate it," said Summers.

"Think nothing of it." Leon waved the gun toward the car. "If you don't mind getting in the trunk, Mr. Summers."

"If I did mind, would it make a difference?"

"No," they both said.

With one last forlorn look, the last he'd ever be afforded, Summers crawled into the trunk. Leon slammed the lid. As he slid into the passenger seat, Nanette slipped the cat into his lap.

"You know its fate, right?" Leon asked.

"Fate? Fate's never been very kind to me."

"Hello! New day! We were just talking about a pet."

"Hmm. Could be, could be."

Nanette started the car.

"So...this is our family?" asked Leon.

"Yep."

"Can I name him Cody?"

"Can't think of a more fitting name," said Nanette.

About the Author

Stuart R. West is a lifelong resident of Kansas, which he considers both a curse and a blessing. It's a curse because…well, it's Kansas. But it's great because…well, it's Kansas. Lots of cool, strange and creepy things happen in the Midwest, and Stuart takes advantage of them in his work. Call it "Kansas Noir". Stuart writes thrillers, suspense and horror, both for adult and young adult audiences. Stuart spent twenty-five years in the corporate sector and now writes full time. He's married to a professor of pharmacy (who greatly appreciates the fact he cooks dinner for her every night) and has a twenty-six-year-old daughter who's still deciding what to do with her life. But that's okay. It took him twenty-five years to figure that out.

Curious about other Crossroad Press books?
Stop by our site:
http://store.crossroadpress.com
We offer quality writing
in digital, audio, and print formats.

www.ingramcontent.com/pod-product-compliance
Lightning Source LLC
Chambersburg PA
CBHW020338180626
46812CB00001B/246